Creed grinned at her

"Just so I can get this straight," he said, reaching into the bag and pulling out a jeweler's box. "You're saying no?"

She stared at the box he opened for her to view. It contained a heart-shaped diamond, which he was pretty proud of picking out this morning.

"Creed," she said, sounding shocked and choked up, and he snapped the box shut and put it back in the bag.

"Too bad," he said. "The jeweler promised me no woman could say no to this ring. He said a woman would have to have a heart of stone to refuse it. He said—"

"You're crazy," Aberdeen said. "I knew it when I first met you. I know you're crazy, and I know better than to throw myself to the wind like this, but I'm going to ride this ride, cowboy, and I swear, if you turn out to be a weirdo, I'll be really ticked at you."

Dear Reader,

We hope you enjoy the Western stories *The Cowboy's Bonus Baby* and *The Bull Rider's Twins,* written by *USA TODAY* bestselling Harlequin American Romance author Tina Leonard.

The Harlequin American Romance series is a celebration of all things Western! These stories are heartwarming contemporary tales of everyday women finding love, becoming part of a family or community—or maybe starting a family of her own.

And don't miss an excerpt of Tina's *Callahan Cowboy Triplets* at the back of this volume. Look for *Callahan Cowboy Triplets,* available September 2013.

Happy reading,

The Harlequin American Romance Editors

The Cowboy's Bonus Baby
&
The Bull Rider's Twins

USA TODAY Bestselling Author

TINA LEONARD

HARLEQUIN® AMERICAN ROMANCE®

ISBN-13: 978-0-373-68913-2

THE COWBOY'S BONUS BABY
& THE BULL RIDER'S TWINS

Copyright © 2013 by Harlequin Books S.A.

The publisher acknowledges the copyright holders of the individual works as follows:

THE COWBOY'S BONUS BABY
Copyright © 2011 by Tina Leonard

THE BULL RIDER'S TWINS
Copyright © 2011 by Tina Leonard

PLEASE RECYCLE
THIS PRODUCT IS RECYCLABLE

Recycling programs for this product may not exist in your area.

40513050 $2.13

HARLEQUIN®
www.Harlequin.com

Printed in U.S.A.

CONTENTS

ABOUT THE AUTHOR

Tina Leonard is a *USA TODAY* bestselling and award-winning author of more than fifty projects, including several popular miniseries for Harlequin American Romance. Known for bad-boy heroes and smart, adventurous heroines, her books have made the *USA TODAY,* Waldenbooks, Ingram and Nielsen BookScan bestseller lists. Born on a military base, Tina lived in many states before eventually marrying the boy who did her crayon printing for her in the first grade. You can visit her at www.tinaleonard.com, and follow her on Facebook and Twitter.

THE COWBOY'S BONUS BABY

Many thanks to Kathleen Scheibling for believing in the Callahan Cowboys series from the start. I have certainly enjoyed the past five years under your guidance. Also, there are so many people at Harlequin who make my books ready for publication, most of whom I will never have the chance to thank in person, and they have my heartfelt gratitude. Also many thanks to my children and my husband, who are enthusiastic and supportive, and most of all, much appreciation to the generous readers who are the reason for my success.

Chapter One

"Creed is my wild child. He wants everything he can't have."—Molly Callahan, with fondness, about her busy toddler.

Creed Callahan was running scared. Running wasn't his usual way of doing things, but Aunt Fiona's plot to get him and his five brothers married had him spooked. Marriage was a serious business, not to be undertaken lightly, especially by a commitment-phobe. Aunt Fiona had just scored a direct hit with Creed's brother Pete, who'd married Jackie Samuels and had triplets right off the baby daddy bat. Creed was potently aware his days as a happy, freewheeling bachelor might come to an end if he didn't get the hell away from Rancho Diablo.

So he'd fled like a shy girl at her first dance. Creed didn't relish being called chicken, but Aunt Fiona was a force to be reckoned with. Creed stared into his sixth beer, which the bartender in Lance, Wyoming, a generous man who could see that Creed's soul was in torment, had courteously poured.

Anyone in Diablo, New Mexico, would attest to the powers of Aunt Fiona. Especially when she had a goal—then no one was safe. His small, spare aunt had raised him and his five brothers upon the deaths of their parents without so much as a break in her stride. She and her butler, Burke, had flown in from Ireland one day, clucked over and coddled the five confused boys (young Sam had not yet been part of the family, an occurrence which still perplexed the brothers), and gave them an upbringing which was loving, firm and heaped with enthusiastic advice.

Creed barely remembered their parents, Jeremiah and Molly. He was the lucky one in the family, in his opinion, because he had a twin, Rafe. It had helped to have a mirror image at his back over the years. Creed was prone to mischief, Rafe was more of a thinker. Once, when the boys had wondered where babies came from—upon Sam's surprising arrival after Fiona had come to be their guardian—Creed had uprooted all of Fiona's precious garden looking for "baby" seeds. Rafe had told Aunt Fiona that he'd seen bunnies in her garden, which was true, but bunnies weren't the reason Aunt Fiona's kitchen crop had to be restarted.

Creed certainly knew where babies came from now. Watching Pete and Jackie go from a casual romance once a week to parents of triplets had underscored for him the amazing fertility of the Callahan men. They were like stallions—gifted with the goods.

With Fiona prodding about his unmarried state, Creed had hit the road. He did not want his own virility tested. He didn't want a wife or children. Pete was solidly positioned to win Rancho Diablo, for that was the deal Fiona had struck: whoever of the six brothers married and produced the most heirs inherited all five thousand acres.

But he and his brothers had worked an agreement out unbeknownst to their wily aunt: Only one of them would be the sacrifice (which had turned out to be the lucky—or unlucky, depending upon how one viewed it—brother Pete), and he would divide the ranch between the six of them. It was a fair-and-square way to keep any animosity from arising between them for the high-value prize of hearth and home. Competition wasn't a good thing among brothers, they'd agreed, though they competed against each other all the time, naturally. But this was different.

This competition wasn't rodeo, or lassoing, or tree climbing. This was a race to the altar, and they vowed that Fiona's planning wouldn't entrap them.

"And I'm safe," Creed muttered into his beer.

"Did you say something?" a chocolate-haired beauty said to him, and Creed realized that the old saying was true: Women started looking better with every beer. Creed blinked. The male bartender who'd been listening to his woes with a sympathetic ear had morphed into a sexy female, which meant Creed wasn't as safe as he thought he was. He was, in fact, six sheets to the wind and blowing south. "Six beers is not that big a deal," he told the woman who was looking at him with some approbation. "Where's Johnny?"

"Johnny?" She raised elfin brows at him and ran a hand through springy chin-length curls. "My name is Aberdeen."

He wasn't *that* drunk. In fact, he wasn't drunk at all. He knew the difference between moobs and boobs, and while Johnny had been the soul of generosity, he'd had girth appropriate for bouncing troublemakers out of his bar. This delightful lady eyeing him had a figure, pert and enticing, and Creed's chauvinistic brain was registering very little else except she looked like something a man who'd had six beers (okay, maybe twelve, but they were small ones so he'd halved his count), might want to drag into the sack. She had bow-shaped lips and dark blue eyes, but, most of all, she smelled like something other than beer and salami and pretzels. *Spring flowers,* he thought with a sigh. Yes, the smells of spring, after a long cold winter in Diablo. "You're beautiful," he heard someone tell her, and glanced around for the dope that would say something so unmanly.

"Thank you," she said to Creed.

"Oh, I didn't—" He stopped. *He* was the dope. *I sound like Pete. I need to leave now.* The beer had loosened his tongue and thrown his cool to the wind. "I'd best be going, Amber Jean." He slid off the bar stool, thinking how sad it was that he'd never see Johnny/Amber Jean again, and how wonderfully fresh and romantic springtime smelled in Wyoming.

"Oh, now, that's a shame," Johnny Donovan said, looking down at the sleeping cowboy on his bar floor. "Clearly this is a man who doesn't know much about brew."

Aberdeen gave her brother a disparaging glance. "You're the one who gave him too much."

"I swear I did not. The man wanted to talk more than drink, truthfully." Johnny gave Aberdeen his most innocent gaze. "He went on and on and on, Aberdeen, and so I could tell he wasn't really looking for the hops but for a good listener. On his fifth beer, I began giving him near-beer, as God is my witness, Aberdeen. You know I disapprove of sloppiness. And it's against the law to let someone drink and drive." He squinted outside, searching the darkness. It was three o'clock in the morning. "Mind you, I have no idea what he's driving, but he won't be driving a vehicle from my bar in this sloppy condition."

Her brother ran a conscientious establishment. "I'm sorry," Aberdeen said, knowing Johnny treated his patrons like family. Even strangers were given Johnny's big smile, and if anyone so much as mentioned they needed help, Johnny would give them the shirt off his back and the socks off his feet. Aberdeen looked at the cowboy sprawled on the floor, his face turned to the ceiling as he snored with luxuriant abandon. He was sinfully gorgeous: a pile, at the moment, of amazing masculinity. Lean and tall, with long dark hair, a chiseled face, a hint of being once broken about the nose. She restrained the urge to brush an errant swath of midnight hair away from his closed eyes. "What do we do with him?"

Johnny shrugged. "Leave him on the floor to sleep. The man is tired, Aberdeen. Would you have us kick a heartbroken soul out when he just needs a bit of time to gather his wits?"

"Heartbroken?" Aberdeen frowned. The cowboy was too good-looking by half. Men like him demanded caution; she knew this from her congregation. Ladies loved the cowboys; they loved the character and the drive. They loved the romance, the idea of the real working man. And heaven only knew, a lot of those men loved the ladies in return. This one, with his soft voice, good manners and flashing blue eyes… Well, Aberdeen had no doubt that this cowboy had left his fair share of broken hearts trampled in the dirt. "If you sit him outside, he'll gather his wits fast enough."

"Ah, now, Aberdeen. I can't treat paying customers that way, darling. You know that. He's causing no harm, is he?" Johnny looked at her with his widest smile and most apologetic expression, which should have looked silly on her bear of a brother, but which melted her heart every time.

"You're too soft, Johnny."

"And you're too hard, my girl. I often ask myself if all cowboy preachers are as tough on cowboys as you are. This is one of your flock, Aberdeen. He's only drunk on confusion and sadness." Johnny stared at Creed's long-forgotten beer mug. "I feel sorry for him."

Aberdeen sighed. "It's your bar. You do as you like. I'm going to my room."

Johnny went on sweeping up. "I'll keep an eye on him. You go on to bed. You have preaching to do in the morning."

"And I haven't finished writing my sermon. Good night, Johnny." She cast a last glance at the slumbering, too-sexy man on the dark hardwood floor, and headed upstairs. She was glad to leave Johnny with the stranger. No man should look that good sleeping on the floor.

A ROAR FROM DOWNSTAIRS, guffaws and loud thumping woke Aberdeen from deep sleep. Jumping to her feet, she glanced at her bedside clock. Seven o'clock—past time for her to be getting ready for church. She grabbed her robe, and more roars sent her running down the stairs.

Her brother and the stranger sat playing cards on a barrel table in the empty bar. One of them was winning—that much was clear from the grins—and the other didn't mind that he was losing. There were mugs of milk and steaming coffee on a table beside them. Both men were so engrossed in their game that neither of them looked up as she stood there with her hands on her hips. She was of half a mind to march back upstairs and forget she'd ever seen her brother being led astray by the hunky stranger.

"Johnny," Aberdeen said, "did you know it's Sunday morning?"

"I do, darlin'," Johnny said, "but I can't leave him. He's got a fever." He gestured to his playing partner.

"A fever?" Aberdeen's eyes widened. "If he's sick, why isn't he in bed?"

"He won't go. I think he's delirious."

She came closer to inspect the cowboy. "What do you mean, he won't go?"

"He thinks he's home." Johnny grinned at her. "It's the craziest thing."

"It's a lie, Johnny. He's setting us up." She slapped her hand on the table in front of the cowboy. He looked up at her with wide, too-bright eyes. "Have you considered he's on drugs? Maybe that's why he passed out last night."

"Nah," Johnny said. "He's just a little crazy."

She pulled up a chair, eyeing the cowboy cautiously, as he eyed her right back. "Johnny, we don't need 'a little crazy' right now."

"I know you're worried, Aberdeen."

"Aberdeen," the cowboy said, trying out her name. "Not Amber Jean. Aberdeen."

She looked at Johnny. "Maybe he's slow."

Johnny shrugged. "Said he got a small concussion at his last stop. Got thrown from a bull and didn't ride again that night. He says he just had to come home."

She shook her head. "Sounds like it might be serious. He could have a fever. We can't try to nurse him, Johnny."

"We can take him to the hospital, I suppose." Johnny

looked at the stranger. "Do you want to go to a hospital, friend?"

The cowboy shook his head. "I think I'll go to bed now."

Aberdeen wrinkled her nose as the cowboy went over to a long bench in the corner, laid himself out and promptly went to sleep. "You were giving milk to a man with fever?"

Johnny looked at her, his dark eyes curious. "Is that a bad thing? He asked for it."

She sighed. "We'll know soon enough." After a moment, she walked over and put her hand against his forehead. "He's burning up!"

"Well," Johnny said, "the bar's closed today. He can sleep on that bench if he likes, I guess. If he's not better tomorrow, I'll take him to a doctor, though he doesn't seem especially inclined to go."

Aberdeen stared at the sleeping cowboy's handsome face. *Trouble with a capital T.* "Did he tell you his name? Maybe he's got family around here who could come get him."

"No." Johnny put the cards away and tossed out the milk. "He babbles a lot about horses. Talks a great deal about spirit horses and other nonsense. Native American lore. Throws in an occasional Irish tale. Told a pretty funny joke, too. The man has a sense of humor, even if he is out of his mind."

"Great." Aberdeen had a funny feeling about the cowboy who had come to Johnny's Bar and Grill. "I'm going to see who he is," she said, reaching into his front pocket for his wallet.

A hand shot out, grabbing her wrist. Aberdeen gasped and tried to draw away, but the cowboy held on, staring up at her with those navy eyes. She couldn't look away.

"Stealing's wrong," he said.

She slapped his hand and he released her. "I know that, you ape. What's your name?"

He crossed his arms and gave her a roguish grin. "What's *your* name?"

"I already told you my name is Aberdeen." He'd said it not five minutes ago, so possibly he did have a concussion. With a fever, that could mean complications. "Johnny, this man is going to need a run to the—"

The cowboy watched her with unblinking eyes. Aberdeen decided to play it safe. "Johnny, could you pull the truck around? Our guest wants to go for a ride to see our good friend, Dr. Mayberry."

Johnny glanced at the man on the bench. "Does he now?"

"He does," Aberdeen said firmly.

Johnny nodded and left to get his truck. Aberdeen looked at the ill man, who watched her like a hawk. "Cowboy, I'm going to look at your license, and if you grab me again like you did a second ago, you'll wish you hadn't. I may be a minister, but when you live above a bar, you learn to take care of yourself. So either you give me your wallet, or I take it. Those are your choices."

He stared at her, unmoving.

She reached into his pocket and pulled out his wallet, keeping her gaze on him, trying to ignore the expanse of wide chest and other parts of him she definitely shouldn't notice. Flipping it open, she took out his driver's license. "Creed Callahan. New Mexico."

She put the license away, ignoring the fact that he had heaven-only-knew-how-many hundred-dollar bills stuffed into the calfskin wallet, and slid it back into his pocket.

He grabbed her, pulling her to him for a fast kiss. His lips molded to hers, and Aberdeen felt a spark—more than a spark, *real* heat—and then he released her.

She glared at him. He shrugged. "I figured you'd get around to slapping me eventually. Might as well pay hell is what I always say."

"Is that what you always say? With every woman you force to kiss you?" Aberdeen asked, rattled, and even more irritated that she hadn't been kissed like that in years. "You said stealing was wrong."

"It is. I didn't say I didn't do it." He grinned, highly pleased with himself, and if he hadn't already rung his bell, she would have slapped him into the next county.

Then again, it was hard to stay mad when he was that cheerful about being bad. Aberdeen put her hands on her hips so he couldn't grab her again. "All right, Mr. Callahan, do you remember why you're in Wyoming?"

"Rodeo. I ride rodeo, ma'am."

Johnny was back. "Truck's out front."

"Johnny," Aberdeen said, "this is Creed Callahan. Mr. Callahan is very happy you're going to take him for a ride. Aren't you, Mr. Callahan?"

"Callahan?" Johnny repeated. "One of the six Callahans from New Mexico?"

"Have you heard of him?"

"Sure." Johnny shrugged. "All of them ride rodeo, and not too shabbily. The older brother didn't ride much, but he did a lot of rodeo doctoring after he got out of medical school. Some of them have been highly ranked. You don't go to watch rodeo without knowing about the Callahans." He looked at Creed with sympathy. "What are you doing here, friend?"

Creed sighed. "I think I'm getting away from something, but I can't remember what."

"A woman?" Johnny asked, and Aberdeen waited to hear the answer with sudden curiosity.

"A woman," Creed mused. "That sounds very likely. Women are trouble, you know. They want to have—" He lowered his voice conspiratorially in an attempt to keep Aberdeen from hearing. "They want to have b-a-b-i-e-s."

Aberdeen rolled her eyes. "Definitely out of his mind. Take him away, Johnny."

Her brother laughed. "He may be right, you know."

"I don't care," Aberdeen said, gathering her self-control. He might have stolen a kiss, but the conceited louse was never getting another one from her. "He's crazy."

"That's what they say," Creed said, perking up, obviously recognizing something he'd heard about himself before.

Aberdeen washed her hands of Mr. Loco. "Goodbye, cowboy," she said, "hope you get yourself together again some day. I'll be praying for you."

"And I'll be praying for you," Creed said courteously, before rolling off the bench onto the floor.

"That's it, old man," Johnny said, lifting Creed up and over his shoulder. "Off we go, then. Aberdeen, I may not make your service today, love."

"It's okay, Johnny." Aberdeen watched her brother carry Creed to the truck and place him inside as carefully as a baby. The man said he was running, but no one ran from their family, did they? Not someone who had five brothers who'd often traveled together, rodeoed together, competed against each other? And Johnny said one of the brothers was a doctor.

People needed family when they were hurting. He'd

be better off with them instead of being in Wyoming among strangers.

Aberdeen went to her room to look up Callahans in New Mexico, thinking about her own desire for a family. A real one. Her sister, Diane, had tried to make a family, but it hadn't worked. Though she had three small adorable daughters, Diane wasn't cut out to be a mother. Then Aberdeen had married Shawn "Re-ride" Parker right out of high school. That hadn't lasted long, and there had been no children. And Johnny, a confirmed bachelor, said he had enough on his hands with his two sisters. They had their own definition of family, Aberdeen supposed, which worked for them. If a woman was looking to be have a baby, though, Creed Callahan probably ranked as perfect donor material— if a woman liked crazy, which she didn't. "I don't do crazy anymore," she reminded herself, dialing the listing she got from the operator.

The sooner crazy left town, the better for all of them.

Chapter Two

Creed was astonished to see his brother Judah when he awakened. He was even more surprised to realize he was in a hospital room. He glanced around, frowning at his snoozing brother—Judah looked uncomfortable and ragged in the hospital chair—and wondered why he was here. Creed tried to remember how he'd gotten to the hospital and couldn't. Except for a ferocious headache, he felt fine.

"Judah," he said, and his brother started awake.

"Hey!" Judah grinned at him. "What the hell, man? You scared me to death."

"Why?" Creed combed his memory and found it lacking. "What's going on? Where am I?"

"We're in Lance, Wyoming. A bar owner brought you in."

"Was I in a fight?" Creed rubbed at his aching head, confused by his lost memory. He didn't remember drinking all that much, but if a bar owner had brought him in, maybe he'd gotten a little riled up. "If I was, I hope I won."

Judah smirked. "The fight you were in was apparently with a bull. And you lost. At least this round."

Creed perked up. "Which bull was it? I hope it was a bounty bull. At least a rank bull, right?"

His brother smiled. "Can I get you something? Are you hungry?"

Creed blinked. Judah didn't want to tell him which bull had thrown him, which wasn't good. Cowboys loved to brag, even on the bad rides. He told himself he was just a little out of practice, nothing more riding couldn't cure. "I feel like my head isn't part of my body."

"You've got a slight concussion. The doctor thinks you're going to be fine, but he's keeping you a few hours for observation."

"I've had concussions before and not gone to the hospital."

"This time you had a high fever. Could have been the concussion, could have been a bug. The doctors just want to keep an eye on you. They mapped your brain, by the way, and said you don't have too much rattling around inside your skull. The brain cavity is strangely lacking in material."

Creed grunted at Judah's ribbing. "Sorry you had to make the trip."

"No problem. I wasn't doing anything."

Creed grunted again at the lie. Callahans always had plenty to do around Rancho Diablo. Five thousand acres of prime land and several hundred head of livestock meant that they stayed plenty busy. They kept the ranch running through sheer hard work and commitment to the family business.

"Anyway, it's been a while since anyone's seen you. Didn't know where you were keeping yourself." Judah scrutinized him. "We really didn't understand why you left in the first place."

Now *that* Creed could dig out of his cranium. "I was next on Fiona's list, Judah. I could *feel* it." He shuddered. "You don't understand until you've had Fiona's eye trained on you. Once she's thinking about getting you to the altar, you're halfway there."

"She's thinking about all of us," Judah pointed out. "Remember, that's her plan."

"But it was supposed to be over when Pete got married. He was the sacrifice." Creed took a deep breath. "And then I realized Fiona was running through her catalog of eligible females for me. I could hear her mind whirring. I've known every woman Fiona could possibly think of all my life. And there's not a one of them I'd care to marry."

Judah nodded. "I feel the same way."

Creed brightened. "You do?"

"Sure. Occasionally I think about a certain gal, but then I think, no, she'd never have me. And then I get over it pretty fast." Judah grinned. "The sacrifice wasn't ever going to be me. I'm not good at commitment for the sake of just having a girl around. Heck, I was never even good at picking a girl to take to prom."

"That was an exercise in futility." Creed remembered his brother's agony. "I had to fix you up with some of my friends."

"And that was embarrassing because of you being a year older than me."

"I didn't exactly mind," Creed hedged. "And I didn't hear you complaining about going out with an older woman."

Judah shook his head. "My dates didn't complain because I'm a good kisser. When you're a year younger than the girls you take out, you learn to make it up to them." He grinned. "You know, it's not that I don't like women, I just like *all* women."

"Amen, bro," Creed said happily, back on terra firma. "Women are a box of candy, you never know what you're going to get."

"All right, Forrest Gump. Go back to sleep." Judah smiled at the nurse who came in to take his brother's temperature. "I had no idea the ladies in Wyoming are so lovely," Judah said. "Why wasn't I living here all my life?"

Creed grinned at his brother's flirting. *Now* he remembered who he was. He was Creed Callahan, hotshot rider and serious serial lover of females. Wild at heart. It was good to be a Callahan. He was love-them-and-leave-them-happy, that's who he was.

And women adored him.

Creed never noticed the nurse taking his pulse and his temperature. Somewhere in his memory a vision of a brunette with expressive eyebrows nagged at him. A female who hadn't quite adored him. In fact, she might even have thought he was annoying.

It wasn't likely such a woman existed, but then again, he couldn't remember ever getting concussed by anything other than a rank bull, either. Creed closed his eyes, wishing his headache would go away, but there was greater pain inside him: His last several rides had been bombs. Not even close to eights. On par with unfortunate.

I need a break, and the only thing I manage to break is my head.

He'd just lie here and think about it a little while longer, and maybe the fog would lift. He heard Judah and the nurse giggling quietly about something, which didn't help. Judah could score any time he liked. The ladies loved all that haunted-existentialist crap that his younger brother exuded. *But I'm not existential. Rafe, he's an existential thinker. Me, I'm just wild. And that's all I'll ever be.*

He felt really tired just connecting those pieces of information. When he got out of here, he was going to remember that a fallen rider needed to get right back up on his reindeer.

Or something like that.

But then Creed thought about dark-blue annoyed eyes staring at him, and wondered if he was running out of good luck.

ABERDEEN SAT RELUCTANTLY at the cowboy's bedside, waiting for him to waken, and not really wanting him to. There was something about him that nagged at her, and it wasn't just that he'd kissed her. Cowboys were typically a good group, but she wasn't sure about this one, though she was trying to give him the benefit of the doubt. She worked to spread faith and good cheer amongst her beat-up flock, and beat-up they were on Sunday mornings. Her congregation consisted of maybe twenty-five people on a busy Sunday, often less. Banged-up gentlemen dragged in for an hour of prayer and sympathy and the potluck spaghetti lunch she and her friends served in the bar afterward. She preached in Johnny's big barn, which had a covered pavilion for indoor riding. The cowboys and cowgirls, wearing jeans and sleepy expressions of gratitude, gratefully headed to the risers.

This man was beat-up, all right, but he didn't seem like he cared to find spiritual recovery in any form. She pondered her transient congregation. Sunday mornings were her favorite part of the week, and she rarely ever missed giving a sermon, though if she did, Johnny was an excellent stand-in, as well as some of their friends. Neither of them had grown up thinking they wanted to be preachers, but missionarying had taken hold of Aberdeen in high school, growing stronger during college. She'd majored in theology, minored in business, and Johnny had done the opposite. The two of them were a good working team. Over the years, Johnny's Bar and Grill had become known as the place to hang out six days a week, crash when necessary, and hear words of worship on Sunday. Aberdeen knew many of the cowboys that pulled through Lance. She couldn't understand why she'd never heard of the Callahans, if they were the prolific, daring riders that Johnny claimed they were.

But she'd gotten busy in the past five years, so busy she barely paid attention to anything more than what the top riders were scoring, and sometimes not even that. Her knowledge had ebbed when she started helping Johnny at the bar and writing more of her sermons. She was twenty-nine, and at some point, rodeo had left her consciousness. She'd focused more on her job and less on fun—although sometimes she missed that. A lot.

Plus she had Diane to think about. Diane was in trouble, real trouble, and nothing she or Johnny did seemed to help her. Their older sister couldn't keep a job, couldn't keep a husband—she was on her third—and had three young children, had had one a year for the past three years. Now she was going through a bitter divorce from a man who'd walked out and was never coming back. It had always been hard for Aberdeen and Johnny to understand why Diane made the choices she did.

Recently, Diane had asked Aberdeen to adopt her daughters, Ashley, Suzanne and Lincoln Rose. Diane said she could no longer handle the responsibility of being a parent. Aberdeen was seriously considering taking the girls in. If Diane didn't want to be a mother, then Aberdeen didn't want to see Child Protective Services picking up her nieces. She loved them, with all her heart.

Diane lived in Spring, Montana, and wanted to move to Paris to chase after a new boyfriend she'd met traveling through the state. Aberdeen lived in fear that their elderly parents would call and say that Diane had already skipped.

"Howdy," the cowboy said, and Aberdeen's gaze snapped up to meet his.

"Hi. Feeling better?" she asked, conscious once again of how those dark denim eyes unsettled her.

"I think so." He brightened after feeling his head. "Yes, I definitely am. Headache is gone." He gave her a confiding grin. "I dreamed about you."

Her mouth went dry. "Why?"

"I remembered your eyes. I didn't remember a lot else, but I did remember your eyes."

She'd remembered his, too, though she'd tried not to. "Good dream or a bad dream?"

He grinned. "Now, sugar, wouldn't you like to know?"

She pursed her lips, wishing she hadn't asked.

"Ah, now that's the expression I recall with clarity," Creed said. "Annoyance. Mainly because it's not what I usually see in a woman's eyes."

"No? What do you usually see?" Aberdeen *was* annoyed, and the second she fell into his trap, she was even more irritated. Mainly with herself.

"Lust, preacher lady. I see lust."

She leaned away from him. "Ladies do not lust."

He raised jet-black brows. "I swear they do."

"They desire," she told him. "They have longings."

He shook his head. "You've been meeting the wrong kind of fellows, sugar cake."

She got up and grabbed her purse. "It's good to see you on the mend, Mr. Callahan. Happy trails."

He laughed, a low, sensual sound that followed Aberdeen to the door. "Thank you, miss."

He hadn't placed an emphasis on *miss,* but it teed

her off just the same. Made her feel naked. She wasn't an old-maid kind of miss; she was a conscientious abstainer from another marriage. *That's right, cowboy. I'm single and okay with it. Almost okay with it, anyway.*

As she rounded the corner, she plowed into a tall cowboy who looked a lot like the one she'd left in his hospital room.

"Whoa, little lady," he said, setting her back on her feet. "Where's the fire?"

She frowned. "You're not one of the Callahans, are you?"

"I am." He nodded, smiling at her. "You must be the nice lady who let us know Creed was down on his luck."

"Yes, I did. He's made a great recovery."

He tipped his hat, dark-blue eyes—just like Creed's—sparkling at her. "My name is Judah Callahan."

She reached out to shake his hand. "Aberdeen Donovan."

"We can't thank you enough, Miss Aberdeen."

He had kind eyes—unlike the flirt back in the hospital bed. "No thanks necessary. My brother Johnny would help anyone in trouble." She smiled at him. "I've got to run, but it was nice meeting you, Judah."

"Thank you, Aberdeen. Again, thanks for rescuing Bubba."

She shook her head and walked away. Bubba. There was nothing little-brother Bubba about Creed. He was all full-grown man and devil-may-care lifestyle. She'd be a fool to fall for a man like him. Fortunately, forewarned was forearmed.

Chapter Three

Judah strolled into Creed's room. By the sneaky smile on his brother's face, Creed deduced that his visit wasn't all about rousing the patient to better health. "What?" Creed had a funny feeling he knew what was coming.

"You've got all the luck," Judah said, throwing himself into a chair. "Finding a little angel like that to rescue you."

Judah grinned, but Creed let his scowl deepen. "She's not as much of an angel as she appears. Don't let her looks fool you."

His brother laughed. "Couldn't sweet-talk her, huh?"

Creed sniffed. "Didn't try."

"Sure you did." Judah crossed a leg over a knee and lounged indolently, enjoying having Creed at his mercy. "She didn't give you the time of day." He looked up at the ceiling, putting on a serious face. "You know, some ladies take their angel status very seriously."

"Meaning?" Creed arched a brow at his brother, half-curious as to where all this ribbing was going. Judah had no room to talk about success with women, as far as Creed was concerned. Only Pete was married—and only Pete had claimed a girlfriend, sort of, before Aunt Fiona had thrown down the marriage gauntlet. Creed figured the rest of the Callahan brothers were just about nowhere with serious relationships.

Including me.

"Just that once a woman like her rescues a man, she almost feels responsible for him. Like a child." Judah sighed. "Very difficult thing to get away from, when a woman sees a man in a mothering light."

Creed stared at his brother. "That's the biggest bunch of hogwash I've ever heard."

"Have you ever wondered exactly what hogwash is?" Judah looked thoughtful. "If I had a hog, I sure wouldn't wash it."

"Hogwash just means garbage," Creed said testily. "Your literal mood is not amusing."

"I was just making conversation, since you're not in a position to do much else."

"Sorry." Creed got back to the point he was most intrigued by. "Anyway, so you met Aberdeen?"

Judah nodded. "Yes. And thanked her for taking care of my older brother. Do you remember any of what happened to you?"

"I don't know. Some bug hit me, I guess." Creed was missing a couple of days out of his life. "I didn't make the cut in Lance, so I was going to head on to the next rodeo. And I saw this out-of-the-way restaurant on the side of road, so I stopped. Next thing I knew, I was here."

Judah shook his head. "A bad hand, man."

"Yeah."

"Never want a woman you've just met to see you weak," Judah mused.

"I wasn't weak. I just got the wrong end of a ride. Or the flu." Creed glared at Judah. "So anyway, how are the newlyweds? And Fiona? Burke? Everyone else?"

"No one else is getting married, if that's what you're asking. You still have a shot. Like Cinderella getting a glass slipper. It could happen, under the right conditions."

"I don't want a wife or children. That's why I'm here," Creed growled. "You can be the ambassador for both of us, thanks."

"I don't know. I kind of thought that little brunette who went racing out of your room might have some possibilities."

"Then ask her out." Creed felt a headache coming on that had nothing to do with his concussion. It was solely bad temper, which Judah was causing.

Just like the old days. In a way, it was comforting.

"I don't know. I could have sworn I felt that tension thing. You know, a push-pull vibe when she left your room. She was all riled like she had fire on her heels, as if you'd really twisted her up."

"That's a recipe for love if I ever heard one."

"Yeah." Judah warmed to his theory. "Fire and ice. Only she's mostly fire."

"Hellfire is my guess. You know she's a cowboy church preacher."

"Oh." Judah slumped. "That was the fire I picked up on. I knew she needed an extinguisher for some reason. I just thought maybe it had to do with you."

"Nope," Creed said, happy to throw water on his brother's silly theory. "You'll have to hogwash another Callahan into getting roped. And you are not as good as Fiona," Creed warned with satisfaction.

Judah shook his head. "No one is."

"I THINK," FIONA TOLD HER FRIENDS at the Books 'n' Bingo Society meeting, "that voting a few new members in to our club is a good idea. Sabrina McKinley can't stay shut up in the house all the time taking care of dreadful old Bode Jenkins." Fiona sniffed, despising even saying Bode's name. It was Bode who'd finally closed her up in a trap, and the fact that the man had managed to find a way to get Rancho Diablo from her rankled terribly. She was almost sick with fear over what to tell her six nephews. Pete knew. She could trust Pete. He would keep her secret until the appropriate time. And he was married now, with darling triplet daughters, a dutiful nephew if there ever was one.

But the other five—well, she'd be holding her breath for a long while if she dreamed those five rapscallions would get within ten feet of an altar. No, they'd be more likely to set an altar on fire with their anti-marriage postures. Poof! Up in smoke.

Just like her grip on Rancho Diablo. How disappointed her brother Jeremiah and his wife, Molly, would be if they knew that she'd lost the ranch they'd built. "Some guardian I am," she murmured, and Corrine Abernathy said, "What, Fiona?"

Fiona shook her head. "Anyway, we need to invite Sabrina into our group. We need fresh blood, young voices who can give us new ideas."

Her three best friends and nine other ladies smiled at her benevolently.

"It sounds like a good idea," Mavis Night said. "Who else do you want?"

Fiona thought about it. Sabrina had been an obvious choice for new-member status, because she was Corinne's niece. So was Seton McKinley, a private investigator Fiona had hired to ferret out any chinks in Bode's so-far formidable armor. "I think maybe Bode Jenkins."

An audible gasp went up in the tearoom.

"You can't be serious," Nadine Waters said, her voice quavering. "He's your worst enemy."

"And we should keep our enemy close to our bosoms, shouldn't we?" Fiona looked around the room. "Anyway, I put it forth to a vote."

"Why not Sheriff Cartwright? He's a nice man," Nadine offered. "For our first male in the group, I'd rather vote for a gentleman."

Murmurs of agreement greeted that sentiment.

"I don't know," Fiona said. "Maybe I'm losing my touch. Maybe inviting Bode is the wrong idea." She thought about her words before saying slowly, "Maybe I should give up my chairwomanship of the Books 'n' Bingo Society."

Everyone stared at her, their faces puzzled, some glancing anxiously at each other.

"Fiona, is everything all right?" Corinne asked.

"I don't know," Fiona said. She didn't want to tell them that in another six months she might not be here. It was time to lay the groundwork for the next chairwoman. She would have no home which to invite them, there would be no more Rancho Diablo. Only one more Christmas at Diablo. She wanted to prepare her friends for the future. But she also didn't want the truth to come out just yet, for her nephews' sakes. She wanted eligible bachelorettes—the cream of the Diablo crop—to see them still as the powerful Callahan clan, the men who worked the hardest and shepherded the biggest ranch around.

Not as unfortunate nephews of a silly aunt who'd gambled away their birthright.

She wanted to cry, but she wouldn't. "I think I'll adjourn, girls. Why don't we sleep on everything, and next week when we meet maybe we'll have some ideas on forward-thinking goals for our club."

Confused, the ladies rose, hugging each other, glancing with concern at Fiona. Fiona knew she'd dropped a bomb on her friends. She hadn't handled the situation well.

But then, she hadn't handled anything well lately. *I'm definitely losing it,* she thought. In the old days, her most gadabout, confident days, a man like Bode Jenkins would never have gotten the best of her.

She was scared.

"I'm thinking about it," Aberdeen told Johnny that night. "Our nieces need a stable home. And I don't know how to help Diane more than we have. Maybe she needs time away. Maybe she's been through too much. There's no way for us to know what is going through her mind." Aberdeen sat in their cozy upstairs den with Johnny. It was Sunday night so the bar was closed. They'd thoroughly cleaned it after going by to see the recovering cowboy. He'd looked much better and seemed cheered by his brother's presence.

There wasn't much else she and Johnny could do for him, either, and she didn't really want to get any more involved. She had enough on her hands. "Mom and Dad say that they try to help Diane, but despite that, they're afraid the children are going to end up in a foster home somewhere, some day." Aberdeen felt tears press behind her eyelids. "The little girls deserve better than this, Johnny. And Diane has asked me to adopt them. She says she's under too much pressure. Too many children, not enough income, not enough… maternal desire."

That wasn't exactly how Diane had put it. Diane had

said she wasn't a fit mother. Aberdeen refused to believe that. Her sister had always been a sunny person, full of optimism. These days, she was darker, moodier, and it all seemed to stem from the birth of her last child. Up until that moment, Diane had thought everything was fine in her marriage. It wasn't until after the baby was born that she'd discovered her husband had another woman. He no longer wanted to be a father, nor a husband to Diane.

"I don't know," Johnny said. "Aberdeen, we live over a bar. I don't think anyone will let us have kids here. Nor could I recommend it. We don't want the girls growing up in an environment that isn't as wholesome as we could make it. We don't even have schools nearby."

Aberdeen nodded. "I know. I've thought about this, Johnny. I think I'm going to have to move to Montana."

Her brother stared at her. "You wanted to leave Montana. So did I."

"But it's not a bad place to live, Johnny." It really wasn't. And the girls would have so much more there than they would living over a bar. "I could be happy there."

"It's not that Montana was the problem," Johnny said. "It was the family tree we wanted to escape."

This was also true. Their parents weren't the most loving, helpful people. They'd pretty much let their kids fend for themselves, believing that they themselves had gotten by with little growing up, and had done fine figuring life out themselves. So Johnny and Aberdeen had left Montana, striking out to "figure life out" on their own. Diane had opted to stay behind with their parents. Consequently, she'd married, had kids, done the wife thing—and left herself no backup when it all fell apart.

"I've been thinking, too," Johnny said. "To be honest, the red flag went up for me when the folks said they were worried. For them to actually worry and not ascribe to their typical let-them-figure-it-out-themselves theory, makes me think the situation is probably dire."

Aberdeen shook her head. "The girls need more. They're so young, Johnny. I don't know exactly what happened to Diane and why she's so determined she can't be a mother anymore, but I think I'm going to either have to get custody or fully adopt, like Diane wants me to do. They need the stability."

Johnny scratched his chin. "We just can't have them here. There are too many strangers for safety."

"That's why I think I have to go to Montana. At least there I can assess what's been happening."

Johnny waved a big hand at her. "Diane is leaving. There's nothing to assess. She's going to follow whatever wind is blowing, and our parents don't want to be bothered with toddlers."

"They don't have the health to do it, Johnny."

"True, but—"

"It doesn't matter," Aberdeen said quickly. "We just need to think of what's best for the girls."

"We can buy a house here. Maybe it's time to do that, anyway."

She looked around their home. It hadn't been in the best condition when they'd bought the building, but they'd converted the large old house into a working/living space that suited them. Upstairs were four bedrooms, with two on either side of an open space, with en suite bathrooms in the two largest bedrooms. They used the wide space between the bedrooms as a family room. For five years they'd lived here, and it was home.

"Maybe," she said, jumping a little when a knock sounded on the front door downstairs. Aberdeen glanced at Johnny. Their friends knew to go to the back door after the bar was closed; they never answered the front door in case a stranger might decide to see if they could get someone to open up the bar. A few drunks over the years had done that. She was surprised when Johnny headed down the stairs. Her brother was big and tall and strong, and he wouldn't open the door without his gun nearby, but still, Aberdeen followed him.

"We're closed," Johnny called through the door.

"I know. I just wanted to come by and say thanks before we left town," a man called from the other side, and Aberdeen's stomach tightened just a fraction.

"The cowboy," she said to Johnny, and he nodded.

"He's harmless enough," Johnny said. "A little bit of a loose cannon, but might as well let him have his say."

Aberdeen shrugged. "He can say it through the door just the same," she said, but Johnny gave her a wry look and opened up.

"Thanks for letting me in," Creed Callahan said to Johnny, shaking his hand as though he was a long-lost friend. "This is the man who probably saved my life, Judah," he said, and Judah put out a hand for Johnny to shake. "Hi, Aberdeen," Creed said.

"Hello, Aberdeen," Judah said, "we met in the hospital."

She smiled at Judah's polite manners, but it was his long-haired ruffian of a brother who held her gaze. She could feel her blood run hot and her frosty facade trying to melt. It was hard not to look at Creed's engaging smile and clear blue eyes without falling just a little bit. *You've been here before,* she reminded herself. *No more bad boys for you.*

"We didn't save your life," Johnny said, "you would have been fine."

Creed shook his head. "I don't remember much about the past couple of days. I don't really recall coming here." He smiled at Aberdeen. "I do remember you telling your brother you didn't want me here."

"That's true." She stared back at him coolly. "We're not really prepared to take in boarders. It's nice to see you on the mend. Will you be heading on now to the next rodeo?"

Judah softly laughed. "We do have to be getting on, but we just wanted to stop by to thank you." He tipped his hat to Aberdeen. "Again, I appreciate you looking out for my brother. He's fortunate to have guardian angels."

Aberdeen didn't feel much like an angel at the moment. She could feel herself in the grip of an attraction unlike anything that had ever hit her before. She'd felt it when she'd first laid eyes on Creed. The feeling hadn't dissipated when she'd visited him in the hospital. She could tell he was one of those men who would make a woman insane from wanting what she couldn't have.

It was the kiss that was muddying her mind. He'd unlocked a desire she'd jealously kept under lock and key, not wanting ever to get hurt again. "Goodbye," she said, her eyes on Creed. "Better luck with your next ride."

He gave her a lingering glance, and Aberdeen could have sworn he had something else he wanted to say but couldn't quite bring himself to say it. He didn't rush to the door, and finally Judah clapped him on the back so he'd get moving toward the exit.

"Goodbye," Creed said again, seemingly only to her, and chicken-heart that she was, Aberdeen turned around and walked upstairs, glad to see him go.

Once in Creed's truck, Judah tried to keep his face straight. Creed knew his brother was laughing at him, though, and it didn't help. "What?" he demanded, pulling out of the asphalt parking lot. "What's so funny?"

"That one is way out of your league, Creed."

Creed started to make a rebuttal of his interest, then shrugged. "I thought you said she'd probably feel responsible for me because she saved me."

Judah laughed. "Works for most guys, clearly backfired on you. Good thing you're not interested in a relationship with a woman, or keeping up with Pete, because you'd never get there if that gal was your choice. I don't believe I've ever seen a female look at a man with less enthusiasm. If you were a cockroach, she'd have squashed you."

He *felt* squashed. "She was like that from the moment I met her," Creed said. "I remember one very clear thing about the night I got here, and that was her big blue eyes staring at me like I was an ex-boyfriend. The kind of ex a woman never wants to lay eyes on again."

"Bad luck for you," Judah said, without much sympathy and with barely hidden laughter. "You're kind of on a roll, bro."

"My luck's bound to turn eventually." Creed was sure it would—he'd always led a fairly charmed existence, but when a man couldn't ride and the ladies weren't biting his well-baited hook and he was evading his wonky little aunt's plan to get him settled down, well, there was nothing else to do but wait for the next wave of good luck, which was bound to come any time.

"Take me to the airport," Judah said, "now that you're on the mend."

"You don't want to ride with me to the next stop?"

Judah shook his head. "I've got a lot to do back home."

Guilt poured over Creed. There was always so much

to do at Rancho Diablo that they could have had six more brothers and they wouldn't cover all the bases. "Yeah," Creed said, thinking hard. He wasn't winning. He'd busted his grape, though not as badly as some guys he knew. Still, it probably wasn't wise to get right back in the saddle.

He was homesick. "Maybe that bump on my noggin was a good thing."

"Not unless it knocked some sense into you."

He couldn't remember ever being homesick before. It was either having had a bad ride or meeting Aberdeen that had him feeling anxious. He wasn't sure which option would be worse. With a sigh he said, "Feel like saving on an airplane ticket?"

"Coming home?" Judah asked, with a sidelong glance at him, and Creed nodded.

"I think I will."

"Suits me. I hate to fly. So many rules to follow. And I hate taking off my boots in a line of other people taking off their shoes. I guess I could wear flip-flops or slip-ons, but my boots are just part of my body." He glanced out the window, watching the beautiful land fly past, clearly happy to have the scenery to admire. "Better luck next time, bro," he said, then pulled his hat down over his eyes. "Wake me when you want me to drive."

Creed nodded. He wasn't as sanguine and relaxed as Judah. He was rattled, feeling that something was missing, something wasn't quite right. Creed kept his eyes on the road, tried to relax his clenched fingers on the steering wheel—just enough to take the white from his knuckles. It had been silly to go back to Johnny's Bar and Grill, but he'd wanted to see Aberdeen. He wanted to take one last look at her, at those springy, dark-brown curls, her saucy nose, full lips, dark-blue eyes. He'd been lying, of course. He remembered something else besides those eyes staring at him with annoyance. He would never forget the soft feel of her lips beneath his, printing her heart onto his soul. He'd felt it, despite the concussion, and he had a funny feeling he would never forget Aberdeen Donovan.

Which was a first for a man who loved to kiss all the girls with his usual happy-go-lucky amnesia. He'd wanted one more kiss from Aberdeen, but it would have taken better luck than he was currently riding and maybe a real guardian angel looking out for him to make that dream come true.

He turned toward home.

Chapter Four

When Aberdeen and Johnny got to Montana a week after the cowboy had left town, they found matters were worse than expected. Diane was already in Paris chasing after her new boy toy, and had no plans to return. Ashley, Suzanne and Lincoln Rose had been left with their grandparents—and as Aberdeen and Johnny had feared, the older folk were overwhelmed and looking to hand off the girls. Quickly.

"Why didn't you call us?" Aberdeen demanded. "How long has Diane been gone?"

"She left two weeks ago. With that man." Fritz Donovan looked at his nieces helplessly. "Seems a mother ought to stay around to raise her own kids. Like we did."

Aberdeen bit her lip. *Some raising. You left us to raise ourselves, so Diane isn't all to blame.*

"You still should have called, Dad."

May Donovan jutted out her chin. "Diane said she'd told you that she was leaving. We figured that since you didn't come, you didn't want the girls. And you know very well Diane needs a break. It's just all been too much for her since the divorce."

Aberdeen counted to ten. May's constant blind eye where her older daughter was concerned was one of the reasons Diane continued to act irresponsibly at the age of thirty-five.

Johnny got to his feet, towering in the small kitchen. "There's no need to lay blame. If Diane is gone, she's gone. Now we need to decide what to do with the little ones."

"You're taking them with you, of course," May said. "Now that you've *finally* arrived."

Fritz nodded. "We're a bit old to take care of three little kids. Not that we can't," he said, his tone belligerent, "but maybe they'll be happier with you. Since that's what Diane wanted and all. You should help your sister since she's not had the breaks in life that you two have had."

Aberdeen told herself their parents' words didn't matter right now. They had always been cold and odd, and strangely preferential toward Diane. Aberdeen loved her sister as much as they did, but she wasn't blind to her faults, either. Diane had a selfish side that one day she might, hopefully, grow out of. For the sake of her nieces, Aberdeen prayed she did. "We'll take them back with us," she said finally, glancing at Johnny for his approval, which she knew would be there. "You can come see them as often as you like to visit."

"Ah, well. That won't be necessary," May said. "We don't travel much."

Their parents had never visited their home in Lance. Aberdeen shook her head. "There's always a first time for everything. I'm heading to bed. We'll be off in the morning."

"That will be fine." The relief on May's face was plain. "You are planning to adopt them, aren't you, Aberdeen? After all, it would help Diane so much. She just can't do this, you know."

Her mother's gaze was pleading. It occurred to Aberdeen that her sister's mothering skills were basically the same as May's. It was always Johnny who kept the family together, Aberdeen realized. Johnny had been adoring of his little sister and helpful to his big sister and they'd always known they had their protective Johnny looking out for them. Not their parents. Johnny.

"I don't know, Mom," Aberdeen said. "We'd have to see if a court would allow it. We don't know what is involved with an in-family adoption when a mother is simply absent by choice. There's finances to consider, too."

"We can't give you any money," May said quickly, and Johnny said, "We're not asking you for money. We just need to proceed in a responsible fashion for the girls' sakes."

"Well, I would think—" May began, but Johnny cut her off.

"Enough, Mom. We have a lot of decisions to make in the near future. For all we know, Diane could come home next week, ready to be a mother. Maybe she just needed a vacation."

Aberdeen hoped so, but doubted it. "Good night," she said, and headed upstairs.

Part of her—the dreamy, irresponsible part she rarely acknowledged—took flight for just an instant, wondering how her life might be different if she, too, just took off, as Diane had, following a man on the whim of her heart.

Like a certain cowboy.

A big, strong, muscular, teasing hunk of six-four cowboy.

But no. She was as different from Diane as night and day. She was a dreamer, maybe, not a doer. She would never fling caution to the wind and follow a man like Creed Callahan.

Yet sweet temptation tugged at her thoughts.

"I'VE BEEN THINKING," Creed told Judah as they made their way through Colorado, "that little cowboy church preacher was a little too uptight for me, anyway."

Judah glanced at him as Creed slumped in the passenger seat, doling out some of their favorite road food. They'd made a pit stop just outside of Denver and loaded up on the junk food Fiona wouldn't allow them to have.

"What made you decide that?" Judah asked, taking a swig of the Big Red Creed had put in the cup holder for him. "Because I was pretty certain uptight might be good for you."

"Maybe in small doses," Creed said, feeling better as every mile took him farther away from temptation. "I'm pretty sure I can't handle uptight in large doses."

"I'd say narrow escape, except I don't think you were in danger of getting caught." Judah munched happily on Doritos from the open bag between the seat. "No, I'm sure you had Free Bird written all over your forehead, bro. No worries."

Creed pondered that. "I've decided to make a run for the ranch."

Judah glanced at him. "Since when?"

Since he'd met the preacher. That was weird, though, Creed thought with a frown. Women usually made him want to get naked, not own a ranch. "I don't know."

"Okay, of all of us, you are not the one to settle down and grow a large family."

"Pete's happy. I could learn by example."

"You ran away from being Pete. Remember? You ran like a hungry wolf to a picnic basket."

Creed considered that as he crunched some chips. "I think I changed when I got my bell rung."

"Creed, you get your bell rung once a year."

"This was different," Creed said. "I saw stars."

"You saw nothing. You weren't yourself for two days," Judah told him. "Anyway, it's not enough to change you. You've always been a loose goose."

"Yeah. I suppose so." Creed lost his appetite for chips and stared morosely at his soda can. "You know, I think Fiona's right. This *is* trash we're eating. I can feel my intestines turning red."

Judah sighed. "This is nectar of the gods."

"Maybe I miss home-cooking. We don't have it bad with Fiona, you know?" The past several months had outlined that to Creed. "We were lucky she raised us."

"Yeah. We could have gone into the system."

"That would have sucked." Creed turned his mind away from thoughts of being separated from his brothers. "Although I met a cowboy who'd been adopted, and he was pretty happy. Things worked out for him."

"It does. But we were in a good place with Fiona and Burke."

"And that's why I intend to fight for the ranch," Creed said with determination. "I just need a woman to help me with this project."

"It'd take you twenty years to *find* a woman," Judah said with some sarcasm, which cut Creed. "I'd say Pete is safe. Anyway, I thought we all agreed that the sacrificial lamb would do the deed, inherit the ranch and divvy it up between all of us. Thereby leaving the rest of us free to graze on the good things in life."

Creed crushed his soda can. "I'm not sure I'm grazing on the good things in life."

"Oh. You want angel food cake." Judah nodded.

"Good luck with that. Let me know how it goes, will you?"

Creed rolled his eyes. Judah didn't understand. "I'm just saying, maybe we shouldn't burden Pete with all the responsibility."

"Why not? He's always been the responsible one."

"But maybe some of us should take a crack at being responsible, too. Take the pressure off him. He's got newborn triplets. It's selfish of us to stick him with all the duties."

"I think Fiona's probably realized by now that she can go ahead and award the ranch to Pete. Who could catch up with him? It would take years for one of us to find a woman and then have tons of kids. And what if the woman we found only wanted one? Or none?"

Creed gulped. He tried to envision Aberdeen with a big belly, and failed. She was such a slender woman. He liked slender, but then again, a little baby weight would look good on her. He liked full-figured gals, too.

Hell, he liked them all.

But he'd especially liked her, for some reason.

"It was the thrill of the hunt, nothing more," Judah said, his tone soothing. "Down, boy. It would have come to nothing."

Creed scowled. "I have no idea what you're babbling about."

"We are not settled men by nature. None of us sits and reads a whole lot, for example."

"Not true. Jonas read a hell of a lot to get through med school. And Sam for law school. And Rafe's been known to pick up a Greek tome or two."

"Pleasure reading. Expand-the-mind reading. That's what I'm talking about."

"Well, we're not reading romance novels, if that's

what you're getting at." Creed put away the chips, beginning to feel slightly sick to his stomach. "Although maybe you should."

"What's that supposed to mean?" Judah demanded.

"Maybe if you read romance novels, you'd be able to see that which has been at the end of your nose for years, dummy." Creed jammed his hat down over his eyes, preparing to get in a few winks. "Think about it. It'll come to you." He pondered Judah's thick skull for a moment, then said, "Or maybe not."

Judah made no reply, which was fine with Creed, because all he wanted to do was sit and think about Aberdeen for a few minutes. *Judah is wrong. I owe it to myself to see if I can find a woman I could fall for. I owe it to myself to try to figure out if I'd be a good father. Maybe I would. I like kids.*

Wait. He didn't know that for sure. Truthfully, Pete's babies kind of intimidated him. Of course, they were no bigger than fleas. And fleas weren't good.

Pete's girls were cute as buttons. And they would grow. But they still made him nervous. Maybe he didn't have uncle-type feelings in him. He'd been uninterested in holding them. But they were so small and fragile. *I've eaten breadsticks bigger than their legs.*

Damn. I'm twenty-nine, and I'm scared of my nieces. That can't be good.

"Have you held Pete's kids yet?" Creed asked Judah.

"Nah. They're kind of tiny. And they yell a lot." Judah shook his head. "I don't want kids. I'm a quiet kind of guy. Organized. Peaceful. Small, squalling things are not peaceful."

Creed felt better. Maybe he wasn't totally a heel for not bonding with his nieces. "I just think I could be good at this, if I put my mind to it."

"At what? Being a dad?" Judah snorted. "Sure. Why not? As long as you give up rodeo and getting dropped on your head, you might be all right."

"Give up rodeo?" Creed echoed, the thought foreign and uncomfortable. He planned on rodeoing in the Grandfather's Rodeo, if they had such a thing. They'd drag him out of the saddle when he was cold and dead and rigor mortis had set in. Cowboy rigor mortis. What man didn't want to die with his boots on?

Of course, if he wasn't good at it anymore… "What the hell am I doing?"

"Search me," Judah replied. "I can't figure you out, bro. It'd take a licensed brain-drainer to do that."

Creed decided not to punch Judah, even though he was pretty certain he should. All he knew was that before his concussion, before he'd met Aberdeen, he'd been sure of who he was. He'd had a plan.

Now, he was asking himself all kinds of questions. Judah was right: It would take a shrink to figure out the knots in his brain.

I should have kissed her again. Then I wouldn't be thinking about her. I'm shallow like that.

I really am.

TWO DAYS LATER, Johnny watched as a man he was particularly displeased to see walked into the bar. This reappearance couldn't have come at a worse time. Johnny shook his head, wondering why bad pennies always had to return when a man needed a lucky penny in his boot.

He wasn't surprised when Aberdeen went pale when she saw their customer. But then, to Johnny's astonishment, Aberdeen brightened, and went to hug the tall, lanky cowboy.

"Hello, Shawn," she said. "Long time, no see."

"Too long."

Blond-haired, smooth "Re-ride" Parker's glance slid over Aberdeen's curves. Johnny felt his blood begin to boil.

"Hello, Johnny," Aberdeen's ex-husband said.

"Re-ride," Johnny muttered, not pleased and not hiding it.

"Fixed this place up nicely." Re-ride looked around the bar. "I remember when it was just a hole in the wall."

"How's the rodeo treating you?" Johnny asked, figuring he could bring up unpleasantries if Shawn wanted. When Johnny had bought this place, it *had* been a hole in the wall—and Re-ride had just left Aberdeen with no means of support. Johnny had settled here to help Aberdeen mend the pieces of her shattered marriage, and seeing the cause of his sister's former distress did not leave him in a welcoming frame of mind.

"I'm not riding much these days," Shawn said, staring at Aberdeen, drinking her in, it seemed to Johnny, with an unnecessary amount of enthusiasm. "A man can't be on the circuit forever."

Johnny grunted. He followed the scores. He chatted to the cowboys who came in. Re-ride had never broken out of the bottom of the cowboy bracket. Maybe he had bad luck. Johnny didn't follow him closely enough to know. What he did know was that he seemed to get a lot of "re-rides," hence the name which had stuck all these years. In Johnny's opinion, Shawn could have quit the circuit ten years ago and no one would have missed him. "Guess not. Want to buy a bar?"

Aberdeen scowled at him. "No, he most certainly does not, I'm sure. Shawn, can we offer you a soda?"

Re-ride glanced at Johnny. "Ah, no. Thanks, though.

Actually, I stopped by to talk to you, Aberdeen. If you have a moment."

Johnny felt his blood, which was already hot, heat up like he was sitting on a lit pyre of dry tinder.

"Johnny, can you listen out for the girls?" Aberdeen took off her apron, put the broom in the closet, and nodded to Shawn. "I do have a few minutes. Not long, though."

"Girls?" Shawn asked, snapping out of his lusting staring for a moment.

"Aberdeen's adopting three small children," Johnny said cheerfully, instantly realizing how to stop the man from using his soft-hearted sister for whatever reason his rodent-faced self had conjured up. What Aberdeen saw in the man, Johnny would never understand. *Sneaky like a rat.*

"Johnny," Aberdeen said, her tone warning as she opened the door. Re-ride followed her after tipping his hat to Johnny. Johnny ignored it, not feeling the need to socialize further.

This was no time for Re-Ride Parker to show up in Aberdeen's life. He resented every time the man appeared—usually about once or twice a year—but this time was different. He could tell, like a wolf scenting danger on the wind. Shawn was up to no good. He was never up to any good, as far as Johnny was concerned, but the way he'd practically licked Aberdeen with his eyeballs had Johnny's radar up. In fact, it was turned on high-anxiety.

Very bad timing, he told himself, but then again, that was Re-ride. Bad, bad timing.

"I'VE CHANGED MY MIND," Fiona told the five brothers who came by for a family council—and to eat barbecue, grilled corn and strawberry cake. Pete was at his house with his daughters and Jackie, probably juggling to keep up with bottles and diapers. Creed had promised to give him the thumbnail sketch of what happened at the meeting.

"I've had a lot on my mind. And I've been doing a lot of thinking about all of you. And your futures." She looked around at them, and Creed noticed Burke give her a worried glance as he served drinks in the large upstairs library. "I can't leave the ranch to the brother who gets married first and has the most children. That was my plan when Bode Jenkins got his cronies to try to legally seize this land for eminent domain purposes. His claim was that this particular property was too large for just one person to own—basically me—when the greater good could be affected by a new water system and schools. So I decided that if you all had children, we could make the case for the greater good, since there were plenty of Callahans. The state wouldn't have the right—nor would they dream, I would hope—of tossing a large family off the only property you've all ever known."

She nodded her head, her silvery-white hair shining under the lights, her eyes bright as she chose her words. Creed was amazed by his aunt's energy. For the hundredth time, he pondered how much she'd given up for them.

He even felt a little bad that he'd tried to thwart her plans. But fate stepped in and, just as soon as he was positive he wanted to thwart her forever, he'd met a girl who made his heart go *ding!* like a dinner bell. Maybe even a wedding bell. That was life for you.

"So," Fiona continued, "I have a confession to make. In my haste to keep the ranch out of the state's hands, and out of Bode's possession, I made a mistake. I played right in to his hands by agreeing to sell the land to a private developer. Fighting the state would have taken years in court, and money I was loath to spend out of your estate. So I chose a private buyer to sell it to, and made a deal that they would allow Rancho Diablo to be taken over by an angel investor. My offer was that we would buy the ranch back from them in five years, when Bode had turned his eyes to someone else's property or passed on, whichever came first." She took a deep breath, appearing to brace herself. "However, Bode was ahead of me, and the private investor I thought was absolutely safe and in our corner turned out to be in that nasty man's pocket. So," she said, looking around at each brother, "we're homeless in nine months. Totally. And for that, I can never say how sorry I am. I'm sorry for not being a wiser manager. I'm sorry that you men won't have the home your parents built—"

She burst into tears. The brothers sat, shocked, staring at their aunt, then at Burke, then at each other. Creed took a couple of quick breaths, wondering if he'd heard her right, if he could possibly have just heard that Rancho Diablo wasn't theirs anymore, and quickly realized this was no playacting, no manipulation, on Aunt Fiona's part.

It scared the hell out of him. His brothers looked just as stunned. But their aunt had been bearing an oh-so-heavy burden alone, so Creed got up and went to pat her back. "Aunt Fiona, don't cry. This isn't a matter for tears. We're not angry with you. We would never be angry with you. You've done the very best you could, and probably better than most people could under the circumstances."

"You *should* be angry! If you had an ounce of common sense, you would be, you scalawag." She pushed his hand away, and those of the other brothers when they came to fuss over her.

"But I probably don't have an ounce of sense," Creed said, "and we love you. Rancho Diablo is yours just as much as ours." He gulped, trying not to think about the yawning chasm that their lives had just turned into with a stroke of an errant wand. This was *home*.

Although perhaps not any more. But he only said, "Let Sam look over whatever papers you have to make certain there are no loopholes. Maybe call in some legal beagles. Right, Sam?"

His younger brother nodded. Creed got down on a knee and looked into her eyes. "You should have told us instead of trying to marry us off. Maybe we could have helped you."

"I wanted babies." She blew her nose into a delicate white handkerchief. "If I was going to lose the ranch, I wanted you to have brides who were eager to marry into the Callahan name, and live at Rancho Diablo. At least get married here, for heaven's sakes. But you're all so slow and stubborn," she said, with a glance around at each of them, "that I realized I was going to have to be honest with you instead of waiting for the spring sap to rise. Goodness knows, even the bulls are looking for mates. But not my nephews."

She sighed, put upon, and Creed glanced around at his brothers with a grin. "We tried to get hitched for you, Aunt Fiona. The ladies just won't have us."

"Well, I certainly don't blame them." She took the drink that Burke handed her, sipping it without energy. "But I'm making other plans. I'm holding a matchmaking ball, right here at Rancho Diablo. I'm inviting every single female that my friends know, and that's a ton, from as far away as the ladies care to come, all expenses paid. It's probably the last big party I'll ever have at this ranch, and I intend for it to be a blowout that will be talked about for years. Your bachelor ball, my going-away party."

"Whoa," Judah said, "there are only five of us, Aunt Fiona. We can't entertain a whole lot of women in a chivalrous manner."

"Goodness me," Fiona said, "most men would leap at the chance to have a bachelor raffle held in their honor."

"Bachelor raffle?" Jonas asked. "That sounds dangerous."

"Only if you're a wienie." Aunt Fiona gave her nephews an innocent look. "And there are no wienies in this room, I hope."

"Definitely not," Creed's twin, Rafe, said.

"No," Sam said, "but as the youngest, I'd like to put forth that I should have the lion's share of the ladies." His brothers scowled at him. "What? None of you wants to settle down. I'm not exactly opposed. At least not for the short term."

"You don't want to settle down," Jonas said, "you want to sow your wild oats. And all of us are ahead of you in the age department."

"Uh-oh," Sam said, leaping at the chance to bait his eldest brother, "do I hear the sound of a man's biological clock ticking? Bong, bong, Big Ben?"

Jonas looked as though he was about to pop an artery, Creed thought, not altogether amused. "We don't need a raffle or a bachelor bake-athon or whatever, Aunt Fiona. We're perfectly capable of finding women on our own. In relation to the ranch, if it isn't ours anymore—potentially—then there's no reason for us to hurry out and find brides. What we need to find are excellent lawyers, a whole team of them, who can unwind whatever Bode thinks he's got you strung with."

"We don't need to hire a lawyer, or a team," Aunt Fiona said, and the brothers looked at her with surprise. "We won't hire a lawyer because I hired a private investigator to keep an eye on him. I'm just positive Bode'll make a slip any day, and I'll be on him like a bird on a bug. And," she said, her doughy little face sad and tearstained with now-dried tears, "it wouldn't look good that I hired a P.I. to dig up dirt on him." She leaned close to Creed to whisper. "However, there's every chance he knows."

Creed winced. "Not unless he's bugged the house." Pete had claimed that someone had locked him in the basement last winter, searched the house and destroyed Aunt Fiona's jars of canned preserves and other stored food in an attempt to find something. What that person could have been looking for was anyone's guess. Nothing had been stolen—no television, none of Fiona's jewelry, no tools. He supposed the house could be bugged, but the room they were currently sitting in was far away from the front doors and not easy to access. Someone would have needed several hours to search the house and plant bugs, and Pete hadn't been locked away that long. "It would be very difficult to bug this place."

"But he might know many things about us anyway," Fiona said, "because he gossips a lot."

"Bode?" Jonas said. "No one would talk about us to him."

"You think Sabrina McKinley might have told him something?" Sam asked, "since she's working as his caregiver?"

"No, Sabrina wouldn't blab," Aunt Fiona said, "because she's working for me."

Chapter Five

"Whoa," Jonas said, "Aunt Fiona, that little gypsy is a private investigator?"

Aunt Fiona nodded. "She's actually an investigative reporter, which is even better because sometimes they're nosier. It's her sister, Seton, who's the actual gumshoe. And don't sound so shocked, Jonas. You didn't think she was a real fortune-teller? She was playing a part I hired her to play."

Creed was having trouble dealing with all this new information. "But didn't she say that our ranch was in trouble, and a bunch of other nonsense?"

"Yes, but I gave her a script. I was trying to warn you, spur you along. As I mentioned, you're all quite slow. Thick, even. Why, I'd say molasses in winter moves faster than my nephews." She gave a pensive sigh. "The problem is, you don't have a home anymore. We don't have a place to run our business. And only Pete got married. At least he's happy," she said. "At least he found a wonderful woman." She cast an eye over the rest of her charges. "The rest of you will have a less favorable position to offer a wife. Your stock has dropped, as they say."

"Okay," Jonas said, "let's not think about our marital futures right now. Let's deal strictly with the business end."

"I say we go kick Bode Jenkins' skinny ass," Sam put in, and everyone shouted, *"No!"*

Sam said, "What a bunch of pansies."

"You have to be more sly than that," Fiona said sternly. "Violence is unacceptable. It's all about the mind, and I simply got out-thought."

"I'll have a friend eyeball the papers," Jonas said thoughtfully. "In the meantime, I'm closing on that land I offered on next week. We're not exactly homeless. If we have about nine months, we have enough time to move Rancho Diablo operations there. And build a house. It won't be like this one," he said, glancing around the room, "but it will be ours."

"What would you supposedly get for the house and land—if the deal is for real?" Rafe asked.

"Only ten million dollars," Fiona said. "A half of what it's worth for all the land, the house, and—"

She stopped, glanced at Burke, who shrugged.

"And?" Creed prompted.

"And mineral rights, and so on," she said, and Creed wondered if she'd just hedged some information. Fiona was known to keep her cards close to the vest. "It's a pittance, when you consider that we won't be able even to use the name *Rancho Diablo* anymore. We will truly be starting our brand from the bottom again."

Fiona's cheeks had pink spots in them and her eyes glittered. Creed could see that not only was her pride stung because Bode had outwitted her, she was crushed to have to give her nephews this hard news.

"We'll talk about it later," Creed said. "For now, this is enough to digest. I don't think you should trouble yourself anymore tonight, Aunt Fiona."

Judah nodded. "I agree. My only question is, Bode hasn't been bothering you lately, has he?"

Fiona shook her head. "He's been pretty quiet since he thinks he got me over a barrel."

"About Sabrina," Jonas said. "What happens if Bode finds out that she's actually a reporter?"

They all took that in for a moment. Bode was known for his hot temper and grudges. He was underhanded, unforgiving. The tall, skinny man was unkind to just about everyone he knew; he kept people in his pocket by making sure he had whatever they needed. Bode was a power broker; he liked that power, and no one crossed him lightly.

Creed looked at his aunt. "Do you think involving her was a good idea, Aunt Fiona?"

"She and her sister came highly recommended. They are the nieces of—"

"Oh, no," Sam said, "not one of your Books 'n' Bingo cronies."

Fiona arched a brow at her youngest nephew. "Yes, as a matter of fact. I always hire friends, whether it's for curtain-making, preserving or tree-trimming. There's no better way to ensure loyalty and fairness in a job than to hire one's friends."

Creed's heart sank a little, too, just south of his boots. Aunt Fiona was in over her head. The expressions on his brothers' faces confirmed his own doubts. His cell phone jumped in his pocket, forestalling his worried thoughts. Glancing at the number, he frowned, wondering why he'd be getting a call from Wyoming.

Probably something to do with the rodeo he'd crashed out of. "Excuse me for a moment, Aunt Fiona," he said, and stepped outside the library. "Hello?"

"Creed Callahan?" a man asked.

"Yes. Who's speaking?"

"This is Johnny Donovan. You were at our place—"

"I remember you, Johnny. How are you doing?" Creed's heart jumped right back up into his chest where it belonged as he wondered if Aberdeen might have put Johnny up to calling him. He could only hope.

"I'm fine. In a bit of a tight spot, actually."

"Oh?" Johnny had seemed capable of handling just about anything. "Something I can help with?"

"Actually, yes, perhaps," Johnny said. "You remember my sister, Aberdeen?"

Did he ever. "Yeah." He made his voice deliberately disinterested, not wanting to sound like an overeager stud.

"Well, I'm wondering—jeez, this is awkward," Johnny said. "I'm wondering if I paid your way back up here for a week, could you come keep an eye on my bar?"

Creed's jaw went slack. "Um—"

"I know. Like I said, it's awkward as hell. I wouldn't ask if I wasn't up against it, and if I didn't know that you were taking a bit of time off from the circuit."

"Yeah, I am." Creed sank into a hallway chair, staring out the arched, two-story windows that looked out over flat, wide, beautiful Rancho Diablo. "What's going on?"

"I need to be in Montana for a few weeks. Aberdeen needs to be there as well. We have a child custody hearing coming up."

Creed frowned. He didn't remember anything being discussed about children. Did Aberdeen have kids? He knew nothing about her personal life—and yet, whenever he thought about her, he got an irrational shot of pleasure. *I'm doomed. I'm damned. She's not only a preacher but one with custody issues. Yee-haw.* "I see," he murmured, not seeing at all, but wanting to prod Johnny into spilling more info.

"Yeah. We can close the bar for two weeks, but I still hate to leave it unattended. This isn't the best area of town, as you know. We're kind of out of the way. I have a ton of friends here who could watch it, but frankly, I was thinking you owed me one."

Creed laughed, detecting teasing in Johnny's voice. "I probably do."

"I believe in doing business between friends," Johnny said. "The pay is generous. My bar's my livelihood. I'd like to keep it in safe hands."

Creed grinned. "And you don't want to keep it open?"

"Not necessarily, unless you want to. You don't have any experience with a bar or family-owned restaurant, do you?"

"Not so much." Creed wondered if he should back away from the offer politely or jump at the chance to see if Aberdeen still smoked his peace pipe the way he remembered she did. He was pretty certain she set him on fire all over. Sure, any woman could probably do that if a man was in the right, open mood, Creed mused—but Aberdeen seemed to do it for him even when she aggravated the hell out him.

He thought that was a pretty interesting juxtaposition. "We do have a family business, but it isn't in the same field as yours. We don't have strangers knocking on our door at all hours, not often anyway."

Johnny laughed. "So you'll do it?"

"I might. Let me run it past the family."

"Sounds mafia-like."

Creed grinned to himself. "Sometimes it can seem

that way to outsiders. I'll get back in touch with you soon, Johnny. Good to hear from you."

He turned off his phone, sitting and considering this new twist for a moment. His gaze searched the wide vista outside, its dusty expanse vibrant even as night was covering the mesa. And then, he saw them, running like the wind across the faraway reaches of the ranch, black as night, fast as wind, free as spirits.

"Los Diablos," he murmured, awed by the hypnotizing beauty. "The Diablos are running!" he called to his brothers, and they came out of the library to stand at his side, watching in silence, shoulder to shoulder, knowing this might be one of the last times they ever saw the beautiful horses materializing across the evening-tinged swath of Rancho Diablo land.

"Are you all right?" Aberdeen asked Johnny as she walked into the upstairs living room. "You look like you're thinking deep thoughts."

Johnny put his cell phone in his pocket. "No deeper than usual."

She smiled at him. "Then why are you frowning?"

"I've just been thinking about how we're going to make this all work out."

"Oh." She nodded and sat down on a worn cloth sofa. "I finally got all three girls to sleep. They are so sweet when they sleep. They look so angelic and happy."

A small smile lifted Johnny's mouth—but not for long. "Has Diane called to check on them?"

Aberdeen shook her head. "I think she probably won't for a while. I did talk to Mom and Dad today. They said Diane has decided to go around the world on a sailboat with her new boyfriend. They expect the trip to take about a year and a half."

Johnny's face turned dark. "You're kidding, right?"

"I wouldn't joke about that." Aberdeen sighed. "We need her at least to sign some forms that state we can make medical decisions for the girls while she's gone."

"I'm going over to France," Johnny said, and Aberdeen could see his jaw was tight. "I'm going to try to talk some sense into her. She just can't abandon her children. I don't know if she needs medication or what is going on—"

"Johnny." Aberdeen patted the sofa cushion beside her. "Come sit down."

He sighed. "Maybe I need a drink."

"It wouldn't help. I think you going to France is a good idea. I'll stay here with the girls and start looking for a house and school and a doctor."

"Have you ever thought how much having the girls here is going to change your life, even more than mine?"

Aberdeen blinked. "There's no point to worrying about the situation. We love the girls. Diane, as much as I hate to say it, appears to be unfit or unwilling at the moment."

Johnny sat silently for a few minutes. "I'll make a plane reservation. I may drag Diane back here kicking and screaming, though."

"Do you want me to go?" Aberdeen asked, and Johnny quickly shook his head.

"No. You've got enough to do in the next two weeks for the custody hearing." Johnny stood, going to look out a window over the parking lot. "I think I might sell the bar, Aberdeen."

She drew in a sharp breath. "Why?"

He didn't turn around. "I think it's time."

"Is this because of Shawn?" she asked, hating to ask but feeling she had to. She was aware Johnny had been biting his tongue for the past two weeks to keep from complaining about her ex-husband's frequent presence. It would be like Johnny to decide to sell the bar and move the newly enlarged family to Timbuktu if he thought he could get rid of Shawn. Johnny didn't understand her rosy daydreams of romance with Shawn were long evaporated. Shawn was comfortable, someone she'd grown up with, in a strange way.

"No," he said, but she wondered if he was being completely truthful. "But on that unpleasant topic, is there a reason he's suddenly hanging around again?"

A flush ran up Aberdeen's cheeks and neck. "I'm not exactly sure what you mean, or if he has a specific reason for his presence. He says he's changed—"

"Ugh," Johnny interrupted. "Changed what? His spots? I don't think so."

That stung. Aberdeen blinked back tears. "Johnny, he's been through a lot. It's not like I'd remarry him. You know that."

"I just think it's not a good time for someone like him to be in your life if we're serious about getting custody of the kids."

"I think he's lonely, and nothing more."

"You're not lonely right now," Johnny pointed out. "You're busy raising three little girls who really need you."

"Shawn knows me. He's a part of my past."

Johnny turned away. Aberdeen took a deep breath. "So, why are you really thinking about selling the bar? You've mentioned it a couple of times. I'm beginning to think you might really be considering it."

"Aberdeen," Johnny said suddenly, ignoring her question, "If your Prince Charming rode up tomorrow on a white horse, would you want that?"

"I think by twenty-nine a woman doesn't believe in fairy tales. The fairy godmother never showed up for me." She touched her brother on the arm, and after a moment, he gave her a hug. They stood together for a few moments, and Aberdeen closed her eyes, drinking in the closeness.

Just for a few heartbeats, she felt Johnny relax. He was sweet big brother again, not worried, not overburdened by life. She let out a breath, wishing this feeling could last forever.

The sound of a baby crying drifted across the hall. Aberdeen broke away from Johnny, smiling up at him. "Don't worry so much, big brother," she said, but he just shook his head.

"By the way," he said offhandedly as she started to leave the room to check on Lincoln Rose and her sisters. "I've got Creed Callahan coming to watch over the bar while we're away."

Aberdeen looked at Johnny. It didn't matter that her heart skipped a beat—several beats—at the mention of Creed's name, or that she'd thought she'd never see him again. "That's probably a good idea," she murmured, going to comfort the baby, wondering if her brother thought he had to play matchmaker in her life. Johnny was worried she was falling for Shawn again. So had he called in a handpicked Prince Charming?

It would be so like Johnny—but if he was meddling in her life, she'd have to slap him upside his big head.

He just didn't understand that Creed Callahan, while handsome enough to tease her every unattended thought, was no Prince Charming—at least not hers.

Chapter Six

The next day, Aberdeen wondered if her brother understood something about men that she didn't. Shawn sat at their kitchen table, watching her feed the girls and wearing a goofy grin.

"I never thought you'd be such good mother material," Shawn said, and Aberdeen looked at him.

"Why would you think I wouldn't be?"

Shawn was the opposite of Creed in appearance: blond, lanky, relaxed. Almost too relaxed, maybe bordering on lazy, she thought. Creed was super-dark, built like a bad girl's dream with big muscles and a strong chest, and not relaxed at all. She frowned as she wiped Lincoln Rose's little chin. Actually, she didn't know much about Creed. He'd been ill when she'd seen him. But she still had the impression that he wasn't exactly Mr. Happy-Go-Lucky.

Not like Shawn.

"You always seemed too career-oriented to want a family." Shawn sipped at his coffee, and smiled a charming smile at her. "I always felt like you were going to be the breadwinner in our marriage."

"Would that have been a problem?"

"For a man's ego, sure. Some men might like their wife being the big earner, but not me. I have my pride, you know." He grabbed one of the carrots she'd put on the three-year-old's plate and munched it.

Not much pride. Aberdeen told herself to be nice and handed him Lincoln Rose. "Let's test your fathering skills, then."

"I'm a family man," he said, holding Lincoln Rose about a foot away from him. Lincoln Rose studied him and he studied her, and then the baby opened her mouth like a bird and let out a good-sized wail. "Clearly she doesn't recognize father material," Shawn said, handing Lincoln Rose back to Aberdeen.

Aberdeen rolled her eyes. "Have you ever held a baby?"

"Not that I can recall," Shawn said cheerfully. "But that doesn't mean I couldn't learn to like it. I just need practice and a good teacher." He looked at her so meaningfully that Aberdeen halted, recognizing a strange light in her husband's eyes. He looked purposeful, she thought—and Shawn and purposeful did not go together well.

"There was no double meaning in that statement, was there?" Aberdeen asked.

Shawn's expression turned serious. "Aberdeen, look, I've been doing a lot of thinking." Idly, he grabbed another carrot; thankfully, the toddlers didn't seem to mind. Aberdeen put some golden raisins on their plates to keep them happy while Shawn got over his thinking fit. "I know you're determined to adopt these little ladies."

"They will always have a home with me."

Shawn nodded. "I think that's a good idea. Diane is a great girl, but even back when you and I were married, she wasn't the most stable person, if you know what I mean."

Aberdeen bit her lip. She didn't want to discuss this with him. "Diane has a good heart," she murmured.

"I know," Shawn said, his tone soothing, "but you're doing right by these girls. I believe they need you." He gave her a winning smile. "And I know you're worried about the temporary-custody situation. I've been thinking about how I could be of assistance."

Aberdeen shook her head. "Thanks, Shawn, but I believe the good Lord will take care of us."

"I'd like to help," he said. "I really mean it."

She looked at him, her attention totally caught. It seemed the little girls in their sweet pink dresses were listening, too, because their attention seemed focused on Shawn. Handsome Shawn with the charming smile, always getting what he wanted. Aberdeen watched him carefully. "What are you getting at?"

"I just want you to know that I'm here for you." He took a deep breath, and she could see that he meant every word—at least, he did while he was speaking them. "I wasn't the world's greatest husband, Aberdeen. You deserved a hell of a lot better. And I'd like to be here for you now if you need me." He gave her the most sincere look she'd ever seen him wear on his handsome face. "All you have to do is say the word. I'd marry you again tomorrow if it would help you with custody or adoption or anything."

Aberdeen blinked, shocked. But as she looked into Shawn's eyes, she realized he was trying to atone, in his own bumbling way, for the past.

And as much as she'd like to tell him to buzz off, she wondered if she could afford to be so callous. She didn't know how the courts would regard her. She thought they would see her in a positive light, as a minister, as Diane's sister, as a caring aunt.

But what if the court preferred a married mother for these children? Aberdeen looked at her nieces. They seemed so happy, so content to be with her. Their eyes were so bright and eager, always focused on her as they banged spoons or pulled off their shoes and dropped them to the floor. Did it matter that she planned to live with them out of the state where they'd been raised? Would she look more stable with a husband? She and Johnny and Diane knew that even two-parent homes lacked stability—but would a court of law see it that way? For her nieces' sake, maybe she couldn't just write Shawn's offer off as so much talk.

"I would hope nothing like that will be necessary."

He shrugged. "I mean it, Aberdeen, I really do. If you need a husband, then, I'm your man."

"What happened to the man who didn't want to be married to the family breadwinner?" she asked, not wanting to encourage him.

He smiled. "Well, I'd feel like things were a bit more balanced since you need me, Aberdeen."

She pulled back a little and tried not to let anger swamp her. Shawn was pretty focused on his own needs; she knew that. But he was harmless, too—now that she wasn't married to him, she could see him in a more generous light. Sometimes. Creed's dark-blue eyes flashed in her memory. She could see him laughing, even as he was in pain from the concussion. The man had a sense of humor, though things hadn't been going his way. He had a roguish charm, and she'd told herself to run from it.

Because it had reminded her of Shawn. *Crazy,* she'd thought of him. *No more loco in my life.*

And yet loco was sitting here right now offering to give her the illusion of stability for the sake of her nieces.

Aberdeen swallowed. Maybe she shouldn't dismiss the offer out of hand. Husband, wife, devoted uncle—not quite a nuclear family here, but close enough.

But it was Shawn. And she wanted something else. "Have some more carrots," she said absently, her eyes on her nieces. She'd been totally attracted to the cowboy from New Mexico, as much as she didn't want to admit it, and no matter how hard she'd tried to forget him, he hadn't left her memory.

But maybe it was better to deal with the devil she knew—if she needed a devil at all.

"Don't mind me," Creed said three days later, as Johnny looked around the bar one last time. "I've got everything I'll need. I'll be living like King Tut here."

"He didn't live long," Johnny pointed out, "and I think somebody might have done him in. Let's hope that your time here is spent in a more pleasant manner."

Creed grinned. "You're sure you don't want me to keep this place open for business?"

"It's too much to ask of a friend," Johnny said.

"Lot of income for you to lose," Creed pointed out. "I'm averse to losing income."

Johnny laughed. "I am, too. But this has got to be done. You just keep an eye on things, guard my castle and I'll be grateful for the imposition on your time."

Creed took a bar stool, glancing around the bar. "You did yourself a good turn buying this place, Johnny. It's nice. Did it take you long to turn a profit?"

"No. Not really. Building business was slow, but it happened over time. People like to hear Aberdeen preach, and then they remember us for snacks and beverages the rest of the week. It's a loyal crowd around here." He took a rag and wiped the mahogany bar with it. "I might sell, you know."

Creed blinked. "Do you mind me asking why?"

Johnny shook his head. "You'll see soon enough."

Creed wasn't sure what he meant by that, but if Johnny didn't want to discuss his business, that was fine by him. He wouldn't want to talk to anyone about Rancho Diablo and all that was happening back home unless he knew that person very well.

Actually, he wouldn't discuss it with anyone but family. Everything had gotten complicated real fast. He looked around the bar, trying to see himself with some kind of business set-up like this, and failed.

But he'd always think of it kindly because it had been his inn in the wilderness. If he hadn't come here—

"Here you go, sweetie," he heard Aberdeen say, and then he heard feet coming down the staircase. He watched the stairs expectantly, wondering how he'd feel about seeing her again. Certainly he hadn't stopped thinking about her. She was a pretty cute girl, any man would have to admit. In fact, probably lots of men noticed. But she was a prickly one. She would never have fitted into one of Aunt Fiona's marriage schemes. The woman was spicy and probably didn't have a maternal bone in her body.

Still, he waited, his eyes eager for that first glimpse of her.

She made it into view with a baby in her arms, holding the hand of a tiny toddler and with a somewhat larger toddler hanging on to her skirt as they slowly negotiated the staircase. Creed's face went slack, and his heart began beating hard in his chest. Three little blond girls?

"Holy smokes," he said, "you guys have been keeping secrets from me." He got up to help the small girls make it down the last few steps so they wouldn't face-plant at the bottom of the staircase. One shrank back from him, wanting to get to the landing herself, and one little girl smiled up at him angelically, and his heart fell into a hole in his chest. They were sweet, no question.

And then he looked up into Aberdeen's blue eyes, and it was all he could do not to stammer. "Hello, Aberdeen."

She smiled at him tentatively. "Hi, Creed. So nice of you to come look after Johnny's bar."

He caught his breath at the sight of those eyes. She was smiling at him, damn it, and he couldn't remember her ever being soft around him. It had his heart booming and his knees shaking just a bit. "It's nothing," he said, trying to sound gallant and not foolish, and Aberdeen smiled at him again.

"Oh, it's something to my brother. He said you're just the man he could trust to keep his bar safe."

Creed stepped back, nearly blinded by all the feminine firepower being aimed at him. "It's nothing," he repeated.

She gave him a last smile, then looked at Johnny. "We're ready for the road. Aren't we, girls?" She looked at Creed. "I'm sorry. These are my nieces. We're going to Montana for a custody hearing."

"Custody?"

She nodded. "I'm filing for temporary custody of the girls for now. And then maybe later, something more, if necessary."

The smile left her face, and Creed just wanted it back. "They sure are cute," he said, feeling quite stupid and confused, but the last thing he'd ever imagined was that Aberdeen Donovan might one day be the mother of three little girls. He didn't know what else to say. Clearly, he didn't know as much about these folks as he'd thought he had. He'd best stick to what he'd been hired for. "Well, I'll keep the floor nailed down," he said to Johnny, his gaze on Aberdeen.

"I'll check in on you soon enough." Johnny helped Aberdeen herd the girls toward the door. "If you have any questions, give me a ring on my cell. And thanks again, Creed. I can't tell you how much I appreciate this."

"I appreciated you saving my life," Creed murmured, letting one of the tiny dolls take him by the hand. He led her to Johnny's big truck, and watched to see that she was put in her car seat securely, and then he waved as they drove away, his head whirling.

"Three," he muttered. "Three small, needy damsels in some kind of distress." He headed back inside the bar, shell-shocked. Aberdeen had never mentioned children. Of course, they'd barely spoken to each other.

At the moment, his swagger was replaced by stagger, and a rather woeful stagger at that.

"I kissed a woman who's getting custody of three children," he said to himself as he locked up the bar. "That's living dangerously, and I sure as *hell* don't want to end up like Pete."

Or do I?

Chapter Seven

A couple of hours later, Creed was lying on the sofa upstairs, nursing a brewski and pondering what all he didn't know about Aberdeen. He was certain he could still smell the sweet perfume she wore, something flowery and clean and feminine, like delicate lilies and definitely not baby powder from the three little darlings—when he heard a window sliding open downstairs. The sound might not have been obvious to most people, but since he and his brothers had done their share of escaping out of windows in the middle of the night, he knew the stealthy sound by heart.

And that meant someone was due for an ass-kicking. He searched around for appropriate armament, finding Johnny's available weaponry lacking. There was a forgotten baby bottle on the coffee table. A few books were stacked here and there, mostly addressing the topic of raising children.

This was a side of Aberdeen he had totally missed. Creed vowed that if the opportunity ever presented itself, he might ask a few questions about parenthood, a subject he found somewhat alarming. He glanced around the room again, but there wasn't a baseball bat or even a small handgun to be found. If Johnny had a gun, he probably had it locked in a drawer now that he had small angels terrorizing his abode. If Creed had children, he'd certainly have the world's most secure gun cabinet with all things that go pop safely locked away.

He was going to have to make do with his beer bottle, he decided, and crept down the stairs. There he saw his uninvited guest rooting around in the liquor bottles like a martini-seeking raccoon.

And then he spied a very useful thing: a long-handled broom. In the dim light, he could barely make out a shadow investigating the different choices the bar had to offer. The man seemed in no hurry to make his selection; apparently he was a thief of some distinction. When he finally settled on a liquor, he took his time pouring it into a glass. Creed wondered if olives speared on a plastic sword, perhaps a twist of lemon, might be next for his discerning guest.

The thief took a long, appreciative drink. Creed picked up the broom, extending the wooden handle toward the intruder, giving him a pointed jab in the side. His guest dropped his beverage and whirled around, the sound of shattering glass interrupting the stillness.

"Who's there?"

Creed grinned to himself, reaching out with the broom for a slightly more robust jab. The intruder was scared, and clearly hadn't yet located Creed in the dark room. Moonlight spilled through the windows, bouncing a reflection back from the bar mirror, so Creed had an excellent view of his shadowy target. "The devil," he said. "Boo!"

The man abandoned his pride and shot to the door. Creed stuck out the pole one last time, tripping his guest to the floor. "Not so fast, my friend," Creed said. "You haven't paid for your drink."

"Who are you?" The thief scrambled to his feet.

"Who are you?" Creed asked. "The bar's closed. Didn't you see the sign?"

"I—I wasn't doing anything wrong. I was just wetting my whistle."

"Do you do this often?" Creed asked. "Because I think the owners might object."

"They don't care. They give me free drinks all the time." He backed toward the window where he'd let himself in, realizing he wasn't going to get past Creed and his broom.

Creed put the handle out, tripping the man from behind. "Why do they give you free drinks, friend?"

"Because I was married to Aberdeen. And I'm going to marry her again. So I have a right to be here," he asserted, and Creed's heart went still in his chest.

"Are you telling the truth?"

"I never lie," the stranger said. "Anyway, I'm sorry I bothered you. I'll just be leaving the way I came in now."

Creed flipped on the lights, curious to see the man Aberdeen was going to marry. They stared at each other, sizing up the competition. "I'll be damned. I know you," Creed said, "you're that dime-store cowboy they call Re-ride."

"And you're a Callahan." Re-ride looked none too happy. "What are you doing in Aberdeen's bar?"

"Keeping it free of snakes." Creed felt the interview to be most unpleasant at this point. He almost wished he'd never heard the man break in. Marry Aberdeen? Surely she wouldn't marry this poor excuse for a cowboy.

Then again, she'd married him before, or at least that's what he claimed. It was something else Creed hadn't known about her. To be honest, Creed hadn't proven himself to be any more of a serious cowboy in Aberdeen's eyes after his rambling night on the plank bench. Aberdeen probably thought he was just as loose as Re-ride.

That didn't sit too well. "Go on," he told Re-ride. "Get out of my face. I'd beat you with this broom, but I've never roughed up a lady and I'm not going to start tonight. So *git.*"

Re-ride looked like he was about to take exception to Creed's comment, then thought better of it and dove out the window. Creed locked it behind him—and this time, he turned on the security system. He couldn't risk more varmints crawling into the bar tonight—he was in too foul a mood to put up with nonsense. He put himself to bed in the guest room, feeling quite out of sorts about life in general.

Babies, beer burglars and a one-time bride—sometimes, life just handed a cowboy lemonade with no sugar in sight.

"I've LOOKED OVER these papers with Sam," Jonas said to Aunt Fiona, "and I think we're selling ourselves short. Maybe."

His aunt looked at him. "How?"

"We should fight it, for one thing. Not roll over for the state or Bode Jenkins. And I'm in a fighting mood. Now that I've sold my medical practice, I have more time to help you with things," Jonas said. "I should have been more available for you all along."

Fiona looked at her oldest nephew. "It shouldn't have necessitated your attention. Darn Bode Jenkins's hide, anyway."

Jonas leaned against the kitchen counter, eyeing his small, spare aunt. She was like a protective bear overseeing her cubs, but actually, things should be the other way around. He and his brothers needed to be protecting her and Burke, now in their golden years. Fiona had tried to convince them that she was one foot from the grave, but he'd been keeping an eye on her, and he was pretty certain Fiona was working their heartstrings. She had never seemed healthier, other than an unusually low spirit for her, which he attributed to her concern about losing the ranch.

He had decided to lift those burdens from his diminutive, sweetly busybodying aunt. "You know that land I put an offer on?"

Fiona brightened. "Yes. East of here. How's that coming?"

"I've changed my mind," Jonas said, after a thoughtful pause. It took him a minute to get his head around the words; every day since he'd made the decision, he'd pondered the situation again and again. "I've withdrawn my offer."

Fiona's eyes widened. "For heaven's sakes, why?"

"Because we're not going anywhere," Jonas said. "That's how Creed feels, and I agree with him."

"Creed! He's had a concussion recently," Fiona said with a sniff. "He's not thinking straight. Then again, when does he?"

"I think he might be thinking straighter than all of us." Jonas reached over and patted her shoulder. "I'm going to need all my resources, both time and money, to fight this theft of our land. I don't regret giving up on Dark Diablo for a minute."

Fiona looked at him. "Dark Diablo? It sounds beautiful."

He thought again about the wide expanse of open land where he could run cattle and horses and have his own place. His own sign hanging over the drive, shouting to the world that this was Dark Diablo, his own spread. But Creed had said Rancho Diablo was their home, and that they should fight for it, and fight hard. They would have to be dragged off their land— instead of rolling over because things looked dark and done. "Otherwise," Creed had said, "we're just cowards. Runners. The family stays together," he'd said. "Sic Sam on them."

Jonas's jaw had dropped. Sam didn't get "sicced" on anyone. Sam liked to ignore the fact that he'd gone to law school, barely broke a sweat passing the bar, and then gone on to prestigious internships, working his way up to cases that garnered him credit for being a steely defender who never failed to make his opponents cry. He'd become famous for his big persona. But only his family had noticed that with every big win to his credit, he became unhappier.

Sam liked winning. Yet he didn't like defending corporate cases where he knew the little guy was getting strung. And after a particularly nasty case, Sam had packed it in. Come home to Rancho Diablo to recover from big-city life. Now he mostly acted as though he hadn't a care in the world.

Except for Rancho Diablo.

Jonas winced. They couldn't sic Sam on Bode, but they could fight. "I've been thinking, Aunt Fiona, and I'm not so certain your marriage scheme doesn't have some merit."

She radiated delight. "Do you think so?"

He shrugged. "It wouldn't be as easy for the state to take a property where there are families. I'm not saying that they care about us, but it certainly makes it easier to win public sympathy when folks realize what happens to us here could happen to them."

"Yes, but Pete doesn't even live here with his family," she said, her shoulders sagging. "And the rest of you are short-timers."

He grinned. "Are you hosting a pity party, Aunt?"

She glared at him. "What if I am? It's my party, and I can cr—"

"When Creed gets back here in a few days, we'll throw that bachelor ball you wanted."

"Really?" Fiona clapped her hands.

"Sure. He needs to settle down."

She looked at him, suspicious. "Why him?"

"He wants to settle down more than anyone. Haven't you noticed? And his days of rodeoing are over, though he'll never admit it. A woman would keep him off the road, and children would keep him busy."

"It's a great plan," Fiona said, "if you think it would work."

Better him than me. With Fiona busy with her usual plotting and planning, I'll try to figure out how to undo this problem with the ranch.

He was going to have to take a firm hand with his aunt and Burke. They weren't telling everything they knew. It was a riddle wrapped inside a mystery, but he agreed with Creed on one thing: It was better to fight than run.

AFTER A COUPLE more beers to help get him over the shock of Aberdeen's babies and the ex-husband who wanted her back, Creed decided maybe he'd be wiser to run than fight. It was three in the morning, but he couldn't sleep, and if he didn't quit thinking about her, he was going to end up having beer for breakfast. Creed sighed, not having any fun at all. Aberdeen tortured him, and she didn't even know it.

"I wouldn't be so bothered if it wasn't for Re-ride," he told a small pink stuffed bear he'd found underneath the coffee table—probably the smallest damsel's bear. He'd placed the bear on the coffee table after he'd discovered it. The bear had looked forlorn and lost without its tiny owner, so Creed had propped it on a stack of books, regarding it as he would a comforting friend. "You have to understand that the man is given to useless. Simply useless."

The bear made no reply but that was to be expected from stuffed pink bears, Creed told himself, and especially at this hour. And the bear was probably tired of hearing him debate his thoughts, because Creed was certainly tired of himself. Everything ran through his mind without resting, like a giant blender churning his conscience. "She's just so pretty," he told the bear, "I don't see what she sees in him. It's something she doesn't see in me." He considered that for a moment, and then said, "Which is really unfortunate, for me and for her. I am the better man, Bear, but then again, a woman's heart is unexplainable. I swear it is."

If his brothers were here, he could talk this over with them. They wouldn't be sympathetic, but they would clap him on the back, rib him mercilessly or perhaps offer him some advice—and at least he'd feel better. It was hard to feel bad when as an army of one trying to feel sorry for yourself, you faced an army of five refusing to let you give in to your sorrows. How many times had he and his brothers dug each other out of their foul moods, disappointments or broken hearts?

There weren't as many broken hearts among them as there might have been because they had each other to stall those emotions. When you knew everybody was working too hard to listen to you wheeze, you got over a lot of it on your own. But then, when it was important, you could count on a brother to clout you upside the head and tell you that you were being a candy-ass.

He wasn't at that point yet. "But she's working on me, Bear." He waved his beer at the toy. "I didn't come here to help Johnny. It wasn't the overwhelming reason I said yes, you know? It was her. And then, I got here, and I found out…I found out that maybe I rang my bell so hard that I didn't really pay attention to her when I met her. I think, Bear," he said, lowering his voice to a whisper, "that I have it *bad*."

Really bad, if he was sitting here talking out his woes on a baby's pink bear. Creed sighed, put the bottle on the table and shut his eyes so he wouldn't look at the bear's black button eyes anymore for sympathy he couldn't possibly find. "Grown men don't talk to bears," he said, without opening his eyes, "so if you don't mind, please cease with the chatter so I can get some shut-eye."

If he *could* sleep—without thinking about Aberdeen becoming a mother, a scenario that in no way seemed to have a role for him.

ALL ABERDEEN COULD BE when the judge had heard her case was relieved. She was sad for her sister and for her nieces, but it was good to be able to have temporary legal custody of her nieces.

"However," the judge continued, "it's in the best interests of the children that they remain here in Montana, where their maternal grandparents are, and paternal as well, who may be able to provide some assistance."

Shock hit Aberdeen. "Your Honor," she said, "my

congregation is in Wyoming. My livelihood is in Wyoming."

The judge looked at her sternly. "A bar isn't much of a place for young, displaced girls to grow up. You have no house for them set apart from the establishment where there could be unsavory elements. And your congregation, as you've described it, is transient. None of this leads me to believe that the situation in Wyoming is more stable for the minors than it would be here, where at least the maternal grandparents can be trusted to oversee the wellbeing of the children."

Aberdeen glanced at Johnny. He would have to go back to Lance. She would be here alone with their parents, who would be little or no help. Tears jumped into Aberdeen's eyes when Johnny clasped her hand. She stared at the judge and nodded her acquiescence.

"Of course, should anything change in your circumstances, the court will be happy to reconsider the situation. Until then, a social worker will be assigned to you." He nodded at Johnny and Aberdeen. "Best of luck to you, Miss Donovan, Mr. Donovan."

Aberdeen turned and walked from the court, not looking at Johnny until they'd gotten outside.

"I expected that," Johnny said, and Aberdeen glanced at him as they walked toward his truck. "That's why I said I'd probably sell the bar. I was hoping it would turn out differently, but I knew Mom and Pop know the judge."

Aberdeen drew in a sharp breath. "Are you saying that they talked to him?"

Johnny climbed in behind the wheel, and Aberdeen got in the passenger side. "I don't know that they did, but I know that he would be familiar with some of our situation. To be fair, any judge hearing this type of case might have decided similarly. But I don't think him knowing Mom and Pop hurt them."

"So now what?" Aberdeen asked.

"Now we're custodians, for the time being," Johnny said. "I've got someone looking for Diane, and if they manage to make contact with her, we'll know a little more. I'll sell the bar, and we'll stay here until matters get straightened out. We're either going to be doing this for the long haul, or it could be as short a time as it takes Diane to come to her senses."

"You don't have to stay here," Aberdeen said. "I've taken this on gladly."

"We're family. We do it together." Johnny turned the truck toward their parents' house.

Aberdeen looked out the window. "I think selling the bar is too drastic, don't you?"

"I can think of more drastic things I don't want to see happen."

Aberdeen looked at him. "I think the worst has already passed."

Her brother took a deep breath, seemed to consider his words. "Look, I just don't want you even starting to think that putting a permanent relationship in your life might be the way to salvage this thing."

"You mean Shawn."

"I mean Re-ride." Johnny nodded. "Don't tell me it hasn't crossed your mind. He as much admitted to me that he wouldn't be opposed to remarrying you."

Aberdeen shook his head. "He mentioned it. I didn't take him very seriously."

"Stability might start looking good to you after a few months of Mom and Pop interfering with your life."

"So you're selling the bar to move here to protect me from myself?" Aberdeen sent her brother a sharp look.

"Johnny, I'm not the same girl I was when Shawn and I got married."

"Look, I don't want to see both my sisters make mistakes is all," Johnny said. "You're not like Diane in any way, but Diane wasn't like this before her marriage fell apart, either."

Aberdeen sighed, reached over to pat Johnny's arm. "I think you worry too much, but thanks for looking out for me. I know you do it out of love and a misguided sense of protection, which I happen to greatly appreciate."

Johnny smiled. "So then. Listen to big brother."

Aberdeen checked her cell phone for messages, then went all in. "Is that why you brought the cowboy back?"

Johnny glanced at her. "I could pretend that I don't know what you're talking about, but I figured you'd suspect, so I might as well just say it doesn't hurt to have an ace in my boot."

"Johnny Donovan," Aberdeen said, "perhaps I'll start meddling in your life. Maybe I'll find a string of cute girls and send them your way to tempt you into matrimony. How would you like that?"

"I hope you do, because I'd like it very much," Johnny grinned. "Make them tall, slender and good cooks. I do love home cooking, and women who want to cook these days are rare."

Aberdeen shook her head. "Creed has no interest in me. And the feeling is mutual. Besides, he wouldn't solve my problem in any way if Diane doesn't come back. Even if he and I got some wild notion to get married, he lives in New Mexico. I don't know that the judge is going to let me take the girls anywhere if you really believe he's influenced by Mom and Pop."

"Still, he'll keep Re-ride busy," Johnny predicted, "and I won't mind that a bit."

"You have a darkly mischievous soul, Johnny," Aberdeen said, but secretly, she had liked seeing Creed Callahan again. It was too bad she and Creed were as opposite as the sun and the moon.

He could make a woman think twice about taking a walk on the *very* wild side.

Chapter Eight

Creed woke up and stretched, hearing birds singing somewhere nearby. It was different here than in Diablo. Everything was different, from the birds to the land, to the—

The pink bear stared at him, and Creed sighed. "Okay, last night won't happen again. You will not be hearing such yak from me again. I had my wheeze, and I'm over it." He carried the bear down to the room where the little girls had been sleeping, and was caught by the sight of tiny dresses, shorts and shoes spread at the foot of a big bed. There were toys scattered everywhere, and even a fragile music box on the dresser top. It was like walking into fairyland, he mused, and he wondered if Aberdeen had had a room like this when she was little.

He backed out of the room after setting the bear on the bed, decided to shower and get cheerful about the day—and there was no better way to get cheerful than to fill his stomach. That would require heading out to the nearest eating establishment, which would be a great way to see Lance. He took a fast shower, jumped into fresh jeans and a shirt, clapped his hat on his head and jerked open the bar door to take in a lungful of fresh, bracing summer air.

Re-ride stared up at him from the ground where he

was sitting, leaning against the wall, clearly just awakening.

"Oh, no, this is not going to happen," Creed said, setting the security alarm, locking the door and loping toward his truck. "You and I are not going to be bosom buddies, so buzz off," he called over his shoulder.

Re-ride was in hot pursuit. "Where are you going?" he asked, jumping into the truck when Creed unlocked the door.

"I'm going someplace you're not. Get out." Creed glared at him.

"Breakfast sounds good. I'll show you the hot spots around here." Re-ride grinned. "I know where the best eggs and bacon are in this town."

Creed didn't want the company, but his stomach was growling, and if the eggs were the best… "If you give me any trouble," he said, and Re-ride said, "Nope. Not me."

Creed snorted and followed his new friend's directions to Charity's Diner two streets over. "I'm pretty certain I could have found this place myself," Creed said, and Re-ride laughed.

"But you didn't. Come on. I'll show you some waitresses who are so cute you'll want more than marshmallows in your cocoa."

That made no sense, Creed thought sourly. In fact, it was a pretty stupid remark, but he should probably expect little else from the freeloader. He followed Re-ride into the diner and seated himself in a blue vinyl booth, watching with some amazement as Re-ride waved over a tiny, gorgeous, well-shaped redhead.

"This is Cherry," Re-ride said, "Cherry, this is Creed Callahan."

Creed tipped his hat, noticing that Re-ride's hand fell

perilously low on Cherry's nicely curved hip. "Pleasure," he told Cherry, and she beamed at him.

"Cocoa?" she asked Creed.

"Coffee," he said, wary of Re-ride's cocoa promise. "Black as you've got it, please."

She showed sweet dimples and practically stars in her big green eyes as she grinned back at Creed. "Re-ride, you've been hiding this handsome friend of yours. Shame on you."

Re-ride shook his head as he ran his gaze hungrily down a menu, his mind all on food now, though he still clutched Cherry's hip. Creed looked at his own menu as Cherry drifted away, surprised when Re-ride tapped the plastic sheet.

"She likes you, I can tell," Re-ride said.

"Look," Creed said, annoyed, "it's plain that you don't want competition for Aberdeen, but I don't—"

"Oh, there's no competition." Re-ride shook his head. "I told you, I'm marrying Aberdeen. I'm just trying to find you someone, so you won't be odd man out."

Creed sighed. "Odd man out of what? I'm only here for a few days."

"Really?" Re-ride brightened. "I might have misunderstood Johnny when I called him last night."

Creed perked up. "You talked to Johnny?"

"Yep." Re-ride lowered his voice. "You know Aberdeen is trying to adopt Diane's little girls, a horrible idea if there ever was one."

"Why?" Creed asked, telling himself that the Donovan family matters were none of his business, and yet he was so curious he could hardly stand it.

"Because I'm not cut out to be a father," Re-ride explained. "I don't want to be a father to Diane's children."

"Oh." Creed blinked. "Selfish, much?"

"What?" Re-ride glared at him, obviously confused.

Creed shrugged. "If you love Aberdeen, wouldn't you want what she wants?"

"No, that's not how it works. I'm the man, and I'll make the decisions about what's best for our family. There's no way a marriage can work when there's no chance for privacy right from the start. A man and his wife need *privacy,* and I'm sure you know what I mean, Callahan."

Fire flamed through Creed's gut. *Jealousy. By God, I'm jealous. I can't be jealous. That would be dumb. But how I wish I could poke this jerk in the nose. I should have beaten him a time or two with that broom handle last night, kind of paying it forward. I sure would feel better now.* "You'd be better off taking that up with Aberdeen than with me," Creed said, keeping his tone mild even as his heart had kicked into over-drive. Maybe he was getting a mild case of indigestion. His whole chest seemed to be enduring one large attack of acid.

"You paying, cowboy?" Re-ride asked. "I'm short a few at the moment."

He was short more things than dollars, but Creed just shook his head, deciding it wouldn't kill him to help out the poor excuse for a man. "I suppose," he said, and Re-ride proceeded to call Cherry back over to give her a list of items that would have fed an army.

Creed sighed to himself. If anyone had ever told him he'd be buying breakfast for the ex-husband and current suitor of a woman that Creed had a small crush on, he would have said they were crazy.

"Turns out I'm the crazy one," he muttered, and Re-ride said, "Yeah, I heard that about you."

Creed drank his coffee in silence.

WHEN CREED AND HIS unwanted companion returned to Johnny's bar, Creed said, "Sayonara, dude," and Re-ride hurried after him.

"No," Creed said, shutting the door in Re-ride's face.

"This isn't how you treat friends!" Re-ride called through the door.

"Exactly," Creed said, turning to study the bar. He decided he'd go upstairs and call his brothers, see how the old homestead was doing. He'd only been gone a day and a half—not much could have changed in his absence. He got out his laptop, too, to surf while he chatted. "This is the life," he said, making himself comfortable in the den. He ignored the banging on the door downstairs. Re-ride would go away soon, or he'd fall asleep outside the door again, and either way, it wasn't Creed's problem.

Until Aberdeen came back. Then Re-ride's constant presence would be a problem.

Yet, no. It couldn't be. Aberdeen was nothing to him, and he was nothing to her, and he was only here to pay back a favor. Not get involved in their personal family business.

Or to fall for her.

"That's right. I'm not doing that," he said, stabbing numbers into the cell phone. Re-ride had ceased banging for the moment, which was considerate of him. "Howdy, Aunt Fiona," he said, when his aunt picked up, and she said, "Well, fancy you calling right now, stranger."

"What does that mean?" Creed's antennae went straight up at his aunt's happy tone. Aunt Fiona was never happier than when she was plotting, but surely he hadn't been gone long enough for her to have sprung any plots.

"It means that you must have telekinetic abilities. We just mailed out the invitations to the First Annual Rancho Diablo Charity Matchmaking Ball!"

Creed blinked. "That's a mouthful, Aunt."

"It is indeed. And we are going to have mouthfuls of food, and drink and kissing booths—"

"I thought—" He didn't want to hurt Aunt Fiona's feelings, so he chose his words carefully. "Why are we having a…what did you call it again?"

"A First Annual Rancho Diablo Charity Matchmaking Ball!" Aunt Fiona giggled like a teenage girl. "Doesn't it sound like fun? And it's all Jonas's idea!"

Creed's brows shot up. He could feel a headache starting under his hatband, so he shucked his hat and leaned back in Johnny's chair. Outside the window ledge, a familiar face popped into view.

"Let me in!" Re-ride mouthed through the window, and Creed rolled his eyes.

"Get down before you kill yourself, dummy," he said loudly, and Aunt Fiona said, "Why, Creed! How could you speak to me that way?"

"No, Aunt. I'm not—" He glared at Re-ride and headed into another room. It was Aberdeen's room, he realized with a shock, and it carried her scent, soft and sweet and comforting. Sexy. And holy Christmas, she'd left a nightie on the bed. A white, lacy nightie, crisp white sheets, fluffy pillows…a man could lie down on that bed and never want to get up—especially if he was holding her.

But he wasn't. Creed gulped, taking a seat at the vanity instead so he could turn his face from the alluring nightie and the comfy bed which beckoned. It was hard to look away. He had a full stomach, and a trainload of desire, and if he weren't the chivalrous man that he was, he'd sneak into that bed and have a nap and maybe an erotic dream or two about her. "When is this dance, Aunt?"

"Be home in two weeks," she commanded, her typical General-Fiona self. "We're rushing this because Jonas says we must. I wanted to have it in a month, when I could order in something more fancy than barbecue, but Jonas says time is of the essence. We need ladies here fast. Well, he didn't say that, but that's the gist of it."

Creed sighed. "None of us dance, Aunt Fiona. You know that."

"I know. I never saw so many men with two left feet. Fortunately," Aunt Fiona went on, "you still draw the ladies in spite of your shortcomings. My friends have put out the calls, and we've already had a hundred responses in the affirmative. This should be a roaring success in the social columns, I must say!"

This didn't sound like one of Jonas's plans. "I've only been gone a few hours," Creed said, reeling, and Aunt Fiona snapped, "We didn't have time to wait on you to get back here, Creed, and heaven knows you're not one for making fast decisions. But Jonas is. And he is light on his feet when it comes to planning. I have great hopes for him."

Creed said to hell with it and moved to Aberdeen's bed, testing it out with a gentle bounce. It was just as soft and comfortable as it looked. "I'm afraid to ask, but why do we need a charity ball?"

"To get your brothers married, of course. And you, but I think you'll be the last to go." Fiona sounded depressed about that. "You're still haring around, trying to figure out what you want in life, Creed."

Right now he wanted a nap in this sweet bed. Telling himself he was a fool to do it—he was treading into dangerous territory—Creed picked up the lacy white nightie with one finger, delicately, as though the sheer lace might explode if he snagged it with his work-roughened hands. "I know what I want in life, Aunt Fiona," he said softly, realizing that maybe he did know, maybe he'd known it from the moment he'd met her, but there were too many things in the way that he couldn't solve. His aunt was right—he was still going after something he couldn't have. "What are we wearing to this shindig, anyway?"

"Whatever you want to wear," Aunt Fiona said, "but I'll warn you of this. Your brothers are going all out in matching black tuxes. Super-formal, super-James Bond. They intend to dance the night away and seduce the ladies in ways they've never been seduced."

Creed stared at the nightgown, seduced already. But what good would it do? There was an eager ex-husband jumping around outside, climbing to second-story windowsills, trying to make himself at home. And Creed was feeding him. "Sounds like fun, Aunt Fiona," he said. "Guess I'll shine up my best boots."

"I'll just be grateful if you get here and ask a lady to dance," Aunt Fiona said, "so hurry home."

"Don't worry. I'll be home very soon."

"You promise?"

"I swear I do."

"Then I hold you to that. I love you, even though you are a wily coyote. I must go now, Jonas is yelling at me to buy more stamps for the invitations. He had them made special in town, and then printed invitations in all the nearby papers. I tell you, your brother's a magician. I don't know why I didn't notice it before."

She hung up. Creed stared at his cell for a moment,

finally turning it off. He was dumbfounded, in a word. Aunt Fiona must have worked a heck of a spell on Jonas to put him in such a partying mood. Jonas was not the ladies' man in the family. Nor did he have the most outgoing disposition. Creed frowned. There was something off about the whole thing, but it was Aunt Fiona and her chicanery, so "off" was to be expected.

Still, it made him tired. Or maybe Re-ride had made him tired. It didn't matter. He'd slept on the sofa last night, and he hadn't slept well, and the eggs had filled him up, and Re-ride was quiet for the moment, so Creed took one last longing look at the white lace nightie he held in his hand, and leaned back against the padded headboard just for a second.

Just for a quick moment to see what it would feel like to sleep in Aberdeen's bed. A guy could dream couldn't he?

His eyes drifted closed.

CREED HAD NEVER slept so hard. Never slept so well. It was as though he was enclosed in angel wings, dreaming the peaceful dreams of newborn babies. He didn't ever want to wake up. He knew he didn't want to wake up because he was finally holding Aberdeen in his arms. And she was wearing the hot nightie, which was short enough and sheer enough not to be a nightie at all. He'd died and gone to heaven. Everything he'd ever wanted was in his arms.

He heard a gasp, and that wasn't right; in his dreams, everyone was supposed to make happy, soft coos of delight and admiration. Creed's eyes jerked open to find Aberdeen staring at him—and Re-ride.

It was a horrible and rude awakening. There was no hope that he wouldn't look like some kind of pervert, so Creed slowly sat up. He removed the nightie from his grasp and shoved it under a pillow so Re-ride couldn't get more of a glimpse of it than necessary. "Hi, Aberdeen. Did everything go well?"

"Yes." She crossed her arms, glaring at him. "Shawn says you've been running all over town, not watching the bar at all. He says he had to come in and look after it last night because he thought he saw a prowler!"

Creed flicked a glance at Re-ride. The traitor stared back at him, completely unashamed of his sidewinder antics. "Did he say that?" Creed asked, his voice soft, and Aberdeen nodded vigorously.

"And may I ask why you're in my bed?"

It was a fair question, and one to which he didn't have a good answer. And he was already in the dog house. Creed sighed. "You can ask, but I don't have a good reason."

"Then will you get out of it?" Aberdeen said, and Creed got to his feet.

"I guess I'll be going." He walked to the door, glancing back only once, just in time to see Re-ride grab Aberdeen and give her the kind of kiss a man gives a woman when he's about to emblazon her hand with a diamond ring fit for a princess. Creed could hear wedding bells tolling, and it hurt.

All his dreams—stupid dreams—were shot to dust. He slunk down the hallway, telling himself he'd been an idiot ever to have trusted Re-ride. "That yellow-bellied coward. I live with Aunt Fiona and five brothers. How could I have let myself be gamed like that?" Creed grabbed up his laptop and his few belongings, and five minutes later he was heading down the stairs, his heart heavy, feeling low.

Re-ride went running past him, hauling ass for the

front door. He jetted out of the bar, running toward town. Creed hesitated in the doorway, wondering if he should check on Aberdeen.

She came down the stairs, lifting her chin when she saw him. "You're still here?"

Creed blinked. "Re-ride just beat me to the door, or I'd be gone already."

She had enough ice in her eyes to freeze him, and Creed was feeling miserably cold already.

"Why were you in my bed?"

"I fell asleep. Is that a crime? It's not like I was Goldilocks and I tried out all the beds in the house and thought yours was the best. Although from my random and incomplete survey, so far it is pretty nice."

"I wasn't expecting to find you in my bed."

"I wasn't actually expecting to be in it, it just happened that way," he said with some heat, still smarting that Re-ride had painted him in a thoroughly unflattering light, and liking it even less that Aberdeen had believed the worst of him. Women! Who needed them? "I went in there, I fell asleep. End of story. And I'm not sorry," he said, "because it was damn comfortable, and I slept like a baby. Frankly, I was beat."

She looked at him for a long moment. "Would you like to sleep all night in my bed?" she asked, and Creed's pulse rocketed. Women didn't say something like that unless they meant something awesome and naked, did they?

"I should probably be hitting the road," Creed said, not sure where he stood at the moment, although the direction of the conversation was decidedly more optimistic than it had been a few moments ago.

She nodded. "Okay. I understand."

He understood nothing at all. "Understand what?"

She shrugged. "Thanks for watching the bar, Creed. And I'm sorry for what I said. I should have known better than to believe anything Shawn says."

"You mean Re-ride?" Creed glanced over his shoulder to see if the cowboy had reappeared, but there was a dust plume from the man's exit. "What changed your mind?"

"He proposed," she said simply. "And I realized he was doing it because of you."

"Yeah, well. I have that effect on men, I guess. They get jealous of me because it's obvious the ladies prefer me." Creed threw in a token boast to boost his self-esteem. Aberdeen had him tied in a cowboy's knot.

"So," Aberdeen slowly said, "the offer's still open if you're not of a mind to hit the road just yet."

Creed hung in the doorway, feeling as if something was going on he didn't quite understand, but he wasn't about to say no if she was offering what he thought she was. Still, he hesitated, because he knew too well that Aberdeen wasn't the kind of woman who shared her bed with just anyone. "Where's Johnny? And the little girls?"

"They're in Spring, Montana. I just came back to get some of our things." Aberdeen looked at him, her eyes shy, melting his heart. "And then I'll be going back."

She wasn't telling everything, but Creed got that she was saying she wouldn't be around. And she'd just told Re-ride to shove off, so that meant—

He hardly dared to hope.

Until she walked to him, leaned up on her toes, and pressed her lips against his.

And then he allowed himself to hope.

Chapter Nine

The first thing Creed noticed about Aberdeen was that she was a serious kisser. There was no shyness, no holding back. When he pulled her close and tight, she melted against him.

That was just the way he wanted her. Yet Creed told himself to go slow, be patient. She'd been married to quite the dunderhead; Creed wanted to come off suave, polished. Worthy of her. He would never get his fill of her lips, he decided, knowing at once that Cupid's arrow had shot him straight through.

She only pulled back from him once, and stared up into his eyes. "Are you sure about this?"

He gulped. That was usually the man's question, wasn't it? And here she was asking him like he was some shy lad about to lose his virginity. "I've never been more sure of anything in my life."

"Then lock the door, cowboy. Bar's closed for the rest of the day. And night."

He hurriedly complied, and then she took his hand, leading him upstairs. Creed's heart was banging against his ribs; his blood pressure was through the roof. *Let this be real, and not that horny dream I'd promised myself.* When Aberdeen locked the bedroom door behind them, he knew he was the luckiest man on earth. "Come here," he told her, "let me kiss you."

If he had the whole night, then he was going to kiss her for hours. He took her chin gently between his palms, his lips meeting hers, molding against her mouth. She moaned and he was happy to hear that feminine signal, so he turned up the heat a notch. She surprised him by eagerly undoing his shirt buttons, never taking her lips from his until she had his shirt completely undone. Then she pulled away for just a moment, her hands slipping his shirt off, her gaze roaming over his chest, her hands greedily feeling the tight muscles of his stomach and the knotted cords of his shoulders.

She looked as though she was starving for love and affection. He'd never made love to a preacher lady, but he'd figured she would have all kinds of hang-ups and maybe a go-slow button. Aberdeen acted as if he was some kind of dessert she'd promised herself after a month-long fast. And he didn't want to get drawn in to any lingering firefight between her and Re-ride, if that was what was going on here. He caught her hands between his, pressing a kiss to her palms. "Aberdeen, is everything all right?"

She nodded up at him, her eyes huge. "Yes."

"You're sure you want this?"

She nodded again. "Yes, I do, and if you don't quit being so slow, I'm going to be forced to drag you into my bed, Creed."

Well, that was it. A man could only play the firefighter so long when he really wanted to be the raging fire. So he picked her up and carried her to her white bed, laying her gently down into the softness. Slowly, he took off her sandals, massaging each delicate ankle. He unbuttoned her sundress, every white button down the front of the blue fabric, patiently, though it seemed to take a year and he wasn't certain why a woman needed so many buttons. He kissed her neck, keeping her still against the bed, his shoulders arched over her body, and still she kept pulling him toward her. In fact, she was trying to get his jeans off, and doing a better job of it than he was doing with the dress, but Creed was determined to have her out of her clothes first and lavish on her the attention he'd been so hungry to give her. Slipping the dress to the floor, he moved Aberdeen's hands to her side and murmured, "Don't worry. I'm going to take good care of you," and she sighed as though a ton of burdens had just slid off her. He slipped off her bra, delighted by the tiny freckles on her breasts, which, he noticed, happened to match the same sprinkles on her thighs. He took his time kissing each freckle, then slowly slipped a nipple into his mouth, tweaking the other with his hand. She moaned and arched against him, but he pressed her against the sheets again, keeping her right where he wanted her.

"Slow," Creed murmured against Aberdeen's mouth. "I'm going to take you very slowly."

She tried to pull him toward her, but there wasn't any way he was going to be rushed. He captured her hands in one of his, keeping them over her head so he could suck on her nipples, lick her breasts, tease her into readiness. Every inch of her was a treasure he'd been denied for so long; he just wanted to explore everything, leave nothing behind. She was twisting against him, her passion growing, and he liked knowing that she was a buttoned-up lady for everyone else but him. He let her hands go free so that he could cup a breast with one hand, shucking his boots with the other, and then started the heavenly trail down her stomach.

There were cute freckles there, too. Aberdeen gasped, her fingers tangling in his hair. He could feel her control completely slipping, which was the way he wanted her, wild with passion. Looping his fingers in the sides of her panties, he pulled them down, bit by bit revealing the hidden treasure.

And there was nothing he could do once he saw all of Aberdeen's beauty but kiss her in her most feminine place. She went still, surprised, he thought, but he had more surprises in store for her. She was too feminine to resist, and he'd waited too long. Her body seemed made for his; she felt right, she fitted him, and he couldn't stand it any longer. He slipped his tongue inside her—and Aberdeen cried out. He spread her legs apart, moving to kiss those pin-sized freckles on her thighs, but she buried her hands in his hair again, and it sure seemed like begging to him, so Creed obliged. He kissed her, and licked her, holding her back, knowing just how close he could get her before she exploded, and then, knowing she was too ladylike to beg—next time, he'd make sure he got her to totally let go—he put a finger inside her, massaging her while he teased her with his tongue.

Aberdeen practically came apart in his hands.

"Creed!" she cried, pulling at him desperately, and he fished a condom out of his wallet, putting it on in record time. Holding her tightly, he murmured, "Hang on," and kissing her, slid inside her.

She felt like heaven. This *was* heaven. "If I do this every day for the rest of my life, it won't be enough," he whispered against her neck, and when Aberdeen stiffened in his arms, he moved inside her, tantalizing her, keeping her on edge. She was holding back in spirit, in her heart, but as Creed brought her to a crying-out-loud climax, he kissed her, thinking she had no clue that she couldn't run him off as easily as she'd run off Re-ride. He just wasn't that kind of shallow.

"Aberdeen," he murmured, his mind clouding, nature taking over his body. He'd only pleasured her twice, but he couldn't stand it any longer. He rode her into the sheets, the pressure commanding him to possess her, never give her up, take her to be his. She cried out, grabbing his shoulders, locking her legs around him, crying his name, surrendering this much passion, he knew, against her will. When he came, he slumped against her, breathing great gulps of air, and murmured her name again. It was engraved in his heart.

Aberdeen just didn't know that yet. She'd be hard to convince. She'd have a thousand reasons why they couldn't be together.

But if he knew anything at all, if he understood one thing about his destiny, it was that Aberdeen Donovan was meant to be his by the glorious hand of Fate.

And he was damned grateful.

ABERDEEN LAY UNDERNEATH Creed practically in shock. Never in her life had she experienced anything like that. She hadn't even known making love could be such... so much fun, for one thing. If you could call that fun. She felt as if she'd had her soul sucked from her and put back better.

She wiggled, trying to see if he had fallen asleep on her. Her eyes went wide. Was he getting hard again? It certainly felt like he was. He was the hardest man she'd ever felt, like steel that possessed her magically. All she had for comparison was Re-ride, and that wasn't much of a comparison. Aberdeen bit her lip as that thought flew right out of her brain. Creed *was* getting hard inside her again! She'd figured he'd want her once and go on his way, the way her ex had—and then she'd pack the things she needed and head to Montana.

He wouldn't miss her—he wasn't that kind of guy. He probably had women in every town. So she hadn't felt too guilty about seducing him. She'd just wanted a little pleasure, something for herself, an answer to the question she'd had ever since she'd seen his admiration for her burning in his navy gaze. He was too good-looking and too much of a rascal—a bad boy a woman fantasized about—for her not to want the question answered. She wasn't an angel. And right now she was glad of that, because he was hard, and he wanted her, and even if she hadn't planned on making love to Creed twice, she wasn't about to say no.

Not after the pleasure he'd just given her.

He looked deep into her eyes, not saying a word. She didn't know what to say to him. He made all the words she ever thought she might say just dry up. He made a lazy circle around one of her breasts, and she could feel him getting even harder inside her. He kissed her lips, sweetly and slowly, and Aberdeen's breath caught somewhere inside her chest.

To her surprise, he rolled her over on her stomach, and she went, trusting him. He reached for another condom, and kissed her shoulders, as if he wanted to calm her, soothe her. So she waited with held breath as he kissed down her spine, finding points which seemed to intrigue him. He kissed her bottom reverently, took a nip here and there, licked the curve of her hips.

And then the hardness filled her again as he slid inside her. She tried not to cry out, but oh, she couldn't stop herself. He held her gently, not demanding, not passionate and eager as he'd been before, and he rocked her against him, filling her with him. He tweaked a breast, rolling it between his fingers as he kissed her neck, and she couldn't stop her body from arching back against him. She didn't know exactly what she wanted, but when he put a hand between her legs, teasing her, the combination of steel and gentle teasing sent her over the edge again. "Creed," she said on a gasp, and he said, "Say it again," against her neck, and she obeyed him as he drove her to another climax. And when she said his name a third time—she heard herself scream it— he pounded inside her, taking her until his arms tightened around her and his body collapsed against hers.

But still he didn't let her go.

And now, she didn't want him to.

WHEN ABERDEEN AWAKENED, Creed wasn't in her bed. She rose, glancing around the room, listening.

There was nothing to hear.

He'd left. He'd gone back to New Mexico. Her heart racing, Aberdeen crawled from the sheets, sore in places she couldn't remember being sore before. And yet it felt good, a reminder of the passion she'd finally experienced.

No wonder the Callahans were famous. She peeked out the window, but his truck was gone. Her heart sank, though she'd expected him to head off. Men like Creed didn't hang around. Hadn't she learned that from Shawn? Oh, he'd come back in the end, but he hadn't really wanted her. She'd figured that out quick enough when Shawn proposed to her.

She'd told him she had custody of her nieces, and he'd told her he didn't want to be a father. That had inflamed her, and she'd told Shawn that if he didn't get out of her room, out of her house, she'd set Creed on him.

Those were the magic words. Her ex had run as though devils were on his tail.

Aberdeen got into the shower, thinking she had a lot to be grateful to the Callahan cowboy for. She'd known there was no future for the two of them—there were too many differences in their lives—but still, she wished he'd said goodbye.

She took a long shower, letting the hot water calm her mind. She didn't want to think about her nieces at the moment, or custody, or cowboys she couldn't have. Raspberry body wash—her favorite—washed all the negative thoughts away, and she grabbed a white towel to wrap around her body and began to dry her hair. If she hurried, she could leave in an hour. She'd close up the bar, put on the security alarm, and drive to the next phase in her life. She doubted she'd ever see Creed again. A tiny splinter of her heart broke off, and she told herself she was being silly. Just because she'd slept with him, that didn't mean they could be anything to each other. But still, she'd started to think of him as someone in her life—

She heard the door downstairs open and close. Her pulse jumped. Creed had left, but surely he'd locked the door. She'd seen the closed sign in the window when they'd come home.

Boots sounded on the stairs. Aberdeen froze, holding her towel tightly around her. She could hardly hear for the blood pulsing in her ears.

When Creed walked into the room, her breath didn't release, as it should have, with relief. If anything, she was even more nervous. "I thought you'd gone."

He smiled at her. He'd showered, but he must have used Johnny's room, which made sense. His longish hair was slightly wet at the ends. His dark-blue eyes crinkled at the sides.

"Did you dress for me, Aberdeen?" he asked, his voice a teasing drawl.

Blush heated her face. She decided to brave this out. "As I said, I thought you'd gone."

He nodded. "I didn't want to wake you up when I went out. You were sleeping like a princess."

Of course he was well aware he'd made her feel like a princess. Her defenses went up. "Why are you here?"

His gaze swept her toes, up her calves, considered the towel she clutched before returning to her face. He gave her a smile only a rogue would wear. "Do you want me to leave?"

She wanted him, and he knew it. He was toying with her. "I don't know why I would want you here," she said, "I'm leaving today, and I'm sure you have places to go."

He took off his hat and laid it on her vanity. Her heart jumped inside her, betraying her inner feelings. "I do have places to go, things to do," he agreed.

She didn't trust the gleam in his eyes. Tugging the towel tighter against her, she lifted her chin. "Where did you go?"

"Out for a little while."

He didn't move closer, so Aberdeen felt on firm footing. "Did you come back to say goodbye? Because if you did, you can say it and go. No guilt." She took a deep breath. "I know you have a long drive."

He nodded. "I do."

She waited, her heart in a knot, too shy suddenly to tell him she wished everything could be different—

"I didn't come back to say goodbye," he said, stepping toward her now. "You need breakfast before you leave, and I need you."

She stood her ground as he came near, and when he reached out and took hold of the towel, she allowed him to take it from her body. He dropped it to the floor, his gaze roaming over her as if he'd never seen her body before. He seemed to like what he saw. He took her face in his hands, kissing her lips, her neck, and Aberdeen closed her eyes, letting her fingers wander into his hair as he moved to her stomach, kissing lower until he licked inside her, gently laving all the sore places until they felt healed and ready for him again. She moaned, her knees buckling, her legs parting for him, and when Creed took her back to her bed, laying her down, Aberdeen told herself that one more time enjoying this cowboy in her bed was something she deserved. She couldn't have said no if her life had depended on it. He made her feel things she'd never felt before, and she wanted to feel those things again, and he knew it.

He took out a new box of condoms. Aberdeen watched him, wanting to say that he wasn't going to need an entire new box since they both had places to be—but by the time he'd undressed and gotten into bed with her, murmuring sweet things against her stomach, telling her she was a goddess, Aberdeen slid her legs apart and begged him to come to her. And when Creed did, she held him as tightly as she could, rocking against him until she felt him get stronger and then come apart in her arms, which somehow felt better even than anything he'd done to her.

She was in heaven in his arms—and she didn't want to be anywhere else.

Chapter Ten

Time seemed to stand still for Creed, suspended between what he wanted and what was realistic. The sleeping woman he held in his arms was what he wanted. Realistically, winning her was going to be hard to achieve.

He had to give it everything in his power. There were a hundred reasons he could think of that Aberdeen had to be his—but convincing her would take some serious effort.

It would be worth it, if he could convince her.

He realized she was watching him. "Hello, beautiful," he said, stroking her hair away from her face.

She lowered her lashes. He liked her a little on the shy side; he enjoyed tweaking her, too. She was so cute, tried so hard to be reserved, and then she was all eager and welcoming in bed. "I want you again," he told her. "I don't know how you have this spell on me."

She stroked a hand over his chest. He kissed the tip of her nose, and then lightly bit it. She pinched his stomach, just a nip, and he grinned at her, giving her bottom a light spank. She jumped, her eyes wide, and he laughed, holding her tighter against him. "I could stay here with you for weeks, just making love to you. I don't even have to eat."

He would just consume her. He kissed her lips, taking his sweet time to enjoy that which he'd wanted for so long.

"I have to go, Creed," Aberdeen said, "as much as I would love to stay here with you."

He grunted, not about to let her go this moment. There was too much he still needed to know. "What happened to Re-ride? Why did he take off?"

She gazed at him, and Creed couldn't resist the pain in her eyes, so he kissed her lips, willing her to forget the pain and think only of the pleasure he could give her.

"He got cold feet," Aberdeen said.

"How cold?"

"Ice." She looked at him. "Arctic."

"He said he was going to marry you again." Creed palmed her buttocks, holding her close against him so he could nuzzle her neck, feel her thighs against his. She slipped a thigh between his, and he nearly sighed with pleasure. She was so sweet, so accommodating. He really liked that about her.

"He talks big." Aberdeen laid her head against his shoulder, almost a trusting, intimate gesture, and Creed liked that, too. "He didn't want me to adopt the girls, but I am going to, if I have to. If it's the right thing for them. If my sister, Diane, doesn't come back, then I'll move to the next phase. Right now, I've been awarded temporary custody. Shawn wanted to be part of my life, so he claimed, knew I was going to adopt my nieces if I had to, but when I told him I had to move to Montana, he went cold." She ran a palm lightly over his chest. "I told him if he didn't get out, you'd throw him out. Or something to that effect. I hope you don't mind."

Creed grinned, his chin resting on top of Aberdeen's head. "I never miss a chance to be a hero."

"So that's my story. What's yours?"

Creed thought his story was too long and too boring to bother anyone with. He didn't want to talk about it anyway. "I don't have a story."

Aberdeen pulled away. "That's dirty pool. You can't pull out my story, and then keep yours to yourself."

She had a point. He pushed her head back under his chin and gave her another light paddling on the backside. "Have I ever told you I don't like opinionated women?"

She made a deliberately unappreciative sound which he would call a snort. "I like my women a little more on the obedient side," he said, teasing her, enjoying trying to get her goat, only because he wanted to see what her retribution would be. He liked her spicy. Spice was good.

"I like my men a little more on the honest side," Aberdeen shot back, and Creed smiled to himself.

"That's my sweet girl," he said, and Aberdeen gave him a tiny whack on his own backside, surprising him. He hadn't expected her to turn the tables on him.

"So, your story?" Aberdeen prompted.

"I need to get married," Creed said, his gaze fixed on the vanity across the room as he thought about his life in New Mexico. "My aunt wants all of us to get married."

Aberdeen pulled away from him to look into his eyes. "And do you have a prospect back in New Mexico?"

"No," he said, pulling her back against him, "I don't. So my aunt—who is a formidable woman—is planning a marital ball of some kind to introduce me and my four unmarried brothers to eligible ladies."

"Why does your aunt care if you're unmarried or not?"

"Because she's bossy like that." Creed loved the smell of Aberdeen's shampoo. Raspberry or strawberry—something clean and fresh and feminine. He took a deep breath, enjoying holding her. "And the women she'll have at the ball will be highly eligible. Socially acceptable. Drop-dead gorgeous."

"So what are you doing here?" Aberdeen asked, and Creed grinned, fancying he heard just a little bite in her words.

"Sleeping with you? Oh, this is just a fling." He kissed her lips, though she tried to evade him. "Didn't you say that you had to leave for Montana? So you're just having a little fun before you go back. I understand that. Men do it all the time." He sucked one of her nipples into his mouth, and Aberdeen went still, though she'd been trying to move to the edge of the bed, putting room between them.

"I don't know what this is," Aberdeen said, and he heard honesty in her voice. He released her nipple and kissed her on the mouth instead.

"You were going to say yes to Re-ride."

She looked at him, her gaze clear. "I hate to admit that I briefly considered it."

"But it didn't work out before."

She shook her head. "I suppose I was desperate enough to wonder if it might have been the best idea."

He hated the sound of that. "Because of your nieces?"

"I only have temporary custody. The judge didn't seem to find me all that compelling as a guardian. I feel like I need more stability in my life to convince him. He pointed out that Johnny and I live over a bar, not exactly suitable for children. The clientele is transient. He doesn't know Johnny and me. He does know our parents, and made the assumption that they'll be available to help us out. What he didn't understand is that our parents didn't even raise us." Aberdeen seemed ashamed to admit this, and Creed put his chin on her shoulder again, holding her tight. "So I can't leave Montana with the kids. I think if my marital status were to change, that would be something in my favor."

"And along came Re-ride, and you saw your prince."

Aberdeen shrugged. "It made sense at the time."

Creed could see the whole picture. He understood now why Johnny had called him to come watch the bar. Johnny didn't like Re-ride. Johnny had called Creed in, hoping Creed might have an eye for his sister.

"Tell me something," Creed said, "why are you here to get your things instead of Johnny?"

"Johnny was going to come, and I was going to stay with the girls. But then Johnny said he thought it would be better if he stayed because our folks give him a little less trouble. Very few people bother Johnny. He's always been my biggest supporter."

"Protective big brother," Creed murmured, and Aberdeen said, "Yes."

And so Creed had run off the competition, just as Johnny had probably hoped. Creed could spot a plot a mile away, even if he was late to figure it out. Fiona had given him good training. He tipped her chin back with a finger. "Preacher lady, you need a husband, and it just so happens I need a wife."

She blinked. Seemed speechless. Her eyes widened, like she thought he was joking. He kissed her hand, lightly bit the tip of a finger before drawing it into his mouth. She pulled her finger away, then glared at him.

"That's not funny."

"I'm not joking." Creed shrugged.

"You're serious."

"Men don't joke about marriage." Creed shook his head. "It's a very serious matter worthy of hours of cogitation."

"Are you suggesting we have some sort of fake marriage? To fool the judge and to fool your aunt?"

"*Fooling's* kind of a harsh word." Creed kissed her neck, ignoring her when she tried to push him away. She couldn't; he outweighed her by a hundred pounds, and he sensed she wasn't serious about moving him away from her delightful body. She just needed distance while her mind sorted the conclusion he'd already come to. "I'm just suggesting we become a stable, responsible married couple for all interested parties."

"You want to marry me just to get your aunt off your back?"

Creed laughed. "You make it sound so simple. Aunt Fiona is not that easy to fool. You'll have to be a very enthusiastic bride. Or she'll find me a better wife."

Aberdeen shook her head. "It's a silly reason to get married. I counsel people on making proper decisions regarding marriage vows. This would be a sham."

"*Sham* is also a harsh word." He kissed the tip of her nose. "I prefer *happy facade.*"

Her glare returned. "*Happy facade* sounds ridiculous. Marriage should be a contract between two people who trust each other."

"Think of all the benefits. I'd sleep with you every night, Aberdeen. I promise." He tugged her up against him, so he could kiss between her breasts. "We're a good fit in bed."

"Sex isn't enough." Aberdeen tried to squirm away.

"It's not enough, but it sure is a lot." He rolled her over so he could spoon against her back and nip her shoulder lightly at the same time. "Good thing you like sex as much as you do. I wouldn't want a frigid wife."

She gasped and tried to jump out of the bed. "Aberdeen, you know you like it. Don't try to deny it." He laughed and tugged her against him. "Were you reaching for the condoms, love? If you hand me a couple, I'll give you an hour you'll never forget."

She went still in the bed. He held her against him, stroking her hips, letting her decide if she was going to be angry with him or take the bait. Either way, he had a plan for that.

"You're too crazy for me to marry," Aberdeen said, "even if you're serious, which I don't think you are."

"I'm as serious as a heart attack, love."

She flipped over to stare into his eyes. "Where would we live?"

"In my house in New Mexico. Wherever that's going to be."

"A house?" He could feel her taste the words, and realized having a house was a dream of hers.

"Mmm," he murmured, unable to resist running a palm down her breasts. "House, yard, school nearby, church, the works. Nothing fancy. But a home."

"Why would you be willing to have my three nieces live with you?" She looked as though she didn't quite believe what she was hearing.

He shrugged. "I don't mind kids. They didn't exactly run screaming from me, and I thought that was a good start. And my aunt wants us to have as many children as possible."

She crooked a brow. "Can't you have your own?"

He laughed. "Come here and let's find out."

Aberdeen squirmed away, studying his face. "Men

don't get married and take on other people's children because of aunts."

"Probably not." He could feel her brain whirring a mile a minute, trying to find the trap. She didn't get it, and even if he told her, she wouldn't believe him. *I like her, I honestly like her. I like her body. I like her innocence. I think she'd like being married to me. That's as much as I know about why people get married anyway. This feels good and real, when it's always felt kind of empty before. And I think I'm falling in love with her.* "If you want to make love again, I'll try to think of some more reasons we should get married. There's probably one or two good excuses I haven't thought of yet, but—" He kissed her neck, burying deep into the curve, smelling her clean scent, wanting her already.

"Creed," she said, "I've been through one marriage. And my nieces have already been through marriages that didn't work out for their parents. Do you know what I mean?"

"I do, my doubting angel." He kissed her hand. "You want something solid for your nieces. You won't settle for anything less than a real family. And you think I'm your man. Hand me that bag on the nightstand, please."

"Not right now, Creed, this is serious." Aberdeen melted his heart with her big pleading eyes that melted his heart. She was such a delicate little thing. He wouldn't hurt her for the world. "I feel like you're playing with me."

"Oh, no. I wouldn't. Well, sometimes I will, in fact a lot of times I will, but not about a marriage agreement. I'm very serious about agreements. Hand me my bag, sugar."

She shook her head. "Creed, I can't make love when

you've got me tied in knots. I couldn't think. I couldn't focus. I just don't understand why you want to marry—"

He gave her a tiny slap on the backside. "Aberdeen, will you please hand me that sack on the nightstand? Or do I have to get it myself?"

"Here's your silly old sack," she said, snatching it up and flinging it at him. "But I'm not saying yes, so don't even ask."

He raised a brow. "No yes?"

"No. Absolutely not." She looked fit to be tied, as if she'd love to kick him out of her bed.

Creed sighed. "Is that your final answer?"

"In fact, it is. No woman can make love when the man who is in her bed is being an absolute ass."

"Whoa, them's fighting words from a preacher." Creed grinned at her. "Just so I can get this straight," he said, reaching into the bag and pulling out a jeweler's box, which he opened, "you're saying no?"

She stared at the box he opened for her to view. It contained a heart-shaped diamond, which he was pretty proud of picking out this morning on his way for the condoms and granola bars.

"Creed," she said, sounding shocked and choked-up, and he snapped the box shut and put it back in the bag.

"Too bad," he said. "The jeweler promised me no woman could say no to this ring. He said a woman would have to have a heart of stone to refuse it. He said—"

"You're crazy! I knew it when I first met you. I know you're crazy, and I know better than to throw myself to the wind like this, but I'm going to ride this ride, cowboy, and I swear, if you turn out to be a weirdo, I'll be really ticked at you."

He kissed her, and she burst into tears, and threw her

arms around his neck. "There, there," he said, "having a weirdo for a husband wouldn't be that bad, would it?"

"Creed, give me my ring," Aberdeen said, trying not to giggle against his neck as he held her.

"Greedy," he murmured, "but I don't mind." He took the ring from the box and slipped it on her finger, and for a moment, they both admired it in the light that spilled into the bedroom through the lace curtains.

"You are a weirdo," Aberdeen said, "and I don't know why I'm jumping off a cliff into alligator-infested waters."

Creed just grinned at her. "I'll let you get on top, future Mrs. Callahan, if you're sweet, and this time, you can ride me bareback."

Aberdeen looked at him, not sure if she trusted him or not, not sure exactly of what she wanted to feel for him. But Creed understood she'd been let down before, so he tugged her on top of him, and then smiled to himself when after a moment she said, "This time, I'm going to please you, cowboy."

Aunt Fiona was right, as usual. This marriage stuff is going to be a piece of cake. I feel like I'm winning again—finally.

Chapter Eleven

Marriage was *not* going to be a piece of cake. It was going to be as nerve-racking as any rodeo he'd ever ridden in—only this time, he was pretty certain getting stomped by a bull was less traumatic than what he was experiencing now. Creed found himself waiting outside Aberdeen's family home, cooling his heels before the big intro. The girls were inside, getting reacquainted with their aunt and Johnny. Aberdeen wanted to introduce him to her family after she had a chance to go inside and prepare them for the big news.

He was nervous. And it was all because of the little girls. He'd thought they'd liked him for the brief moments they met him before—but what if they'd changed their minds? Kids did that. He knew from experience. He wasn't certain he would have wanted a new father when he was a kid. Maybe he wouldn't. He and his brothers probably would have given a new father a rough road—he was certain they would have. They'd given everybody a rough road on principle, except Fiona. She wouldn't have put up with that type of nonsense, and besides, she'd always been able to out-think them.

He was pretty certain the little girlies might be able to out-think him, too. Girls had mercurial brains, and at their tender ages, they probably had mercurial set on high.

He was sweating bullets.

He should have brought some teddy bears or something. Big pieces of candy. Cowgirl hats. Anything to break the ice and get the girls to see him in a positive light.

"Creed, come in." Aberdeen smiled out the door at him, and he told his restless heart to simmer down. It was going to be okay.

He stepped inside the small Montana house—and found himself on the receiving end of frowns from everyone in the family except Johnny.

"Good man," Johnny said, clapping him on the back, and Creed felt better.

"You might have warned me you were setting me up," Creed groused under his breath, and Johnny laughed.

"You struck me as the kind of man who didn't need a warning," Johnny said. "These are our parents. Mom, Dad, this is Creed Callahan."

He was definitely not getting the red carpet treatment. Mr. and Mrs. Donovan wore scowls the size of Texas. "Hello," he said, stepping forward to shake their hands, "it's a pleasure to meet you."

He got the fastest handshakes he'd ever had. No warmth there. Creed stepped back, telling himself he'd probably feel the same way if he had little girls and some cowboy was slinking around. The girls looked up at him shyly, their eyes huge, and Creed had to smile. He did have little girls now—three of them—and he was going to scowl when boys came knocking on his door for them.

"Well," Aberdeen said, "Creed, sit down, please. Make yourself comfortable."

"You're marrying my daughter," Mr. Donovan said, and Creed nodded.

"That's the plan, sir."

"I don't think I care for that plan."

Creed glanced at Johnny, surprised. Johnny shrugged at him.

"I'm sorry to hear that," Creed finally said, trying to sound respectable. "Your daughter will be in good hands, I promise."

"We know nothing about you," Mrs. Donovan said.

"Mom," Aberdeen said, "I'm marrying him. You can be nice, or you can both be annoying, but this man is my choice. So you'll just have to accept it."

"You're not taking the girls," Mrs. Donovan said, and Creed went tense.

"Yes, I am, as soon as I clear it with the judge." Aberdeen got to her feet, abandoning the pretense of a welcome-home party. Creed felt sorry for her. Aunt Fiona had kept them in line over the years, but she'd never been rude to them. He glanced at the tiny girls, and they stared back at him, not smiling.

His heart withered to the size of a gumdrop. He wanted them to like him so badly, and at the moment they just seemed confused.

"The judge won't approve it." Mr. Donovan seemed confident about that. "He feels they are better off here, near us."

"All right. Come on, Creed." Aberdeen swept to the door. Creed recognized his cue and followed dutifully, not understanding his role in the script but sensing his bride-to-be was working on a game plan.

Mrs. Donovan shot to her feet. "Where are you going?"

"Back to Wyoming," Aberdeen said, and Johnny followed her to the door. Johnny might have set him up, Creed realized, but he definitely had his sister's back.

"You can't just leave!" Mrs. Donovan exclaimed.

"I can. I will. And I am."

"Wait!" Mrs. Donovan sounded panicked. "What are we going to do with the girls?"

"Raise them," Aberdeen said, and Creed could see her lips were tight. She was angry, loaded for bear, and he didn't ever want to see her look at him like that. "Maybe you'll do a better job with them than you did with us."

"Hang on a minute," Mr. Donovan said. "Let's just all calm down."

"I'm past calm," Aberdeen said. "Calm isn't available to me at the moment."

The little girls started to cry. Creed's heart broke. "Oh," he murmured, not sure what to do, completely undone by the waterworks. "I think I'll wait outside," he said, and headed toward Johnny's truck. This was such bad karma that he was going to kiss Aunt Fiona as soon as he got back to Rancho Diablo. He'd never realized before how much her steadfast parenting had colored his existence happy. Of course, she was going to box his ears when she found out he was getting married and she didn't get to arrange it, and that made him feel a bit more resourceful.

He sat in the truck, feeling like a teenager. After a few moments, Mrs. Donovan came to his window. "Mr. Callahan," she said, her eyes bright. He thought she'd been crying.

"Yes, ma'am? Please call me Creed."

"Will you please come back inside and have a cup of tea before you depart?"

He looked at her, and she looked back at him with a sad expression, and he realized she was scared.

"You know," he said softly, "I'm not taking her away from you forever. And you will always be welcome at Rancho Diablo. We like having family around."

Tears jumped into her eyes. She nodded. "Tea?"

"I'd be honored," he said, and followed his future mother-in-law into the house.

"WHAT DID YOU SAY TO HER?" Aberdeen asked, watching her mother ply Creed with cupcakes and tea.

"I said I liked tea a whole lot."

Creed filled his plate up with sweets, and balanced Lincoln Rose on his knee as though he'd done it a thousand times before. Aberdeen was astonished. Good father material wasn't something she'd put on her checklist when she'd decided to seduce Creed. The shock of discovering that he might have potential in this area warmed her heart. The most important thing in the world to her right now was the welfare of her nieces— she'd do anything to protect their futures, make sure their lives were as comfortable and normal as possible under the circumstances.

Never had she suspected that Creed might be a truly willing participant in her goal. He sure looked like it now, with all her nieces standing close to him, eating him up with their eyes like they'd never seen a real man before. They'd had Johnny, but she and Johnny hadn't been around much, not knowing that Diane's marriage was in trouble. So Creed garnered a lot of attention from the girls. And he seemed to return that attention, with affection thrown in.

*It's an agreement. We made an agreement. He's
merely keeping up his part of the bargain. I wanted
stability, and he wanted stability, and neither of us ever
said anything about permanent. Or love.*

*So don't do it. Don't go falling in love when you know
that's not a realistic ending to the story. Wild never set-
tles down forever—and he never said forever anyway.*

"More tea?" she said to Creed, and he smiled at her,
his gaze kind and patient as he held the girls, and she felt
heat run all over her. And another chip fell off her heart.

"To be honest," Johnny said to Creed when they'd gone
outside to throw a ball for the little nieces, "I didn't
mean for you to propose to my sister."

Creed looked at him, then back at the porch where
Aberdeen was standing with her parents, watching the
game. The small house framed them. If he hadn't known
better, he would have thought this was a happy family. However, it wasn't anything he wasn't experienced
with, so Creed felt pretty comfortable. "What did you
have in mind, then?"

"I thought it would be a good idea to give Aberdeen
something new to look at. Re-ride was old, you were
new." Johnny grinned. "I wanted her to know that there
were other fish in the sea."

"I'm sure there've been plenty of fish swimming her
way," Creed said, his tone mild.

"Yeah, but she's not much for catching them." Johnny
tossed the ball, and the pink toy bounced toward the
girls who squealed and tried to catch it with uncoordi-
nated hands. "Anyway, I just wanted you to know that
you're taking on a pretty tall order with us."

"Tall doesn't bother me." Creed looked at the girls,
then glanced back at Aberdeen. Her hair shone in the

Montana sunlight and she was smiling at him. "However, you'll have to come to New Mexico to see her, my friend, so I hope you thought through your plan in its entirety."

"That's the way it is, huh?"

"That's the way it is." Creed nodded. "We've got plenty of space for you, too, if you're of a mind to see a different topography."

Johnny grinned. "I hear New Mexico is nice this time of year."

Creed nodded, but his gaze was on Aberdeen again, and all he could think about was that New Mexico was going to be really nice, better than nice, when he had his little preacher lady sleeping in his big bed. Naked. Naked, warm and willing.

She waved at him, and he smiled, feeling like the big bad wolf. The happiest wolf in the canyons.

AFTER HE'D CHARMED Aberdeen's folks—who warmed to him quickly after their initial resistance—and after he'd cleared hurdles with the judge, Creed placed one last phone call to warn his family of their impending change in lifestyle.

"Hello," Rafe said, and Creed grinned.

"Hello, yourself. If you've got the time, we need a ride."

His twin sighed. "I'm not flying up there just to pick up your lazy butt."

Creed had taken himself out to the small backyard after dinner to have this conversation. Johnny and Aberdeen were tucking the little girls into bed, so he had time to sound the alarm. "You'll be picking up my lazy butt and a few very busy little bottoms."

"Well, now, that sounds more interesting. How are these bottoms? Female, I hope?"

Creed grinned. "Very much so."

"Round and cute?"

"The cutest, roundest tushes you ever saw."

"So I should shave."

"Definitely. You'll regret it if you don't. You don't want to scare them." Creed thought about the small dolls that would be traveling with him and held back a laugh.

"You flying your own entertainment in for Fiona's charity ball?"

"You might say I am."

"Well, consider me your eager pilot. Where and what time do you need a pick-up?"

One of the benefits of having an ex-military pilot who'd spent time flying for private corporations was that the family had their own plane. Rafe was an excellent pilot, and letting him fly them home would be easier on the girls. Creed hadn't yet told Aberdeen, but he was looking forward to surprising her. "Tomorrow, in Spring, Montana. Plan on me, a friend and four damsels, you might say."

Rafe whistled. "You *have* been busy."

"Be on your best behavior. And ask Aunt Fiona to get the guest house ready for visitors, will you?"

"She's going to be thrilled that you're falling into line." Rafe laughed. "I should have known that all this talk of watching over a bar for some guy was just a ruse."

"Probably you should have."

"I don't know if Fiona's going to be cool with you sleeping in the guest house with a bunch of women. On the other hand she's not totally uptight, and she is hoping to marry you off," Rafe mused. "She did say she thought you were the least likely of all of us to ever set-tle down. So she'll probably be okay with it."

"My ladies are pretty fine. Aunt Fiona will be all right after the initial shock."

"Bombshells, huh? Are you sharing?"

"You can hold them any time you like. Except for my particular favorite, of course. Oh, and bring your headset. They can be loud. Girl chatter and all that. Wild times."

"You old dog," Rafe said, his tone admiring. "And everyone says you're the slow twin. Boy, did you have everybody fooled."

"See you tomorrow," Creed said, and turned off his phone. He went to find Aberdeen, who was sitting in the family room alone. She appeared slightly anxious as her gaze settled on him. "Hello."

"Hi." She smiled, but he thought she looked nervous. "Girls asleep?"

"Johnny's reading to them. Lincoln Rose is asleep, the other two are excited about the trip tomorrow."

Creed nodded, sitting next to her on the sofa. "I hope you don't mind flying."

Aberdeen looked at him. "We're flying to New Mex-ico?"

"It'll be easier on the girls than a few days' drive."

"Thank you." Aberdeen smiled. "That's consider-ate of you, Creed."

"It is. I plan to get my reward after we're married."

Aberdeen's eyes widened. "After?"

"Well, yes. You'll have to wait to have me until you've made an honest man of me." He was pretty proud of his plan. He knew she had probably been thinking of how everything was going to work out between them. Sooner or later, she'd get worried about the silly stuff.

Like, she wouldn't want to sleep with him at his ranch until they were married; it wouldn't be decent. She was, after all, a minister. She would worry about such things. She was also a new mother to children. She would be concerned about propriety. He intended to take all those worries right out of her busy little mind.

"I think you are an honest man," Aberdeen said shyly.

"Well, aren't you just a little angel cake," he said, pleased, and dropped a kiss on her nose. "But you're still not having me until you put the ring on my finger."

Aberdeen laughed. "You're horrible."

"But you like it." He put her head against his shoulder, enjoying holding her in the quiet family room.

"I'm so glad you weren't bothered by my folks," Aberdeen said softly. "They can be busybodies."

"Oh, I know all about well-meaning interference. I'm an experienced hand. I just hope you know what you're getting yourself into, little lady."

She smiled and leaned closer, and Creed closed his eyes, contented. Of course she had no idea what she was stepping into. He wasn't certain what was waiting back home for them, either. All he did know was that he'd told her she had to wait until they were married to have him again.

But they hadn't set a wedding date.

He felt like he was holding his breath—and he needed to breathe again. Soon.

Chapter Twelve

When Rafe met them at the plane, he was in full wolf
mode. Dark aviator glasses, new jeans, dark Western
shirt, dress boots. Even a sterling bolo with a turquoise
stone. The kind of lone wolf any woman would lick her
chops over.

Only Creed's ladies didn't really have chops yet, just
gums. "Here you go," he told Rafe, and handed him the
baby. "This is Lincoln Rose. Lincoln, don't be scared
of ugly, honey. He tries hard but he's just not handsome like me."

Lincoln Rose stared at Rafe. Rafe stared back at her,
just as bemused. Creed grinned and went to walk the
next little girl up the stairs. "This is my brother, honey.
You can call him Uncle Rafe if you want to, Ashley,"
Creed said, even though she didn't talk much yet. "Let's
figure out how to strap your car seat in, okay? This
plane has never seen a baby seat. But I'm pretty sure
we can figure it out." He put her favorite stuffed animal and a small book beside her, then went back to the
front of the plane. "And I see you've met my last little
girl." Creed grinned at his brother, who still held Lincoln Rose as he latched eyes on Aberdeen with appreciation. "And this is the lady I mentioned was my special
girl. Aberdeen, this is my brother, Rafe. Rafe, this is my

fiancée, Aberdeen Donovan, and this little munchkin is Suzanne. Her sisters call her Suzu. And bringing up the rear is our nanny, Johnny Donovan."

"You look just like Creed," Aberdeen said. "Creed, you didn't tell me you had a twin."

"No reason to reveal all the sordid details." Creed waved Johnny toward the back and took Lincoln Rose from his brother.

"Details like how you travel in style?" Johnny said. "This is a sweet ride."

"Well, it helps to get around the country fast. We do a lot of deals here and there." Creed looked at Aberdeen. "Do you want to be co-pilot, honey?"

"No," Aberdeen said, "Thank you. I'll just sit back and try to decide how I got myself into this."

Creed grinned. "Make yourself comfortable. I'm going to help Rafe fly this rust bucket. Are we good to go, pilot?"

Rafe still seemed stunned as he looked over his new cargo of toys and babies. "Three little girls," he said, his tone amazed. "Are you trying to beat Pete?" he asked, and Creed glared at him.

"Do you see a fourth?" Creed asked.

"Who's Pete?" Aberdeen asked.

"Our brother who was first to the altar, and first to hit the baby lotto," Rafe said cheerfully.

"What were you supposed to beat him at, Creed?" Aberdeen asked.

Rafe glanced at Creed, who wished his brother had laryngitis. "I'm not trying to beat anybody at anything," Creed said. "Don't you worry your pretty little head about anything my numbskull of a brother says."

Rafe nodded. "That's right. Ignore me. I'm a pig at times."

"Most of the time. Let's fly." Creed dragged his brother into the cockpit.

"She doesn't know, does she?" Rafe asked as they settled in.

"I saw no reason to mention the baby-making aspects of Fiona's plan. It had no bearing on my decision."

"You sure?" Rafe asked.

"More than sure. Otherwise, there would be a fourth."

"And there's not?"

"Do you see a fourth?" Creed glared at Rafe again.

"I'm just wondering," Rafe said. "As your twin, it's my duty to wonder."

"Skip your duty, okay?"

Rafe switched on some controls. "I should have known that when you said you were keeping an eye on a bar, you meant a nursery."

"No, I meant a bar. I didn't have plans to get engaged when I left."

"So you found yourself in a bar and then a bed." Rafe sounded tickled. "And there were three bonuses, and so you realized this was a primo opportunity to get out of Fiona's line of fire. And maybe even beat Pete."

"No," Creed said, "because there's nothing to beat Pete for. We have no ranch, per se. Therefore, no need to have children by the dozen."

"Oh. You hadn't heard. You've been gone." Rafe slowly taxied on to the runway. "We're all supposed to settle down, if we want to, to try to keep Bode from getting the ranch."

"It's no guarantee."

"But you don't know that Fiona says that competition begets our more successful efforts, so he who winds up with a wife and the biggest family will get the biggest chunk of the ranch—if we keep it."

Creed frowned. "That has no bearing on my decision."

"It might when you've had a chance to think it over. You'll probably think about it next time you crawl into bed with your fiancée," Rafe said, his tone annoyingly cheerful.

Creed scowled. "Let's not talk about marriage like it's a rodeo, okay? I'm getting married because…because Aberdeen and the girls are what I need."

"To settle you down." Rafe nodded. "Believe me, I understand. I'd settle down if I could find the right woman."

That wasn't it, exactly. Creed was getting married because he and Aberdeen had struck a bargain that suited them both. He got up to glance out at his precious cargo, wanting to make certain everyone was comfortable, particularly the little ladies. Aberdeen and Johnny were staring at him. Aberdeen looked as if she might be on the verge of throwing Lincoln Rose's bear at him. Johnny looked as if he was considering getting out of his seat to squash Creed's head. "Is something wrong?" he asked, instantly concerned for the babies.

"The mike's on," Johnny said, "or whatever you call that loudspeaker thing."

Creed groaned. They'd heard everything—and probably misunderstood everything, too. "We'll talk later," he said to Aberdeen, but she looked out the window, not happy with him at all.

That made two of them.

Creed went back into the cockpit, flipping the switch off as he sat down. Rafe glanced at him.

"Uh-oh. You may be in trouble," Rafe said. He looked honestly concerned. "Was that my bad?"

"I'm not certain whose bad it was. Just think about flight patterns, bro. The sooner I get her on terra firma at Rancho Diablo, the clearer things will be."

He hoped Aberdeen was the type of woman who was willing to forgive and forget. Otherwise, he might be in for a bit of a rough ride, and, as he recalled, he'd been thrown recently. Which was how he'd ended up here in the first place.

He had no intention of being thrown again.

"THIS IS HOME," Creed told Aberdeen when they arrived at the ranch a few hours later. Rafe had left a van at the small regional airport where they kept the family plane in a hangar, and very little had been said on the ride to the ranch. The girls had been sound asleep in their car seats. Though Johnny had ridden up front with Rafe, and Creed had sat next to her, neither of them had felt like talking. The bigger conversation was later. If he thought she was marrying him out of a sense of obligation, he was dead wrong. And she had no intention of "settling him down," as he'd told Rafe. He could just go settle himself down, she thought.

Now, at the family ranch, Aberdeen couldn't help but be surprised. She glanced at Johnny for his reaction to the huge house on the New Mexico plains. In the distance a couple of oil derricks worked. Cattle roamed behind barbed-wire fencing. The sky was a bruised blue, and canyons were red and purple smudges in the distance. It was in the middle of nowhere, and a sense of isolation hung over the ranch.

Until, it seemed, a hundred people flowed out of the house, coming to greet them. Creed opened his door, turning to help her out. A tiny, older woman made it to the van first.

"Aunt Fiona, this is Aberdeen Donovan," Creed said. "Aberdeen, this is the brains of the outfit, Fiona."

"Hello, Aberdeen," Fiona said. "Welcome to Rancho Diablo."

Fiona's smile enveloped her. Aberdeen thought that the same wonderful navy eyes ran in the Callahan family. She felt welcomed at once, and not nervous as she had been after listening to the men discuss their "tyrant" aunt. "Hello. Creed's told me so many wonderful things about you."

"I doubt it." Fiona smiled. "But you're sweet to fib, honey. This is Burke, the family overseer. He's the true brains of the outfit, as my rascal nephew puts it."

A kindly white-haired gentleman shook her hand. "It's a pleasure, Aberdeen. And Fiona, I think we have some extra guests." Johnny had unstrapped Lincoln Rose and handed her out to Aberdeen. Fiona gasped.

"What a little doll! Creed, you didn't tell us you were bringing a baby!"

His brothers came forward, eager for their introduction and to catch a glimpse of the baby. Johnny handed out the last two, and Aberdeen smiled.

"This is Lincoln Rose, and Suzanne and Ashley. These are my nieces, and this is my brother, Johnny Donovan."

Johnny finally made it from the van and introduced himself to the rest of the Callahans. Fiona shook her head at Creed. "You told Rafe you were bringing bombshells, you ruffian."

"I couldn't resist, Aunt Fiona." Creed grinned, clearly proud of himself.

"These are the prettiest bombshells I've ever seen,"

Fiona said. "I'll have to send out for some cribs, though. And anything else you require, Aberdeen. We don't have enough children at Rancho Diablo, so we'll be happy to gear up for these. You'll just have to let us know what babies need. My nephews have been a wee bit on the slow side about starting families." She sent Creed a teasing smile. "Is there anything else you'd like to spring on us, Creed?"

"Introductions first, Aunt Fiona." He went through the litany of brothers, and Aberdeen felt nearly overwhelmed by all the big men around her. Johnny seemed right at home. But then, another woman came forward, pushing a big-wheeled pram over the driveway, and Suzanne and Ashley went over to see what was inside.

"Babies," Ashley said, and Creed laughed.

"This is Pete's wife, Jackie. Jackie, this is Aberdeen Donovan."

Jackie smiled at her; Aberdeen felt that she'd found a friend.

"We'll have a lot to talk about," Jackie said.

"Yes, we will," Fiona said. "Come inside and let's have tea. I'm sure you're starving, Aberdeen." She took Lincoln Rose in her arms and headed toward the house. Aberdeen and Jackie followed.

"I'm starving, too," Creed said, watching the ladies walk away.

Sam laughed. "Not for love."

Jonas shook his head. "Did you buy that big diamond she's wearing?"

Creed shrugged. "It isn't that big."

"You're getting married?" Judah asked. "You were only gone a few days!"

"It feels right," Creed said, grinning at them.

"You're trying to win," Pete said. "You're trying to beat me."

Creed clapped his brother on the back. "Nope. I'd have to go for four to win, and I'm pretty good at knowing my limits, bro. The gold medal is all yours."

Pete grinned. "I hope you warned Aberdeen."

"About what?" Creed scowled as he and his brothers and Johnny walked toward the house, each carrying a suitcase. Burke tried to help carry one, but the brothers told him diaper bags were their responsibility, and Burke gladly went to park the van instead.

"About the bet. Which is a really dumb bet, if you ask me," Pete said. "I wasn't even trying, and look what happened to me. I just wanted to get married."

"It's almost like you got hit by a magic spell," Sam mused. "Who would have ever thought you could father three adorable little girls?"

"I don't know what to say about that," Pete groused. "I think it was more like a miracle. But besides that, I'm more than capable of fathering adorable, thanks. You'll be the one who has ugly."

"There's no such thing as an ugly baby." Jonas opened the door. "Have you ever seen an ugly baby? They don't exist. I'm a doctor, I know."

"You're a heart specialist, don't overreach your specialty." Creed shook his head. "But no, we're not going to bring up the baby bet, and we're not going to talk about ranch problems or anything like that. I'm trying to get the woman to marry me, not leave in a dust cloud." It could happen. Aberdeen could get cold feet. She had that cold-feet look about her right now. Creed knew she was still annoyed about Rafe's conversation with him in the plane. He also knew she'd been a bit rattled by the size of Rancho Diablo. Or maybe by its faraway location. Whatever it was, he needed time to iron it out of her without his brothers bringing up Callahan drama. "So just pull your hats down over your mouths if you have to," he told his brothers, "and let's not talk about anything we have going on that's *unusual*."

"Oh, he likes this one," Sam whispered to his brothers.

"You're talking about my sister like I'm not here," Johnny said.

"Sorry," Sam said. "You look like one of us. You could be a Callahan. We can be easily confused." He grinned. "We separate ourselves into the bachelors and the down-for-the-count."

"I'm not down—oh, never mind." Creed shook his head. "Johnny, don't listen to anything we say. We mean well. Some of us just blab too much."

Johnny shrugged. "I hear it all the time in the bar. Yak, yak, yak."

Jonas jerked his head toward the barn. "While the ladies chat, let us show you the set-up."

Creed hung back as his brothers headed out. He was pretty certain that if he was smart—and he thought he was where women were concerned—he'd better hang around and try to iron some of the kinks out of his little woman. She had a mulish look in her eyes whenever he caught her gaze, and he knew too well that mulish females were not receptive to men. He sat down by Aberdeen and pulled Lincoln Rose into his lap. "Take you for a buggy ride around the property when you've had a chance to rest?"

Aberdeen looked at him. "Is it story time?"

"I think so." Creed nodded. "Better late than never, huh?"

"We'll babysit," Jackie said, and Fiona nodded eagerly.

"And it's romantic on the ranch at night," Jackie said. "Trust me, Aberdeen, you want to take a spin on the ranch."

Aberdeen looked at Creed, and he smiled, and though she didn't smile back at him, he thought, she wasn't beaning him with a baby bottle, either—and that was the best sign he had at the moment.

"Romance," he said so only she could hear, "are you up for that?"

"We'll see how good your story is," she said, and Creed sank back in the sofa, looking at Lincoln Rose.

"Any tips on good stories?" he asked the baby, but she just looked at him. "I don't know any, either," he said, and Fiona said, "Then I suggest you get it in gear, nephew. Once upon a time, cowboy poets lived by their ability to tell stories. Live the legend."

Aberdeen raised a brow at him, and he decided right then and there that whatever she wanted, the lady was going to get.

Chapter Thirteen

Aberdeen could tell Creed was dying to get her alone. She wasn't entirely reluctant. Story time didn't sound horrible—and in spite of the conversation she'd overheard between Creed and his twin, she was willing to give him a chance to explain.

And to kiss her breathless.

Burke entered the room with a tall, distinguished-looking guest, and the room went silent.

"Well, Bode Jenkins," Fiona said, rising to her feet. "To what do we owe this unpleasant occurrence?"

Bode smiled at her thinly, then glanced at Aberdeen's daughters. "A little bird told me that you were welcoming visitors. You know how I hate not being invited to a party, Fiona." He sent a welcoming smile to Aberdeen, but instead of feeling welcomed, her skin chilled.

Creed stood, and Jonas stood with him. Sam followed, as did Rafe, Pete and Judah. Aberdeen glanced at Creed, whose face seemed suddenly set in granite. The brothers looked ready for an old-style Western shoot-out, which bewildered her.

"Now, Bode," Fiona said, "you have no business being here."

"You should be neighborly, Fiona," Bode said, his tone silky. "When Sabrina told me you were expecting visitors, I just had to come and see what good things were happening around my future ranch. One day," he ruminated, "I'm going to cover this place over with concrete to build the biggest tourist center you ever dreamed of."

The brothers folded their arms, standing silent. If this man's visit was about her arrival, then Aberdeen wanted no part of it. She grabbed Lincoln Rose and held her in her lap, either for comfort or to protect her from what felt like an oncoming storm, she wasn't certain. Her sisters naturally followed Lincoln Rose, hugging to Aberdeen's side for protection.

But then Ashley broke away and went to Creed, who picked her up in his big, strong arms. Bode smiled, his mouth barely more than a grimace. "Looks like you're growing quite the family, Fiona," he said, glancing at Pete's and Jackie's three daughters. "Another birdie told me that you're paying your sons to get wives and have babies so you can make the claim that Rancho Diablo has its own population and therefore shouldn't be subject to the laws of the nation. It won't work, Fiona, if that's what's on your mind."

"Never mind what's on her mind," Creed said, his voice a growl. "If you've stated your business, Jenkins, go."

Bode looked at Aberdeen. Her skin jumped into a crawling shiver. She clutched her two nieces to her. "I'm not going without giving my gift to the new bride-to-be," he murmured, his gaze alight with what looked like unholy fire to Aberdeen. "Will you walk outside with me, my dear?"

"I'm sorry that I can't," Aberdeen said. "My nieces wouldn't like me leaving them. We've just gotten in from a long day of traveling. I'm sure you'll under-stand."

Creed shot her a look of approval.

"That's too bad," Bode said. "There's someone I want you to meet."

"Is Sabrina outside?" Fiona frowned. "Why don't you bring her in?"

"Sabrina says she thinks she's coming down with a cold. She didn't want to give it to anyone." Bode shrugged. "I've just learned Sabrina is a fortune-teller. I wanted her to tell your fortune as a gift, Miss—"

"Donovan," Aberdeen said. "I don't believe in fortune-telling, Mr. Jenkins. Please tell your friend I'll be happy to meet her at another time when she isn't under the weather."

But then she realized that Fiona was staring at Bode, her brows pinched and low. Aberdeen sank back into her chair, glancing at Creed, who watched Bode like a hawk.

"Sabrina is a home-care provider," Fiona said, "who happens to have a gift. Why do you sound so irregular about it, Bode?"

He smiled at Fiona, but it wasn't a friendly smile. "I think you've tried to set me up, Fiona Callahan. And I don't take kindly to trickery."

"I don't know what you're talking about," Fiona snapped. "Don't be obtuse."

"Then let me be clear. You hired Sabrina McKinley to spy on me."

"Nonsense," Fiona shot back. "Why would I do that?"

"You'll do anything you can to save your ranch." Bode tapped his walking stick with impatience. "My daughter Julie figured it all out," he said. "She learned from one of your sons that Sabrina had been here one night."

"So?" Fiona said, her tone rich with contempt.

"So it was an easy feat for Julie to run a background check on Sabrina. Turns out she was traveling with some kind of circus."

"Is that a crime?" Jonas asked. "Last I knew, a circus was a place for hard-working people to have a job with some travel and do what they like to do."

"I'd be careful if I was you, Jonas," Bode said, his tone measured, "your little aunt can get in a lot of trouble for helping someone forge documents of employment and employment history."

Creed snorted. "How would Aunt Fiona do that?"

"Why don't you tell them, Fiona?" Bode stepped closer to Aberdeen, gazing down at the little girls she held. "I'd be cognizant, my dear, were I you, that this family loves games. And not games of the puzzle and Scrabble variety. Games where they use you as a pawn. You'll figure out soon enough what your role is, but only you can decide if you want to be a piece that's played."

"How dare you?" Aberdeen snapped. "Sir, I'll have you know that I'm a minister. I've met people from all walks of life, heard their stories, ached with their troubles, celebrated their joy. You know nothing about me at all, so don't assume I don't know how to take care of myself and those I love."

"I only wish to give you the gift of knowledge," Bode replied.

Aberdeen shook her head. "Gift unaccepted and unneeded. Creed, I'd like to take the girls to their room now." She stood, and Burke materialized at her side.

"I'll take Miss Donovan to her room," Burke said. "The golf cart should carry everyone nicely."

"I'm going out to see Sabrina," Jonas said, and Bode said, "She's not up to seeing—"

"She'll see me," Jonas snapped.

Judah trailed after Jonas. "I'm not being a bodyguard or anything," he told Bode as he walked by him, "I'm just damn nosy."

The two men left. Creed handed Lincoln Rose to Burke. Fiona stood, looking like a queen of a castle.

"You've caused enough of an uproar for one night, Bode. Out you go."

"We're at war, Fiona," Bode said, and she said, "Damn right we are."

"That's enough," Creed said. "If you don't go, Jenkins, we'll throw your worthless hide out."

Aberdeen followed Burke outside, with a last glance back at Creed. He'd stepped close to Bode, protectively standing between his aunt and the enemy, and Aberdeen realized that Creed was a man who guarded his own. He looked fierce, dangerous, nothing at all like the man who romanced her and seduced her until she wanted to do whatever it took to make him happy.

Yet, looking back at Creed, Aberdeen also realized she had no idea what was going on in this family. It was as if she'd landed in a strange new world, and the man she'd agreed to marry had suddenly turned into a surly lion.

Johnny took one of the girls in his arms, following her out, and as their eyes met, she knew her brother was re-thinking her cowboy fiancé, too.

"BUSTED," SAM SAID, and Creed nodded. Bode had left, his demeanor pleased. Whatever he'd come to do, he felt he'd succeeded.

"I think you are busted, Aunt," Creed said. "He

knows all about your plan. I don't think Sabrina would have ratted you out unless he threatened her."

"Oh, pooh." Fiona waved a hand. "Bode is my puppet. He jumps when I pull his strings."

Creed crooked a brow at his aunt. "You told Sabrina to enlighten him with the fortune-teller gag?"

"Seemed simpler than having him fish around and find out she's actually an investigative reporter." Fiona shrugged, looking pleased with herself. "Now he thinks he knows something he probably won't go digging around in her background. At the moment, he thinks he stole her from me, so he's pleased. It's not that hard to do a search on the computer for people these days, you know."

Creed shook his head. "You deal with her," he told his brothers. "I have a fiancée and three little ladies to settle in to the guest house."

His brothers looked as though they wished he would keep on with the line of questioning he'd been peppering the cagey aunt with, but he had promised romance to a pretty parson, and he was going to do just that.

CREED WALKED INTO the guest house right after Aberdeen had finished tidying the girls up and putting them in their jammies. The girls were tired, too exhausted for a bedtime story, so Aberdeen kissed them and put them in their little beds with rails—except for Lincoln Rose, who had her own lovely white crib. "Your aunt is amazing," she told Creed, who nodded.

"She amazes everyone."

"She's thought of everything." Aberdeen pointed around the room, showing the toys and extra diapers and even a tray of snacks and drinks on a wrought-iron tray on the dresser. "How did she do all this so quickly?"

"A lot of this is Burke's doing," Creed said, "but Fiona is the best. We were spoiled growing up."

"I could guess that." Aberdeen looked around the room. "It's clear that she spent a lot of time thinking about what children need to be comfortable."

Creed frowned. Aunt Fiona hadn't known about the girls. He hadn't told anyone, not even Rafe. He'd wanted them to get to know Aberdeen and the girls on their own, and not from anything he mentioned on a phone call.

Somehow Aunt Fiona had figured him out. He sighed. "No moss grows under her feet."

"Well, I'm very grateful. And now, if you don't mind, I'm going to bed." She turned her back on Creed, letting him know that he need not expect a good-night kiss. She wasn't ready to go into all the details of everything he was keeping from her, but at this moment she was bone-tired. And her nieces would be up early, no doubt. Tomorrow she'd make Creed tell her what was going on with the scary neighbor and Rancho Diablo.

At least those were her plans, until she felt Creed standing behind her, his body close and warm against her back. She closed her eyes, drinking in his nearness and his strength. He ran his hands down the length of her arms, winding her fingers into his, and Aberdeen's resistance slowly ebbed away.

He dropped a kiss on the back of her neck, sending a delightful shiver over her.

"I'm sorry about tonight," he murmured against her skin. "I had romantic plans for us."

"It may be hard to find time for romance with all the

commotion you have going on here. I thought my family tree was thick with drama."

He turned her toward him, his dark gaze searching hers. "I know you're wondering about a lot of things. I'll tell you a few family yarns in between riding lessons with the girls."

"Not my girls," Aberdeen said, her heart jumping.

"No time like the present for them to get in the saddle." Creed winked at her. "And you, too. You'll make a wonderful cowgirl."

"Sorry, no." Aberdeen laughed. "Lincoln Rose is staying right in her comfy stroller. My other two nieces can look at the horses, but there'll be no saddle-training for them."

"We'll see," Creed said, his tone purposefully mysterious. "Learning to ride a horse is just like learning how to swim."

"Will not happen," she reiterated, and stepped away from his warmth. She already wanted to fall into his arms, and after everything she'd heard today, she'd be absolutely out of her head to do such a thing. If she'd ever thought Creed was wild, she had only to come here to find out that he probably was—at the very minimum, he lived by his own code. And the judge was looking for stability in her life before he awarded her permanent custody of her nieces. An adoption application needed to be smooth as well. She shot Creed a glance over her shoulder, checking him out, noting that his gaze never left her. He was protective, he was kind, he was strong. She was falling in love with him—had fallen in love with him—but there were little people to consider. Her own heart needed to be more cautious, not tripping into love just because the man could romance her beyond her wildest imaginings. "Good night, Creed," she said, and after a moment, he nodded.

"Sweet dreams," he said, and then before she could steel herself against him, he kissed her, pinning his fingers into her waist, pulling her against him.

And then he left, probably fully aware that he'd just set her blood to boil. Tired as she was, she was going to be thinking about him for a long time, well past her bedtime—the rogue. And she was absolutely wild for him.

She wished Creed was sleeping in her bed tonight.

Chapter Fourteen

"You can't marry her," Aunt Fiona said when Creed went back to the main house. Fiona was sitting in the library in front of a window, staring out into the darkness. Burke had placed a coffee cup and a plate of cookies on the table. Creed recognized the signs of a family powwow, so he took the chair opposite Fiona and said, "I'm surprised you'd say that, Aunt. Doesn't Aberdeen fill the bill?"

Fiona gave him a sideways glance. "If there was a bill to be filled, I'm sure she'd do quite well. However, I don't believe in doing things in half measures, and I think that's what you're doing, Creed."

He nodded at the cup Burke placed beside him, and sipped gratefully. He didn't need caffeine to keep up with Fiona, but he did need fortification. It was going to be a stirring debate. "You're talking about the little girls."

Fiona shrugged. "They're darling. They deserve your best. We don't have a best to give them at the moment, as Bode's untimely visit indicates."

"We'll be fine. Give me the real reason you're protesting against me marrying her."

"Stability. We don't have that." Fiona sighed. "Have you told Aberdeen about this situation?"

"No. It didn't seem necessary. I'll take care of her and the children."

Fiona nodded. "I would expect that. However, we're at war here. Bode was sizing us up. I don't mind saying I'm afraid."

Creed shrugged. "I'm not afraid of that old man."

"You should be. He intends to make trouble."

"What's the worst he can do?"

Fiona looked at him. "You should know."

"I think the choice should be Aberdeen's."

Fiona nodded. "I agree. Be honest with her. Let her know that we're not the safe haven we may appear to be at first glance."

Creed didn't like that. He wanted to be able to give Aberdeen and the girls the comfort and safety he felt they needed. Protecting them was something his heart greatly desired. And yet, he knew Aunt Fiona's words of caution probably warranted consideration. "I'll think about it."

"Do you love her, Creed?" Fiona asked, her eyes searching his.

"Aberdeen is a good woman." He chose his words carefully, not really certain why he felt he had to hold back. "I think we complement each other."

After a moment, Fiona sat back in her chair. "Of course, you know that it's my fondest wish for you boys to be settled. I haven't hidden my desire to see you with families. But I wouldn't want to bring harm to anyone, Creed."

He stared at his aunt. Harm? He had no intention of causing Aberdeen any pain. Far from it. All her wanted to give her was joy. He wanted to take care of her. That's what they'd agreed upon between themselves: Each of them needed something from the other. He intended to keep his side of the bargain.

But as he looked at his little aunt fretting with her napkin and then turning to stare out the window, searching Rancho Diablo in the darkness, he realized she really was worried.

For the thousandth time in his life, he wished Bode Jenkins would somehow just fade out of their lives. But he knew that wasn't going to happen. They just couldn't be that lucky.

"If I only believed in fairy tales," Fiona murmured. "But I have to be practical."

"You pitting us against each other for the ranch is very practical." Creed smiled. "Nobody is complaining, are they?"

Fiona gave him a sharp look. "Is the ranch why you're marrying her?"

Creed drew in a deep breath. Why was he marrying Aberdeen—really? Was he using the ranch as an excuse to bolster his courage to give up rodeo, give up his unsettled ways and get connected to a future? Aberdeen, a ball and chain; the little girls, tiny shackles.

Actually, Creed thought, he was pretty sure the little girls were buoys, if anything, and Aberdeen, a life preserver. Before he'd met them, he'd been drowning in a sea of purposelessness. "I can't speak to my exact motivation for marrying Aberdeen Donovan," Creed said. "I haven't had time to pinpoint the reason. It could be gratitude, because I think she saved my life in the literal sense. It could be she appeals to the knight in me who feels a need to save a damsel in distress. It might even be that she's gotten under my skin and I just have to conquer that." Creed brightened. "Whatever it is, I like it, though."

Fiona smiled. "You do seem happy."

He grunted. "I haven't got it all figured out yet. But when I do, I'll let you know."

TWO WEEKS LATER, the magic still hadn't worn off. Mornings bloomed so pretty and sunny that Aberdeen found herself awestruck by the beauty of the New Mexico landscape. Riding in the golf cart with Burke, who'd come to get her and the girls for breakfast, Aberdeen couldn't imagine anything more beautiful than Rancho Diablo on a summer morning.

And the girls seemed tranquil, curious about their surroundings, staring with wide eyes. Horses moved in a wooden corral, eager to watch the humans coming and going. Occasionally she saw a Callahan brother walking by, heading to work—they always turned to wave at the golf cart. She couldn't tell which brother was which yet, but the fact that Creed has such a large family was certainly comforting. She liked his family; she liked the affection they seemed to have for each other.

She was a little surprised that Creed was a twin, and that his brother, Pete, had triplets. What if she had a baby with Creed? What were the odds of having a multiple birth in a family that seemed to have them in the gene pool? The thought intimidated her, and even gave her a little insight into why Diane might have become overwhelmed. *One at a time would be best for me. I'd have four children to guide and grow and teach to walk the right path. I wonder if I'll be a good mother?*

When Aberdeen realized she was actually daydreaming about having Creed's baby, she forced herself to stop. She was jumping light years ahead of what she needed to be thinking about, which was the girls and putting their needs first. They were so happy and so sweet, and she needed to do her best by them. She saw Johnny ride past in one of the trucks with a Callahan brother, and they waved at her and the girls, who got all excited when they saw their uncle. Johnny, it seemed, was fitting right in. He hadn't come in to the guest house last night, and she suspected he'd slept in the bunkhouse with the brothers. "Your uncle thinks he's going cowboy," she murmured to the girls, who ignored her in favor of staring at the horses and the occasional steer. It was good for Johnny to have this time to vacation a little. He'd had her back for so long he hadn't had much time to hang out, she realized. They'd both been tied to the bar, determined to make a success of it, buy that ticket out of Spring, Montana.

She hugged the girls to her. "Isn't this fun?"

They looked at her, their big eyes eager and excited. For the first time she felt herself relax, and when she saw Fiona come to the door, waving a dish towel at them in greeting, a smile lit her face. It was going to be all right, Aberdeen told herself. This was just a vacation for all of them, one that they needed. If it didn't work out between her and Creed, it would be fine—she and Johnny and the girls could go back home, create a life for themselves as if nothing special, nothing amazing, had happened.

As if she'd never fallen in love with Creed Callahan.

She took a deep breath as Burke stopped the golf cart in front of the mansion. Aberdeen got out, then she and Burke each helped the girls to the ground. Aberdeen turned to greet Fiona.

"Look who's here!" Fiona exclaimed, and Aberdeen halted in her tracks.

"Mommy!" Ashley cried, as she and Suzanne toddled off to greet Diane. Aberdeen's heart went still at the sight of her older sister, who did not look quite like the Diane she remembered. Cold water seemed to hit her in the face.

"Aberdeen!" Diane came to greet Aberdeen as if no time had passed, as if she hadn't abandoned her children. She threw her arms around Aberdeen, and Aberdeen found herself melting. She loved Diane with all her heart. Had she come to get her daughters? Aberdeen hoped so. A whole family would be the best thing for everyone.

"How are you doing?" Aberdeen asked her sister, leaning back to look at her, and Diane shook her head.

"We'll talk later. Right now, your wonderful mother-in-law-to-be has welcomed me into the fold," Diane said, and Aberdeen remembered that they had an audience.

"Yes. Aunt Fiona, this is my older sister, Diane." Aberdeen followed her nieces, who were trying to get up the steps to Fiona. Aberdeen carried Lincoln Rose, who didn't reach for her mother. The minute she saw Fiona, she reached for her, though. Fiona took her gladly, and Aberdeen and Diane shared a glance.

"I'm good with children," Fiona said, blushing a little that Diane's own daughter seemed to prefer her. "It's the granny syndrome."

"It's all right," Diane said quickly. "Come on, girls. Let's not leave Mrs. Callahan waiting."

"Oh." Fiona glanced back as they walked through the entryway. "Please, just call me Fiona. I've never been Mrs. Callahan."

"This is gorgeous," Diane whispered to Aberdeen. "How did you hook such a hot, rich hunk?"

"I haven't hooked him," Aberdeen said, hoping Fiona hadn't heard Diane.

"Well, find a way to do it. Listen to big sister. These are sweet digs."

"Diane," Aberdeen said, "what are you doing here? And how did you get here?"

"Mom and Dad told me where you were, and it's not that difficult to buy a plane ticket, Aberdeen."

"What about the French guy?"

"We'll talk later," Diane said as Fiona showed them in to a huge, country-style kitchen. At the long table, the largest Aberdeen had ever seen, settings were laid, and each place had a placard with their names in gold scrolling letters. There were even two high chairs for the youngest girls, with their own cards in scrolled letters. Each of the children had a stuffed toy beside her plate, and so they were eager to sit down, their eyes fastened on the stuffed horses.

"I hope you don't mind," Fiona said. "We have a gift shop in town and the owner is a friend of mine. I couldn't resist calling her up to get a few little things for the girls."

"Thank you so much," Diane said, and Aberdeen swallowed hard.

"Yes, thank you, Fiona. Girls, can you say thank you?"

The older ones did, and Lincoln Rose saw that her sisters were holding their horses so she reached for hers, too. And then Burke brought them breakfast, and Aberdeen tried to eat, even though her appetite was shot.

They were being treated like princesses—but the thing was, she wasn't princess material. She eyed her sister surreptitiously; Diane seemed delighted by all the attention Fiona was showering on them, and Aberdeen felt like someone dropped into a storybook with a plot she hadn't yet caught up on.

"Quit looking so scared," Diane said under her breath. "Enjoy what the nice lady is trying to do for you. This is great." And she dug into the perfectly plated eggs and fruit as though she hadn't a care in the world.

"Diane," Aberdeen said quietly, so Fiona couldn't hear, even though she had her head in the fridge looking for something—a jam or jelly, she'd mentioned. "What are you doing here? Really?"

Diane smiled. "Little sister, I'm here to see my daughters. Who will soon be your daughters, by the looks of things."

"I think you should reconsider," Aberdeen said, desperation hatching inside her. "If you're not traveling with that guy, and you seem so happy now, I mean, don't you think…" She looked at her sister. "These are your children, Diane. You can't just abandon them."

"I'm not abandoning them." Diane took a bite of toast. "I simply recognize I'm not cut out to be a mother. I wish it were different, but it's not. I get depressed around them, Aberdeen. I know they're darling, and they seem so sweet and so cute, but when I'm alone with them, all I am is desperate. I'm not happy. I think I was trying to live a dream, but when my third husband left, I realized the dream had never been real." She looked at Aberdeen. "Please don't make me feel more guilty than I do already. It's not the best feeling in the world when a woman realizes she's a lousy mother. And, you know, we had a fairly dismal upbringing. I just don't want to do that to my own children."

Fiona came over to the table, setting down a bowl full of homemade strawberry jam. "I'm pretty proud of this," she said. "I had strawberries and blackberries shipped in special, and I redid my jam stock after I lost all of last year's." She beamed. "Tell me what you think of my blue-ribbon jam!"

Aberdeen tore her gaze away from her sister, numb, worried, and not in the mood for anything sweet. She glanced around at her nieces who seemed so amazed by all the treats and their stuffed horses that all they could do was sit very quietly, on their best behavior. They were obviously happy to see Diane, but not clingy, the way kids who hadn't seen their mother in a while would be. Aberdeen sighed and bit into a piece of jam-slathered toast. It was sweet and rich with berry taste. Perfect, as might be expected from Fiona, as she could tell from everything Creed had said about his aunt.

Her stomach jumped, nervous, and a slight storm of nausea rose inside her. Aberdeen put her toast down. "It's delicious, Fiona."

Fiona beamed. It *was* delicious. If Aberdeen had eaten it at any other time in her life, she'd want to hop in the kitchen and learn Fiona's secrets. There were probably secrets involved in making something this tasty, secrets that could only be passed from one cook to another. Her stomach slithered around, catching her by surprise. She felt strangely like an interloper, a case taken on by these wonderful people and Creed. That wasn't the way she wanted to feel.

And then he walked into the kitchen, big and tall and filling the doorway, her own John Wayne in the flesh, and sunshine flooded Aberdeen in a way she'd never felt before.

"It's wonderful jam," Diane said, and Aberdeen nodded, never taking her eyes off the cowboy she'd come to love. He grinned at her, oblivious to her worries, and if she didn't know better, she would have thought his eyes held a special twinkle for her. Ashley got down from her chair and tottered over to him to be swept up into his arms. Lincoln Rose and Suzanne sat in their high chairs, patiently waiting for their turns for attention from Creed. Creed walked over and blew a tiny raspberry against Lincoln Rose's cheek, making her giggle, and did the same to Suzanne. They waved their baby spoons, delighted with the attention.

Then Creed winked at Aberdeen, in lieu of a good-morning kiss, and Aberdeen forced a smile back, trying to sail along on the boat of Unexpected Good Fortune.

But life wasn't all blue-ribbon strawberry jam and gold-scrolling placards. At least not her life.

Diane poked her in the arm, and Aberdeen tried to be more perky. More happy. More perfect.

She felt like such a fraud.

Chapter Fifteen

Pete and Jackie strolled in, carrying their three babies and a flotilla of baby gear, and the mood in the kitchen lifted instantly. Creed rose to help his brother and sister-in-law settle themselves at the breakfast table.

"We figured there'd be grub," Pete said, "hope you don't mind us joining you, Aunt Fiona."

She gave him a light smack on the arm with a wooden spoon. "The more, the merrier, I always say." She beamed and went back to stirring things up on the stove. Jackie seated herself next to Aberdeen.

"So, how do you feel about the royal treatment, Aberdeen?" Jackie asked.

"It's amazing. Truly." Aberdeen caught Creed's smile at her compliment. "Jackie, Pete, I'd like you to meet my sister, Diane."

Diane smiled, shaking her head at the babies Pete and Jackie were trying to get settled in their baby carriers. "I had my babies one at a time and I still felt like it was a lot. I can't imagine it happening all at once."

Jackie smiled. "We couldn't, either. And then it did." She got a grin from her proud husband, and Aberdeen's gaze once again shifted to Creed. He seemed completely unafraid of all the babies crowding in around him—in fact, he seemed happy.

"It hasn't been bad," Pete said. "We're catching on faster than I thought we would. Jackie's a quick study."

Aberdeen didn't think she'd be a quick study. She pushed her toast around on her plate, trying to eat, wishing the nausea would pass. She caught Creed looking at her, and he winked at her again, seeming to know that she was plagued by doubts. Cold chills ran across her skin. She didn't think she'd be radiant sunshine like Jackie if she found herself with three newborn triplets. He'd probably be dismally disappointed if she didn't take to mothering like a duck to water. "Excuse me," she said, getting up from the table, feeling slightly wan, "I'm going to find a powder room."

"I'll show you," Jackie said, quickly getting up to lead her down a hall.

"Thanks," Aberdeen said, definitely not feeling like herself.

"You look a bit peaked. Are you feeling all right?" Jackie asked.

"I'm fine. Thank you." Aberdeen tried to smile. But then she wasn't, and she flew into the powder room, and when she came back out a few moments later, Jackie was waiting, seated on a chair in the wide hallway.

"Maybe not so fine?" Jackie said.

"I suppose not." Embarrassment flashed over her. "I've always been a good traveler. I can't imagine what's come over me."

"Hmm. Let's sit down and rest for a minute before we go back to the kitchen."

Aberdeen sat, gratefully.

"It can be overwhelming here, at first."

"I think you're right." Aberdeen nodded. "Johnny and I live a much simpler life. And yet, everyone here is so nice."

"Did you know your sister was coming?"

Aberdeen shook her head.

"Well, you've got a lot going on." Jackie patted her hand. "Let me know if there's anything I can do to help."

"You have three newborns." Aberdeen realized the nausea had passed for the moment. "I should be helping you."

"We all help each other." Jackie looked at her. "Your color is returning. Are you feeling better? You were so pale when you left the kitchen."

"I feel much better. I've always been very fortunate with my health. I don't think I've had more than a few colds in my life, and I'm never sick. I can't imagine what's come over me." Aberdeen wondered if she was getting cold feet. But she wouldn't get cold about Creed. He made her feel hotter than a firecracker.

"Not that's it's any of my business," Jackie said, "but the nurse in me wonders if you might be pregnant?"

Aberdeen laughed. "Oh, no. Not at all. There's no way." Then the smile slipped slowly off her face as she remembered.

There *was* a way.

Jackie grinned at her. Aberdeen shook her head. "I'm pretty certain I'm not."

"Okay." Jackie nodded. "Can you face the breakfast table?"

Aberdeen wasn't certain. Her stomach pitched slightly. "I think so."

Jackie watched her as she stood. "You don't have to eat breakfast, you know. It's a lovely time of the day to take a walk in the fresh air. And I'd be happy to keep an eye on your little ones."

"I think…I think I might take your suggestion."

Something about the smell of eggs and coffee was putting her off. She felt that she'd be better off heading outside until her stomach righted itself. "I'm sure it's nothing, but…would you mind letting Fiona know I'm going to head back to the guest house?"

"Absolutely." Jackie showed her to a side door. "Don't worry about a thing."

Aberdeen *was* worried, about a lot of things.

I can't be pregnant. I was in the safe zone of the month when we—

She walked outside, the early-morning sunshine kissing her skin, lifting the nausea. "No, I'm not," she told herself, reassuringly.

A baby would really complicate matters. As wonderful as Rancho Diablo was, Aberdeen felt as though she was on vacation—not at home. Being here was fairy-tale-ish—complete with a villain or two—and any moment she should wake up.

She didn't know how to tell Creed that as much as she wanted to keep to their bargain, she didn't know if she could.

CREED GLANCED UP when Jackie came back into the kitchen, his brows rising. "Where's Aberdeen?"

Jackie seated herself, looking at him with a gentle smile. "She's taking a little walk. Fiona, she said to tell you she'd see you in a bit." Jackie smiled at her husband, and resumed eating, as though everything was just fine and dandy.

But Creed knew it wasn't. Jackie had high marks in this family for her ability to cover things up—look at how skillfully she'd gotten Pete to the altar. So Creed's instinctive radar snapped on. "Is she all right?"

"She's fine."

Jackie didn't meet his eyes as she nibbled on some toast. "Maybe I'll go join her on that walk," he said, and Diane said, "Good idea."

Jackie waved a hand. "I think she said she was looking forward to some solitude."

That was the signal. It just didn't sound like something Aberdeen would say. Creed got to his feet. "I think I'll go check on the horses."

Diane nodded. "My girls and I are going to sit here and enjoy some more of this delicious breakfast." She whisked her sister's abandoned plate to the sink. "Fiona, if I could cook half as well as you do, I might still have a husband."

Fiona grinned. "You think?"

"No." Diane laughed. "But I would have eaten better."

Diane seemed comfortable with Fiona and company, much more so than Aberdeen did. Creed got to his feet. "I'll be back, Aunt Fiona."

"All right." His aunt beamed at him, and Creed escaped, trying not to run after Aberdeen as he caught sight of her walking toward the guest house. "Hey," he said. "A girl as pretty as you shouldn't be walking alone."

Aberdeen gave him a slight, barely-there-and-mostly-fakey smile. Creed blinked. "Are you okay, Aberdeen?"

"I'm fine. Really."

"Hey." He caught her hand, slowing her down. "You trying to run away from me, lady?"

She shook her head. "I just need a little time to myself." She took her hands from his, gazing at him with apology in her eyes.

"Oh." Creed nodded. "All right." He didn't feel good

about the sound of that. "Call me if you need anything. Burke keeps the guest house stocked pretty well, but—"

"I'm fine, Creed. Thank you."

And then she turned and hurried off, smiting his ego. *Damn.* Creed watched her go, unsure of what had just happened. He wanted to head after her, pry some answers out of her, but a man couldn't do a woman that way. They needed space sometimes.

He just wished the space she seemed to need didn't have to be so far away from him.

ABERDEEN FELT GUILTY about disappearing on Fiona, and Diane—and Creed. She didn't want to be rude, but she wanted to wash up, change her clothes, shower. Think. Just a few moments to catch her breath and think about what she was doing.

She felt like she was on the Tilt-A-Whirl at the State Fair, and she couldn't stop whirling.

At least I'm not pregnant, she told herself. *I'm a planner. Planning makes me feel organized, secure.*

I've got to focus.

"Hey," Johnny called, spying her. "Wait up."

He caught up to her, following her into the guest house. "It feels like I haven't seen you in days."

"That's because we're in this suspended twilight of Happyville." Aberdeen went into the bathroom to wash up. When she came out, Johnny was lounging in the common area.

"That didn't sound particularly happy, if we're hanging out in Happyville." Johnny shot her a worried look. "What's up?"

Aberdeen sat on one of the leather sofas opposite Johnny. "I don't know, exactly."

He nodded. "Feel like you're on vacation and shouldn't be?"

"Maybe." Aberdeen considered that. "I need to wake up."

"An engagement, three kids that aren't yours, a new place ..." His voice drifted off as he gazed around the room. "Saying yes to a guy who lives in a mansion would freak me out, I guess, if I was a woman."

"Why?" Aberdeen asked, and Johnny grinned.

"Because your bar was set too low. Re-ride wasn't much of a comparison, you know?"

Aberdeen nodded. "I lost my breakfast, and Jackie wanted to know if I was pregnant."

"Oh, wow." Johnny laughed. "That would be crazy."

Aberdeen glared at him.

"Oh, wait," Johnny said, "is there a possibility I could be an uncle again?"

"I don't think so," Aberdeen snapped, and Johnny raised a brow.

"That's not a ringing endorsement of your birth-control method."

Aberdeen sighed. "I don't want to talk about it." The best thing to do was to concentrate, and right now, she just wanted to concentrate on what was going on with Diane. "Johnny, have you noticed that Diane seems to like her children just fine?"

"Mmm. She's just not comfortable with them. She's like Mom."

Aberdeen felt a stab of worry. "I wonder if I'd be like that."

Johnny crooked a brow. "You're not pregnant, so don't worry about it. Unless you might be pregnant, and then don't worry about it. You're nothing like Mom and Diane."

"How do you know? How does any mother know?" Aberdeen was scared silly at the very thought that she might bring a child into the world she couldn't bond with.

"Because," Johnny said, "you're different. You were always different. You cared about people. I love Diane, but she pretty much cares about herself, and whatever's going on in her world. You had a congregation that loved you, Aberdeen."

Aberdeen blinked. "I miss it. Maybe that's what's wrong with me."

"Well, I don't think that's all that's going on with you, but—" Johnny shrugged. "The pattern of your life has been completely interrupted. The bright side is that you can build a congregation here, if you want. I'm sure there's always a need for a cowboy preacher."

Aberdeen wasn't certain she wanted a new church. "What if I want my old church? My old way of life?" she asked softly.

Johnny looked at her. "I think that bridge has been crossed and burned behind us, sis."

Creed burst in the door, halting when he saw Johnny and Aberdeen chatting. He was carrying a brown paper bag, which caught Aberdeen's suspicious gaze.

"Sorry," Creed said, "Didn't realize you two were visiting."

"It's all right," Johnny said. "I'm just taking a break from ranching. I think I'm getting the hang of this cowboy gig." He waved a hand at the paper bag. "Did you bring us breakfast or liquor?"

Creed set the bag on a chair. "Neither."

Aberdeen shot her fiancé a guarded look. "Is that what I think it is, Creed Callahan?"

"I don't think so," Creed said. "It's a...lunch for me. That's what it is. I packed myself a lunch."

"You're going to go hungry, then," Johnny observed. "You can't work on a ranch and eat a lunch the size of an apple."

"It's for me," Aberdeen guessed.

"It's for us," Creed said, and Johnny got to his feet.

"I'll leave you two lovebirds alone," he said, and Aberdeen didn't tell him to stay.

"Goodbye," Johnny said, and went out the door.

"Creed, that's a drugstore bag," Aberdeen said, "and since you just bought a huge box of condoms when we were in Wyoming, I'm betting you bought a pregnancy test."

He looked sheepish. "How'd you guess?"

"Because you looked scared when you ran in here, like your world was on fire. Jackie told you, didn't she?"

"Well, everyone was worried. We thought something was really wrong with you. And Fiona started fretting, worrying that you didn't like her food, and Jackie said it was a girl thing, and she'd tell Fiona later, and then Diane blurted out that maybe you were pregnant, and I—" He looked like a nervous father-to-be. "Could you be?"

"I don't think so." Aberdeen sighed. "I mean, I guess it's possible. But not likely."

"It wasn't likely for Pete to have triplets, either," Creed said. "Maybe we'd better find out."

"I don't have to pee," Aberdeen said, feeling belligerent. She didn't want everyone at Rancho Diablo discussing her life.

"I'll get you a glass of water," Creed said, jumping to his feet, and Aberdeen said, "No!"

"Well, I might get a glass of water for me. With ice. It's hot in here."

Aberdeen closed her eyes. Just the thought of being a dad clearly was making him nervous. He'd have four children, Aberdeen realized, all at once.

"It wouldn't be what we agreed on," Aberdeen said, and Creed said, "We'll make a new agreement. After I drink a tall glass of water." He went into the kitchen and turned the faucet on full-blast. "Do you hear water running, sweetheart?"

Aberdeen shook her head. "I'm not going to take the test."

He shut off the faucet and came back in with a glass of water. "We'll drink together."

"You pee in the cup." Aberdeen ignored the glass Creed set beside her.

"I didn't get a cup," Creed said cheerfully. "I bought the stick one. It looked more efficient. And it said it could detect a pregnancy five or six days before a skipped—"

Aberdeen swiped the bag from him. "I'm not going to do it while you're here."

"Why not?" Creed was puzzled.

"Because," Aberdeen said. "I need privacy. I have a shy bladder."

He grinned at her. "No, you don't. I happen to know there's nothing shy about you, my little wildcat."

Aberdeen looked at him, her blood pressure rising. "I just want to avoid the topic a little while longer, all right?"

"Well, I feel like a kid on my birthday trying to decide which present to open first," Creed told her. "Pregnancy will probably be a very healthy thing for me."

"Is this about the ranch?" Aberdeen asked, and Creed looked wounded.

"No," he said, "that's dumb."

"Why? You said yourself—"

"I know." Creed held up a hand. "I told you getting married was about getting the ranch. I'd have three built-in daughters, and it would get Fiona off my back. I told you all that, it's true. But it's not anymore."

She looked at him, wanting to kiss him. Maybe he was falling for her as hard as she was falling for him! "What is it, then?"

"Our agreement?" Creed considered her question. "I don't know. Grab out the pee stick and we'll renegotiate based on whether you come up yes or no." He rubbed his palms together. "It's almost as much fun as a magic eight ball."

Aberdeen closed her eyes for a second, counting to ten. "Did anyone ever tell you you're a goof?"

"No. They just call me handsome. And devil-may-care." He came to sit next to her with his icy glass of water. "Drink, sweetpea?"

Chapter Sixteen

Twenty minutes later, Creed tapped on the bathroom door. It seemed like Aberdeen had been in there a long time. "Aberdeen? Are you taking a nap in there?"

"Give me a second," she said, and he wondered if her voice sounded teary. Was she crying?

His heart rate skyrocketed. "Let me in."

"No."

"Is something wrong?"

"I don't think so."

He blinked. That sounded foreboding, he decided. "Do you want your sister?"

"No, thank you."

He pondered his next attack. She couldn't be in there all day. He was about to relinquish his sentinel position outside her door when it opened.

Aberdeen walked out, and he saw at once that she *had* been crying. "Guess we're having a baby?"

She nodded.

He opened his arms, and she walked into them, her body shaking. Creed held her, and she sniffled a second against his chest, and then she pulled away.

He wanted her back. "I'm really amping up the pressure on my brothers," he said cheerfully, seeing a whole world of possibilities kaleidoscoping before him. He'd have a son to play ball with, to teach how to rope. Was there anything better than a boy to help him on the ranch?

Even if they didn't have a ranch anymore, he'd have a son.

"Aberdeen, sweetie, this is the best news I've had in my entire life. Thank you."

She looked at him. "Really?"

"Oh, hell, yeah." He sat down, checking his gut and knew every word he was speaking was true. "I feel like a superhero."

She wiped at her eyes, then looked at him with a giggle. "I feel strangely like a villainess."

"Uh-uh." He shook his head. "I mean, you're sexy and all, but there's nothing evil about you, babe, except maybe what you do to my sense of self-control. I don't suppose you'd like to have a celebratory quickie?"

She laughed but shook her head.

"It was worth a try." He liked seeing the smile on her face. "Hey, you know what this means, don't you?"

"It means a lot of things. Name the topic."

He felt about ten feet tall in his boots. "We need to plan a wedding."

She looked at him, surprised. "Isn't that rushing things a bit?"

"Not for me. I'm an eight-second guy. I'm all about speed and staying on my ride."

Aberdeen crossed her arms in a protective gesture, almost hugging herself. "When I met you, you hadn't stayed on your ride. In fact, you had a concussion. What if—"

"What if I decide to bail?" He grinned at her and pulled her into his lap. "Lady, you're just going to have to stick around to find out."

She looked down at him from her perch. "I'm way over my head here, cowboy. Just so you know."

"Nah. This is going to be a piece of cake. Fiona can help you plan a wedding. Or we can elope. Whichever you prefer." He nibbled on her neck. "Personally, I'd pick eloping. We'll get to sleep together faster. And you'll make a cute Mrs. Callahan. I'm going to chase my Mrs. Callahan around for the rest of my life."

"I can run fast."

"I know," he said, "but I think we just learned that I run faster."

She laughed, and he kissed her, glad to see the waterworks had shut off. She'd scared him! No man wanted to think that the mother of his child didn't want him. But he was pretty certain Aberdeen did want him, just as much as he wanted her. It was just taking her a little longer to decide that she wanted him for the long haul.

He wasn't letting her get away from him. "When are you going to make an announcement?"

She sighed. "I think something was foreshadowed when you ran in here with a paper bag from the drugstore. I won't be surprised if Fiona has already ordered a nursery. And I don't even know anything about you." For a moment, she looked panicked. "You know more about me than I do about you."

He shrugged. "No mysteries here. Ask a question."

"Okay." Aberdeen pulled back slightly when he tried to nibble at her bottom lip. Maybe if he got her mind off the pregnancy, he could ease her into bed. He did his best romancing between the sheets, he was pretty certain. Right now, her brain was on overdrive, processing, and if she only but knew it, he could massage her and kiss her body into a puddle of relaxation. He felt himself getting very intrigued by the thought.

"Who's the scary guy who visited?" Aberdeen asked. "That Bode guy?"

Uh-oh. It was going to be hard to lure her into a compromising position if she was up for difficult topics. "He's just the local wacko. No one special."

"I felt like I'd been visited by the evil Rancho Diablo spirit."

He sighed, realizing he was getting nothing at the moment—even his powers of romance weren't up to combating a woman who was still trying to figure out if she wanted to be tied to his family, friends and enemies. "I'm a very eligible bachelor," he said, "you don't have to examine the skeletons in my closet. Why don't we hop down to Jackie's bridal shop and look at dresses?" he said. Surely if romance wouldn't do it, shopping might get her thinking about weddings—and a future with him.

"Bode Jenkins," she said. "Was he threatening me?"

"He was being a pest. We're used to him showing up uninvited, trying to throw a wrench into things. Don't take it personally."

"He wants your ranch."

"Yep." Creed shrugged. "I think he may be delusional. He doesn't really want the ranch. He just wants to stick it to us. That's my personal assessment." He nuzzled at her cheek. "I'll be a lot stronger in my fight against evil and doom if I'm married. Let's talk about our future, all right?"

She moved away from his mouth. "Quit trying to seduce me. You're trying to get me off topic, and it isn't going to work."

He sighed. "Most women in your shoes would be more than happy to talk about tying me down, sister."

She took a long time to answer, and when she did, it

wasn't what he wanted to hear. "I can't get married at the snap of a finger, Creed. Mom and Dad would want me to get married at home—"

"We can fly them here."

"They would want me to have a church wedding—"

"But what do you want?" he asked, wondering why she was suddenly so worried about her parents. Her folks didn't seem to be all that interested in what she did. He moved his lips along her arm, pondering this new turn of events.

"I don't know. I just found out I'm having a baby. I can't really think about a wedding right now." She slid out of his lap and walked over to the window. "I'd better get back to the girls. I've left them alone too long."

"They're not alone," Creed said, surprised. "They're with their mothe—"

The glare she shot him would have knocked him back two feet if he'd been standing. She went out the door like a storm, and Creed realized he had a whole lot of convincing to do to get his bride to the altar.

In fact, it was probably going to take a miracle.

"I NEVER THOUGHT it would be so difficult to get a woman to jump into a wedding gown," Creed told his twin a few minutes later, when Rafe sat down next to him in the barn. Creed still felt stunned by the whirling turn of events in his life. "I'm going to be a father. I want to be a husband. I don't want my son coming to me one day and saying, 'Mom says you were half-baked with the marriage proposal.'" He looked at Rafe. "You know what I mean?"

Rafe shook his head. "Nope."

Creed sighed, looking at the bridle he was repairing. Trying to repair. This should have been mental cotton candy for him, and he was muffing the repair job. His concentration was shot. "Imagine finding out the best news in your life, but the person who's giving you the news acts like you're radioactive. You would feel pretty low."

"Yeah. But I'm not you. I'd just make her say yes."

Creed looked at Rafe. "Thanks for the body-blow."

Rafe grinned and took the bridle from him. "Give her some time, bro. She's just beginning to figure out that you've turned her life inside out. She needs some time to adjust."

"Yeah," Creed said, "but I want her to be Mrs. Callahan before I have to roll her down the aisle in a wheelbarrow."

Rafe looked at him. "And you wonder why Aberdeen isn't running a four-minute mile to get to the altar with you. Is that the way you romance a woman? 'Honey, let's get hitched before my brawny son expands your waistline?'"

"I never said a word about that. I just want sooner rather than later. I don't really care if she's the size of an elephant, I just want her wearing white lace pronto." Creed scratched his head, and shoved his hat back. "Truthfully, I think I wanted to marry that gal the moment I laid eyes on her. Even in my debilitated state, I knew I'd stumbled on something awesome." He looked at Rafe. "Aberdeen *is* awesome."

Rafe considered him. "You really are crazy about her, aren't you? This isn't about the ranch for you."

"Nope. I've tried every song-and-dance routine I know to get her to take me on. I've offered short-term marriage, marriage-of-convenience, and the real deal. She just doesn't set a date." He sighed, feeling worn down. "It's killing me. I really think I'm aging. And I'm pretty sure it's supposed to be the woman who plots to get the guy to wedded bliss. She sure can drag her feet."

"I don't know, man. All I know is you better shape up before the big dance tomorrow night."

Creed straightened. "That's not tomorrow night, is it?"

Rafe nodded.

"Oh, hell. I've got a bad feeling about this."

Aberdeen already seemed overwhelmed by the ranch, by Rancho Diablo, by him. How would she feel about a bachelor rodeo? He already knew. She would see his brothers hooting and hollering, trying to catch women and vice versa, and figure that he was no different from those lunkheads. That's how a woman thought. "I bet pregnant women probably jump to conclusions faster than normal, because of their hormones and stuff."

Rafe smacked him on the head. "Of the two of us, you are definitely the dumbest. Why do you talk like Aberdeen has no common sense? When beautiful, husband-hunting women are throwing themselves at you tomorrow night, she'll totally understand. It'll probably make her want you. Jealousy is catnip to a woman."

Creed groaned. If he knew Aberdeen the way he thought he did, she was going to run for the mountains of Wyoming. She was like a piece of dry tinder just waiting for a spark to set her off. He could feel her looking for reasons not to trust him. Damn Re-ride, he thought. He'd convinced her that all men were rats.

"Most men are rats," he said, pondering out loud, and Rafe nodded.

"Very likely. And women still love us."

Creed didn't think Aberdeen was going to love him if she could convince herself that he was a big stinky rodent. "I've got to get her out of here," he said, but his twin just shrugged.

"Good luck," Rafe said, and Creed figured he'd need a turnaround in his luck pattern if he wanted his bride.

He knew just who could advise him.

DIANE SAT ON a porch swing, watching her daughters play in a huge sandbox the brothers had constructed for all the new babies at Rancho Diablo. Maybe it was dumb, Creed thought, to make a sandbox when the babies were all still, well, babies. Ashley and Suzu were big enough to play in the soft sand dotted with toys, but Lincoln Rose would catch up in time, and so would Pete's daughters.

Creed couldn't wait to see all the kids playing together one day. The vista of Rancho Diablo land made a beautiful backdrop for children to view, panoramic and Hollywood-like. Burke had helped, drawing off precise measurements and finding the best type of sand to make wonderful castles.

And now Diane sat on the porch swing alone, watching her two oldest, and holding her baby. He watched her for a second, and then went to join the woman he hoped would be his sister-in-law one day.

"Hi," he said, and Diane turned her head.

"Hello."

"Mind if I join you?"

"Not at all. Please do." She smiled when he sat down. "My girls really like it here. There's something about this ranch that seems to agree with them."

He nodded. "It was a pretty great place to grow up."

Diane looked back at her girls. Creed realized her gaze was following her daughters with interest, not the almost cursory, maybe even scared expression she'd worn before.

"Are you comfortable here?" Creed asked.

"I am." She nodded. "Your aunt and uncle have been very kind."

Creed started to say that Burke wasn't his uncle, then decided the tag was close enough. Burke was fatherly, more than uncle-like, and a dear friend. "How long are you staying?"

She smiled, keeping her gaze on her daughters. Creed mentally winced, his question sounding abrupt to him. He sure didn't want Diane to think he was trying to run her off.

"Your aunt has offered me a job," Diane said, surprising Creed.

"She has?"

"Mmm." She turned to look at him, and he saw that her eyes were just like Aberdeen's and Johnny's, deep and blue and beautiful. But hers were lined with years of worry. She'd had it hard, he realized—no wonder Aberdeen and Johnny were so bent on helping her. "She says she needs a housekeeper/assistant. She says all her duties are getting to be too much for her. Yet your aunt Fiona seems quite energetic to me."

Creed shrugged. "I wouldn't blame Fiona a bit if she felt like she needed some help. She's got an awful lot she does on the ranch."

"So it wasn't just a polite invitation?" Diane looked at him curiously.

"I doubt it. While my aunt is unfailingly polite, she's never offered such a position to anyone else that I'm aware of, and she wouldn't fancy giving up any of the reins of the place if she really didn't feel the need."

He smiled. "She's pretty fierce about doing everything herself."

"So why me? Because I'm Aberdeen's sister?"

He shrugged again. "Probably because she likes you. Fiona prefers to run her own business, so if she offered, she must have felt that you'd be an asset to the ranch."

"She doesn't discuss hiring with you?"

He laughed. "She may have talked to some of my brothers. I can't say. But Fiona's business is her own. So if you're interested in a job with her, that's a discussion between the two of you. The only tip I could positively give you is that if you accept her offer, you will work harder than you ever have in your life. Ask Burke if you don't believe me."

She finally smiled. "I'll think about it, then."

"Yeah. Well, glad I could help. Not that I have any useful information to impart." He grinned at the pile of sand the two little girls were pushing around in the box with the aid of a tiny tractor and some shovels. "So now I have a question for you."

"All right," Diane said. "You want to know how I can help you to get Aberdeen to marry you."

He blinked. "Well, if you could, it would help."

She smiled. "Look, Creed. I'm going to be just as honest with you as you were with me. Aberdeen doesn't always talk about what she's thinking. If she does, she'd go to Johnny first, and then maybe she'd come to me. I'm a lot older than Aberdeen, in many ways. But I can tell you a couple of things. First, she's afraid she's turning out like me. The fact that she's pregnant makes it feel real unplanned to her, for lack of a better word, and Aberdeen is all about planning everything very seriously. People who plan are *responsible*. Do you understand what I'm saying?" She gave him a long, side-ways look.

Creed nodded. "Thank you for your honesty."

She went back to watching her daughters. "It's good to self-examine, even when it's painful. I know who I am, and I know what I'm not. I'm not a good mother, but I know I'm a good person. That probably doesn't make sense to you, but I know that in the end, the good person in me will triumph."

Creed thought she was probably right. There was a kind streak in Diane, a part of her that acknowledged strength in family, that he'd already noticed. "No one's perfect," he said. "Neither my brothers nor I would claim we've come within a spitting distance of perfect. So you're probably amongst like-minded people."

Diane placed a soft kiss atop Lincoln Rose's head. Creed wondered if she even realized she'd done it. "Back to Aberdeen. The B-part to my sister that I know and understand—though I'm not claiming to be an expert—is that there will never be another Re-ride in her life."

"I'm no Re-ride," he growled.

"I mean that, even if she married Re-ride again, it would be no retread situation. Aberdeen is not the same shy girl who got married so young. She would kick his butt from here to China if she married him and he tried to do the stupid stuff he did before."

"She's not marrying Re-ride," Creed said decisively, "and I'm no green boy for her to be worrying about marrying."

Diane sighed. "I'm sure Aberdeen is well aware that it was a real man who put a ring on her finger this time, cowboy. All I'm saying is that she's going to make her own decisions in her life now. She'll do things when she's comfortable and not before—and right now, I'd say she's not totally comfortable. Some of that is probably due to me, but—" She gave Creed a long look and stood. "I feel pretty comfortable in saying that most of her indecision is due to you," she said, kissing him on the cheek, "future brother-in-law."

He looked at her. "I don't wait well."

She smiled. "I guessed that. You may have to this time, if you really want your bride." Diane went to the sandbox and said, "Girls, we need to get washed up now," and they dutifully minded their mother. Creed watched with astonishment as they followed Diane like little ducklings. It was one of the most beautiful things he'd ever seen. He wondered if Diane had yet realized that she had no reason to be afraid of being a mother— she seemed to have all the proper components except confidence. He watched the girls go with a little bit of sentimental angst, already considering himself their father in his heart, knowing that they needed their mother, too. He'd have thought Lincoln Rose would have at least reached for him.

But no. They'd been content to spend time with their mother, an invisible natural bond growing into place. Creed wished he could grow some kind of bond with Aberdeen. She seemed determined to dissolve what they had. "I'm not doing this right," he muttered, and jumped when Burke said, "Did you say something, Creed?"

Creed glanced behind him as Fiona's butler materialized with a tray of lemonade and cookies. "Are those for me?"

"They're for the little girls and their mother." Burke glanced around. "Are they done with playtime?"

"I'm afraid so. Bring that tray over here to me. I need fortification."

Burke set the tray down on the porch swing.

"There's only one glass," Creed said.

"Yes. The lemonade is for you. It has a little kick in it, which I noticed you looked like you needed about twenty minutes ago when you ran through the house."

Creed looked at Burke. "Okay. Tell me everything you're dying to say."

"I'm not really an advice column," Burke said. "I see my role more as fortifier."

Creed waved a hand, knocking back half the lemonade. "You're right. That does have a kick. And it's just what I needed."

Burke nodded. "The cookies are for the girls. They get milk with theirs, usually."

Creed blinked. "Well, my ladies have departed me. All of them, I fear."

Burke cleared his throat. "If you don't need anything else—"

"Actually, I think I do." Creed looked at the butler, considering him. "Burke, your secret is out. We all know you and Fiona are married."

Burke remained silent, staring at him with no change in expression.

Creed let out a sigh. "I guess my question is, how did you do it?"

"How did I do what?"

"How did you convince my aunt to get to the altar?"

Burke picked up the tray. "I sense the topic you're exploring is Miss Aberdeen."

"I could use some advice. Yes." Creed nodded. "Wise men seek counsel when needed, Burke, and I know you have some experience with handling an independent-minded female. My problem is that I've got a woman who seems a little more cold-footed than the average female, when it comes to getting to the altar."

"I may have mentioned my role isn't giving advice," Burke said, "but if I had any, I would say that the lady in question seems to know her own mind. Therefore, she undoubtedly will not take well to being pushed." Burke handed him a cookie. "I must go find the young ladies. It's past time for their afternoon snack and nap."

Creed nodded. "Thanks, Burke."

The butler disappeared.

"I'm not hearing anything I want to hear," Creed muttered. "I know a woman needs her space. But I'm no Re-ride." He munched on the cookie, thinking it would taste better if Aberdeen was there to share it with him.

Between Burke's special lemonade, the cookie and the advice, he thought he was starting to feel better. Not much, just a little, but better all the same.

He was going to be a father.

He wanted to be a husband, too.

He wanted Aberdeen like nothing he'd ever wanted in his life. If his aunt had sprung the perfect woman on him, she couldn't have chosen better. He would easily trade Rancho Diablo if Aberdeen would be his wife. He wanted to spend the rest of his days lying in bed with her, holding her, touching her.

He was just going to have to hang on.

Chapter Seventeen

"I'm worried about Sabrina McKinley," Fiona said to Creed when he rolled into the kitchen. She was making a pie, blueberry, he was pretty sure.

For once, he had no appetite for Fiona's baking. "You mean because of Bode?"

"Well, I certainly didn't like his tone the other night. He made it sound like she was a prisoner or something. The man gives me the creeps." She shook her head and placed the pie on a cooling rack. "I begin to rethink my plan of planting her, I really do, Creed."

"Jonas checked on her. He'd know if something was wrong." Creed sometimes wondered if his oldest brother had developed a secret penchant for Fiona's spy. Then he dismissed that. Jonas was nothing if not boring. He'd never go for the Mata Hari type.

"I suppose." She fluffed her hands off over the sink, brightening. "On the other hand, we have news to celebrate!"

"Yeah." Creed didn't know how his aunt always managed to hear everything lightning-fast. "I'm going to be a father." He beamed, just saying the words a pleasure.

Fiona's mouth dropped open. "You're having a baby?"

He nodded. "Isn't that the news you were talking about?"

She slowly shook her head. "I was going to say that we have one hundred and fifty beautiful, eligible bachelorettes attending the ball tomorrow night." Her gaze was glued to him. "Is the mother Aberdeen?" she asked, almost whispering.

"Yes!" He stared at his aunt, startled. "Who else would it be?"

"How would I know?" Fiona demanded. "You were gone for months. I thought you had only just met Aberdeen when you got thrown at your last rodeo."

He nodded. "Absolutely all correct."

"That means you two got friendly awfully *quickly*." She peered at him, her gaze steadfast. "Goodness, you've barely given the poor girl a chance to breathe! No wonder she left."

He blinked. "Left?"

Fiona hesitated, her eyes searching his. "Didn't she tell you?"

His heart began an uncomfortable pounding in his chest. "Tell me what?"

"That she was going back home? She left an hour ago."

Creed sat down heavily in a kitchen chair. Then he sprang up, unable to sit, his muscles bunched with tension. "She didn't say a word."

"I think she said something about a letter. Burke!"

Her butler/secret husband popped into the kitchen. "Yes?"

"When Aberdeen thanked us for our hospitality and said she was leaving, did she leave a letter of some kind?"

Burke's gaze moved to Creed. "She did. I am not to give it to Creed until six o'clock this evening."

"The hell with that," Creed said, "give it to me now."

Burke shook his head. "I cannot. It was entrusted to me with certain specifications."

Creed felt his jaw tightening, his teeth grinding as he stared at the elderly man prepared to stick to his principles at all costs. "Burke, remember the chat we had a little while ago out back?"

Burke nodded.

"And you know I'm crazy about that woman?"

Burke nodded.

"Then give me the letter so that I can stop her," Creed said, "please."

Burke said. "Creed, you're like a son to me. But I can't go against a promise."

"Damn it!" Creed exclaimed.

Fiona and Burke stared at him, their eyes round with compassion and sympathy.

"I apologize," Creed said. He ran rough hands through his hair. His muscles seemed to lose form suddenly, so he collapsed in a chair. "I don't suppose she said why?" he asked Fiona.

Fiona shook her head. "She said she needed to be back home. I asked her to stay for the ball, and she said she felt she'd only be underfoot. However," she said brightly, "Diane, Johnny and the girls stayed."

"Good," Creed said, shooting to his feet, "I've got a future brother-in-law to go pound."

"He's a guest!" Fiona called after him. "He saved your life!"

Creed strode out to find Johnny—and some answers.

FIVE HOURS LATER, at exactly six o'clock—and after learning that Johnny and Diane knew nothing at all about Aberdeen's departure—Burke finally presented Aberdeen's letter to Creed, formally, on a silver platter.

The envelope was white, the cursive writing black and ladylike. Creed tore it open, aware that his family was watching his every move. News of Aberdeen's departure—and pregnancy—had spread like wildfire through Rancho Diablo. No one had had a clue that Aberdeen had wanted to leave.

Of course he'd known. In his heart, he'd known she was questioning their relationship from the minute she'd seen the ranch and the jet to the moment she'd learned she was pregnant.

Creed,
I want you to know how sorry I am that I will be unable to keep our bargain. As you know, at the time we made it, I was under the belief that Diane wanted me to adopt her children. I had no idea when, or if, Diane might return. But now I am hopeful that, given a little more time with her daughters and the gentle comfort of Rancho Diablo, my sister is gaining a true desire and appreciation of what it means to be a mother. This is more than I could have ever hoped for. For that reason, I'm leaving her here, in good hands, as Fiona has offered her employment. I know Diane is happy here, happier than I might ever be. It seems a fair trade-off.
My part of the bargain to you was that marriage might cure your aunt's desire to see you married to help keep Rancho Diablo. I don't think

you'll need my help. All of you seem quite determined to keep fighting, and I pray for the best for you. Mr. Jenkins seems most disagreeable, so I hope the good guys win. After the ball tomorrow night, perhaps all of your brothers will find wonderful wives. That is something else I will be praying for.

As you know, I have a congregation and a life back in Lance that means a lot to me. When I met you, I believed you were basically an itinerant cowboy. Marrying you for your name on an adoption application didn't seem all that wrong, considering that you, too, had a need of marriage. Now that I've met your family, I know that it would be wrong for me to marry you under false pretenses. That's just not the kind of person I am. Yours is a different kind of lifestyle than I could ever live up to. In the end, though you are a wonderful, solid man, I realize that my life and your life are just too different. With Diane finding her footing with her girls, I think this is a happy ending. I have you and your family to thank for that. So I'd say that any debt that may have existed before is certainly wiped out.

I know too well that you will want visitation rights once the baby is born. You no doubt have lawyers available to you who can draw up any documents you wish to that effect.

I know we will be talking in the future about our child's welfare, so I hope we can remain friends.

All my best,

Aberdeen

P.S. I have entrusted Burke with the engagement

ring. Thank you so much for the gesture. For a while, I did feel like a real fiancée.

He looked up from the letter, his heart shattered. "She left me," he said, and his brothers seemed to sink down in their various chairs.

The silence in the room was long and hard. No one knew what to say to him. His hands shook as he stared at the letter again. She didn't feel like a real fiancée.

How could she not? Had he not loved her every chance he got? "She says she didn't feel like a real bride-to-be," he murmured. "But she's having my baby. How can she not feel like she's going to be a real wife?"

Jonas cleared his throat. "Women get strange sometimes when they're pregnant," he said, and Fiona gasped.

"That's not kind, Jonas Callahan!" She glared at him.

"It's true," Pete said. "Jackie gave me a bit of a rough road when she found out she was pregnant. There we were, this perfectly fine relationship—"

"That went on and on," Sam said. "Every woman has heard that a man who sleeps with her for a hundred years isn't serious about her, so you were only a Saturday-night fling, as far as she knew."

Pete stiffened. "But that wasn't how I felt about her. She just saw our relationship on a completely different level."

"I am never going through this," Judah said, "and if I do find a bride—and I hope I don't—but if I do, I'm going to do it right. None of this bride-on-the-run crap." He leaned back in the sofa, shaking his head.

"Maybe it's not that simple," Rafe said. "Maybe she didn't like it here."

"She didn't seem quite herself," Creed said, "but I

put it down to the fact that she was worried about her nieces." Yet he'd known deep inside that hadn't been all of it. "I guess she didn't love me," he said, not realizing that he'd spoken out loud.

"Did you tell her you did?" Rafe asked.

Creed glanced up from the letter. "Not specifically those very words. I mean, she knew I cared."

"Because she was clairvoyant," Sam said, nodding.

"Hey," Jonas said, "your time is coming, young grasshopper. Go easy on Creed."

"I'm just saying," Sam said, "that it's not like she's some kind of fortune-teller like Sabrina."

Everyone sent him a glare.

"Well, I did think she was the more quiet of the two sisters," Aunt Fiona said. "I wondered about it, I must say. I put it off to her being shy, perhaps, and—"

"That's why you offered Diane a job," Creed said, realization dawning like a thunderclap. He sent his aunt a piercing look. "You knew Aberdeen wasn't happy here, and you were trying to keep her little nieces here at the ranch!"

Fiona stared at him. "Oh, poppycock. That's a lot of busybodying, even for me, Creed. For heaven's sake."

He was suspicious. "Did Aberdeen tell you she wasn't happy here? With me?"

Fiona sighed. "She merely thanked me for my hospitality and said she had parents and a congregation to get back to. It wasn't my place to ask questions."

"So she never told you we'd had an agreement based on her feeling that a husband might put her in a more favorable light to an adoption committee?" Creed asked.

"So when Fiona offered Diane a job, and Aberdeen could see that things might be working out for her sister, the marriage contract between you two could be nullified," Judah said, nodding wisely.

"Oops," Aunt Fiona said. "I had no idea, Creed. I was just thinking to help Diane get on her feet again."

It wasn't Fiona's fault. He and Aberdeen had an agreement which, to her mind, was no longer necessary, so she'd chosen to leave him. She couldn't be blamed for that, either, since he'd never told her that he was wolf-crazy about her. Creed grunted. "What happens if Diane doesn't accept your offer of employment?"

Fiona straightened. "She will." She looked uncertain for a moment. "She'd better!"

"Because you fell for the little girls?" Creed asked, knowing he had, too. It was going to drive him mad if they left—and yet, if Diane chose to leave with her daughters, he would wish them well and hide his aching heart.

"No," Fiona said. "I would never dream of interfering in someone's life to that extent. She just happens to have recipes from around the world, thank you very much, due to all her travels. And she has experience taking care of elderly parents. And I could use a personal secretary." Fiona sniffed.

Groans went up from around the room. Fiona glared at her nephews. "Oh, all right. Is there anything wrong with giving a mother time to bond with her daughters? Perhaps all she had was a little bit of the blues. Does it matter? I like Diane. I like Johnny. And I like Aberdeen." She shook her head at Creed. "Of course I didn't mean to do anything that would give Aberdeen the license to leave you, but I didn't know the nature of your relationship. It was up to you to discuss your feelings with her, which I'm sure you did amply."

Creed grunted. "I was getting around to it."

A giant whoosh of air seemed to leave the room. His brothers stared at the ceiling, the floor, anywhere but at him. Creed's shoulders sagged for a moment. He hadn't, and now it was too late.

"Give her time," Fiona said. "If I was in her shoes, I'd want time."

He held on to this jewel of advice like a gold-miner. "You really think—"

"I don't *know*," Fiona said, "although all of you seem to think I know everything. I don't. I just think Aberdeen has a lot on her mind. I would let her figure it out on her own for a while, perhaps."

"It might be sound counsel, considering the lady in question is mature and independent-natured," Burke murmured in his soft Irish brogue. Burke didn't hand out advice willy-nilly, so he was sharing knowledge of how he'd won Fiona.

"And the baby?" Creed asked, his heart breaking.

Fiona shook her head, silent for once.

The minutes ticked by in still quiet. Creed read the letter again, feeling worse with every word. Judah got up, crossing to the window of the upstairs library. "The Diablos are running," Judah said, and though the joy of knowing the wild horses were still running wild and free on Callahan land sang in Creed's veins, he stared at out at them, not really believing their presence portended mystical blessings anymore.

Chapter Eighteen

Aunt Fiona's First Annual Rancho Diablo Charity Matchmaking Ball was a knock-out success, Creed acknowledged. Ladies of all makes and models came to the ranch by the carload. If he'd still been a single man, he might have been as holistically lighthearted as Sam, who was chasing ladies like a kid at a calf-catch. He thought Johnny Donovan garnered his fair share of attention, though the big man never seemed to do more than dance politely with any lady who lacked a partner. Jonas was his usual stuck-in-the-mud self. If anybody was ever betting on Jonas to finally have a wild night in his life, the bettor was going to lose his money to the house. Jonas was a geek, and that was all he was going to be.

The one shocker of the evening was that Judah and Darla Cameron—who'd had her eyes on Judah forever, not that his clown of a brother had the sense to realize it—actually seemed to engage in a longer-than-five-minute conversation. The chat lasted about twenty minutes, Creed estimated, even more surprised to see his brother initiate said conversation. To his great interest, he saw Darla head off, leaving Judah standing in the shadows of the house. Creed spied with enthusiasm, watching his boneheaded brother watching Darla walk away.

And then, just when he thought Judah was the dumbest man on the planet, beyond dumb and moving toward stupid-as-hell, Judah seemed to gather his wits and hurried after Darla. Creed snickered to himself and drank his beer. "Dumb, but not terminal," he muttered to himself, and thanked heaven he'd never been that slow where a good woman was concerned.

Or maybe he was. Creed thought about Aberdeen being up north, and him being here, and fought the temptation to give in and call her. Johnny said Aberdeen was stubborn. And on this Creed thought Johnny probably had a point.

He was willing to give her time, but it seemed like the cell phone in his pocket cruelly never rang with a call from her.

Creed went back to pondering Aunt Fiona's wonderful party. As bachelor busts went, it was one for the ages. Any of them should get caught. *Not me, I'm already caught, even if my woman doesn't know it. But it'll be fun for us all to get settled down, and then we'll raise a bunch of kids together, and instead of marriage feeling like a curse, we'll all look back and laugh about how determined we were to stay footloose and fancy-free.*

Except for my dumb twin. Rafe is a worm that will never turn. He watched Rafe go by, stuck in wolf mode, a bevy of absolutely gorgeous women tacked on to him like tails pinned on a donkey. Disgusting, Creed thought, that anyone considered his brother deep-thinking and existential when he was really a dope in wolf's clothing. Rafe looked like a man on his way to an orgy, dining at the table of sin with great gusto.

Disgusting.

Johnny sat down next to him on the porch swing. "You're not doing your part, dude. Aren't you supposed to be dancing?"

Creed shrugged. "I danced with a couple of wallflowers, so Aunt Fiona wouldn't be embarrassed. But I'm wallflowered out now."

"Nice of some of the local guys to show up and help out with the chores of chivalry," Johnny said.

"Everyone loves a lady in a party dress," Creed said morosely. "Heard from your sister? She's not coming back tonight to make sure I have my dance card filled? Induce me to give up my swinging-single lifestyle?"

Johnny laughed, raised a beer to Creed. "You know Aberdeen. She's the kind of woman who'll let a man hang himself with his own rope."

Creed leaned back. "It's dangerous dating a woman who's fiercely independent."

Johnny nodded. "Tell me about it."

Creed gave him a jaundiced eye. "Oh, hell, no. You're not dating anyone. Don't give me that commiseration bit."

"I'm hanging on," Johnny said. "For the right one to come along and catch me."

"Yeah, well, good luck," Creed said. "I found the right one. She threw me back."

"Patience is a virtue," Johnny said, and Creed rolled his eyes. Patience was *killing* him. He'd never been a patient man. Fiona said that he'd always wanted everything he couldn't have. He was a worker, a planner, a man of action—the crusader who rode into a forest and plucked out a maiden in the midst of battle, if need be, even before he discovered treasure and liberated it from the evil dragon.

Princess first. Ladies first. Absolutely, always.

At least that's the way he'd always seen himself. Aberdeen had him sitting on the sidelines in his own fish story. He was chomping at the bit.

"Wanna dance, handsome?" Creed heard, and glanced up, fully prepared to wave off a charming and buxom beauty, only to realize she was staring at Johnny, her eyes fast to the man whom Creed had thought might be his brother-in-law one day.

"Mind if go do my duty?" Johnny asked Creed. "I hate to leave you here alone, nursing that dry bottle, but as you can see, duty calls, and it's a beautiful thing."

Creed waved the empty bottle at Johnny. "Never let grass grow under your feet."

"Nor your ass, my friend," Johnny said with a grin, and went off with a lovely lady dragging him under the strung lights and a full moon to join the other dancers.

Creed shifted, feeling as if grass might have grown under him, he'd sat here so long. Johnny was right: He was moping after Aberdeen. If he didn't quit, he was going to end up Rip Van Winkle-ish, waking up one day to find time had passed and nothing had happened in his life. The phone wasn't going to ring; Aberdeen wasn't going to call.

He was waiting on a dream.

He had a baby on the way, a child who would bear his name. But he couldn't force Aberdeen to love him.

He would just have to be happy with knowing that at least his future had a blessing promised to him. And he was going to be a hell of a father. Because he remembered how much it had hurt when he'd lost his own father, how much it had stung not to have a dad around on the big occasions. So maybe he couldn't be a husband, and maybe his Cinderella had thrown her slipper at his heart, but this one thing he knew: He was going to wear a World's Best Father T-shirt as if it was a king-size, golden, rodeo buckle.

And his kid would know he was there for him. Always.

Eight months later

ABERDEEN HAD GROWN like a pumpkin: blue-ribbon, State-Fair size. At least that's the way she felt. Johnny worried about her incessantly. "You should have stayed, accepted the Callahans' offer of employment, because you're driving me nuts," she told her brother.

"I could have," Johnny said, turning on the Open sign at the bar door, "but my livelihood is here. I'll admit I toyed briefly with the idea of staying in New Mexico and working with the Callahans. They seemed to need the help. And they sure know how to throw a heck of a dance. There were ladies from everywhere just dying to find a husband. I had a feeling if I'd hung around, Fiona might have fixed me up with a wife, too. From what I've gleaned over the past several months, no weddings went off and no one got caught, though."

Aberdeen wondered if Johnny was trying to reassure her that no one had caught Creed. She decided to stay away from that painful subject. She nodded at his pleased grin. "You could use someone looking after you."

"Women are not that simple, as I know too well." Johnny smiled and wiped off the bar. "No, it was fun at the time, and I enjoyed the break, but I had to be near my new nephew."

She shook her head. "I don't know the sex of the baby. Quit angling for a hint."

Johnny laughed. "Okay. So what happens when the baby is born?"

"I'm going to keep doing what I'm doing. Occasionally preaching, working here, looking for a house."

Her answer was slightly evasive because she knew Johnny was asking about Creed. The truth was, she never stopped thinking about him. Yet she knew their bargain had been a fairy tale. He'd been grateful to her and Johnny; he'd wanted to help her out. She wouldn't have felt right keeping him tied to an agreement for which there was no longer a need.

"As soon as that baby is born, you know he's going to be here."

Aberdeen nodded. "That's fine." She was over her broken heart—mostly. "You know what the bonus is in all this? Diane is happy at the Callahan ranch. Her daughters are flourishing."

At that Johnny had to smile. He flew down there once a month to visit the girls and Diane, always bringing back reports of astonishing growth and learning skills. Teeth coming in. New steps taken. First pony rides. He'd even taken their parents down to visit once. They'd been impressed with the girls' new environment, and the change in Diane.

Johnny never mentioned Creed when he took his monthly sojourn to New Mexico, and Aberdeen never asked. She knew he would come to visit his baby. It would be the right thing, for the baby's sake. And he would want his baby to spend time at Rancho Diablo. *It will all work out,* Aberdeen told herself. *We're two adults, and can make this work. We are not Diane and her ex-husbands, who turned out to be sloths and degenerates of the first order. Creed will be an excellent father.*

She turned her mind away from Creed and back to the new sermon she was writing. After the baby was born, she intended to go back to school for some additional theology classes. The bar would bring in some income as she did the books for Johnny, and then she could afford a separate house.

It might not be the kind of situation she'd dreamed of with her concussed cowboy—but those had been just dreams, and she knew the difference between dreams and real life.

She went upstairs to the temporary nursery, smiling at the few things she'd put in the small room. A white crib, with white sheets and a white comforter. A lacy white valance over the small window. Diapers, a rocker, some tiny baby clothes in neutral colors: yellow, white, aqua.

It had seemed better not to know if she was having a boy or a girl. She would love either.

In fact, she couldn't wait.

Voices carried up the stairs. Johnny was welcoming some customers. She'd be glad to find her own little house, she realized. Something about having a baby made her feel protective, made her need her own space.

Her tummy jumped with a spasm, bringing another smile to Aberdeen's face. This was an active child, always on the go. The ob/gyn had said that Aberdeen needed to take it easy; the baby could come any day now.

It was too hard to sit and wait, though. The feeling of nesting and wanting everything just right had grown too great for her to ignore. She touched the baby's tiny pillow, soft satin, and told herself that in a few days, she'd be holding her own precious child.

"Aberdeen," a deep voice said, and she whirled around.

"Creed," she said, so astonished she couldn't say anything else. Her heart took off with a million tiny tremors. The baby jumped again, almost as if recognizing that its father had walked into the room.

"I bribed Johnny to let me up here without telling you I was here. Blame me for that, but I wanted to surprise you."

"I'll yell at him later," Aberdeen said.

His gaze fell to her stomach. Aberdeen put a hand over her stomach, almost embarrassed at her size.

"You look beautiful."

"Thank you." She didn't, and she knew it. Her dress was a loan from a mother in her congregation. She hadn't wanted to spend money on clothes when she was too big to fit into much other than a burlap potato sack, the kind that could hold a hundred pounds of potatoes easily. "Why are you here?" she asked, not meaning to sound rude, but so shocked by his sudden appearance that she couldn't make decent conversation.

She'd never been so happy to see anybody in her entire life. She wanted to throw herself into his arms and squeal for joy that he'd come.

But she couldn't.

"I came to see you. And my baby," he said. "I didn't want to miss you having the baby."

She swallowed. "Any day now. I guess Johnny told you."

Creed smiled. "He gives me the occasional update."

Drat her brother. "I guess I should have known he would."

"So this is the nursery?"

She ran a hand proudly along the crib rail. "For now. At least until I find a small house."

He nodded. He gazed at her for a long time. Then he said, "I've missed you."

She blinked, not expecting him to say anything like that. "I—"

He held up a hand. "It was just an observation. Not said to pen you into a corner."

She shook her head. "I know."

Another cramp hit her stomach. Her hands went reflexively to her tummy.

"Are you all right?" Creed asked, and she nodded.

"I think I'll go lie down. It's good to see you, Creed," she said. "Thanks for coming."

He nodded. "Guess I'll go bug Johnny. He's promised to teach me how to make an Expectant Father cocktail."

"Oh, boy," Aberdeen said, backing toward the door. "You two just party on."

She disappeared into the hallway, but as she left, she glanced over her shoulder at Creed. He was staring at her, his gaze never leaving her—and if she hadn't known better, she would have thought he looked worried.

If he was worried, it was because of the baby. He'd never said he loved her, never told her anything except that he'd take care of her and Diane's daughters, so she knew she'd done the right thing by letting him go.

Another cramp hit her, this one tightening her abdomen strangely, and Aberdeen went to check her overnight bag, just in case.

"So, DID THE HEART GROW FONDER in absentia?" Johnny asked.

Creed shook his head and slid onto a bar stool across

from Johnny. "Can never tell with Aberdeen. She keeps so much hidden."

"Have confidence," Johnny said, putting a glass in front of him, "and a New Papa cocktail."

"I thought you were going to teach me about Expectant Father cocktails."

Johnny grinned and poured some things into the glass. Creed had no idea what the man was putting in there, but he hoped it took the edge off his nerves. He'd waited eight long months to lay eyes on Aberdeen again, and the shock, well, the shock had darn near killed him.

He'd never stopped loving her. Not one tiny inch, not one fraction of an iota. If he'd thought he had any chance with her, any at all, he'd ask her to marry him tonight.

And this time he'd spend hours telling her how much he loved her, just the same way he'd spent hours making love to her. Only now, he'd do it with a megaphone over his heart.

"Give her a moment to think," Johnny said, "and drink this. It's for patience. You're going to need it."

"I've never had to chase a woman this hard," Creed grumbled. "I'm pretty sure even a shot from Cupid's quiver wouldn't have helped. The shame of it is, I know she likes me."

Johnny laughed. "No, this is a drink for patience as you wait to become a father. The doctor said today was her due date. Did I mention that?"

"No," Creed said, feeling his heart rate rise considerably. "All you said was today was a great day to get my ass up here. Thanks, you old dog. Now I think I'm going to have heart failure."

"You are a weak old thing, aren't you?" Johnny laughed again. "Relax, dude. I predict within the next week, you'll be holding your own bouncing bundle of joy."

Creed felt faint. He took a slug of the drink and winced. "That's horrible. What is it?"

"A little egg, a little Tabasco, a little bit of this and that. Protein, to keep your strength up."

Creed frowned. "Ugh. It's not going to keep my strength up, it's going to bring my lunch up."

"Trust me on this. It grows on you."

Creed shuddered. And then he froze as Aberdeen's voice carried down the stairs.

"Johnny?"

"Yeah?" her brother hollered up the stairs.

"I think perhaps you might bring the truck around."

Creed felt his jaw give. His gaze locked on Johnny. "What does that mean? Is that code for kick me out?"

"No." Johnny flipped the open sign to Closed and locked the door. "I think it means she wants to make a little run to the county hospital."

Creed blinked. He felt fainter. "What am I supposed to do?" He jumped up from the bar stool. "Should I carry something? Help her pack?"

Johnny said, "Hold on," and went upstairs.

A moment later, he came back down. "You might jog up there and keep an eye on her while I bring the truck around. I'll meet you out back in a minute."

Creed's anxiety hit high gear when he realized Johnny was totally rattled. The man knocked over a liquor bottle and broke a glass—Creed had never seen him anything but sure-handed around his bar—in his haste to put things away.

But he didn't hang around to analyze his friend. He shot up the stairs to check on Aberdeen. She sat on the bed, looking puzzled.

"Do you need something?" he asked. "A glass of water? A...hell, I don't know. What can I do?"

"Nothing," Aberdeen said, panting a little. "Except I have some concerns."

"Shoot," he said, "I'm your listening ear."

She gave him a wry gaze. "Are you going to want to be in the delivery room?"

"Nothing could keep me out of there," he said, "unless you don't want me, in which case I'm not above bribing you."

Aberdeen started to laugh, then quit abruptly. "Ugh. Don't make any jokes."

"I'm not joking in the least. I have to be there every step of the way."

"Okay." She took a deep breath. "You can't look under the sheet, and if things get tricky, you have to leave. Deal?"

"I don't know," he said, "you didn't keep to our last deal. I don't guess I can trust you with another one unless it's in writing."

"Creed!" Aberdeen said, looking like she was torn between laughing and crying.

"Oh, all right," he said, "although I reserve the right to judge what is tricky."

"If I say go, then you go," Aberdeen explained, with another gasp and a pant.

He sighed. "You'll want me there. Pete's already told me that my main role is to bring you ice chips and let you squeeze the skin off my fingers. Oh, and if you cuss me out, I'm to ignore all that and tell you how beautiful you are, and how you're the most wonderful woman in the world."

Aberdeen groaned. "If you can do all that, you'll be a true prince."

A truck horn honked outside, and Creed helped Aberdeen to her feet. "Guess I got here in the nick of time," he said, to make conversation. "Isn't that what princes do? Show up to help the fair damsel?"

Aberdeen didn't say anything for a moment.

But then she looked up at him, about halfway down the stairs. "Thank you for being here," she told him, and Creed's heart soared.

Maybe, just maybe...

Chapter Nineteen

"I can't believe my mother had six of us," Creed said, after Aberdeen let out a loud groan. "Can't she have some medication to dull the pain?"

"She's too far along," the nurse said.

"Can I have some pain medication?" Creed asked.

The nurse smiled at him, at the edge of tolerance. "Perhaps you'd like to go sit outside in the waiting area. We'll take good care of Mrs. Callahan."

Aberdeen let out another gasp. Creed's gaze flew to her, his teasing spirit gone. He was panicked. There seemed to be a lot of pain involved, and he hadn't meant to do this to her. She was never going to become Mrs. Callahan.

She was going to hate him forever.

He went through his litany of jobs Pete had suggested: Ice chips, tell her she's beautiful, stay out of the way except when she wants to squeeze your fingers to the bone. Try to be helpful. Try.

Creed stayed at the bedside, scared out of his wits. Good-and-stomped cowboys suffered, but even they hadn't seemed to be in this much agony.

Creed closed his eyes and prayed.

Thirty minutes later, Aberdeen gave one final shriek

that went through Creed—he seemed to feel her every pain—and suddenly the doctor smiled with satisfaction.

"It's a girl," the doctor said, and Creed went light-headed. He sank onto a chair as nurses scurried to clean up baby and Aberdeen. He was out of breath; there was no more strength in his body.

Then it hit him. The baby that was squalling up a storm and being fussed over by the nurses was *his*. He jumped to his feet and hurried over to get a glimpse.

She was beautiful.

He went to tell Aberdeen. His heart constricted as he saw how exhausted she was.

"How are you doing?" he asked, and Aberdeen gave him a wan smile.

"How are you?" she asked. "I thought you were going to fade on me."

"No," he said. "I'm tough. Not as tough as you, though. You win." He bent down and kissed her on the lips, so she'd know she was beautiful. A kiss seemed to express his feelings better at this moment than words.

Then he remembered he was in this predicament be-cause he'd never said the words (Sam's shot about clair-voyance came to mind), so he just threw himself out on the ledge. "You're beautiful," he told her. "I may never get you pregnant again, but I want you to know that I love you fiercely, Aberdeen Donovan. And this may not be the time to tell you, but if you don't put my ring back on your finger and marry me, I'm going to…I'm going to cry like my daughter."

Aberdeen smiled. But she didn't say anything for a long moment. She closed her eyes and he thought she looked happy. Content. He brushed her hair back from her face, thinking she really was the most beautiful woman he'd ever seen in his life. Of course he was in love with her, had been always, but now she'd given him an amazing gift, so he loved her even more.

"I saw him one day," Aberdeen murmured, and Creed said, "Who?"

"The Native American. He was on your ranch, probably a thousand feet from the house. He waved to me, so I went to talk to him. He was tall, and had long, braided hair and such kind eyes. He said he was watching over the horses."

"The Diablos?"

"He called them that, but I didn't know what he meant at the time. And he said not to be scared, that all things worked out for the Callahans. That you would know your parents through this baby."

He blinked. "He told you that?"

"I didn't understand what it meant. But now I do. He said he'd known your parents a long time ago, and this baby was a gift to them. And then he left."

Creed was shocked. He'd never spoken to Aunt Fiona's friend; neither had any of his brothers, as far as he knew. "Our parents died long ago," he said. "I'm not sure how a baby can be a gift to them. But I'm okay with the theory."

"Have you ever talked to him?"

Creed shook his head. "He comes around to talk to Fiona about once a year. I don't know why. It's one of those things Aunt Fiona is mysterious about—one of many things, I suppose."

"He was nice. I liked him. I've never seen so much peace in someone's eyes." She looked at him. "I'll marry you, Creed Callahan."

His heart soared. "You will?"

She smiled. "Yes."

A nurse came between them for a moment, handing Aberdeen her pink-blanket-wrapped baby, and a delighted smile lit Aberdeen's face. "She looks just like you."

"Don't say that," Creed said, "I want her to look just like her wonderful mother. There are no beauties in my family tree, just unfortunately unhandsome brothers."

"There's a beauty now." Aberdeen kissed the top of her baby's head. "She's so sweet."

"That she gets from your side of the family." Creed was so proud he was about to burst. "Are you really going to marry me?"

Aberdeen handed him the baby, which he took carefully, lovingly. "I am, cowboy. I've decided you're the prince I've been waiting for."

He was so happy he wanted to cry. "What took you so long?"

"I was afraid you might be the wolf in my fairy tale, not a prince. You had me fooled for a while." Aberdeen smiled. "I was determined not to make any more mistakes. But I never stopped thinking about you, and after a while, I knew you were the only man I could ever love."

"When were you going to tell me?" Creed asked. "Because I'm pretty sure the last several months have just about killed me."

"After you told me," she said simply, and he groaned.

"I'm going to tell you every day of your life how much I love you," Creed said. "I'm going to keep you convinced that you made the right decision."

"I am," Aberdeen said with conviction. "I know exactly what I'm doing. I'm marrying the most wonderful man in the world. Now name your baby."

He hesitated, glancing down at the sleeping child in his arms. "I don't know anything about naming babies. What if I pick something she hates later on?"

She smiled. "Don't you have a favorite female name?"

"Aberdeen," he said with a decisive nod.

That made her laugh as she lay back against the pillow. "I'm going to sleep now, but when I wake up, I want you to have named your little girl. Surprise me with your creativity."

"No pressure or anything," he said, and he looked down at the tiny lips, adorable closed eyes, sweet cheeks of his daughter, knowing the old Navajo was right: This baby connected him to the past he could barely remember. But he knew his parents had loved him, just as he loved this child. Joy filled him, and then it came to him. "Joy," he said, and Aberdeen opened her eyes.

"That's lovely," she said.

"It's what I feel when I look at you," he said, and she knew his heart was in his words. "And when I hold this little baby..." He leaned down to give Aberdeen a kiss. "Thank you is all I can say. And I will love you until the end of time."

"You're going to make me cry," Aberdeen said, but he sat down next to her, and touched her face, and suddenly Aberdeen didn't feel like crying, only smiling, with joy.

Creed Callahan wasn't loco, she knew. He was her prince, her man, and the hottest cowboy she'd ever laid eyes on. All hers.

All her dreams come true.

Creed leaned against her and Aberdeen drifted, loving feeling him by her side, holding their baby. It was the sweetest moment, starting their family. She murmured, "I love you," and Creed said, "Joy says you'd better," and then he kissed her again.

It was perfect.

Joy.

Epilogue

In February, the month after Joy Patrice was born, Aberdeen finally walked down the aisle into Creed's waiting arms.

Only it wasn't that simple.

First, he had to convince her that baby weight was no excuse not to marry him. Then he had to tell her that getting married at Rancho Diablo on Valentine's Day during the coldest month of the year was a swell idea—red was a great color for bridesmaid's gowns. She only had one attendant and that was Diane, but still, it took some doing. Aberdeen kept talking about waiting until springtime, when she'd lost some weight, when Joy would be a little older, when the weather would be warmer—but he wasn't about to let her weasel out of marrying him for any reason.

He'd nearly lost her before. If he'd learned anything, it was that he had to do a lot of talking with this woman. So talk he did.

And today, a day that dawned clear and sunny, he didn't relax until Aberdeen finally said, "I do." And even then, he asked her to say it again, which made her and the guests laugh.

Judah said later he'd never seen such a desperate case. Jonas told Judah he'd better hush, because one day it might be him begging some poor woman to marry him. Sam said he thought it was romantic, if a bit weinie, of his brother to go down on bended knee and promise to love and adore Aberdeen for the rest of their lives, and Rafe said his twin had finally showed some depth of character and soul. Pete said he didn't care as long as they hurried up and cut the cake because he was starving. Keeping up with the demands of three little girls kept his appetite fired up.

Valentine's Day was a perfect day to catch his bride, in Creed's opinion. When they were finally declared husband and wife, he swept Aberdeen off her feet and carried her back down the aisle, intent on putting her right into the waiting limousine.

He intended to spend their week-long honeymoon in Bermuda making love to her constantly, and as far as he was concerned, the honeymoon began *now*.

"Wait," Aberdeen said, laughing, "Creed, put me down. We have guests. There's cake to cut."

"Oh." He put her down, reluctantly. "I'm not letting you out of my sight, though."

She took him over to the three-tiered cake. "I know. But there are some duties required—"

"Cut fast," he told her, and she made a face at him.

"We have to dance, and tell everybody thank you for coming," she said. "Creed, we just can't desert our guests. And there's Joy. I feel so guilty about leaving her. Don't you think we should wait for our honeymoon until—"

"That's it," he said, "here's the knife. Cut the cake, take a bite and let's shazaam before you get cold feet. I know you too well, parson, and I worked too hard to get you." He put cake into her mouth, waved at the applauding guests, let the photographer snap a few more photos of them, and then went over to Aunt Fiona who was holding Joy in her arms.

"This is a great party, Aunt," he said.

"But you're leaving."

He kissed her cheek. "Yes, we are. My bride wants me all to herself. Mrs. Callahan is demanding like that."

"Creed," Aberdeen said, laughing, as she bent to kiss Fiona's cheek, and then reached up to kiss Burke's.

"It's all right," Fiona said. "I've succeeded beyond my wildest dreams, so I just want to say welcome to the family, Aberdeen. And congratulations on catching Creed. I never thought I'd live to see the day, did you, Burke?"

Burke shook Creed's hand. "The limo has all your items in it, and is waiting for your call."

"Thanks for everything," Creed said, and kissed his aunt goodbye. Then he bent to kiss his baby's head. "Joy, you be sweet to your family. Aunt Diane is going to take very good care of you."

"Yes, I am." Diane closed her sister in her arms. "Congratulations, sis," she said, "I'm going to be as good an aunt to your daughter as you were to mine. I can never thank you enough for giving me time to figure out my life."

Aberdeen smiled. "I knew you would."

Johnny nodded. "I'm going to practice my uncle skills. I can't wait. Seems like I've been waiting months for this, and now I've got four babies to uncle. It's pretty cool."

"Yes," Creed said, prouder about new fatherhood than about winning all his rodeo buckles. "All these new women in my life. Who would have ever thought it?"

"I would," Fiona murmured to Burke, who hugged

her as she gazed at her growing family. "I always knew he had it in him."

"I always knew I had it in me," Creed said to Aberdeen, and she kissed him.

"Let's go, cowboy," she said, for his ears only. "I've got a special gift to give you in the limo. Because I'm pretty sure you said I wasn't having you until I made an honest man of you, and now I have."

"Hot dang," Creed said. "I'm already there, my love."

They waved goodbye to their guests under a shower of pink paper hearts, and, as Creed helped his bride run to the white limo in her long, lacy gown, he caught sight of the black mustangs running, tossing their manes and pounding their hooves, free and wild, as they chased the spirits in the wind.

Enchanted.

* * * * *

THE BULL RIDER'S TWINS

Many thanks to my editor Kathleen Scheibling,
for believing in this series, always having faith in me
and editing my work with a sure hand.

There are many people at Harlequin
who make my books ready for publication, most
of whom I will never have the chance to thank in
person, and they have my heartfelt gratitude.

Also many thanks to my children, who by now are
both off to college, leaving me with an empty nest.
It's not hard to envision me writing a series about
babies—I had an extremely blessed experience with
my two kids, and I thank you for your faith
and encouragement.

And many, many thanks to the very generous
readers who are the reason for my success.
I could not write without your caring words
and loyal support.

Chapter One

"Judah is my seeker," Molly Callahan said of her toddler son, to which her husband, Jeremiah, replied, "Then the apple didn't fall far from the tree, my love."

Judah Callahan couldn't believe the woman of his dreams was waiting in his bed. Unless he missed his guess, Darla Cameron was as naked as the day she was born.

"I've been waiting for you," she said, sitting up and holding the sheet to her chest. His throat went dry as a bone in a New Mexico desert. Blond hair cascaded over pale shoulders, and big blue eyes gazed at him with apprehension. She was nervous, Judah realized, closing the door and locking it behind him.

He wanted to say he'd been waiting for her for years. "I'd think you'd been in the champagne, but I noticed you didn't go near it except to toast Creed and Aberdeen."

She shook her head. "It was a lovely wedding. Really beautiful. All the valentine decorations were so romantic."

He couldn't take his eyes off her. Whatever she thought was romantic about Creed's wedding was nowhere near as attractive as Darla showing up nude in his bed. A little worry crossed her face, and he realized she was afraid he might turn down what she was obviously offering.

Not a chance.

He seated himself on the foot of the bed, the sight of her creamy skin setting him on fire. "If not an excess of champagne, why tonight?"

She blushed. "I wish I could tell you."

That didn't sound like the Darla he knew. Darla was forthright. An excellent businesswoman—her new calling since she'd hung up her nurse's badge and gone into business as wedding shop owner with Jackie Samuels. "Try."

She shook her head. "Be with me."

He wasn't going to put her, or himself, through any more agony. He kissed Darla, amazed at the sweet taste of her. "Peaches," he said, his mind fogging up. "I always wondered what you smelled like, and now I know. You even taste like peaches."

She moved his hand to the sheet, and he was beset by the urge to tear it away, feel what lay hidden beneath.

"There's a hook here," he said, knowing full damn well Darla Cameron wasn't the type of woman who slept around. "Someone put you up to this, or you want something."

"I do want something," she said, her voice soft in the darkness. "Tonight I want you."

So there it was. Tonight was only a simple hookup. Outside, music played, and fireworks streaked across the sky, popping and hissing. If he opened the window to his second-story bedroom, they would see clouds streaking the moon on a cold Valentine's night. This would all be so romantic, if he wasn't suffering from the sixth sense that something wasn't right.

"How did you know I'd be sleeping in here and not the bunkhouse?"

"I know all the guests who are staying in the bunk-house," she told him, moving his hand slightly so the sheet barely covered her breasts. He could feel heavenly softness just a brush away. Being this close to her at long last was killing him. Parts of him felt like the fireworks, ready to explode.

"And Fiona mentioned that you and some of your brothers were sleeping in the house so the guests could have privacy."

"So here you are."

"Here I am," she said, so sweetly breathless that he didn't have the heart to keep looking the gift horse in the mouth. Luckily, he had condoms in the nightstand, a groom's gift from Creed, who had a penchant for stupid gags. No silver letter opener for his groomsmen; no, just boxes of condoms with peace signs and neon inscriptions on the side. Creed's last laugh, since the brother with the most progeny won Rancho Diablo. Creed was the most competitive of the Callahans.

"All right," Judah said. "I've never thrown a woman out of my bed, and I certainly won't start now."

He didn't get why she was here, but he wasn't going to worry about it. Since the lady had hunted him down, he intended to make tonight very much worth her while.

Two hours later, something made Judah start awake. After the hottest sex he'd ever experienced, he'd fallen asleep, holding Darla in his arms, grateful for the good fortune heaven had thrown his way.

Darla jumped from the bed. "I heard someone in the hall!"

"It's all right," he said, trying to tug her back for another helping of delicious blonde.

"It's not all right!"

She eluded his grasp, so he snapped on the lamp. She was tugging on her party dress like a woman fleeing a crime scene. "Hey," he said, "we're consenting adults. No one's going to bust in here and—"

"Shh!" She glanced at the door nervously. "I think the guests have all left. Your brothers will come upstairs any minute."

"And my aunt Fiona and Burke," Judah said, and Darla let out a squeak of fear.

"Get me out of here! Without anyone seeing me. Please!"

He'd prefer it if she stayed until dawn crested the New Mexico sky, but it was clear she was determined to pull a Cinderella and disappear. He got out of bed and pulled on his jeans.

"Can you zip me? Please?" She turned her back to him and Judah drank in all the smooth skin exposed to his hungry gaze.

"Are you sure you won't—"

"Judah, please!"

He zipped her, taking his sweet time as he pressed a kiss against her shoulder. "Even if any of my family were to see you, Darla, it's not like they'd brand you with a scarlet *A*."

"I shouldn't have done this. I don't know what came over me." She yanked on her heels, bringing her nearly four inches closer to his height. He reached for her, determined to show her how well suited they were, but she unlocked the door and dashed out before he could convince her to stay.

Shoving his shirt in his jeans, he hurried after her. He caught sight of a full blue skirt disappearing around the corner as she made it to the landing.

And then she was gone.

"Damn," Judah said. "I'm think I'm going to have to marry that girl."

Which was really funny, because of all his brothers, Judah had always known he would never marry. Not for his aunt, who dearly wanted to see all the Callahan boys married. Not for Rancho Diablo, which would go to the brother with the largest family. And not for love, because he really didn't believe in love. At least not with one woman.

But perhaps he'd espoused that view because he'd always secretly had a crush on the unattainable Darla Cameron. She'd never so much as glanced his way. She'd been a serious student in high school, gone on to be a serious student in college, gotten a grad degree and then become a serious nurse. No, she'd never really given any of the guys in town a look, so he'd figured his chances were slim. He couldn't even strike up a conversation with her.

All that changed tonight, he thought with a self-satisfied smile. And now that he'd had her, he was pretty certain he wouldn't be able to give her up.

FOUR MONTHS PASSED quickly when you weren't having fun, and Judah wasn't having any fun at all. Darla had barely spoken to him since that Valentine's Day evening. He'd tried to chat with her, done everything but go by the bridal salon and corner her, which his pride would not allow him to do. For a woman who'd seduced him, she'd certainly taken off fast. And lately, he'd heard she'd been lying low. Maybe wasn't feeling great. Aunt Fiona was no help to him, but had dared to nonchalantly ask after his Valentine's night surprise.

Obviously, Darla hadn't been as enthused about their lovemaking as he'd been.

The realization stung like gritty wind. This was worse than when he'd only worshipped Darla from afar. Now he knew what he was missing out on, and it made him hunger for her more. She was constantly on his mind. People said she wasn't taking phone calls, except from her mother, Mavis, who'd put out the word that Darla wasn't accepting visitors at her small bungalow.

He would bide his time. He *had* to have her. There was no other option. She was a treasure he alone was going to possess.

If he could just figure out how.

"The first annual Rancho Diablo Charity Matchmaking Ball was such a success, not to mention Creed and Aberdeen's wedding," Aunt Fiona announced to Judah as he slunk into the kitchen, "that I'm in the mood to plan another party."

He grimaced, not interested in discussing Fiona's die-hard love of partying. It was all an excuse for her to marry off her nephews. The trouble with having a committed matchmaker in the family was that it was embarrassing when said matchmaker couldn't fix his problem even if he wanted her to. He was sunk. "Do we really need another social function?"

"I think we do," Fiona said. "We raised a lot of money for the Diablo public library, and we made a lot of new friends. And we irritated the heck out of Bode Jenkins, which, as you know, is my life's goal. Not to mention you could stand a little perking up."

Judah grunted. "What do you have in mind?"

"Well," she said, moving around the sunny kitchen, "we need to find our next victim. The easiest way to do that is to keep ladies visiting the ranch." She sent him a questioning glance. "Unless you know something I don't know."

"Like what?" He settled in to eating the eggs and bacon she put in front of him. There were strawberry jam-smothered biscuits on the side, and a steaming cup of brew. Life was too good to mess up with another extravaganza. The feed bag was definitely better when Fiona's concentration was on the Callahans and not on impressing females far and wide. "I'm usually the last to know anything about anything."

"That's no surprise. What I meant was that unless you know that romance is blooming somewhere on the ranch—"

He shook his head, silencing that train of thought. "Dry wells around here, Aunt."

"Then let's choose a victim and get on with it. Time is running out."

He looked up reluctantly from his breakfast. "You got Pete and Creed married off. That's a third of us who've given up the flag of freedom. Maybe no more weddings are needed. Or children," he added, knowing that was Fiona's real goal. "Pete has three, and Creed has Joy Patrice, but he brought three more with him if you count Diane's. Either way, that's a grand total of seven new kids on the ranch." He smiled, but it was pained. "Plenty, huh?"

She scowled. "Seven is hardly enough to make the case that our ranch shouldn't be sold for public land use. Bode'll never let us get off that easily. We need more."

Judah looked with sorrow at his eggs, his appetite

leaving him. "Well, you could try Sam, but I think he likes the ladies a little too much to settle down with just one."

"And he's just a baby," Fiona said. "Twenty-six is too young when I've got hardened bachelors sitting around this place shirking their futures."

Judah rubbed at his chin. "Well, there's Jonas, but that would take too much work."

Fiona huffed. "You'd think a thirty-three-year-old surgeon would be a bit more anxious to find a wife, but *no-o-o.* I don't think he has the first clue about women, honestly. He's such a—"

"Nerd," Judah said, trying to be helpful, which earned him another scowl from Fiona.

"He's not a nerd. He's just a deep thinker."

That was an understatement. "You could pick on Rafe. He's next in line behind Jonas, and as Creed's twin it would make sense. He'll probably start missing that twin camaraderie now that Creed's got his hands full."

Fiona looked hurt. "Is that what you think I'm doing? Picking on you boys?"

"Oh, no. No, Aunt Fiona." Judah looked at the hurt tears in his delicate aunt's eyes. "We know you just want us all to be happy."

She nodded. "I do. And how do you think I feel about having to make you all settle down before your time—if you have a sense of time at all, and I don't think any of you boys do—when I've lost Rancho Diablo?"

"We haven't lost it yet," Judah soothed. "Sam's gotten a continuance. We may get out of Bode's trap eventually. Somehow."

"But it's better to load our deck for success." Fiona waved at him. "Eat your breakfast. It's getting cold."

Burke, Fiona's lifelong butler (and her secret husband, which she seemed keen for no one to know about, though all the Callahan brothers had figured it out) brought the mail in, handing it to her.

"Oh, look!" she exclaimed, as Judah pushed the now cool eggs around his plate. She waved an envelope in the air. "Cream-colored stock. Always a good sign!"

"Why?" he asked, his gaze on the calligraphed envelope.

"It's a wedding invitation, if I know my wedding invitations, and I think I do!" Fiona tore into the envelope. She stopped, staring at the contents. "Well," she murmured, "I didn't see this coming. No, I really didn't."

Burke looked over her shoulder, peering at the invite. "Uh-oh," he said, and Fiona nodded.

"Who's getting strung?" he asked, feeling cheerful that it wasn't him. Some other poor sack was getting the marital ball and chain, but it wasn't him. *Pity the fool who falls into the clutches of a beautiful woman,* he thought, as his aunt handed him the invitation silently.

"'Ms. Mavis Cameron Night requests the honor of your presence at the wedding of her daughter, Darla Cameron, to Dr. Sidney Tunstall, on June 30,'" he read out loud, his breath going short and his heart practically stopping. His gaze shot to Fiona's. "Didn't you know about this? She's one of your best friends."

"Mavis didn't say a word to me," his aunt exclaimed. "I can't understand why. And the wedding is in a few days, which I also can't understand. What's the rush?"

She studied the invitation for another moment, then lifted her gaze to his again. Oh, but she needn't have worn such a worried expression. He had a good idea why a woman might marry so quickly—Darla was pregnant.

The thought burned his gut.

"Oh, dear," Aunt Fiona said, her eyes huge.

Judah shoved back his chair.

"Shall I say all the family will be in attendance?" she asked, and he yelled over his shoulder, "I wouldn't miss it," as he dashed out into the hot dry wind. Darla hadn't wanted any emotional connection between them. And he, spare Romeo that he was, had fallen into her arms and dreamed of a future.

He was a fool. But not a fool on his way to the altar, and there was something to be said for that.

Still, Judah wondered if he heard an empty echo in his bravado. And his broken heart drove him onto the range, riding hell-bent to nowhere.

An hour later, Judah was positive he saw the mystical Diablos down in a canyon, well past the working oil derricks and the fenced cattle land. Legend said that the wild horses ran free on Rancho Diablo, and no one could get close to them because they were spirits. They were also a portent of something magical to come. The Callahans didn't see the herd of horses often, but when they did, they respected the moment.

They were not spirit horses, as far as Judah was concerned. He could see them drinking from a small stream that threaded through the dust-painted canyon, though his eyes blurred in the bright sunlight. Nearby, a large cactus offered a little shade, but Judah ignored it, easing back in the saddle to watch the horses. Their untamed beauty called to his own wild side.

They turned as one and floated deeper into the canyon. Judah followed, watching for snakes, hawks and other critters. He and his brothers had explored this canyon many times, knew all its secrets.

His horse went to the thin stream, too. Judah slid

from the saddle and took a long drink from the pale water. When he looked up, he saw a rock shelf he didn't remember.

Closer inspection showed the opening to a cave so hidden from the main canyon path that he would never have seen it if he hadn't bent down to drink. Cautiously, he went inside, his gun drawn in case of wild creatures he might startle.

But the cave was empty now—clearly some kind of once-used mine. Judah went past a rough shaft and a basic pulley and cart.

He'd found the legendary silver mine.

But it wasn't much of one, and appeared to have been long deserted. This couldn't be why Bode was so determined to get Rancho Diablo land—unless he thought there was more silver to be discovered. Still, what difference could silver mean to the wealthy man? And even if the Callahans were forced to sell Rancho Diablo, they would make certain they retained the mineral rights.

A loomed rug lay on the cave floor, hidden from casual visitors. There was also evidence of footprints, visible in the fading light that filtered into the cave. Still deeper, what seemed to be a message in some cryptic language was written on the wall, and it looked fresh. He touched the letters, smearing them a little. Underneath, silver coins and a few silver bars were stacked on a flat rock, like an offering.

Judah realized he'd stumbled on a smuggling operation, or perhaps a thruway for travelers who shouldn't be using Rancho Diablo land.

He left the cave, grabbed his horse's reins and swung into the saddle to ride in the opposite direction the Diablos had taken, as he wondered who might be using Callahan land and why.

For the moment, he would say nothing, he decided—until he understood more about why he'd been led to this place.

THE NEXT DAY, Judah realized drastic steps would have to be taken. The whole town of Diablo, it seemed, was atwitter over Darla's impending marriage. No detail was too small to be hashed over—the bridal gown she'd bought from the store she co-owned with Jackie Samuels Callahan, Pete's wife; the diamante-covered shoes she'd purchased. She'd scheduled an appointment for her hair, which had been dutifully reported. It would be worn long, crowned with an illusion veil that had orange blossoms cascading at the hem, which would just touch her shoulders.

Judah was sick to death of details. He wouldn't know an orange blossom if it grew out of his boot.

Strangely, the bride had not been seen since her invitations were mailed. Nor had the groom, though he was expected in town any day now. Judah knew him. Sidney Tunstall was a popular rodeo doctor and a one-time bronc buster, a man with a spine like a spring, who seemed to be kissed by good fortune. He was also wealthy. And he'd been after Darla for some time, if scuttlebutt was to be believed. Tall and lean and focused, the doctor seemed like a guy who loved what he did and did it well.

Which pretty much stank, but that was how it went. A man could lose to a better rival if he had slow-moving feet, and Judah reckoned his feet had been slower than most.

He flung himself inside the bunkhouse, anxious to sit alone in front of the fireplace to gather his thoughts.

It wasn't to be. Jonas was like a hulking rock in the

den, taking up space with Sam and Rafe. And they'd been talking about him, Judah realized, by the way they shut their yaps the instant he entered.

"What's up?" he asked, eyeing them. "Don't stop talking about me just because I'm here."

"All right," Sam said. "Are you going to the wedding?"

The wedding. As if it was the only wedding in Diablo.

Actually, he hadn't heard of any other Diablo weddings lately, and if there'd been some, Fiona would definitely have been keeping the scoreboard updated for everyone, particularly him and his brothers. He sighed. "I might. Then again, I mightn't."

Jonas shrugged. "Let us know if you need anything."

"Yeah," Rafe said, "short of a shot of pride."

Judah blinked. "What's that supposed to mean?"

Sam gazed at him. "Look, bro. It's not like we haven't known forever that you've been carrying an inextinguishable torch for Darla Cameron. What we can't figure out is why you're letting her waltz off with another man."

"Maybe that's not how I see it," Judah said, "and maybe it's none of your business, anyway."

Jonas leaned back. "We could be wrong. Maybe you haven't always been in love with her."

"Darla and I are friends. That's it."

Sam sniffed. "As long as you're cool with it, we are, too. We support you, whatever you decide. I mean, if you get an itch to crawl through her bedroom window, we'll hold the ladder for you."

"No ladders will be necessary." Judah tried not to think about the few moments he'd held Darla in his arms. "She's chosen her man, and—"

"Ah-ha!" Rafe exclaimed. "You admit she didn't choose you!"

"She didn't choose any of you, either. It's not a special situation," Judah said, feeling cranky.

"So you admit you were in a position to be chosen," Sam said, sounding like the lawyer he was. "You were a candidate, if a slightly lazy one. But there's still time to present your case. Females change their minds like the wind. And ladies love it when a last-minute challenger shows up to yodel his heartstrings under ye olde bedroom window. I say go for it. Yodel away. You can borrow my guitar."

"Darla's doing just fine," Judah said. "Everything is in the works. She's got her shoes, her flowers and no doubt something blue."

"The really blue thing at that wedding is going to be you," Jonas said, "if you don't get up off your duff and speak before the forever-hold-your-peace."

There was no use. He was going to be harried to death by the people who should have supported his wish to be a silent sufferer. And this was light treatment, Judah realized, compared to what he'd probably be treated to in town, and especially at the wedding. Pitying looks, questioning gazes—

"What about the baby?" Sam asked. "What if it's yours?"

Judah frowned, aware of a sudden urge to stuff a fist in Sam's mouth. "What baby?"

Rafe studied him. "You know Darla is pregnant."

"Is that known?" Judah asked, his heart beating hard. "Or is it gossip based on her apparently whirlwind marriage?"

"She was seen buying a pregnancy test a while ago," Jonas said with a shrug. "This is a small town, and though she sent a friend in to purchase it, the bag made a clear exchange, which was duly noted by several people."

"Who were spying like old-time geezers," Judah said, not happy to hear confirmation of his own suspicions. "It doesn't mean she's pregnant. It could have been a negative test. She could have been giving it to Jackie, for all you know. And," he said, finishing with a flourish, "there's every possibility she's getting married because she wants to, and is in love, and the lure of owning her own bridal shop finally got to her. If you owned a machine shop, wouldn't it kill you if you could never use the tools?"

"Boy, are you caging your inner lion," Rafe said. "Hey, we've got your back, bro. We know how to shine the old badge of pride. No one will ever get from us how you got left in the dust." He shook his head, more sympathetic than Judah could stand.

"That's it," he said. "I've just seen a flash of my future, and I'm taking a rain check on it. The only way to get away from you bunch of know-it-alls is to disappear on you." Judah waved an expansive arm. "With no forwarding address. Don't even try to find me. Consider me gone with the wind, in order to save the dregs of my life." He crammed his hat on his head and turned to depart, with one last thought making him swing back around to his brothers, who watched him with open curiosity.

"And you can tell everybody in Diablo that my heart was not broken, thank you very much. You can tell them that rodeo was always my only love, and is to this day." He made a grandiose exit, proud of himself for the charade he'd perpetrated.

No one would ever know he was lying like a rug.

His brothers looked at each other after Judah left.

"Are we going to tell him that the boxes of condoms we all received at Creed's bachelor party were gag gifts? Creed's parting wish that we'd all get hung by our own family jewels?" Sam asked. "It's possible Judah didn't get the joke."

"I think we leave it alone," Jonas said. "Judah doesn't seem to want to consider that the child Darla might be carrying is his."

Rafe nodded. "*If* she is four months pregnant, as we hear she is, and the birth coincides with Creed and Aberdeen's wedding night, then it may be obvious."

"Why wouldn't Darla tell Judah?" Sam's forehead wrinkled. "That's the only thing that's not making sense. Wouldn't she just say, hey, that night of passion resulted in some passion fruit?"

"They've been running away from each other for so long, admitting that she's pregnant by Judah is the last thing Darla would do. He never acts as if he likes her, much less loves her. Ladies do not dig the strong, silent type when they need some reassurance, and Judah's been playing the role of Macho Man with gusto," Jonas said. "What woman wants a man if she thinks he doesn't love her?"

"Anyway, we're in way over our heads here," Rafe said. "We could have this all wrong. Maybe they never did the deed that night. Maybe Creed never saw them go off together. Darla could be pregnant by the bronc buster doctor, not that anyone ever mentioned them dating. It's not like we can ask her, because she's not even telling anyone she's in a family way. Rumors may be flying, but no one's going to mention them to the blushing bride."

They thought about the problem some more, then Jonas shrugged. "We'll know by November, I guess."

"Or not," Sam said. "She may choose to never reveal the real father."

"And Judah loses out on being a dad," Rafe mused. "Which would really be a loss, because he'd probably make a decent one. I mean, if Creed and Pete can do it, why not Judah?"

But there was nothing they could do about it. Darla was getting married, and Judah was gone, and neither one of them seemed to care that true love was being held captive by stubborn hearts.

"I hope I'm not that dumb when a beautiful woman loves me," Sam said with a sigh, and both his brothers immediately said, "You will be."

"But not as dumb as Judah," Sam muttered to himself, listening to Judah's truck roar away.

"I say it's time we engage Aunt Fiona," Jonas suggested, and his brothers nodded. "This situation could be dire."

"Maybe, maybe not," Sam said, "but Judah certainly isn't going to do anything to save himself."

Chapter Two

Rafe, Sam and Jonas went to the kitchen to find Fiona. As a rule, she or Burke could be found there, or nearby, at least. It was nearly the dinner hour, a very odd time for Judah to decide to depart, which just showed that even an empty stomach hadn't deterred his boneheadedness.

The kitchen was empty. The scents of wondrous culinary delights (Fiona could cook like no other, and Burke was no slouch in their shared gastronomic hobby) were absent. Rafe felt his stomach rumble and figured this might be an unannounced catch-as-catch-can night. They had those at Rancho Diablo, though rarely. Usually on the nights their fearless aunt had bingo or her book reading club or a church group, she cut them loose. But at least a pie would be left on the kitchen counter, with a note on the Today's Meal chalkboard that read something to the effect of "Tough Luck! You're Stuck!"

Tonight, all that was on the counter was a single bar of something silver. Rafe, Jonas and Sam crowded around it, perplexed.

"That's not cherry pie," Sam said.

"It's mined silver," Jonas said. "Mined and pressed into a bar. See the .925 on it?"

Rafe blinked. "Why would Fiona leave us a bar of silver?"

"All those years people have whispered about there being a silver mine on our land suddenly comes to mind," Sam said, his voice hushed.

Rafe's gaze went back to the bar. "We've been over every inch of Rancho Diablo. There's no way."

"I don't know," Jonas said. "Why else would Aunt Fiona have a silver bar?"

"Because she's putting it in her stock portfolio," Sam said. "She bought some through a television advertisement, or a jeweler, to diversify her nest egg. It's not sound to leave all one's investments in the stock market or the national currency. She's just taken physical possession of some of her holdings, I would guess."

"But what if it's not part of her nest egg?" Rafe asked. "What if there really is a silver mine on Rancho Diablo? That would explain why Bode Jenkins is so hot to get this place."

They heard Burke whistling upstairs, and the chirping sound of Fiona's voice.

"Quick," Jonas said. "Outside."

They hustled out like furtive thieves. Rafe closed the door carefully behind him. His brothers had already skedaddled down the white graveled drive toward the barns.

Rafe hurried after them. "Why don't we ask her what it is? What if there is silver on the ranch? What if Bode is sniffing around for it?"

"Then she probably wouldn't have left proof of its existence lying out on the kitchen counter," Sam said. "By now, Bode's had this place satellite mapped, I'm sure. He's had the geographic and mineral composition of the land gone over. If there was silver around here, he would know before we would."

"All I'm suggesting," Rafe said, "is that maybe it's time we quit being so worried about offending Fiona. That we just ask her."

His brothers stopped, gave him a long eyeballing. Rafe shrugged. "I mean, what the hell?" he asked. "If we have a silver mine, hurrah for us. It doesn't change anything."

"If there's a silver mine, and Fiona's been putting away dividends all these years, I don't want to know." Jonas shrugged. "Look, I love Fiona. I don't give a damn if there's solid gold under this ranch from corner to corner, and she plans to ferret all of it off like a conquistador. I really don't care. So I'm not asking."

Jonas had a point. Rafe didn't want to hurt Fiona's feelings, either. She'd given up a pretty decent life in Ireland to come take care of them, which couldn't have been easy. They had not been a snap to raise. "All right," Rafe said, "by now she's probably hidden the damn thing. So can we go back now, act like we didn't see it and go over the Judah problem with her? I'm pretty certain we need a guiding hand here."

They went back to the house, and this time, Jonas banged on the kitchen door.

Fiona flung it open. "For heaven's sake. Can't you open a door by yourselves? Three big strong men can't figure out how to use the key?" She glanced at the doorknob. "The door isn't locked. Why are you knocking, like this isn't your house?"

They stared at their tiny aunt. Her eyes were kind, her voice teasing, but she seemed truly mystified. Rafe swallowed. "Aunt Fiona, we wonder if you have a moment so we might pick your brain?"

"So you're standing on the porch? You won't pick it out there. When you're ready, come inside."

They went in, glancing at each other like errant school boys. "You bring up the joke condoms," Rafe said quietly to Jonas. "You're the oldest. I'm not comfortable talking about sex with my aunt."

Jonas straightened his shoulders. "It's not a conversation I want to have, but no doubt she's heard worse."

"That's true," Sam said. "You go for it, Jonas. We support you."

Fiona waved them into the kitchen, where they leaned against the counters. The silver bar was gone, which Rafe had expected. His brothers gave him the same "You see?" look, to which he simply shrugged. He was more worried about condoms than silver bars at the moment.

"Rafe wants to tell you something," Jonas said. "Right, Rafe?"

He gulped, straightened. "I guess so." He flashed Jonas an irate glare with his eyes. "Judah has departed."

Fiona nodded. "He said he longed to test his mettle on the back of an angry bull. I told him to have at it. Judah's been restless lately."

Rafe swallowed again. "Aunt Fiona," he said carefully, not sure how to begin, and then Sam said, "Oh, come on. It's not that hard."

Rafe gave his brother a heated look, wishing he could swing his boot against Sam's backside.

"Spit it out," Fiona said. "You're acting like you have something horrible to tell me. I've got butterflies jumping in my stomach just looking at you, like the time you came to tell me you'd burned down the schoolhouse. You hadn't, but you thought you had—"

Rafe cleared his throat. "Creed gave us all boxes of prank condoms at his bachelor party as a send-off."

Fiona looked at him. "Prank condoms?"

He nodded. "Different colors, different, uh, styles. In the box, there were 'trick' condoms. You were supposed to guess which of the twelve was the trick."

Fiona wrinkled her nose. "What ape thought of that?"

"Creed," Sam and Jonas said.

"I mean, the product." Fiona sighed. "Only an imbecile would buy… Oh, never mind. None of you were dumb enough not to get the joke, so ha-ha."

"We hear rumors," Jonas said, trying to help his brother out, for which Rafe was relieved, "that Darla might be expecting a baby."

Fiona frowned. "What does that have to do with us?"

"Well, is she?" Sam asked.

"It seems there may be a reason for the marital haste." Fiona opened the refrigerator and took out a strawberry icebox pie. She cut them each a generous slice, and the brothers eagerly gathered around with grateful thanks. "I have a Books 'n' Bingo Society meeting tonight, and I intend to ask my dear friend about this rumor."

"Creed thinks," Sam said, around a mouthful of pie, "that Darla and Judah may have had a…"

She glanced at him. "Romantic interlude?"

All three brothers nodded.

"Did you ask Judah?" she inquired.

They shook their heads.

She gazed at all of them. "Do we suspect joke condoms might come into play?"

"We fear they might have," Sam said. "They could have. I threw my Trojan horse away," he said hastily. "But then, I'm a lawyer. I read fine print. When a box says 'Gag gift only, not for use in preventing pregnancy,' I hurl it like a ticking bomb into the nearest trash can."

"Too bad," Fiona shot back. "I like babies, and four of you are dragging your feet."

"Worse than dragging our feet. Judah's gone away with a broken heart," Rafe said.

"And the joke may be on him?" Fiona eyed each of them. "You believe Darla's marrying this other man as a cover for a relationship she may have had with Judah?"

"What we're theorizing," Jonas said, "is that he may have thought the condoms *were* the gag gift, not that they were useless." Jonas sighed. "I, too, threw Creed's gift in the trash. I didn't want hot-pink condom sex with anyone I know."

They all looked at him with raised brows.

"I threw mine away, too," Rafe admitted. "I'm afraid of children. At least I think I am. Or maybe I'm afraid of getting married," he said cheerfully. "When I watched Creed go down like a tranquilized bull, I said, 'Rafe, you are not your twin.'"

"It's possible Judah tossed them as well," Fiona said. "And for all we know, Darla isn't pregnant, although I wouldn't bank on it at this point." She wrapped up the strawberry pie and returned it to the fridge. "Rafe, run upstairs and look in Judah's nightstand, since that's where he stayed that night because of the wedding guest housing situation."

"Not me," Rafe said, "I never snoop."

Fiona elevated a brow. "We can't let him go all over several states rodeoing and maybe scattering his seed, so to speak. If he took the condoms with him, and if he honestly needs glasses so much that he can't read a box—"

"Who reads the label on a box of condoms besides

Sam?" Rafe said. "You just whip the foil packet out and—"

"Go," Fiona said. "Your brother's future may be at stake."

"I'm not doing it," Rafe said, and he meant it.

Fiona plucked three straws from a broom. "Draw," she told the brothers. "Short straw plays detective."

A moment later, Rafe held the short straw. "It's not fair," he grumbled. "I'm the existential one in the family. I believe in reading, and thinking deep thoughts, not nosing into places I don't belong." But he went up the stairs. In his heart Rafe knew that Judah and Darla belonged together. But they couldn't just fall into each other's arms and make it easy on everybody. "Leaving me with the difficult tasks," he muttered, reluctantly opening his brother's nightstand.

And there was the black box of joke condoms with the hot-pink smiley faces, peace signs and lip prints.

"Hurry up!" Fiona bellowed from the stairs. "You're not panning for gold! The suspense is killing us."

Rafe grunted. He opened the box.

There were nine left.

"Uh-oh," he muttered, and went downstairs with his report.

"Three?" Fiona said, when Rafe revealed his findings. "Three have been...are missing?" She looked distressed. "I hope Judah hasn't had more than one situation where such an item might be called for."

They all looked at her, their faces questioning.

"One woman," Fiona clarified, and they all said, "Oh, yeah, yeah, right."

The brothers glanced at each other, worried.

Rafe shifted. "What do we do now?"

They all gazed expectantly at Fiona. This was the counsel they had come to hear.

She shrugged and put on her wrap. "Nothing you can do. No one can save a man if he decides to give up his ground to the enemy. Faint heart never won fair lady and all that. Good night, nephews," she said. "Wish me luck at bingo tonight!"

And she tootled out the door.

The brothers looked after her.

"That was not helpful," Sam said.

"I agree," Rafe said. "I thought she'd give us the typical, in-depth Fiona strategy."

"She's right," Jonas said. "And we should be taking notes to remember this unfortunate episode in our brother's life."

"We probably won't," Rafe said morosely, and sat down to finish his pie. "I heard once that men are slow learners." And he wasn't going to tell anyone that it was Judge Julie Jenkins, next-door ranch owner and Bode's daughter, who had thrown that pearl of wisdom at his head.

DARLA LOOKED AT Jackie Callahan, co-owner of the Magic Wedding Dress Shop. "Pull harder," she said. "I'm not letting out my dress. I just bought it."

Jackie tugged at the fabric. "The satin just doesn't want to give. And I don't think it's good for the baby...."

Darla looked at herself in the triple mirror. "I've been eating a lot of strawberries. I crave them."

"That shouldn't cause so much weight gain," Jackie said. "Not that you look like you've gained *so* very much."

"On ice cream," Darla said, aware that her friend

was trying to be tactful. "Strawberries on top of vanilla ice cream."

"Oh." Jackie looked at her. "Maybe switch to frozen yogurt?"

"There's only a week before the wedding. I think the waistline isn't going backward on the measuring tape." She looked at herself, turning around slowly, and then frowned. "Something's not right."

"I think the dress is beautiful on you."

"Thank you," Darla murmured. "I'm not sure what's not quite right, but there's definitely something."

"Nerves?" Jackie said. "Brides get them. They want everything to be perfect. We've certainly seen our share of Nervous Nells in here."

"I'm not nervous," Darla said. *What I am is not in love. And that's what's wrong. I'm not in love with the man I'm marrying. And he's not in love with me.*

"Do you want to try a different gown?" Jackie asked, and Darla shook her head.

"No. This one will do." She went to change. The gown was not what was wrong. She could wear a paper bag, or a gown fit for a royal princess, and it wouldn't matter.

"Well," Jackie said as Darla came back out, "I think I know what the problem is."

She looked at her, hoping her dear friend, business partner and maid of honor didn't.

"You're not wearing the magic wedding dress," Jackie said. "You always said it was your dream gown." She smiled at Darla. "It worked for me."

Darla's gaze slid to the magic wedding dress. It was true. Ever since Sabrina McKinley had brought the gown to her, saying that it brought true luck to the wearer, she had known it was the only gown for her. It was the most beautiful, magical dress she'd ever seen. Sparkly and iridescent, it made her catch her breath.

But she couldn't wear it, not to marry someone she didn't love with all her heart. She was fond of her fiancé. Dr. Sidney Tunstall was a perfect match on paper. Even he'd said that. He needed a wife for his career, and she…well, she needed not to think about the fact that somehow she'd gotten pregnant by Judah Callahan even though she knew he'd conscientiously used a condom every time they'd made love that incredible night.

He would never believe this was his baby.

"I don't think I believe in magic," Darla said.

Jackie looked at her. "Magic is what we sell."

"I know," Darla said, "but these days, I'm concentrating on the practical." *Practical, not romantic. No magic, just the bare business proposal. And one day, I'll tell Judah the truth—after I've backed it up with a DNA test.*

She'd had hopes that he was in love with her—but she knew better. Hijacking a guy just because he'd spent one evening giving her the pleasure of her life was no way to win his heart. And especially not when he'd been so very careful with protection. Judah was definitely a hunk who didn't want to get caught. He'd always been the favorite of the ladies, and he never stayed with just one.

Practical. That was how it had to be.

JUDAH WAS INTO LIVING lucky. That was his new approach. He was going to swing by his tail in the jungle of life until he beat the jungle back. He was feeling mean and tough, and resolved to win. Focused.

He put his entry in for the rodeo in Los Rios, New

Mexico, and smiled at the cute brunette who took his money.

"Haven't seen you in a while, Judah," she said. "Where have you been hiding?"

"On the ranch." He didn't want to think about Rancho Diablo right now. "But now I'm back, and I plan on winning. How many entries are there?"

"Nearly a hundred, all events totaled. You're just in time. We were about to close registration."

"Then I'm lucky," he said.

"You could get luckier," she said with a smile.

He took that in, maybe half tempted, then shrugged. "You're too good for me, darlin'," he said. He winked at her and headed off to find some drinking buddies, telling himself that he hadn't accepted the brunette's generous offer because he was in a dark mood—really dark. Refusing her hadn't anything to do with Darla Cameron.

But thinking about Darla reminded him that she was marrying another man, and he definitely didn't want to think darker thoughts than necessary, so he pushed her out of his mind. Broken hearts were a dime a dozen, so his wasn't special. He headed to the bar, glad to see some cowboys he knew.

He was welcomed up to the bar with loud greetings.

"You're in?" someone asked, and Judah nodded.

"I'm taking nine months on the circuit to see what I can do. If I can break even and stay healthy, maybe I'll stay until I'm old and gray." He took the beer that the bartender handed him, raising it to the crowd. "And one for all my friends."

His buddies cheered. Judah grinned. This was what he needed. A buddy chorus of men who understood life as he did.

The little brunette slid into the bar, sending a smile

his way. Female companionship wouldn't kill him, either. He couldn't slobber in his beer over Darla forever.

He'd left his condoms at home.

And that was probably lucky, too. Judah sighed and looked at his already empty bottle. He didn't need to sleep with a female. He needed Darla, but Darla—damn her lovely just-right-for-him body—didn't need him at all. Just when he'd finally kissed the princess of his dreams—after forgoing the temptation for years—the princess had turned into a faithless frog.

Which just showed you that fairy tales had it all wrong. It wasn't the woman who always kissed the frog—sometimes it was the guy who got gigged.

Chapter Three

Darla wondered if she was making the right decision. Her whole world reeled as she left the doctor's office.

Twins. She was having twins. It was the last thing she'd expected to hear at her prenatal checkup. And now she knew why she was getting so big so fast, why her wedding gown was already tight. And her babies' father was the wildest of the Callahans.

Her phone rang, startling her. The display read Rancho Diablo. She didn't necessarily want to talk to Fiona at the moment, but a friendly voice was probably just what she needed. "Hello?"

"Darla, it's Sam Callahan. Get your jeans on, doll. We'll be by in five minutes to pick you up."

"Why?"

"We're getting up a convoy to go watch Judah ride. He needs all the hometown support he can get. He's in the finals, and we're borrowing Fiona's party van to take the cheering squad over to Los Rios. So get your boots on and put the cat out for the night."

She didn't have a cat, nor any reason to follow this Pied Piper. Nothing good could come of it. "Sam—"

"And we're picking up Jackie, Sabrina and Julie just for fun. You don't want to be the only girl left in town, do you?"

Put that way, no. But she was getting married in four days, and she was having twins. She was exhausted.

Then again, the last thing she wanted to do was sit around and think about how her life had spun out of control. And if everybody was going to the rodeo, what harm was there in going, too? "I'll bring my pom-poms."

"That's my girl," Sam said. "We'll take good care of you."

She hung up, feeling like a moth attracted to a bright, hot light. "All right, babies. We're going to go see Daddy ride a big piece of steak around an arena. Your first rodeo."

Her children might go to rodeos for years, and they would never know that strong, handsome Judah Callahan was their father. She shivered, thinking about that one wonderful night in his arms.

It would never happen again.

Fiona, Rafe and Jonas waited as Sam hung up the phone.

"No woman wants to be left out of a party." Sam grinned. "Just like you said, Aunt Fiona."

She nodded. "Now remember, when two immovable objects are forced to move into the same space—"

"It's highly combustible," Rafe said. "Your play on physics is unique, Aunt."

She nodded again. "And remember step two…."

"I feel like a spy," Jonas said. "You'd better not ever play any of these tricks on me, redoubtable aunt."

"Oh, I wouldn't *think* of it," Fiona said, her eyes round.

Her nephews grunted in unison, not falling for that, and headed off to pick up the other ladies.

"Did you hear my oldest nephew, Burke, my love?"

"I did." He placed a gentle kiss against her temple. "I do believe he offered you a challenge."

Fiona smiled. "That's exactly what I heard, too. And I wouldn't dream of not accepting a challenge."

JUDAH WASN'T NERVOUS about his rides. He'd almost been carried by angel's wings on every one so far, so high did his bulls buck and thrash, so easily did he hit eight on every ride. Never in his life had he ridden so well. Somehow the bulls he'd drawn were rank, and somehow, he was unbeatable. If rodeo could always be so easy…and yet, in all his years of rodeoing, he'd never ridden like this. He was living in the moment, blessed by the rodeo-loving gods.

And then it happened. He was sitting outside, thinking about his next ride, pondering the bull he'd drawn— Lightfoot Bill was known for tricks, and better cowboys than him had come flying off—when the hometown crowd came whooping and hollering over to him. It wasn't a huge scene they made, just enough to let him know they'd brought practically every one of their friends, including Darla Cameron.

She was definitely pregnant. Even he, who had little experience with the changes of a woman's body, could see that the lady he loved was with child. Her tummy protruded despite the pretty blue dress she wore, and if his eyes didn't deceive him her breasts were taking on the shape of sweet cantaloupes.

Yum.

She was beautiful, Madonna-like. Judah's heart thundered as he met Darla's gaze.

His concentration went haywire. "Hello, Darla," he said, and she said, "Hi, Judah. Good luck."

And then she went inside the arena, and the other ladies kissed his cheek and wished him a long ride, and his brothers clapped him on the back with hearty thuds, telling him he was *the man!*

But he didn't feel like *the man.* What man wanted to see his ladylove pregnant by another guy? The thought cramped his gut.

He was a wimp. A romantic fool.

He dragged himself inside. A couple of his brothers rallied around, giving him a pep talk he didn't hear. "Why'd you bring her?" he asked dully.

"Who?" Rafe asked.

"Darla." He couldn't speak her name without feeling pain.

"We couldn't leave her behind," Sam said. "Now buck up, bro, and think about your ride. I heard Lightfoot took his last rider for a spin into the boards."

"Yeah." That rider had busted his leg and would be out for a few months. Judah put his mouth guard in, a preride ritual that always focused his mind on the next few moments.

His mind wouldn't cooperate. "She's beautiful," he said, and Sam said, "What?"

Judah couldn't form words clearly around the mouth guard and his rattled brain. It didn't matter. Darla wasn't his, wasn't ever going to be his, and that baby she was carrying was going to have a rodeo doctor for a daddy. Not him.

And then he realized why Darla was here. She hadn't come to see him. Her fiancé—husband-to-be in just a few days—was working the rodeo tonight.

"Well, I'm not going to need his services," he said, and Sam said, "What, ass? I can't hear you with that mouth guard in. Why'd you put it in if you were going to go all Oprah on me?"

Lightfoot Bill was in the chute. Judah got on the rails.

It was time to score big. All he needed was to keep riding like he'd been riding—and then it wouldn't matter that his heart was blown out.

Nothing was about to matter, except hanging on.

DARLA DIDN'T KNOW when she'd ever been so nervous. Jackie held her hand, and Sabrina McKinley clutched her fingers on the other side. "Having any visions?" Darla asked Sabrina.

"Only that you're having twins," Sabrina whispered back.

Darla looked at her in shock. "You really are psychic, aren't you?"

"I was teasing. Nice to know I can occasionally guess right." Sabrina smiled at her. "He'll be fine. At least I hope so."

Darla hoped the row of Callahan men behind them—and most especially Fiona—hadn't heard her big news. "Don't tell anyone. I'm still trying to get over the shock."

Sabrina laughed, and Jonas said, "What's so funny? My brother's about to ride down there." So the women shared an eye roll and went back to watching the arena.

The gate swung open and the bull came out jacked and on a mission. Darla was pretty certain her breath completely stopped. She didn't realize she was squeezing Jackie's and Sabrina's hands until the buzzer went off.

The brothers jumped to their feet, cheering for Judah. So did everyone else from Diablo. Darla sat back down, closing her eyes for a moment, awash in conflicting emotions. Judah scared her to death. He loved living dangerously. He always had. Her heart had always been drawn to that. She herself was practical, calculating risks and making sure she stayed in a safe zone.

She wasn't safe anymore. She was wildly in love with Judah Callahan, and in four days she was marrying someone who was not the father of her children. Her babies' father was down there being congratulated, so far away from her they might as well be in different hemispheres.

Judah's score shot him into second place, and Darla tried to breathe.

"Man, that was something!" Jonas said. "That bull laid out all the tricks it knew to get Judah off."

"He's got to be happy with that score," Rafe said. "Now, if he can just keep it going."

Darla closed her eyes, wishing she'd never agreed to come. The nurse in her wished Judah had a safer calling; the practical side of her knew he was doing what he loved best.

Which was why she hadn't said a word to him about being a father.

"You'll have to tell him sooner or later," Sabrina said.

Darla stared at her. "Tell him what?" she asked, hoping her secret was still safe.

"That he's going to be a dad," her friend said.

"Hey, Sabrina," Fiona said from behind them. "I'm thinking about hiring you away from Bode. What would you say to that?"

They all turned to look at the older woman.

"Is that wise?" Sam asked. "Not that I don't approve, but won't that get Bode on you all over again?"

Fiona shrugged. "I'm in the mood to annoy Bode."

Burke said, "We could really use the extra help.

There's been so many babies, and Fiona wants to spend all her time holding them."

Darla felt her heart drop again. Her children would never be part of the love in the Callahan household. It was their rightful place. There were a lot of people at Rancho Diablo who would love the twins, if they knew about them. And she had no right keeping Judah in the dark.

Suddenly, Darla knew Sabrina was right. She had to find a way to tell Judah—before she said "I do."

It wasn't going to be easy, and he probably wouldn't believe her. But her children deserved an honest start in life—no secret-baby surprises. Her gaze found Judah in the arena—though she should have been looking at her rodeo physician fiancé—and it seemed Judah glanced her way before he disappeared.

I'll tell him tonight.

It wasn't Judah's policy to make love to a woman the night before a big ride. He had two more rides tomorrow. He was sitting on a big score tonight—second place was sitting pretty. It left him room to chase, but he wasn't the target. Second was great.

Therefore, lovemaking was the last thing on his mind.

Well, not the last thing. Every time he glanced up at Darla in the stands, looking like a hot dream, he had to fight his mind to focus.

He wasn't planning on making love.

But when she came to him and asked him if he had five minutes to talk to her—alone—a devil jumped to life inside him. "My room's across the street."

She stared at him, her cheeks pink. Oh, he knew her fiancé was here. He'd spoken to the good doc at least five times tonight. He didn't hold a grudge against the man.

If he held a grudge against anyone, Judah thought, it was this woman. She'd snared his heart, then trashed it. He didn't feel bad about reminding her that she'd once been behind a locked door with him.

"I can't go to your room." Darla's face was pale.

"Then talk here." He crossed his arms. "I'm listening."

"I can't talk to you here," she said, glancing around. "Isn't there someplace we can talk privately?"

Judah shrugged and turned back to taking off his gear. "My room."

She took a deep breath. "All right."

He was surprised that she relented. "Here's my key. I'll be there in five." He handed it to her, and she snatched it, looking around furtively, which almost made him smile. Darla did not do sneaky well. She was more sweet than sneaky. She must have something big on her mind if she was willing to rendezvous with him. Idly, he wondered about it, decided he'd never understand the mysteries of the female mind, and promptly dismissed it. She was probably going to do the guilt trip thing, like how the night they'd spent together hadn't meant anything, and now that she was getting married, if he would keep the little detail about their evening under his hat, she'd be eternally grateful, blah-blah-blah.

He'd act as if it hadn't meant a thing to him, either, and let her go on to her newly married life with a clear conscience.

But first he let her stew in her juices for a little bit. Then he followed after her, tapping on his door. She let him in.

"Well? What's so urgent?" He put *I'm a busy man* in his voice, so she'd get her soliloquy over with, thereby sparing both of them the agony.

Darla's eyes were huge as she stared at him; he could tell she was nervous. Judah kept his gaze away from her belly. Looking at her, knowing she was pregnant, was killing him. No man should be in love with a woman and know she was carrying another man's child.

"I'm pregnant."

"I can see that. Congratulations."

"Thank you." She swallowed. "Congratulations to you as well."

"Yeah. It was a lucky ride. I need a couple more tomorrow." He didn't look toward his bed, because if he did, he'd be tempted to drag Darla there. And he was a gentleman. Barely.

"I mean, congratulations to you, because you're having a baby, too."

He laughed. "Not me. I'm—" He stopped, looked at her carefully. Her face was drained of color. "You're not saying—"

She nodded. "I'm afraid so."

He stared at her, gazing deep into her eyes. Darla was not a dishonest woman. She wouldn't tell him this unless she believed it to be true. "I don't get it. How?"

"I don't know! Maybe there was a tear." She glared at him. "You'd know better than me."

He blinked. The condoms had been given to him by Creed at his bachelor party. The side of the box had read *For The Guy Who's Large and In Charge.* Judah remembered vaguely thinking all that might be true, and that it was pretty damn competitive of Creed to try to keep the other brothers from getting themselves in the family way, just so he could stay in the lead for the ranch.

Judah sank into a cracked vinyl chair near a tiny round table. "Why are you telling me this now?"

She breathed in deeply, obviously trying to calm herself. "I wasn't going to tell you at all. But then I realized that was wrong. I don't want to have secret babies."

"Babies?" His heart ground to a halt in his chest. *"Babies?"*

She nodded. "We're having twins."

Judah's world opened up, chasmlike. His pulse jumped, more fiercely than when he'd been on the back of Lightfoot. "You say we're—"

"Yes."

He passed a hand across his forehead, realized he was sweating under his hat. "I don't mean to be coarse, but how do you know that you're pregnant by me and not by your fiancé?" He wasn't about to say the man's name.

"Because I've never slept with him."

"Why not? Not to be indelicate—"

"It doesn't matter," Darla said. "We don't have that kind of relationship."

Maybe the man was an idiot. Maybe his thing didn't work. Judah couldn't believe that a guy who was fortunate enough to get a ring on Darla's finger wouldn't be making love to her like a madman every night. "Every man has *that* kind of relationship, darlin'."

She wore embarrassment like a heavy winter cloak. "When Sid asked me to marry him, we agreed on a business relationship. That's it, and no more."

Sid. Judah leaned back, trying to take in everything he was hearing. "That's why you were so eager to get in my bed that night. You wanted a good time before you tied yourself to this *business* relationship."

She hadn't been interested in business with Judah.

A blush crossed her cheeks. "I—yes. And I'm not sorry about it. Even now."

"Nice to know you don't regret it." He couldn't help the sour tone in his voice. "So what does Tunstall think about you being pregnant?"

Darla stared him down. "It was unexpected, obviously, but he's not opposed to being a father."

Judah jumped to his feet, crossing to her. "Let me tell you something, Darla Cameron. If you're telling the truth—and something tells me you are—no one will be a father to my children but me. Let's just get that straight up front." He studied her, deciding it was time this relationship got on the right track. "Something's going to have to change about your wedding plans, sweetheart."

Darla shook her head at him. Judah was angry. She'd expected anger, but not his statement about her wedding. "What exactly does that mean?"

He went back to his chair, dropping into it with an enigmatic smile shadowing his lips. "It means you've got the tiger by the tail, and now you're going to have to tame it. I shouldn't have to spell anything out for you. You knew when you told me this that your wedding to the good doc was never going to happen."

"I know no such thing!"

"You're not marrying another man while you're carrying my children. So put all that out of your sweet head."

Darla felt her own stubbornness rise. "I'm not having children out of wedlock when I've got a perfectly good groom planning to be my husband, Judah. It's no inconvenience to you if I'm married. You're not planning on being around."

She could see by Judah's expression that he was fighting to be civil. But he didn't have the right to tell her how to run her life.

"It'll be inconvenient for you when two grooms are standing at the altar with you on your wedding day," Judah said.

"You're not suggesting that you want to marry me?"

He nodded. "If you're pregnant by me, the only man you're marrying is me. That's the way *I* do business, babe."

Annoyance rose inside her. "Not that I expect romance in a proposal, but I don't want to be told what I'm going to do, either."

"And I don't want to be told that I'm going to be a father, and that someone else is planning to raise my children." He gave her a determined stare. "I'm being very reasonable, under the circumstances."

This was awful. No woman wanted the man she loved this way. Darla wished she could walk out the door and forget these past ten minutes had ever happened. But she couldn't. Her pride couldn't be the most important thing to her right now—she had her children's welfare to consider. "I'll think about your proposal," she said coolly, going to the door.

"You do that, and don't forget to tell the good doc your business merger's off." Judah followed, putting his hand on the doorknob to open the door for her—at least that's what she thought he was going to do—before pressing his lips against her cheek, his stubble grazing her skin ever so slightly. "Just so you know, Darla, I don't plan on mixing business with my marriage."

His meaning was unmistakable. His hand moved to

her waist in a possessive motion, lingering at her hip just for a second, capturing her. She remembered everything—how good he'd made her feel, how magical the night in his arms had been—and wished his proposal was made from love and not possessiveness.

Judah pulled the door open. "Next time I see you will be at the altar. Till death do us part, darlin'."

Darla stared at him for a long, wary second before stalking off.

If Judah Callahan thought she was going to marry a hardheaded, mule-stubborn man like him, then he was in for a shock.

Chapter Four

Judah had never been one to let someone else fight his battles. So it wasn't even a stretch for him to hunt up Dr. Sidney Tunstall. The good doctor was taking a breather in a bar down the street, which was good because Judah needed a drink himself.

First things first. "Tunstall," he said, seating himself next to the ex-bronc buster. "We have business to discuss."

Sidney put down his beer and gave him a long look. "Do we?"

Judah nodded. "I think it's only fair to let you know that you'll be hearing from Darla that your wedding is off."

The doctor raised a brow. "And how would you know?"

"Because," Judah said, "we just finished having a chat, Darla and I. And we came to the same conclusion. She can't marry you."

Sidney finished his beer, waved for another. "I'll wait to hear that from her, if you don't mind, Callahan."

"See, though, I *do* mind." He put down the money to pay for the beer. Sidney grunted, not about to utter any gratitude, and Judah couldn't blame him. "Darla says she's expecting my children. So that means she'll be taking the Callahan name. *My* name."

Sidney turned. "I happen to know that Darla thinks you're an ass she wishes she'd never met. And she's never mentioned you being the father of her children, so as far as I'm concerned, you're not even in the picture." He raised his bottle in a sardonic wave. "Thanks for the brew, but buzz off and let me drink it in peace."

Judah elected to ignore the insult. "What do you mean, you don't know about her being pregnant by me?"

The doctor shrugged. "We never talked about it. I don't need to know everything in her past. And until I know better, you *are* her past."

Judah slumped on his bar stool for a moment. He couldn't be mad at Tunstall—the man clearly wasn't in possession of all the facts. Just like a woman to leave out important details. Judah stood, tossed some tip money on the bar. "Look, Tunstall, you're an innocent party here, so I'm going to cut you some slack. But don't get in my way. I'll be standing at the altar with Darla, I'll be raising my own sons, and that's just the way it is."

"Maybe," Sidney said, "and maybe not."

The man had no idea how thin Judah's temper was at the moment. It was all he could do not to pound good sense into him. But Darla was the person he needed to be setting straight, so he took a deep breath and sauntered off to collect his wits before his rides tomorrow.

It wasn't going to be easy. His concentration had never been so scattered.

He couldn't decide if it was suddenly finding himself altar-bound or becoming a father that had him the most bent.

"HOW *DARE* YOU?" Darla demanded when Judah made it to his motel room an hour later, where she was waiting outside the door. He cast an appreciative eye over the snapping fire in her blue eyes, and her long blond hair. She looked like an angel, but she was going to bless him out like a she-devil.

Which meant that Tunstall had given her the bad news. And that suited Judah just fine.

"I dare," he said, unlocking his door and stepping inside his room with her on his heels, "because that's what I do. *I dare.*"

Her lips compressed for a moment. "You have no right to interfere."

He tossed his hat into the chair. "Just one man chatting with another. Don't get your panties in a twist over it, sugar." Grinning, he pulled a beer from the six-pack his brothers had thoughtfully left in his room, satisfied that matters should be straight as an arrow between him and his buttercup.

"I'm not going to marry you, Judah." Darla's chin rose, and her tiny nose nearly pointed at his chin. He so badly wanted to run his finger down her face and tell her everything was going to be just fine, if she'd only settle down and let him take care of her.

"We'll talk about it tomorrow after I ride. There's a lot of things we'll have to plan, like naming my sons. You'll need to enroll in a prenatal yoga class, too. I hear it's very beneficial for the mother and the babies."

Darla's cheeks went pink. "I'm leaving now," she told him, "and I *am* marrying Sidney. Quit trying to take over my life."

"Whew," Judah said, pulling her close against his chest. "You'll know when I'm trying to take over your life, babe. I'll say, 'Get in my bed,' and you'll go happily because you'll know I'm going to make you feel like a princess."

Irate as Darla was, she leaned into him, and for a moment, completely relaxed.

But she suddenly pulled herself away and marched to the door. "Not a chance, Judah. Goodbye."

THE NEXT DAY Darla carried the magic wedding dress to the back of the store where she couldn't see it. Lately, it had begun to call to her with a siren song of such temptation that she could barely resist it.

"Just try on the gown," Jackie urged. But Darla didn't want to fashion hopes and dreams through simple fabric.

"I don't need fairy tales and magic in my life. I'm making a solid, practical decision to marry a man who's as even-keeled as I am. Judah is a winter wind blowing through a canyon. I could never rely on him."

"But he's the father of your children," Jackie said. "You don't want to do something in the heat of passion, Darla."

"I already did that," she replied, "which is why I'm choosing to be quite selective with my children's futures now. Sidney will be a good father. He comes from a very small family, and has always wanted a large one. We're good friends. I'll be an organized, supportive doctor's wife." Darla stowed the magic wedding gown in the very back of the stock closet, behind back-stock dresses. It did lure her. Sometimes in the night, she could hear a faint rustle of musical chimes, like an antique jewelry box opening to play a lilting melody. The dress was beautiful.

And she wanted it so badly. But she wouldn't admit that to Jackie. Darla wanted to believe in romance and dreams and fairy tales, just like any other bride. Yet she couldn't afford any mistakes. Her whole makeup was geared toward thoughtful, careful decision making. There really wasn't any room for loving a bonehead like Judah.

Unfortunately for her, that bonehead made her body shiver and ache every time she thought of him. It was like that wild winter wind blew over her skin, reminding her of how much she loved him.

But that was the problem. She did love Judah—and she was just another responsibility for him, much like the ranch, and his family, and rodeo. Nothing special or different. Something he had to rule over, boss, command. Before their night together, he'd never spoken to her, nothing more than a passing hello and chitchat about the weather. And he hadn't so much as sought her out at the store since that night, either.

A woman knew when she was the object of a man's passions, and she wasn't that to Judah. He was too wild for her, too unsettled for a woman who liked calm rational choices in her life. Judah was her one moment of reckless abandon—and it didn't take a psychic gift to know they were not meant to be.

"Speaking of psychic," Darla said, and Jackie glanced up.

"Were we?" she asked.

"No, but is Sabrina really going to work for Fiona?"

"I think so. Why?"

"Because I was thinking about asking her if she wanted to work in the shop while I'm out after the babies are born. You can't do it all by yourself," Darla said, staying in practical mode.

"I'll be fine," Jackie assured her.

"You have three little ones. We need backup."

The door swung open, sending the bells over the shop door tinkling. Judah strolled in, the man of her dreams obviously on a mission, judging by the hot gleam in his eyes. Darla's heart jumped into overdrive.

"We need to talk," he stated, and Jackie said, "I'll be heading out for a coffee break. Nice ride last night, Judah."

He tipped his hat to her, and when the door swung shut behind her, he put the closed sign in the window.

"You can't close my shop," Darla said.

"We have to talk."

"Not while I'm working."

"The brides of Diablo will just have to wait while you take a fruit and juice break." He handed her a small bag. "Organic. Every bite."

She began to seethe. "I eat healthy, Judah. You don't need to concern yourself with my diet."

He nodded. "A husband takes care of his wife."

"Not to point out the obvious—"

He handed her a box. "Darla, you have to quit being so stubborn."

"What's this?" She eyed the small dark box as if it were a bomb.

"What a man gives a woman he wants to marry." He grinned, clearly pleased with himself.

She handed it back. "I'll keep the organic breakfast. You can keep your Pandora's box."

He put it on the counter. "If you don't want me to romance you, I'll stop."

"Thank you." She folded her arms.

He shrugged. "If that's the way you want it."

She didn't say anything to confirm his statement because it really wasn't the way she wanted it. But under the circumstances, "no" was the only option. Judah was a conqueror. He wanted to bulldoze her ivory tower and take her prisoner—but letting him do so would be a mistake.

"Why aren't you at the rodeo?"

"I can't ride when I'm all torn up like this."

That stopped her. She checked his eyes for signs of amusement, found none. Surely he was jesting, though. Judah wasn't a man whose emotions ruled his life. He was all action, sometimes even brave, fearless action. She again checked his expression for teasing, but he looked just as deadly serious as he had a moment ago. It was like gazing into the eyes of an Old West gun-slinger in a classic movie: resolute, determined, honest.

She caught her breath. "We don't know each other at all."

He looked at her. "We know each other well enough to be parents."

"It's not enough, Judah. Marriage between two people who don't love each other is a mistake."

"So marrying Sidney would be just as big a mistake," he pointed out.

She took a step back. "I meant that marrying you when you never loved me would be a mistake. And you can't say that you do, Judah."

He remained silent, and she felt he'd conceded her point.

"If you're worried about having access to the children, you'll always have that."

"That can be taken care of legally," Judah growled. "I don't waste any energy worrying about that."

She blinked. "Legally?"

"Sure." He shrugged. "I could have Sam draw up custodial papers tonight if I was worried about you keeping me from my children. That's the least of my concerns."

"It's very nice to know that you've considered all your options, even as you bring me a token of your questionable affection."

His lips thinned. "That's not what I meant."

She turned away. "It doesn't matter, Judah. I don't want to marry you."

"Guess I'll have to take the good doc out and ask him what his secret is."

She whirled around to face him. "There isn't a secret. We have a lot in common. I like the security of knowing that I'm marrying someone a lot like me."

"Sounds boring." Judah leaned against the counter, giving her a lazy smile. "You're too sexy to be boring."

"Sexy?" She looked at him, startled.

"I think so." He shrugged. "Does Sidney?"

"I don't...I don't know," Darla said, confused. "I don't believe so. I mean, why would he?"

Judah grinned at her, and suddenly Darla felt like a mouse in the paws of a playful lion.

"I don't know why he wouldn't," Judah said. "Maybe you should ask ol' Sid." He pushed himself away from the counter, approaching her too quickly for her to step away, even if she'd wanted to, which she didn't. Not really. She was kind of curious to see what new trick he had up his sleeve.

And she wanted him to kiss her. Just once more, to see if it was as good as she remembered.

He stopped in front of her, towering like a strong redwood tree. "I'm sure almost anyone would say that the good doctor is the better man. I know you'll rest comfortably with your very prudent decision."

"Quit being a rat," Darla snapped, and Judah kissed her—on the forehead.

The jerk. She wanted his lips on hers, and she had a feeling he knew it.

"I know when I'm beat." Judah strode to the door, tipped his hat, then placed it over his heart. "Congratulations. And I'll let ol' Sidney know that I have stood aside, his bride having made her choice."

Darla stared as he flipped the closed sign to Open, and loped down the main street of Diablo. Judah Callahan was the most maddening man she'd ever met. Why she'd ever slept with him, she didn't know.

Passion. She'd wanted one night of passion, which she knew Judah would give her, before she did the practical thing and married Dr. Sidney Tunstall. She'd wanted a lusty bedding before her marriage of convenience shut her up in a gilded prison of diligent routine for the rest of her life.

"I have no regrets," she murmured, and then her gaze fell on the small jeweler's box Judah had left on the wrap stand, next to the healthy snack he'd brought her.

She glanced once at the door to make certain he wasn't outside spying in on her, ready to tease her if she gave in to temptation. But Judah was long gone. There was a crowd on the sidewalk, so she knew that several women had run to chat with him, Judah being a female magnet like all the Callahan men.

Darla's hand rested on the jeweler's box.

Chapter Five

It was one of those days, Judah thought, as he picked himself off the ground. Some days you were the hero, and some days you were the dust between the hero's toes.

Today he might have been the dust under a very ordinary man's feet. Crazy Eight had thrown him within three seconds. It hadn't even been a decent ride. Crazy Eight hadn't been anything spectacular. But just as he'd left the chute, Judah had seen Sidney Tunstall out of the corner of his eye, and somehow his concentration had gone to hell.

He'd gotten thrown so easily a child could have ridden better. Judah slowly wandered over to the rail, slapping his hat against his leg. And somehow, he didn't seem to care. He wondered if Darla had opened the box with his offering in it. A man had to be prepared to fight like a soldier, and Dr. Tunstall was nice enough, but Judah understood women. And what he understood best about women was that a big sparkly diamond sometimes won the fair maiden.

Dr. Tunstall hadn't ponied up yet, so Judah had no compulsion about trying to get the jump on the competition. He'd called Harry Winston's and given a description of exactly what he wanted, then flown to pick it up. And it was a sparkler, like a star plucked from the sky.

No woman could resist it.

"And you know," he said to Sidney when the doc came over to check him out, "I went for the biggest star I could find."

Sidney looked at him. "How do you feel, Judah?"

"Like a winner," he said. "How do you feel, Doc?"

Sidney grunted. "Let's get you where I can take a look at you." He slipped an arm under Judah's, and helped him to a seat.

Then he passed one finger in front of Judah's face. "How many?"

"How many what?" Judah asked.

"Fingers?"

Judah sighed. "I see five fingers, which are going to be a knuckle sandwich, Doc, if you don't get your bony hand out of my face."

Sam came over to stare into his eyes. "Hey, bro. Hearing little birdies or anything? Faraway music? Fairy whisperings?"

Judah drew in another deep breath. "I don't have a concussion. I wasn't paying attention and I got thrown. That's all."

Rafe bent to stare into his face. "That was a doozy of a toss you took. Hit your head or anything?"

It was impossible to convince anybody that his problem wasn't in his head. His problem was in his heart. "If everyone will get out of here, I'm going to get ready for my next ride."

"Assuming I approve you to ride," Sidney said, and Judah glared at him.

"If you don't pass me to ride, I'll kick your ass."

Sidney nodded. "Unprovoked aggression. Loss of concentration. Could be a concussion."

Judah narrowed his eyes. "Don't pull that doctor mumbo jumbo on me. If you keep me from riding, it'll only be because you're trying to keep me from winning. You don't want me to win because you know ladies love cowboys who do. And I am in a serious position to be loved."

Dr. Tunstall shook his head. "I should let you ride. It would serve you right if I let you land on your already cracked head. Maybe it would knock some of the hot air out of you and serve to flatten that outsize ego of yours. But as it is," Dr. Tunstall said, "you're going to have to scratch."

"I will not scratch," Judah declared, and Sidney said, "Then I'll scratch you myself. Either way, your rodeo-ing is over for the next month."

"Month!" Judah hopped to his feet, heading after the departing doctor. "You can't keep me out for a month. I need to ride to make up the points for the finals. You know that as well as anyone."

"I do." Sidney glanced at him before he went back out to the arena to observe the next riders. "Go home and rest, Judah. Don't do any handsprings or jump off any houses, and you should be fine in a few weeks."

"I don't remember hitting my head," Judah muttered, glaring after him. "He's trying to keep me out of the rodeo."

"Well, that's a shame," Sam said. "Now you'll just have too much time on your hands to hang around Diablo and convince Darla that you'd make a better husband than a cowboy."

Light dawned. "Yeah," he said, "that's what I'll do.

I'll cede this hallowed ground and grab territory closer to where yonder princess lays her fair head."

"Oh, jeez," Sam said. "Let's get you to the E.R., bro. I think you've stripped a gear."

DARLA HAD BEGUN to open the box Judah left, but then, not wanting to know what she was passing up, she'd snapped it closed without getting past the first crack in the hinge.

There was no point in torturing herself, since she wasn't marrying him. Ever. He wasn't above tempting her, but she would not succumb. Especially not since she had a wedding in a couple days.

The very thought made her break out in nervous hiccups, something she hadn't done in years. Jackie had gone home, the store was closed for the night and Darla was alone with her thoughts, and a hundred wedding gowns mocking her. She hiccupped twice in rapid succession. The magic wedding gown secreted in the storeroom called to her, dragging her thoughts to it. Temptation—wondering how she would look in the gown of her dreams—tugged at her.

She hiccupped again, painfully and loudly, in the silent store.

She had to know. It would wipe the last questions from her mind, and she could go on with her marriage to Sidney, knowing that a gown was just a gown, after all. It was the groom who made the day special for a bride, a man a woman knew she could trust to be at her side and...

And what? Take care of her? She didn't need that.

But Sidney would expect to take care of her. Judah wouldn't, she mused. He would expect to make love to her most days of the week, and be the guiding light in her life.

Sidney would not expect such hero worship.

Why she was even thinking about both men, comparing them, was a mystery. One of them was about to become her husband. The other wasn't going to be anything more to her than he'd ever been, just a casual acquaintance—with whom she now shared future parenting.

"Argh!" Darla hiccupped wildly. Dashing into the stockroom, she tore the magic wedding dress off its hangar and slipped it on, entranced by the luscious whisper it made sliding over her skin. The dress seemed to enfold her in its beauty, pouring dreams into her heart. The hiccups ceased; her nerves unfurled.

Taking a deep breath, she stepped to the mirrors.

The gown was simply stunning, glinting and sparkling with sequins and crystals, and a luminescence all its own emanating from the fabric. Darla's breath caught as she looked at herself, turning slowly to see all views in the mirrors. It was everything Sabrina had claimed. The same spell that had captured Jackie was now shimmering around her, gentle motes of magic that made her feel like a real bride.

Slowly, Darla gave in and opened the jeweler's box, gasping at the lovely diamond ring. Never had she seen a ring so utterly perfect. Unable to resist, she slipped it on her finger. It fitted perfectly, as if made to order.

Her gaze bounced to the mirrors and caught. She stared, astonished to see herself transformed into a fairy-tale bride.

And behind her, smiling a sexy *you're-all-mine* smile, was her handsome prince.

DARLA WHIRLED AROUND. He wasn't here. Her prince was a figment of her imagination—fantasy, wishful thinking, whatever. She hurried to take off the ring, shut it back in its box. She'd had no business trying it on.

And then she felt it, like a butterfly wing brushing against her neck: his lips, pressing against her fevered skin. Darla glanced into the mirror with longing as she watched Judah's ebony head dip to the cradle of her shoulder.

Before she could totally lose herself in the fantasy, she tore the magic wedding dress off and rapidly dressed, fingers shaking as she put on her own clothes. It was unsettling how much time Judah spent in her thoughts. He practically *lived* there, teasing her subconscious.

"It can't go on like this, buddy," she muttered, slipping on her shoes. "Once I'm married to Sidney, you are banished to the bin of ex-boyfriends."

Ex-lover, to be exact, but she'd fudge a little, one day in the future, when her children asked her about their real father. She'd say Judah Callahan had been a boyfriend, someone she'd cared about, but that they just hadn't loved each other.

Except she did love Judah. Darla swallowed against a tight throat and quickly turned off the store lights, locked the door, ran to her vehicle. Of course she loved him. She'd had a crush on him forever. Once they'd made love, she was lost to him.

And, she thought fiercely, *I'm glad I'm having his babies. It's a piece of him I never dreamed I'd have.*

"KEEPING IN MIND THAT you've always been a bit irascible," Fiona said, "Judah, this is irritable, even for you."

He sighed, taking the piece of triple chocolate fudge

cake she'd brought him. He was going to get fat if Fiona didn't stop ministering to him. Once he'd scratched from the rodeo—very much against his will—and come home, his aunt had appointed herself his watchful angel. He was in bed reading at eight o'clock at night only because he didn't want to hang out with his brothers, who were playing, of all stupid things, badminton under the lights with their wives.

Judah munched dutifully on the delicious cake. "Aunt, you're going to make me fat. I'm not supposed to ride, I can't even play hopscotch with the kids for exercise. Every time I open my eyes, you're stuffing my face with some delicacy." He waved his fork. "You don't have to feed me. I'm capable of making a run to the kitchen myself."

"I'm sure you are." Fiona seated herself on the foot of his bed with a little bounce. "Are you certain you're comfy? Pillow soft enough for your aching head?"

Sighing, he put the cake on his nightstand and sat up, already wishing he had a handful of aspirin. Or an aunt-chaser, like a double whiskey. "What's this all about?"

"Judah," she said, her gaze pinned on his, "I know you found the cave. And I need for you to keep its existence under your hat."

He blinked. "How'd you know I found it?"

"I found your big boot prints there. And Burke had seen you riding that way. Promise me that you won't breathe a word about it. To anyone. Not even...not even Darla."

Judah studied the determined gleam in his aunt's eyes. She was really worked up about this, hence the angelic caregiving she'd been heaping on him. He should have remembered she liked to bake when she was worried about something. "I haven't mentioned it to anybody. I've been preoccupied, and I also needed time to think about why it might be there. But I'd like to know why you're keeping it a secret. Is it because of Bode?"

"Partially," Fiona said, "and partly because we use it often."

"So is that the silver mine everybody's asked about over the years?" Judah reflected on that for a moment. "At one time or another, I guess just about the whole town has gossiped about it. Do we own a silver mine?"

"Not exactly," Fiona said carefully. "You might consider that cave a gift from a friend."

"What friend?"

She glanced at her hands. "I need to know that I have your absolute confidence."

He took another bite of cake, transfixed by his aunt's caginess. It was almost like when she'd told them childhood bedtime stories. She was spinning a great one right now—he could practically hear her thoughts churning. "I wouldn't breathe a word of this to my closest brother."

She sniffed. "Since you have five of those, I guess that's plural."

"Absolutely." He waved his fork again imperiously. "Speak on, aunt of many tales."

She gave him a sharp look. "This is not a fairy tale. More than you can realize hangs on the complete secrecy of that cave."

"I know, I know. But you shouldn't be crawling around in that place," Judah said. "It makes me nervous to think about you being there. What if you stumbled onto a snake? What if a coyote was in there? We never knew you had a secret hangout."

"Nothing will happen to me. Burke usually goes with me."

"Oh, so Burke is in on this as well," Judah said,

growing more fascinated by the moment. "Do the two of you make midnight runs out there to dig up silver?"

She sighed. "I'm going to pop that concussed head of yours if you don't pay attention."

"Go. I'm all ears." He set down the plate and swigged the milk she'd set on his nightstand. The copy of *Death Comes to the Archbishop* he'd been reading fell to the floor, but he didn't notice.

"I have a friend who comes once a year to visit," Fiona began, and Judah said, "The Chief."

She nodded. "The silver is his. The cave is his home, of sorts."

"Is there a tribe around here?"

She nodded again. "But he sometimes stays in the cave. Alone. We won't ever tell anyone that."

"Is he a fugitive? Illegal?" Judah arranged a stern look on his face. "Aunt, we shouldn't be harboring someone who has some kind of record—"

She shook her head. "The cave is his. Your parents bought Rancho Diablo land from him—from the tribe, actually. The cave and the mine stay in his hands, all of those mineral rights being signed over to him."

"Why?"

"It was a fair exchange," Fiona said simply. "Your father negotiated for the land with the stipulation that the mine remained in the tribe's possession. It will be this way for always." She took a deep breath. "And one more reason why I absolutely must keep this ranch from falling into Bode's clutches."

"Oh." Judah had the whole picture now. "So Bode really wants the mine?"

"He wants everything. The mine, which he's only heard rumors about, but which he suspects must be real. The two working oil derricks, the land, the Diablos. He wants it all."

"No one can own the Diablos. They're free."

"For now," Fiona said. "As long as they are on Callahan land, the spirits are free."

A cool breeze passed over his skin. "And if we lose the ranch?"

"Everything is lost. The mine, and the secret that the mine hides."

"Surely there's not all that much silver. It was a small cave, as caves go."

Fiona looked at him sharply, her mouth opening as if to say something. Then she closed it, before rising to put his book on the nightstand and collecting his dishes. "Try to rest. I believe the doctor said a concussion requires absolute stillness for forty-eight hours, in your case."

"Funny thing is, I don't remember hitting my head," he complained. "I swear it's a conspiracy to keep me from riding."

"You'll live to ride another day if you rest now," Fiona said with a smile. "Good night, nephew."

"Good night, Aunt. Thanks for telling me about the cave. I'll take the secret with me to my grave."

She looked at him, her eyes deep and troubled. "You have no idea how much is riding on your ability to do just that." Then she left his room.

Judah felt restless now that he'd heard so much family lore. Inaction was never his strong suit.

What he needed was someone to annoy, to take his mind off all the family stuff. Nothing like a little late-night foray to make a man feel less starved for adventure.

Instead of staying here and allowing Fiona to put ten

pounds on him, he decided to go make a different kind of midnight raid. After hearing about Bode bothering his aunt and the family treasure, he was in a dangerous mood.

JUDAH HESITATED ONLY ONCE, and that was in the hall outside Jonas's old room, where Sabrina now resided. Normally, the brothers slept in one of the large bunkhouses, having moved out once they hit the teen years, though occasionally they slunk back to their old rooms in the main house if they had an injury, which, thankfully, wasn't often. But it was easier to be where Fiona wouldn't have to run out to check on them twenty times a day, which she did when they were injured, no matter how many times they told her it wasn't necessary. His brothers hadn't even asked him where he wanted to sleep off his trifling—in his opinion—concussion; they'd dumped him unceremoniously at the house.

But Jonas shouldn't be in residence, nor any of the other brothers. Judah froze outside Sabrina's room, surprised by the answering murmur of a man's voice. If he didn't know better, he'd think...

He didn't know better. He knew nothing at all, Judah told himself, tiptoeing past her room. He had bigger fish to fry tonight than who was paying a nocturnal call on Fiona's personal secretary.

He sneaked past Fiona and Burke's room without any trouble, and flitted past the family library where they held their meetings, just in case any of the brothers were hanging out in there. One never knew where a Callahan might be loitering, and Judah didn't want to answer any questions.

Then he was out the door and into his truck. Not a soul would know he was laying his pride on the line.

"Where are we going?" Sam asked through the window of the truck, and Judah swallowed a good-size howl.

"*We* are going nowhere," he said. "*I'm* taking a short, *private* drive."

"Ah. To see Darla." Sam leaned his arms on the door. "You know what your problem is?"

"Tell me," Judah said. "I'm just dying to know."

"Your problem is that she's getting married in two days, and it's not to you. Getting that concussion is the best thing that ever happened to you."

"Why?" Judah asked, irritated.

"Because you need to be defending your castle, not riding rodeo."

"There's nothing to defend. I don't have a castle."

"If my lady was pregnant, there wouldn't be any discussion of her marrying another man. That sucker wouldn't dream of encroaching on my territory, because he'd know I'd knock his block off. In fact, my lady wouldn't be thinking about marrying another dude, because she'd be so wild to get into my bed." Sam gazed at him. "Like I said, you have a problem."

"Thanks for letting me know," Judah said, "because I hadn't figured that out on my own."

"You need to buck up. Now is the time for all good men to come to the aid of the party," Sam said.

"If there was a party to be had. Will you get out of my truck so I can go?" he demanded.

"You don't know of any women I could go carousing with tonight, do you?" his brother asked. "I'm in the mood for *looove*."

"Do I look like a dating service? Did you lose your little black book?" Judah was getting steamed. "Why would any sane woman want to carouse with you?"

Sam sighed. "This case is getting on my nerves. I could use a distraction."

Judah straightened. "Are there new developments?"

"Well, Bode's pretty endless with his tricks and appeals. He's got a pretty seamy team of lawyers. And as you know, law isn't my strong suit."

Judah blinked. "You're the best lawyer around. No one bites the pants off the enemy like you. You're legendary for being a butt—ah, bulldog-like in the courtroom."

"But this is personal," Sam said, and Judah realized his brother needed to talk.

"Come on," Judah said. "Let's go carousing."

"Thought you'd never admit that you need a break from hearth and home." He got in the truck, grinning.

"Fiona's driving me nuts," Judah admitted. "She feeds me like a lost lamb."

"Ah, the benefits of home life." Sam looked at him. "So where are we going? Howling at Bode's bedroom window? I wouldn't mind giving the old goat a good fright."

"How about Darla's?" Judah turned down the drive.

"That doesn't sound like much fun unless the doc is there. We could run him off. *That* would be fun."

Judah's thoughts instantly ground to a halt. He'd never considered Darla might be having company. In his mind's eye, she was tucked up in her pristine bed waiting for his embrace—not the good doctor's.

"I'm not sure this is going to be as much fun as I thought it would be," he growled.

"Kind of tame stuff," Sam said, "when we should be painting 'Bode Sucks' on the water tower."

"That's kid's stuff." Judah frowned, thinking about Darla in bed with a rangy, loose-limbed retired bronc buster-turned-doctor. He had a horrible vision of Dr. Tunstall using his stethoscope to listen to Darla's heart going thumpety-thump for him—or even worse, listening to Judah's babies cooing inside Darla's nicely watermelon-shaped tummy. "I need something dangerous."

"Thinking about Darla sleeping with the good doc after the 'I do's' are said?" Sam asked, his tone commiserating.

Judah turned onto the main road. He was loaded for bear, his mood as territorial as he could ever remember it being. He was tired of Bode looming over them; he was tired of Tunstall, nice as he might be. But nice and in-the-way were two different things. "'Hang on to your ass, Fred,' to quote a favorite movie of mine. We're going to look in the face of danger with no regret."

Sam rubbed his hands together with enthusiasm. "Danger, here we come!"

Chapter Six

"This is your idea of dangerous?"

Sam glared at Judah as he held Jackie and Pete's girls, Molly and Elizabeth, on his lap. Judah waved a small stuffed pony he'd bought at the rodeo at the toddlers; he'd bought one for every Callahan child, passing them out like Santa Claus.

Judah grinned at Sam. "This is definitely my idea of dangerous. What did you have in mind, bro?"

Sam allowed little Fiona to crawl up in his lap. The triplets were dressed in their jammies, and old enough to realize they were being given a special treat of staying up past their bedtime. Jackie and Pete looked on fondly and with some amusement as Judah tried on daddy skills.

"I don't know," Sam said, "maybe lobbing a peck-happy chicken through Bode's bedroom window? Perhaps heading into town and seeing if we could rustle up some female attention? That's my idea of living on the edge. Of course you *are* darling," he said to mini-Fiona. "You're my niece, so what else would you be?"

"This is plenty dangerous for me," Judah said. "I'm not good with kids. I'm not cut out for fatherhood."

Pete laughed. "No one is. It just creeps up on you and you deal with it."

Jackie gave her husband a light smack on the arm. "You *are* cut out for being a dad," she told Judah. "You're a Callahan. All the brothers have a latent dad gene. I'm positive."

Judah grunted. "I can't convince Darla of that."

"But did you try?" Jackie asked, smiling. "Did you give her a reason to believe you were interested?"

"I suggested prenatal yoga. And vitamins. And good nutrition." Judah kissed his niece on the top of her head. "What more can I do?" He glanced to Jackie, puzzled, very aware that Pete was trying not to snicker.

"You offer to go *with* her to prenatal yoga," Jackie said gently. "And offer to cook those nutritious meals for her. Things like that. And offer to rub her belly."

"She won't let me rub anything of hers," Judah said morosely. "I'm pretty sure she thinks her pregnancy is a result of my, um, mishandling of the situation."

"It was," Sam said, unable to keep from tossing in his two cents.

"I used protection," Judah said defensively, frowning when everyone started laughing. "What?"

"You never read the box, did you?" Sam asked.

"The box of what?" Judah knew he was the butt of some secret joke, but he wasn't certain why. He'd come here for a little sympathy, and a bit of no-pressure, hands-on baby guidance. Not guffaws.

"Condoms," Sam said. "Creed gave us all joke condoms."

Judah blinked. "There's nothing funny about condoms."

Sam grinned at him. "You don't read directions."

"I'm a man of action," Judah shot back.

"And you fired away and asked questions later." Sam nodded. "That's the reason you're going to be a father."

"No," Judah said, "my box said something like 'For the Man Who Has Almost Everything.' *That* was the joke."

His family laughed harder. Judah shrugged. "It doesn't matter. Even if I begged to attend prenatal yoga, or promised to attend a cooking school for pregnant parents, Darla would still be determined to marry Doc Skin-and-Bones," he said. "You'd think she'd want a fellow with a little more muscle and meat to him. Those bronc busters always look like a string bean reverberating on the back of a horse to me. I'd rather my sons have a man to look up to who has muscles," he said with a sigh. "Strength."

"Meathead," Pete said, his tone kind. "You've got to quit letting Sidney bother you. Tell Darla—without being an ape—how you really feel about her."

"I don't know how not to be an ape." Judah stood, clapped his hat to his head, kissed the little girls goodbye. "Thank you for letting me be an uncle who doesn't call before he drops in at bedtime. I promise not to make a habit of it."

"Come anytime you like," Jackie said, giving him a hug. "We love you, Judah. We want you to be happy. You're a good man."

"Sometimes," Sam said. "When he's not a stupid man. Now can we go do something dangerous? Something that'll really rock the epicenter of wild-n-crazy? Like maybe drive to the Sonic, at least?"

Pete thumped Judah on the back. "It's always darkest before the dawn, dude. It'll work out."

"It's pretty damn dark out there," Judah said. "She's getting married in two days."

"You better rescue the princess *tout suite* then," Pete told him. "You can do it. You're a Callahan."

Judah nodded. "Thanks."

"Danger, here we come!" Sam said, kissing his nieces and hugging his sister-in-law goodbye.

Judah shook his head. Sam had no idea just what kind of danger lay in wait. And he couldn't tell him.

"YOU DID NOT inform me that babysitting was your idea of dangerous," Sam said with a groan twenty minutes later, when they'd made their way to Creed's house. Sometimes Creed's sister-in-law Diane's three daughters stayed in the house with their little cousin, too, but tonight, it was just Creed and Aberdeen and their daughter, Joy Patrice.

"Not only is it dangerous," Judah said, holding out a stuffed pony for the baby, "it's essential. You should do one thing every day that scares you. It's important for your growth. And in my book, diapers are dangerous."

"Growth comes in the shape of luscious, eager females, too," Sam said, "but I can tell you're on a mission, so never mind." He sighed heavily and took the pony from Judah. "She's a baby. She can't hold a stuffed animal, idiot."

Judah gave Creed a stern eyeing. "Did you give us condoms that were basically party balloons?"

He grinned. "Seemed like a great groom's gift, as far as I was concerned."

"Why?" Judah demanded. "Do you mind me asking why?"

"To help you along. And clearly it did." Creed put on an innocent face. "It would be selfish of me to cheat you out of marital bliss. A little lambskin shouldn't stand between you and the most happiness you will ever know."

Judah snorted. "The mother of my children wants to marry someone else. Is that what you had in mind?"

"Now that sounds like a personal problem to me. Can't blame that on a neon party favor." Creed handed him a beer. "The box clearly said—"

"I know. I know. Only I'm not an owl. I don't see things in the dark, like very small print." Judah took the beer, more in the mood to bean his brother with it than to drink it. "I just thought that if a lady bothered to make love with a guy, then surely she had some kind of feelings for him."

Aberdeen looked at him with sympathy. "Darla does have feelings for you, Judah."

"What those feelings are could be anything," Creed said unhelpfully, and Sam laughed. Judah hugged the baby in his arms, setting down his beer to gaze into her face. "Hey," he told her, "your uncles are pigs. But me, I'll rescue you. Don't worry, little princess. You'll always know Uncle Judah had your back."

"Knowing you," Creed said, "you've tried overwhelming Darla with your machismo. You've even given her the ol' I-know-what's-best-for-you treatment." He glanced at Judah. "So that only leaves romancing her socks off."

"Darla doesn't wear socks," Judah said, and everyone groaned.

"You have to go slowly for him," Sam said. "He's not the sharpest knife in the Callahan knife block."

"So, romance," Creed said, speaking slowly for Judah's benefit, as if he didn't know what to do with a woman, "is done with a gentle conductor's baton, a wand, if you will. Not a crashing bull-in-a-flower-bed thunderclap."

"Like you did with me?" Aberdeen said sweetly, and Judah and Sam hooted at their brother. "Judah, don't let Creed tell you he had all the answers, because he didn't."

"But he still won your heart," Judah said. "Though I don't know what you see in him."

That earned him a glare from Creed, which made Judah feel better.

"He won my heart by being persistent."

Creed stared at his wife. "No, I didn't. I won your heart by being the most awesome, irresistible—"

Aberdeen waved at Creed to be quiet. "Trust me, your brother made some mistakes in the wooing process. He was not a perfect prince. Nor was he a love machine, as he might lead you to believe."

Sam and Judah snickered as Creed was put in his place.

"But," Aberdeen said, "he hung in there, no matter what hoops I made him jump through, and I admired that. It made me realize that he actually loved me, in spite of all the doubts I had about us being together. And so he won my heart." She smiled at her husband, and Creed perked up like a plant in the sunshine.

"So how do I hang in there, when Darla doesn't even want me hanging in there? I left her a ring—a ring I was guaranteed would make a lady jump into my arms. And I got nothing," Judah said sadly. "Not even a phone call."

"Well," Aberdeen said, "perhaps it would be good to present your case in person."

"Yeah, dummy. You don't just leave a ring for a woman and hope she gets the clue. It takes more effort than that," Sam said. "Now can we go do something dangerous?"

Judah kissed his niece on the head. "Why is it that all we have on the ranch are baby girls?" he asked, thinking about the sons who would be in his arms before he knew it. A few months was nothing. He could hang in there.

He *could* hang in there. Just like Aberdeen said.

"We have baby girls," Creed said, "because it takes a real man to pack pink booties. Deal with it."

"WHERE'S THE DANGER?" Sam asked, when Judah pulled in front of Darla and Jackie's wedding shop. "This is just a dress store. It's a *wedding dress* store, but unless there's man-hunting brides around—and there's not, since it's nearly midnight—then I don't see the danger. Enlighten me."

Judah took a deep breath, wondering if he was going to be standing at an altar in two days or not. It was going to take everything he had to do it. "The danger is that you get to find a ride home," he told his brother. "I travel alone from here."

Sam gawked at him. "You would leave me in town with no ride?"

Judah nodded. "You wanted danger."

"I get it." Sam hopped out of the truck, wearing a sour expression. "This is not my idea of danger."

"Yes, but your day is coming." Judah waved at his brother. "I'm going to go find an ex-nurse and see if she wants to take my temperature."

"Huh," Sam said, "good luck with that."

He loped off, heading toward the town's only secret night spot, in the back of Banger's Bait and Tackle. Judah drove away, thinking about everything he'd seen in his brothers' homes. It was true that they probably hadn't had the smoothest routes to the altar. They were certainly not hard-core princes.

But they had made it across the finish line.

And that's where Judah wanted to be.

Chapter Seven

It was rude to pay a visit at midnight, particularly without calling first, but time was of the essence. Judah figured he could blame his lack of manners on his nonexistent concussion, which he considered overcautiousness, and maybe even passive-aggressiveness, on Sidney's part. The bronc buster had known that Judah was winning. He hadn't wanted to give his rival any reason to look like a hero, so he'd scratched Judah.

Therefore, it was completely legit to be here. And there was a lamp shining in the window, so a tap on the door would let him know whether Darla wanted company.

There were no vehicles in the drive, and Judah figured she had no nocturnal guest sleeping over. "That's a good thing," he murmured. "I would have hated to toss ol' Sid out on his bony butt."

He knocked.

"Who is it?" Darla asked, and Judah took a deep breath.

"The father of your children."

"Judah," Darla said through the door, "it's late. I have work tomorrow, and I have a doctor's appointment. I don't have time for fun and games."

Fun and games? Was that how she saw him? "I could

play the pity card and tell you I had to scratch from the rodeo due to a slight concussion, and that only a nurse would understand, but—"

The door opened. She looked out at him, her expression wary. "Did you really?"

"Yes. And no. I actually don't think I hit my head, but Tunstall scratched me, and the E.R. said I had a hairline concussion, or stage one. Something like that—I wasn't paying attention." He shrugged. "I think it was Tunstall's evil plot to get me out of the rodeo."

She shook her head. "Sidney's not like that."

"I was fine," Judah insisted. "I've ridden with worse injuries."

She sighed and opened the door. "Come in, but only for five minutes."

He took off his hat and sat awkwardly on the sofa. She looked so cute in her blue robe and little flip-flops. Okay, maybe those weren't sex-goddess garments, but he liked her comfy. It felt homelike here. "This is a nice place."

"No room at the inn." She crossed her arms. "Judah, what did you want to talk about?"

He forced himself to pay attention to why he'd come in the first place. "I don't think you should get married. It's too soon. You could be making the biggest mistake of your life, which will affect my sons."

She frowned. "I don't know the sex of my children, because I haven't asked the doctor. I don't want to know until they're born. So please don't refer to them as males."

"They'll be boys," Judah said. "Pete and Creed might not be capable of manly offspring, but I am."

Darla sighed. "Judah, I'm getting married in two days. Whatever you think about what I'm doing isn't important."

"Can I get a restraining order or something?" Judah pondered this. "There has to be a law where a man can stop a woman from making a foolish mistake in his sons' lives."

Her frown deepened. He could see he'd landed in deep cow droppings with that tack. He decided to change course before he got thrown out on his ear. "What I'm trying to say, Darla, is that I don't think you've given us a chance."

Once he'd said it, it was like a cork popping out of a bottle. "We've started off on the wrong foot for a number of reasons, but there's a spark between us."

"And we should blow on that spark and see if it bursts into flame or goes out altogether?" Darla didn't look convinced. "Judah, there isn't one compelling reason you can offer for me to call off my wedding. I'm not convinced you and I have any sparks, but where you're concerned, I'm pretty flame-resistant."

Well, wasn't that just a pearl every man wanted to hear falling from his beloved's sweet lips? She didn't think there were sparks.

There was only one thing to do. He could be run off by his pumpkin's frosty ways, or he could be a fireman.

He pulled Darla into his lap and said, "I don't know why you're fighting so hard. Maybe you just like a chase. But I'm good at running. And as long as I know you haven't returned my ring, I'm going to believe that you're just fighting your practical side."

She slid from his lap onto the sofa. "You make me sound...like a tease."

He kissed her neck. "Mmm, you smell delicious. And don't put words in my mouth. You're a hot little number, Darla Cameron, and I'm not afraid of a little teasing. You tease me all you like, and I'll tease you back. Although, that night we shared might have been a one-off, come to think of it," he said, angling for a kiss, which he adroitly stole. He noticed she wasn't exactly fighting him. "What's holding us back from having a really kinky lovefest, anyway? Just me and you and a bowl of fruit, maybe?"

"Sidney."

Judah raised a brow. "Didn't you tell me that you and Tunstall aren't exactly burning holes in the bedsheets?"

She stiffened like a dress mannequin with a pole up its back. "That isn't how I phrased it, thank you, speaking of putting words in someone's mouth."

He leaned back comfortably against the sofa and indicated she should go on with her explanation. "I think a woman who is planning on a sexless marriage—a business arrangement—probably has a very good reason for locking herself in a gilded cage."

"You don't know everything," Darla said, "and it's really none of your affair. Now, if you don't mind, I have to be at work early in the morning. We have a shipment of gowns arriving."

He nodded. "And you need all the beauty sleep you can get before the wedding. I understand. It's a bride thing." He stood. "Not that I think Tunstall's much of a catch, but—"

"It doesn't matter what you think," Darla said. "Anyway, what's wrong with him?"

"Nothing," Judah said, a tad too quickly. "Nothing at all."

"You're just annoyed because he made you scratch. That's why you're here, isn't it?"

"No," Judah said, "I'm here to kiss you good night."

He kissed Darla like he might not ever kiss her again. He held her, framing her face with his hands, touching her skin, telling her with his kisses how he felt about her. He couldn't bear the thought of her marrying another man. Darla belonged with him, and he couldn't imagine why she didn't see it the same way he did. He kissed Darla with his whole heart and soul, thrilled to finally have her in his arms. So it was a horrible shock to his soul when banging erupted on the front door.

Darla jumped away from him as if she'd been zapped by a cattle prod. "Who is it?"

"Sidney."

"He can't find you here!" She started shooing Judah toward the bedroom.

"I'm not hiding," he declared. "But even if I would hide like a weasel, don't you think the bedroom is the last place he'd want to find me?"

Darla shook her head. "He won't come in here. Don't move! If you do, I swear I'll…you'll wish you only had a slight concussion!" She closed the bedroom door.

Judah shrugged. "Well, this wasn't how I planned to get in here," he said to himself, "but I'm okay with it." He pulled off his boots, his shirt, his jeans, his socks, hesitated at the black Polo briefs, then shrugged and tossed them on the pile, too. What the hell. He didn't sleep in anything at home; no reason to stand on ceremony now. No telling how long Boy Wonder would be pressing his case with his not-gonna-be-bride, so Judah slid into Darla's bed wearing nothing but a grin.

"Now *this* is living dangerously," he said in the dark, briefly wondering if Sam had made it home and was as comfortable as Judah was at this very moment. Impossible. This bed—Darla's bed—was simply the best place to be in Diablo. And then Judah fell asleep in Darla's soft, cozy, clean smelling sheets, wondering when she'd remember that Judah's truck was parked out front where even Tunstall couldn't miss it.

Sam was right. It was huge fun living dangerously.

"Do you have company?" Sidney asked, and Darla glanced nervously at the bedroom door. She wasn't certain she could trust Judah not to come popping out like a jack-in-the-box to annoy Sidney. Even now, she was pretty sure Judah had his big ear pressed flat to the door, listening to every word, carefully choosing his moment to spring.

"I actually do have company," she said, unable to lie to Sidney. He'd been too kind to her. He really was a nice man, and they made a good team. Sometimes she suspected that he felt a little more than friendly toward her, and then other times he was strictly professional.

Yet Judah wouldn't play nice and understand the unique situation she was in. *Stubborn ass.*

"Do you mind me asking who it is?" Sidney asked, and Darla sighed.

"It's Judah."

"He's in there?" Sidney jerked his head toward her bedroom.

"He'd be happy to come out, if you want. I told him to go in there while you were here. I wasn't aware you'd planned to stop by." She looked at him, gauging his reaction, but he seemed like the Sidney of always, calm and unconcerned.

Not in love with her. Which was a relief.

"No." Sidney sat on the sofa, making himself comfortable. "I'm happy for him to cower in there if you're okay with it."

Darla sat at the other end of the sofa. "So what's on your mind?"

"I just want to make certain you still want to go through with this, now that Judah knows he's the father." Sidney looked at her. "I'd completely understand if you feel that your circumstances have changed."

"There's nothing between Judah and me," Darla

said. "He wants to be a father to his children, which I'm grateful for. But there's no reason…" She stopped, thinking about the beautiful diamond ring Judah had given her. She remembered the satiny feel of the magic wedding gown as she'd slipped it on. It had felt so right, so real, like she was meant to wear it and be a beloved bride.

Then she thought about Judah standing behind her in the mirror, his handsome face gazing at her with love and passion—yes, she'd seen passion in those dark blue eyes—and she shivered. He'd made love to her with an intensity that had rocked her. She knew that side of Judah Callahan.

But not much else. And she didn't want a man who simply felt that she should be his because he'd made children with her. "Nothing needs to change between us, Sidney. You still need a wife to satisfy your inheritance, and I'm more than willing to be a stand-in."

Sidney looked as if he was about to say something, then closed his mouth. His lips, she noticed, weren't full and capable of being demanding—like Judah's. Sidney's lips were thinner, almost nonexistent, as if he was used to holding back his emotions a lot. She considered his dark brown hair, dark eyes, kind face. "Sidney, why haven't you ever married, anyway?"

He shrugged. "I'm always on the road. I have a house that's nice enough, but no woman wants to go home alone at night for months on end."

"That's true, I guess." Darla thought about how nice it was that Judah was so close to his family. They were always around. Sometimes they aggravated each other, but most of the time it was obvious that they all loved each other a lot.

She really wanted a big family for her babies.

"I guess I'll be alone much of the time," she murmured.

He winced. "If you marry me, that's unfortunately part of the deal. I will take very good care of you, when I'm around. And financially you won't lack for anything. Nor will your children, whom I'm willing to adopt as my own."

She took a deep breath. She really didn't need to be "taken care of," as nice as Sidney was trying to be. She'd always taken care of herself just fine. What she really wanted was a father for her babies, a name for them to own, so that they wouldn't grow up wondering why they'd had no daddy.

But she hadn't counted on Judah being so determined to be a father. He was Mr. Footloose, Mr. Don't-Tie-Me-Down.

The huge diamond he'd bought her almost made her change her opinion of him.

Almost.

She owed it to the children to find out. "I think," Darla said softly, "maybe I'd better wait and see how this turns out, Sidney." She looked at him. "I'm so sorry. I hope you can forgive me."

He shrugged. "Nothing to forgive. I completely understand. It's why I came out tonight."

She nodded. "You're a good doctor. And a good man."

"I know," he said, standing. "You've heard that good guys always win, haven't you?"

She smiled. "It's true. You'll win."

He pressed a gentle kiss against her knuckles. "I have half a mind to go in there and tell Judah that I lied about his concussion."

She blinked. "You did?"

"I said I thought he had one. I felt it was important

to get him off the road. The hospital never really found anything, either. They just told him he needed rest. He ran with the advice—quickly, I might add, right to your door." Sidney glanced toward the bedroom. "Part of me wants to go in there and tell him we've decided to elope tonight, and would he mind keeping an eye on the house while we're gone." He grinned at Darla. "What do you think he'd say?"

"I don't know," she answered.

"I do." Sidney smiled at her, tipped his hat and left. She listened as his truck gunned to life and he drove away.

Then she went to her bedroom, opening the door abruptly just in case Judah did have his ear pressed tight to it. She fully intended to smack him a good one for being so nosy.

But he was asleep in her bed—nude, judging by the pile of clothes on the floor. And obviously not worried one bit by what was transpiring in the other room.

It stung. He could have been pacing a little at least.

All he really wanted was to be a bad-ass. And it wasn't going to work with her.

But here they were, bound together. She placed a hand on her belly.

Her babies' father was sleeping blissfully, unconcerned that he did not love their mother. But he would do his duty, just like any of the Callahans would.

There was only one option that would solve their dilemma.

Chapter Eight

Dear Judah,
You and I aren't in love. You want to get married because of the babies, but I have a proposal of my own for you. Let's agree to stay together until after the twins are born, and then we'll reevaluate the situation. That's the best deal I can come up with right now, because I really don't think we're meant for each other as married partners. But we'll try it your way for the sake of the children, if only temporarily. If you agree to a divorce after the babies are born, I'll be at the altar in two days, ready to say I do.
Darla

She put the letter in an envelope, decided to leave it on the kitchen counter where Judah would easily find it. She laid his beautiful ring beside the letter. The diamond caught the light from the overhead hanging fixture, sending prisms dancing over the counter. Her breath caught just looking at it. A princess would wear such a lovely ring.

She was not a princess. She was an unwed mother with a scoundrel for a one-night-stand daddy. "Oh, boy," she murmured, and closed her eyes for a moment. Did she really want to be married only until the children were born? It sounded so prenup, so planned.

At least she was giving him the freedom to leave. And for the sake of her pride, she had to know that he had an escape hatch built in to their agreement. She felt tears pool behind her eyes, told herself she'd spent far too much time staring at dreamy white gowns. She'd gone from a no-nonsense nurse to a woman who dreamed fairy-tale dreams—and it hurt.

Strong arms closed around her, making her jump. Warm lips pressed to the back of her neck, sending sizzles zipping along her skin.

"Is that a Dear John letter you're leaving me?" Judah asked against her nape, and Darla closed her eyes.

"Not exactly." His hard body pressed against her and her knees went weak. "Please tell me you're wearing something."

He kissed the side of her neck. "I think you'd be very disappointed if I was wearing clothes, Darla. You don't have to pretend you're a straight-laced nurse who'll read me the riot act for making a pass at you. Although if I was one of your patients, I definitely would have tried—"

"Judah," Darla said, unable to think about where he was going with that while he was driving her out of her mind with kisses. "I could have a better conversation with you if you weren't nude."

"I don't want to chitchat, doll. I want to hold you and make you scream like a wildcat. Which I know you can do very well." He nipped her shoulder lightly, then ran a tongue over the spot he'd bitten. "The question is, are Dear John letters supposed to be written on pink stationary with a purple pen? It seems to send a romantic signal, dressing it up like that. Black and white would be a lot more impersonal for bad news, I would think. But I wouldn't know," he added, his voice husky. "I have to admit no lady of my acquaintance has ever tried to write me off."

"I'm sure." Darla didn't dare turn around. He was rascal enough to not have a stitch on, and she didn't want to see his firm, well-muscled body. She wasn't strong enough to deny herself a naked Judah whose body was carved by a master sculptor.

"Where's the good doc?" he asked, his breath warm against her neck, tickling the tiny hairs at her nape. "Not trusting me alone with the treasure, is he?"

"Judah, I'm not treasure. And yes, Sidney would trust me. Totally."

"I guess he was trusting you when you sneaked into my room that night?"

She swallowed. "Sidney…Sidney and I aren't getting married anymore. So quit bothering me about him. And please put something on! And leave. I want you to leave."

He took the envelope from her fingers. "Is that what this says? Go away, big bad wolf, and never come back?"

She didn't nod, because she hadn't written anything of the sort. Now she felt foolish for what she had written. Why hadn't she realized how unwise it was to try to bargain with a devil? She tried to snatch the envelope away from him, but Judah eluded her easily.

"Ah," he said, running the envelope down her back so it rasped along her zipper, "you don't want me to read something that has my name on it? I find that strange, Darla Cameron. And one thing you usually aren't is strange."

"Judah, there is a robe in my closet. If you'll at least put on a robe, we can have an adult conversation."

"Now, my love," he said, kissing the shell of her ear, "being an adult is one thing no one's ever accused me of. Besides, I like your backside so much. I remember it fondly."

She closed her eyes, wishing she wasn't pressed against the kitchen counter. He'd teased her enough, she decided. She was going to turn around, was going to face this strong, naked man and tell him she'd changed her mind. She just wanted her letter back, and to give up her unwise attempt at taming this lion.

She was melting, knowing full well what wonderful pleasures lay in store for her if she just gave in.

She couldn't.

Whirling around, she kept her eyes forcefully averted from the masculine glory. "Judah, give me back that envelope right now." Her gaze ran the length of him in astonishment. "You're not naked! You're fully dressed!"

"Disappointed?" he asked, grinning as he stole a kiss. "Sorry about that, babe, but I've got to go. Duty calls back at the ranch. Sleep well." He waved the envelope at her before tucking it in his shirt pocket. "I'll save this for my nightly bedtime reading. I'm sure it'll prove to be interesting, even fascinating. I never expected a letter from my lady." He winked at her, so devil-may-care it was maddening.

"I want it back!"

"Ah, no. I bid you good night. I would stay, sugar, but at this hour, I'm afraid I only have one thing on my mind. And I'm sure you know what that is." He stole another kiss and departed, leaving Darla lathered up and pink-cheeked.

She spun around and saw that the ring was still there,

sparkling on the counter. He knew she wanted it. He knew it tempted her. He knew *he* tempted her.

In fact, she was drowning in temptation.

There was nothing she wanted to do more than run after him and beg him to come back, spend the night with her, make love to her. He probably knew that about her, too. He'd so shamelessly teased her about his nudity, making her think about him naked, making her remember. Oh, he was baiting her, and it was working.

She didn't know how she was going to sleep tonight.

"WELL, IF IT ISN'T Roughriding Romeo," Sam said when Judah dragged himself into the bunkhouse well after midnight. "Mr. Danger himself."

"Glad you made it home, bro. I figured you would." Judah hung his hat on the hook in the mudroom and looked at his brothers in front of the fireplace. Jonas, Rafe and Sam stared at him with raised brows and expectant expressions.

"So, did you find any danger?" Sam asked.

"Nope," Judah said, "nothing but lambs and cotton candy in my world."

"What's that pink thing poking out of your shirt?" Jonas asked.

"This," Judah said proudly, "is my first Dear John letter."

"Nothing to brag about there," Rafe said. "You weren't even a 'dear' as far as Darla was concerned in the first place. So if she's writing you off, you're going backward, bro."

"This Dear John letter means," Judah said, running it under his nose to smell the scent of Darla's perfume, "that she cares about me enough to try to run me off.

She's fighting it, brothers, every step of the way. And that's the way I like my lady."

"Reluctant? Distant? Icy, even?" Sam said. "You always were the peculiar one of us."

"Darla's none of the above." Judah threw himself on the sofa lengthwise, cradling his head on a sofa pillow. "She's fighting herself. And she's losing."

"You can tell all that without even opening the letter? Maybe you've picked up some of Sabrina's psychic skills. But I advise you to read it before you go crowing about how hot your runaway bride is for you," Jonas said.

"She won't run from our wedding, that's for sure. She'll be too practical for that. I'm a catch." Judah shrugged and tore open the envelope to hoots from his brothers, pulling out the letter to read it. "This is better news than I'd hoped, even," he murmured. "She's given the skinny bronc buster the wave-off."

"Really?" Sam perked up. "He's cleared the field for you?"

"And she's planning on marrying me in two days. I told you!" Judah looked up at his brothers in triumph. "I hope I still fit in my tux."

"Dummy," Rafe said. "Sidney wasn't going to wear a tux. Why should you?"

"Why not? It's a special occasion. It calls for a tux." Judah was pretty certain that in spite of her protestations to the contrary, he and Darla would be married forever. He planned to make rock-solid vows in two days, and no way was he ever letting her give him the slip like she'd given Tunstall. Oh, she might think that was what she wanted, and certainly he would agree to her darling little last-ditch attempt to keep herself from falling head over heels in love with him. But this agreement she wanted bought him time. And he could do a whole lot of convincing in four or five months. Judah squinted at the ceiling. "Which one of you dunces wants to be my best man?"

"I'm not feeling it," Jonas said. "Something tells me nothing good can come of marrying a woman who's Miss Reluctant."

"I'm telling you she wants me. Read it for yourself." He handed the letter to Jonas, who snatched it and read it before passing it to his brothers. They all looked at him with worried expressions. Judah shrugged at their hangdog faces. "Don't worry. She's crazy about me."

Rafe sighed. "If I have to, I'll be the sacrificial lamb who stands next to you at the altar while you sign on to get burned a few months hence. But it doesn't feel like happy ever after to me."

"Thanks, tough guy." Judah closed his eyes, annoyed. He waved the letter in the air again. "This is my ticket, my golden chance, my checkmate, if you will. I win."

"We see," Sam said. "We see that you're nuts. Darla's telling you up front she has every intention of marrying you so her babies will have a name. Then she's divorcing you, dude."

"So? I'd rather her marriage-of-convenience be with me than with Sidney. That puts me in her bed, and therefore, in medal contention."

"You think of everything in terms of winning or losing," Sam said. "I don't know if that's healthy."

"Yeah," Rafe said, "what if Darla gives you the boot, as per this agreement? Don't you have to be a gentleman and honor that? Or else it's not valid. She doesn't have to say yes until you agree."

Judah shrugged. "Just be ready in two days to toss birdseed, bros. That's your only job."

His brothers grimaced, then went back to what they'd been doing, which looked to be high-stakes, boring Scrabble. Judah smiled to himself. They had no idea that he had everything completely under control. And they could keep their bachelor jealousy to themselves. He was going to be in contention for Fiona's ranch-o-rama, and they weren't.

Darla was going to be Mrs. Callahan, and he was going to be the hero with strong boys who'd ride rodeo just like him. A bull rider and his bundles of joy—how great was that? He knew all about what Darla wanted, and what the practical side of her wanted was a fab dad. Once she saw how great he was with the little lads, she'd never want to let him go.

Just two days.

It seemed like forever.

Chapter Nine

"I'm worried about Judah," Jonas said, after Judah had conked out. "He thinks he's got this all planned down to a script, but I think the situation's more explosive than he realizes." Jonas squinted at the Scrabble board, considering his options.

Rafe nodded. "I was thinking the same thing."

"Still," Sam said, "it's his business if he wants to get burned like an onion on a grill. We can't save him from being stupid."

"The problem," Jonas said, glancing over at the peacefully snoring Judah, "is that he believes he can convince Darla that she loves him. The two of them have lived in the same town almost all their lives, and never even played doctor with each other."

Rafe and Sam blinked at him. "Doctor?" Sam said.

"Yeah." Jonas grimaced. "You know. Doctor."

Rafe considered that. "I've never played doctor with any of the girls in this town. Spin the bottle, maybe. Pin the tail on the donkey, definitely." He frowned at Jonas. "You don't strike me as the type to play doctor, Jonas."

Sam snickered. "I played doctor. I also got slapped. Ah, good times." He looked at Jonas. "Is that why you became a doctor, because you liked playing it so much?"

"No," Jonas said, "I became a doctor because I'm smart, and I like helping people. I like puzzles."

"It had nothing to do with beautiful nurses," Rafe said. "Good thing, too, or that would have been a waste of your time, considering you've never brought a beautiful nurse home. Or any nurse."

Jonas sighed. "All I was trying to say is that Judah and Darla never had the hots for each other before. So why get married?" He glared at his brothers. "There, was that plain enough for you boobs?"

"Plain enough for me," Rafe said. "I don't think we can save him, though. He's on a mission to marry."

"I think we should test that mission," Jonas said, "to make certain true love exists. After all, it's easier to call off a wedding than to get a divorce later on. Some people have marital counseling, you know, to help them decide if they're on a successful path with their chosen—"

"Bah," Sam said. "I say let him fall on his face."

Jonas looked at Rafe. "That leaves you the deciding vote."

Rafe appeared troubled. "I see your point about saving pain for him and for Darla and for the children later by not putting them through a divorce. I also see Sam's point about it being Judah's business what he does. How exactly do you plan to test this marriage-of-convenience adventure?"

"Simple," Jonas said. "We tell Judah we think he's making a mistake. We just be honest. Nothing underhanded, just plain old honesty."

Rafe shook his head. "I don't want to be punched, thank you."

"Me, neither," Sam said. "I'm the brains of this outfit, you know. I'm trying to save us from Bode. Since it's your idea, it should probably be you, Jonas. You are eldest, after all."

"And I'm the surgeon," Jonas said, "who will stitch Rafe up when he busts his lip on Judah's knuckles."

Rafe shrugged. "Anyway, I still say the deciding factor is it's his life. The truth is, those babies do need a name. And it is all Creed's fault that a Callahan got Darla into this mess, so a Callahan should bail her out."

Sam and Jonas looked at him. Then they looked at Judah, who was snoring, his chin practically pointing toward the ceiling.

"He really isn't much of a catch," Rafe said. "I guess if all Darla needs is a name for her children, I can do the marriage-of-convenience thing as well as anybody. If it would save Darla from making a disastrous mistake."

"You mean Judah," Sam said.

"I mean Darla," Rafe retorted. "He really isn't much of a catch, like I said."

They sat silently, mulling over the situation. Then Jonas leaned over, kicked at Judah's leg with his boot. Judah's eyes snapped open.

"What?" he said. "Are you losers still playing Scrabble? Don't you know how to spell a word longer than three letters?"

"Rafe has something to tell you," Jonas said.

Rafe looked miserable. "We think marrying in haste means repenting in leisure."

"Whatever." Judah moved his hat down over his eyes and shifted to a more comfortable position on the leather couch.

"We think," Rafe said, trying again bravely, "that marriage isn't your style. You're more of a drifter."

"No, I'm not," Judah said from under the hat. "I'm a pragmatic romantic."

They went dead silent for a moment. He grinned, but the felt of his Stetson covering his face kept them from knowing he was laughing at them. They thought they were being so Fiona, but they weren't. No one could plot like Fiona, and Judah had learned at her knee.

"I'm going to tell Darla I'm willing to marry her so her babies will have a name," Rafe said.

Judah rolled his eyes. "You do that."

Silence met his pronouncement. Judah snickered. His brothers were always trying to help, though not successfully, and he had to admire their ham-handed ways.

"You don't mind?" Rafe asked, sounding a little less sure of himself.

"Nope," Judah said. "Have at it."

"I vote we resume this game later," Jonas said, and Sam said, "A fine idea, since Rafe has to be somewhere."

Sam said it importantly, as if Rafe was about to run right over and pop the question to Darla. *These goofballs,* Judah thought. *I don't know what they're up to, but Darla would never want to marry anyone but me. She wants me bad.*

"Okay," Rafe said, "see you later."

The door opened, and Judah heard boots moving out the door. "Called your bluff, didn't I?" he said, sliding the hat from his face. He was alone. They'd gone, ostensibly to scare him into thinking Rafe was actually heading off to save Judah's princess from her self-declared dilemma. But Darla wanted only one cowboy. *And that's me,* he assured himself.

He glanced over at the Scrabble board, seeing a lack of imagination in the chosen spellings. "'Marriage, wife, convenience, bad idea,'" he said out loud, eyeing the tiles. "Oh, very funny. You guys are a laugh a minute." He went back to sleep, completely unconcerned. He had everything under control.

"MARRY YOU?" DARLA asked twenty minutes later, when Rafe had hotfooted it over to her house and banged on her door. He'd told her he'd just left Judah, after telling him he was going to propose. Darla didn't know what to think about the Callahans anymore, except that maybe they were just as crazy as everyone said. "Why would I want to marry you?"

"You'd like me better in the temporary sense," Rafe said, "and after all, it was my twin's gag gift that got you into this dilemma. I feel a certain irony to putting matters right."

She frowned, wondering why Judah hadn't told her about a gag gift. "Gag gift?"

Rafe nodded. "Judah didn't tell you?"

She shook her head.

"Creed gave us all prank condoms as groom gifts. Clearly, the joke was on Judah." Rafe stood straighter. "Like I said, I'm here to put things right."

Darla's heart was sinking. "Judah didn't mind you proposing to me?"

Rafe shook his head. "No, he said to have at it."

Darla wondered what new game Judah had up his sleeve. Her pride came to the fore as she said, "I don't understand why this would solve anything."

"Well, if it's a temporary situation you're looking for, and I guess it is, due to the pink ultimatum you gave Judah, it would be better to marry me, because I am all about temporary. Short Term is my middle name. In fact, No Term is what they should have named me—"

"You don't think Judah will honor the divorce?"

"Nope," Rafe said. "We're territorial in my family.

He's not going to give you up once he has those little cherubs under his control. I mean his, uh, loving guidance."

Darla considered that. "But Judah doesn't love me."

Rafe shrugged. "Hasn't he told you that he does?"

"No." Darla looked at Rafe. "I can raise these children on my own. I don't need anyone to help me with that. I want to marry for love."

"I know. But it may not happen." He looked properly saddened by this revelation, which didn't make her feel any better. "As you know, you're like a sister to me. I've always loved all women, but you have a special place in my heart. I don't want to see you get hurt." Rafe wondered if he was carrying his role a little too far. The more he talked, the more he believed his story. The truth was, Darla and Judah didn't love each other; getting a divorce after the babies were born was going to hurt them, their children and the family.

But if Rafe married Darla, and she knew he was doing it to give her children a name, then there was no ulterior motive. But there was the small matter of him carrying a super-secret torch for Judge Julie, Bode's daughter. He sighed deeply.

"Darla, I'm here for you if you don't want to marry Judah, and probably no sane woman would want to, I suppose."

"I guess you're right," Darla said, thinking that she'd have loved to marry Judah, if things had been different. If they'd fallen in love gently and slowly, finding each other of their own will and choosing, not this slamming together of their separate galaxies. "It's nice of you to offer, Rafe, but actually, I don't want to marry you, either."

He blinked. "Either?"

She sighed. "No. I don't want to marry you, of course, because you're right. You are a brother to me. And I don't want to marry Judah. I'd always feel like the wallflower that got asked to dance because the guy felt sorry for her." She felt tears prickle her eyes, but stood her ground. "Thank you for coming by, Rafe. It's been helpful."

"It has?" Rafe wasn't certain the conversation hadn't gone wildly off the guided track. She wasn't supposed to be saying she didn't want either of them. She was supposed to insist that Judah was the only man for her, once she realized it was true. Clearly, she'd realized something of a totally different sort. "So what are you going to do?"

Darla smiled. "What I should have done all along."

"I HAVE TO GIVE THIS BACK to you," Darla said, laying the magic wedding dress carefully over the bed in Sabrina's room at Rancho Diablo. "It's lovely." She gave Sabrina a smile she didn't realize was sad until she felt it on her face. "Thank you for offering it to us. Jackie felt like a princess when she wore it to her wedding."

Sabrina studied Darla. "Do you want to talk about it?"

"There's nothing to talk about. I think our customers just aren't looking for gowns that are quite so vintage."

"I meant do you want to talk about your wedding? Or anything else?"

Darla shook her head. "There won't be a wedding. For one thing, Sidney and I have decided to remain simply friends."

"And Judah?"

"Judah and I have a complicated situation. We're

still trying to figure out how to say hello to each other without feeling awkward."

"Is there anything I can do?"

Darla shook her head again. "I don't think so. Callahans are different types to deal with, as I'm sure you know."

Sabrina smiled. "It's true."

"Do you think you and Jonas will ever—"

"No." Sabrina shook her own head. "You and Judah do not have the market cornered on awkward."

Darla smiled. "Why that makes me feel better, I don't know."

"Misery loves company."

Sabrina hung the gown in her closet, closing it away. Darla fancied she could still hear the lovely song of its allure calling to her. It was like looking at a sparkling diamond a woman dreamed of one day owning—

"Oh!" Darla jumped to her feet. "I'm sorry to cut this short. I just remembered something I have to do."

Sabrina nodded. "Judah's in the bunkhouse. And if you change your mind about the dress, it'll be here, ready to go on short notice."

"Thanks," Darla said, thinking that short notice and her wedding would never go together. She'd learned about being hasty—and next time, if there ever was a next time she planned a wedding, she was taking the long route.

"So then what did she say?" Jonas asked. Sam was glued to Rafe's every word. They sat around the Scrabble board, but they weren't playing. Judah was nowhere to be found. There were chores that had to be done—ASAP—but at the moment, Jonas and Sam were spellbound by Rafe's bungling of the Darla Problem.

"She said she didn't want to marry me or Judah," Rafe said. "She was pretty definite about it, too."

"Judah's going to kill you," Sam said. "You were supposed to help Darla see that Judah is the only man for her."

"She doesn't think like most women," Rafe said in his defense. "She's pretty independent. And I think Judah annoys her fiercely."

"What does that have to do with anything?" Jonas demanded. "We don't care if she's annoyed. We care that she takes Judah off our hands and keeps him forever."

"It was scary," Rafe said. "For a minute, I thought she was going to take me up on my offer." He shuddered. "I don't think Judah understands how thin a thread he's hanging by with Darla."

"This isn't good." Jonas considered the information about Judah's precarious nuptials. "We could talk to Fiona, tell her that the lovebirds are planning to get a divorce *inmediatamente*. That would frost her cookies. I think that falls under the heading of no fake marriages, and puts him out of contention for the ranch. She won't be happy."

Sam swallowed. "I've got to have a fake marriage if I play the game. I'm never letting a woman lead me around by the nose."

Rafe sighed. "If you don't think that women are doing that every day of your life already, you're dumb."

Sam sniffed. "Well, we can't tell Fiona. She'd just throw a party. That's her answer for everything. Party, party. It's her stress buster."

"Any news on the filing?" Jonas asked. "What's the update on our legal status?"

Sam shrugged. "We could stand for Judah to get

married and populate this joint. If we had a small city of kiddies here, maybe we could make a case that we are the people. The people would be best served by us keeping the ranch and opening an elementary school for the community. Something like that, anyway."

Rafe straightened. "That's a great idea. We need an elementary school. I like kids. I like school bells. Let's build a school with a school bell!"

Jonas sighed. "Let's not put the bell before the babies, all right? First we have to get Judah to slide over home plate."

"Yeah," Rafe said, "and since he told me I could marry the mother of his children, I'm pretty sure he's not in love. It would stand to reason."

"Yeah," Sam agreed. "You wouldn't even need a lawyer to make that case. If I was in love with a woman, I wouldn't let any of you fatheads near her. Probably not even to offer her a glass of water."

"You're selfish, though," Jonas said. "Maybe Judah is more generous."

His brothers blew a collective raspberry at him.

"Judah's not in love," Sam said, "or he would have kicked Rafe's ass when he told him he was going to pop the question to Darla."

"Yeah," Rafe said, "and my ass is un-kicked. It's depressing."

"Look at that," Jonas said, waving at his brothers to come to the bunkhouse window. "Darla just came out of the house. She's heading this way." He glanced at Rafe. "Suppose she's changed her mind about you?"

"Hide me," Rafe said. "She's got a gleam in her eye that doesn't bode well."

"Where's Judah?" Jonas asked. "We need him front and center to catch this incoming fireball."

"Probably in the tub with his rubber ducky. How would I know?" Sam asked.

"Let's sneak out the back," Jonas said. "They'll find their way to each other eventually, and I don't want to be in the path of love."

"Or not," Rafe said. "Last one out the back door has to tell Fiona we screwed up Judah's life."

The brothers did their best Three Stooges impersonation getting out the door. Judah heard the back door slam, looked out his bedroom window in time to see the trio of siblings running for the barn.

"Immature," he muttered, pulling on a shirt. "Always competing."

"Judah?" a female voice called, and he grinned. *I knew that little gal couldn't resist me.*

"Hi," he said, framing himself in the bedroom doorway. "Little Red Riding Hood must be looking for her wolf," he said, taking Darla by the hand and tugging her into his room. He locked the door. "Lucky for you, I just happen to be *very* hungry."

Chapter Ten

"Very funny." Darla swallowed her unease. "I'll wait out in the den."

"Don't be scared. I'll be good to you. No biting."

Warily, she removed her hand from his. She hesitated to be anyplace that contained Judah and a bed, but he was hardly going to jump on her and eat her like a chocolate bunny. As he said, no biting.

"I brought you this," she said, trying not to look at him as she set his ring on the nightstand. She glanced around, curious in spite of herself. His bunkhouse room was sparsely furnished, but he kept it neat. The quilt on the bed was vintage, a beautiful patchwork pattern that must have taken months. Someone had cared deeply about the project. But Darla could hardly pay attention to the room's decor when Judah's shirt was open and he was zipping up his work jeans. She wished she hadn't accepted his invitation to enter his lair.

Bedroom. It was just four walls. Four walls and a bed where they could be together.

There was a time she'd dreamed of nothing more.

"I'm not marrying you, Judah," Darla said, and he grinned at her, a slow, confident grin that unsettled her and got her off her planned script.

"I got that part." He jerked his head toward the ring. "Rafe talk you out of it?"

"No." Darla frowned. "Did you want him to?"

He shrugged. "Only if you could be talked out of marrying me. I knew you wouldn't say yes to him. He's too wild and woolly for a straight-laced little mama like you."

She raised her brows. "You're not exactly tame yourself."

"But the difference is," Judah said, sitting on the bed to pull on his boots, "I'm willing to be tamed."

"I'm pretty sure every single woman in this town has set her cap for you at one time or another," Darla said, "and you've never been available for more than a one-night stand. Two nights at the most, according to gossip."

Judah grinned. "I wouldn't pay attention to gossip, darlin'. This town loves to talk, but talk's cheap."

"It may be cheap," Darla said, "but it's usually pretty much on the money."

He laughed. "Let's just say I'm trying to mend my ways, then."

"Anyway," Darla said, "let's go back to being the way we were before we ever…you know. Next time I talk to you—"

"I'll be a father?" He winked. "I think you're going about this all wrong, sweetheart."

"What do you mean?"

He leaned back, lounging on the bed. "This Dear John business. It's premature."

She edged toward the door, not trusting the look in his eyes, which had turned distinctly predatory. "How so?"

"Usually a Dear John letter is reserved for people

who are breaking up, which implies that there was a relationship of some sort. We have no relationship. I would suggest, therefore, that you don't know what you're missing out on."

She blinked, trying to follow his thought process. "What exactly *am* I missing out on?"

He moved off the bed and took her in his arms. "Let me show you what you're trying to write off, babe."

She could feel warmth, and strength, and full-on sex appeal radiating from him. It made her weak in the knees, faint in the heart. The problem was, she'd always been in love with this man. She couldn't remember a time she'd ever wanted someone else. He ran his hands along her forearms up to her shoulders and she froze, mesmerized by his touch. She had no wish to escape him; she'd wanted to be in his arms for too many years. "This isn't a good idea."

"We don't know that it's a bad idea, either."

He kissed her on the lips, and she melted into his embrace. It hadn't been a dream; she hadn't imagined the overwhelming passion that swept her when he held her. At some point, she wondered why she was bothering to fight him when she wanted to be with him so much.

It was something about pride, she reminded herself, and not wanting to trap him. But it felt as if he was trying to entice *her* into a trap. "Judah," she said, breaking away from his kiss, "parenthood isn't a good reason to marry."

"It's not the worst reason. Ships have been launched because of babies, fiefdoms have risen and fallen. I say you let me kiss you for a while before we try to solve the world's big questions. Let's just figure out if you even like kissing me before you Dear John me." He slipped his hands along her waist, holding her against him. "You'd hate to kick yourself later for giving away a very good thing."

He was so darn confident that he held all the keys to her heart. Darla supposed he was like this with every woman. "Maybe the only way to prove that you're not as irresistible as you think you are is to prove you wrong."

"I'll take that dare," Judah said. "What time do you have to open the shop?"

She looked at him, her blood racing. "What difference does that make? You just kissed me, and I can live without it," she fibbed outrageously. "There's nothing between us that neither of us can't live without."

"I never said that," Judah said, "and you need to stop thinking so hard, my jittery little bride. I haven't even begun to kiss you."

TWO HOURS LATER, Darla opened her eyes. "Oh, no!" she exclaimed, trying to leap from the bed, where Judah had seduced her until she was nothing but a boneless mush of crazy-for-him. He lay entangled with her so that she couldn't free herself from him, possessive even in sleep. He'd made her gasp with pleasure, cry out with delight, and then the man slept practically on top of her, assuring himself that she wouldn't get away without him knowing. She tried to move his big arms and legs off her, and he opened sleepy eyes, grinning at her.

"Move, Judah," she said, pushing at him. "I'm late to open the store!"

"Bad girl," he said, running a lazy hand over her hip. "Have the customers been waiting long?" he asked, kissing her shoulder.

"An hour." She felt his sneaky hand caress her backside, slip a finger inside her. She pushed at him with a little less enthusiasm, and he licked at one of her nipples, teasing it into instant hardness.

"Ready to tear up that Dear John letter yet?" he murmured.

"No," she said with determination. "Just because we had sex does not mean we're right for each other, Judah."

"Hmm," he murmured. "Clearly I have more convincing to do. The customers will have to wait while I plead my case."

He pressed her into the sheets, kissing her, torturing her with sexy passion, giving her no room for thinking of anything but him. Darla felt herself giving in once again. He knew exactly what he was doing to her.

The problem was, she didn't know if she worked the same magic on him.

"WHAT IF THERE'S no such thing as forever?" Darla asked Jackie that afternoon. "What if forever is just smoke and mirrors?"

Jackie glanced at her as she put away hand-beaded garters. "If you're talking about being audited, I'd say forever would be a real pain and I would hate it. I'd break the mirror and blow the smoke away."

Darla wrinkled her nose. "Forever as in marriage."

"Sometimes you have to throw caution to the wind. We sell the prepackaging to the dream here." Jackie waved a hand around the room. "We never thought we'd be so successful when we were planning this little adventure. We said, 'let's give it a shot and see how dumb we are to give up a good job, and try to sell dreams in a bad economy.'"

Darla nodded. "We did jump off a cliff without knowing what was beneath us."

Jackie nodded. "Marriage is the same thing."

Darla stared at her. "Does Pete know you feel like this? That you just took a leap of faith?"

"He took a leap of faith, too. I think it's harder for guys." Jackie giggled. "They don't know if we're going to decorate with lace doilies and leopard-skin rugs. They don't know if we're going to cook for them, or if we can. When Pete married me, he knew little about my cooking and less about how I might decorate. And then there's the biggest question of all."

Darla's eyes went wide. "Do men have all these deep thoughts? Or do they just dive in and hope it goes well?" Judah was probably a "diver." He didn't seem interested in her cooking or decorating. "What's the super-question?"

"Whether we're going to give them a lot of sex after marriage, or if we're just trying to drag them to the altar with lassos of lust."

Darla blinked. "They worry about that?"

Jackie shrugged. "It's a fact that there's a lot more nookie going on in the beginning than later. But that could be for any number of reasons, not necessarily lack of enthusiasm on the female's part."

"Have you been reading these bride magazines?" Darla sank onto a cabbage rose-printed sofa. "I don't think Judah worries too much about lovemaking."

"Because he's in romance mode right now. But on a subconscious level, he's figured out whether he wants to make love to you all the time, and if you'd like it. They like enthusiasm, too."

"Gee," Darla said, "all I was worried about was whether there was such a thing as forever."

"You're thinking romantically. Guys think logically.

With their need barometer." Jackie giggled. "The comforts of hearth, home, kitchen, bed."

Darla liked being in bed with Judah—too much, if anything. "But there has to be more."

"Not for men. They don't get caught up in the fairy tale. It's pretty cut-and-dried."

"It doesn't sound very romantic."

"A moment ago you were wondering if forever was practical. It's not an illusion if both people have the same goals." Jackie laid some white gloves in the case. "Have you ever listened to the brides who come in here? They never talk about how wonderful their guys are. They talk about the dress, the flowers, the cake. Nothing that lasts."

"That's true," Darla said.

"They're in love with the icing," Jackie said, "when they should be focused on the cake."

"I don't remember you being so focused," Darla said. "When did this happen?"

"After I let Pete sweep me off my feet." She smiled. "You should let Judah sweep you. Trust me, it's a whole lot of fun to be romanced by your man."

Jackie and Pete had gotten married after Jackie had a surprise pregnancy. Pete appeared to be gaga over his bride—still.

"Even with three newborns, the romance is—"

"Hotter than a pistol." Jackie closed the cabinet. "I wouldn't worry about forever so much, Darla. I'd be enjoying my nights, if I was you. And coming in late every once in a while is a good thing, too. I can cover opening the store."

Darla blushed, wondering if Jackie knew that she hadn't been late because she'd overslept. Darla never overslept. "I can't think about anything else when he makes love to me," she admitted. "I'm holding out to see if we have anything in common that's not physical, but I'm not sure I'm going to be any good at telling him no. I gave Sabrina the magic wedding dress back, and then I found myself in bed with Judah. And it was wonderful."

"You *are* running in place, aren't you?"

Darla blinked. "You're right. I need a new plan."

Chapter Eleven

Darla called Judah that night and told him she was rescinding her offer of a marriage of convenience.

"Good," Judah said. "I'll be right over."

He hung up. Darla stared at the phone for a moment before racing to brush her hair. She should have anticipated him jumping the gun! She'd meant to tell him that she'd decided that they should wait to get married until after the children were born, when they'd had time to get to know each other better—and naturally, he'd drawn the conclusion he preferred.

Which was pretty much how it always was with Judah.

When she opened the door to him, she redoubled her vow to stick to the plan: no-nonsense laying out of the rules. It wouldn't be easy with him looking like a dark renegade cowboy ready to ravish her at any moment. She hadn't changed out of the comfy, dark gray sweat bottoms and pink polka-dotted halter maternity top, and still he looked at her as if she were edible.

"Tonight we lay everything on the table," Darla said.

"I'm all about tables," Judah said, "and I'm glad you're loosening up a bit. Let me show you what tables are best for, love."

And then to her shock, and beyond her wildest imaginings, Judah made love to her on the beautiful antique dining table where she usually laid out holiday dinners. "I'm afraid I'm too heavy for you," she whispered as he carefully placed her over him. He said, "No, baby. You're just right." And it was completely all right.

She felt like a million dollars as she collapsed with delicious shivers in Judah's arms.

"NO MORE OF THAT," Darla said, after the storm of lovemaking had abated. "We have to talk." She picked up her panties from the floor, collected her sweatpants from a chair and her halter top from the fruit bowl. Her sweats had been far too easy for Judah to take off—*she'd* been too easy. Far too much so.

He grinned. "I know talking is important, but I've always preferred action. I speak better with my hands."

She backed away from his dark appeal. "It doesn't surprise me that you would say that."

"Anyway," he said, "I can't really talk on an empty stomach. Can what you have to say wait until we eat?"

"Eat? At eight o'clock at night?"

He grinned. "Yeah. If this is a girlie chat, you really want me to have a full stomach."

"Girlie chat?" Outraged, she said, "First, just because you're near a table, Judah, doesn't mean all your needs have to be satisfied. Second—"

He kissed her to interrupt her, and pulled her close as he leaned back against the table. "Now, listen, missus, when you *are* my missus, I'll expect you in nothing but an apron, until my children are old enough to know that their mom is a dedicated nudie. Once the kiddos are off to college, you can return to cooking for me in the buff." Kissing her neck, he massaged her bottom, holding her tightly against him. "Questions?"

When she tried to open her mouth to give him the scolding of his life, he kissed her until she was breathless. He sighed, enjoying her quivering with rage. "Your limo driver will be here in about ten minutes. My guess is you'll want to change."

Darla's ire was drowned out by curiosity. "Limo driver?"

Judah released her, waving a negligent hand. "Or coachman. Whatever you romantic gals prefer to call them. I think they were called coachmen in the fairy tale, but they were mice first, and I thought ladies didn't like rodents and things. However, we will be attended by a first-rate rodent tonight."

Darla stared at Judah, wondering what kind of loose cannon had fathered her children. "What in the world are you talking about?"

The doorbell rang, and Judah bowed. "Better get your gown on, Cinderella. It's time for the ball."

"Ball?"

"Our date." Judah grinned. "Every woman wants to be swept off her little glass slippers, doesn't she? Though again, you'll have to forgive the rodent who's driving us." He flung open her front door. "She's not quite ready, bro," he said to Rafe, who walked in wearing some kind of chauffeur's uniform, or maybe a pilot's. Darla wondered what was going on. Rafe had proposed to her in sort of a bee-in-Judah's-eye way not twenty-four hours ago—why was he here now?

"Women are slow to get ready," Judah told Rafe. "And this one wanted to talk first," he said in a loud whisper to his brother.

Darla's gaze jumped to Judah, assessing whether he was trying hard to be a jackass, or if it just came naturally.

She decided it was the most natural thing in the world to him.

Rafe tipped his hat. "Can you hurry it up a bit, Darla? You look lovely the way you are, but I booked a flight plan, and there's a certain window of opportunity I should probably follow."

"Shh," Judah said, "don't give her too many details. She argues when she has detail overload." He went over and kissed Darla. "Hurry, darling, the rodent gets nervous around midnight. He has a phobia about leaving on time."

She opened her mouth to argue, but Judah had claimed she liked to argue, so she really had no choice except to go into her room to examine her options.

There weren't many, she decided, as she tossed off the sweats and took a quick rinse. She wanted to talk, and Judah had left the door open for that. All he wanted to do was eat, he claimed, and though she had some organic veggies in the fridge, she sensed that wasn't what he had in mind. She slipped into a casual dress and tied her blonde hair up in a ponytail. Maybe this was his boneheaded way of being romantic. Judah probably didn't understand that a man didn't barge into a woman's house, ravish her on the dining room table and then announce he wanted to eat.

Yet it sounded romantic, as if Judah had put some thought into whatever his plan was. She slipped on some high heels—it would help her look him almost in the eye when she told him *no* the next time he tried to undress her. Had Rafe said something about a flight plan?

She went back into the den.

"Five minutes flat," Rafe said to Judah. "Dude, you can't do better than a girl who can beautify in five minutes."

Judah's gaze went from Darla's face to her dress, then slowly made its way up again. He grinned at her, and Darla knew instinctively he was thinking *dessert*.

She blushed. Or maybe *she'd* thought it.

"Come on," Rafe said, laughing. "There's so much electricity in this room there's going to be a fire."

Judah opened the door for her, and they left. She went to the Callahan family van, which was apparently serving as the limo tonight.

As soon as Rafe opened the door for her and Judah, she heard giggles and squeals.

"We're going to Chicago!" Sabrina exclaimed, and Darla saw that Jonas was in the back with her. "This is my sister, Seton," Sabrina said. "Seton, this is Darla Cameron, who is engaged to Judah." Sabrina smiled as Rafe took his place behind the wheel, next to her, completely missing the uncomfortable look on Darla's face. Judah slipped in next to Darla and whispered, "Are you okay with this?"

"Almost," she said. "Let me get over the shock."

He squeezed her shoulders gently. "I thought you might enjoy something fun."

No one else could hear Judah over the light jazz music softly playing and the excited chatter in the van, but Darla noted the kindness in his tone and realized he'd been acting like a rascal in her house just to bait her, knowing he had a romantic evening all planned, which delighted her. Dessert in Chicago would be so much fun.

And it was so much better than talking.

In fact, just about everything Judah wanted to do was better than talking. She sent a sidelong glance his way, enjoying him laughing as the girls teased him, and Rafe and Jonas ribbed him about being a worse date than he was a bull rider. And before long Darla felt herself falling for her man of action.

She'd fallen, she realized, completely under his spell. It was too late to do anything but enjoy the ride.

"YOU SHOULDN'T HAVE LET her get away from you like that," Bode Jenkins said, over a gin and tonic that same evening. Sidney Tunstall shrugged his shoulders, not certain what difference it made to one of the wealthiest ranchers in these parts whether he got married or not.

It made a huge difference to Bode. He intended to make certain the nuptials of Darla and Judah never happened. If there was one way to thwart Fiona—and he knew all about her little plan to grow her own zip code—it was to derail this wedding. "Your inheritance is all tied up in you getting married, and as the executor of your grandfather's estate, I have to make certain everything is proper." He gave Sidney a pensive look. "Who are you going to marry, since you've let Darla get away?"

Sidney shrugged. "I don't know."

"You have only another month before it all goes to charity." Bode shook his head. "It sure would be a shame to lose out on a couple million bucks."

Sidney shrugged again, not happy about the situation, but not fighting it, either. "That's just pocket change to some people, I guess. I lived without it before, and I can keep living without it."

Bode slammed a palm down on the mahogany table, one of the few nice furnishings he'd bothered to splurge on for his home. Julie had insisted on it. Lately, she'd been decorating a lot, despite his propensity to groan over the money spent. "You younger generation don't know what money is. I wouldn't let a penny get away from me, much less two million." Bode considered the man across from him. "You don't throw away a fortune, son."

"Under the parameters it was left to me, I can." Sidney straightened. "There's nothing wrong with waiting until I find the woman I love, Mr. Jenkins. And in a world where people now live to be a hundred, being a thirty-five-year-old bachelor isn't an emergency."

"Well, your grandfather thought you were dragging your feet. That's all I know." Bode shrugged, wondering how he could get the good doc to get off the dime and grab Darla away from that wild-eyed Callahan. Fiona's nephew had just stormed in there and thrown Sidney off the train, and apparently put stars of romance in Darla Cameron's eyes. He'd heard all about that from her mother, Mavis, who was the silliest, most cotton-headed woman he'd ever met. It was all love-this, and love-that, and Bode'd had it to the back teeth with all the Callahans and their ability to get everything they wanted. "If you liked Darla, why'd you surrender your ground, son?"

"Because I liked her," Sidney said, "I didn't love her. And she didn't love me."

"I see," Bode said thoughtfully. "You were going to take the money and run."

"No," Sidney said, showing a flash of temper, "I was going to take the money that was left to me, and be a husband to Darla and a father to her children. That's what the plan was."

"And you were never going to divorce?"

Sidney looked at him. "I suppose no one could ever say never, but I don't know why anybody would want to give up Darla. She's a nice lady."

Bode blinked, lit a cigar. "I do not understand your lack of competitiveness."

"I don't understand your thirst for it, so we're square." Sidney looked at Bode. "Is there anything else you need, Mr. Jenkins? I should probably be out looking for another wife, don't you think?" He said it sarcastically, and Bode caught that, but what he also caught was the *angle*.

"It will be hard to get another so quickly," Bode said, "one who has so much going for her. A man can find a woman anywhere, they're like fleas on a dog. But a good woman is tougher to find."

"Not exactly, Mr. Jenkins," Sidney said, getting his gentleman's ire up, which was just what Bode was hoping for. "They're nothing like fleas on a dog."

"Now, now, what I meant was that they are numerous, but not necessarily quality."

"I don't know what you meant, but it sounded pretty demeaning to me."

Bode laughed. "I never remarried after I lost my wife, Sidney. I think I know the value of a good woman."

Sidney looked at him, not appeased.

"Now, take my daughter, Julie—"

Sidney stood. "I'll find my own wife, Mr. Jenkins, if it's all the same to you."

Bode nodded. "Well, be quick about it. I'm very eager to write this check out to you instead of a charity. To be honest, I don't think much of charities, Sidney. I'm not certain that all that lovely money ever gets to the deserving folks who need it."

Sidney, white knight that he was, looked outraged. "There are many charities that do necessary, vital work."

"Yes, and it would be better in your pocket where

you could decide on the charities of your choice. I'm not much for charity, as I said."

Sidney stared at him. "Are you trying to say that you decide where the money goes, if not to me?"

Bode pretended surprise. "Who else would?"

"My grandfather left no directive?"

Bode shook his head. "Nope. He figured you'd want the money badly enough to find your way to an altar, son. So maybe you ought to rethink letting Darla go, since the two of you had this nice little thing worked out."

Sidney sighed. "Tell me again how my grandfather came to choose you to be the executor of his estate?"

"Business, Sidney. We did business together. You might say we understood each other's world view, to a certain extent. And we went to school together, so we went back a long ways. He knew he could trust me."

Sidney looked at him a long time. "You're not trying to jump this will, are you, Mr. Jenkins?"

Bode grinned at him. "Sidney, from where you sit, two million dollars is a world of money. You can do a lot of good with it. You can have a nice house, send your kids to college. But for me, now, because I never let a penny go that had my name on it—unless Julie makes me—two million is good money, but it's not going to change my standard of life."

"I'm not sure you have a standard."

"That's where you're wrong." Bode smiled. "Your grandfather was a good man. And I always honor my friends."

Sidney put his hat on. "Thanks for the drink."

Bode nodded. "By the way, I have my doubts about Darla and Judah working out."

Sidney stopped. "What do you mean?"

"A little bird told me that they're planning to divorce as soon as the children are born. Now if you ask me," Bode said, his gaze sad, "that's a crying shame."

"I don't believe you."

"Ask Darla," Bode said, and Sidney said, "I will."

He closed the door.

Bode grinned and hummed a wedding march.

"It was a lovely evening, Judah," Darla said at her front door when the "limo" returned her home. "Thank you."

"My pleasure," Judah said. "My truck's here, so I can leave, but of course, I can also stay if you want company."

Darla thought about the dining table and how she'd never be able to eat there again without remembering Judah loving her into a delirious frenzy. "It's been a long day. I have to be up early."

He nodded. "I understand."

She wondered if he understood something she wasn't necessarily saying. "Judah, why did you really plan the surprise trip tonight?"

He shrugged. "We haven't ever dated, for one thing, and for another, I'm kind of hoping that tomorrow will be the day we get married."

A truck door slammed, and Sidney appeared.

"Hello, Darla," he said. "Judah."

She glanced at Judah, then at Sidney. "What are you doing here, Sidney?"

"Just feeling a bit wistful. Tomorrow's supposed to be our big day," he said. "Hope you don't mind me saying so, Callahan."

"Not at all," Judah said, "but I guess this is awkward. You two probably have things to discuss. Plans to end."

"Actually, I need to talk to both of you," Darla said.

Chapter Twelve

Darla seated her beaus on the sofa, gave them some tea, wondered if she should serve something stronger. They looked at her expectantly.

"Sidney," she began, "you and I were making a deal when we agreed to get married. That wasn't fair to you."

"I was okay with it," Sidney said. "I still need a wife. In a really bad way."

"There's a lot of women running around Diablo," Judah said helpfully. "Let me introduce you to some."

"I like this one," Sidney said, and Darla could tell he was baiting Judah.

"And Judah," she said, "there are some things between us that make me nervous. The condom prank, for one thing, which you never told me about. We shouldn't even be in this position." She took a deep breath. "I'm still in shock that I'm having twins."

"I'm a Callahan," Judah said. "Magic happens for us."

"Awkward," Sidney said. "And as a doctor, may I remind you that the female is responsible for some of the genetic coding?"

Judah shrugged. "But babies by the bunch are what we do at Rancho Diablo."

He said it in a *top that!* tone, and Darla sighed.

"Also," she said, "Sidney wasn't honest with you about your concussion."

Judah looked at Sidney. "Tunstall, you're a dirty dog. You made me think I'd cracked my nut. Did I even have a scratch?"

Sidney shrugged. "Perhaps there was something minor. Maybe." He sighed. "No. But I saved you from yourself. You needed to be here, with Darla, figuring out your future."

"You see," Judah said, "he's a gentleman, if not a good M.D."

Sidney shrugged again. "Whatever. I've had crankier patients."

"So," Darla said, interrupting their digging at each other, "this is my dilemma."

"No," Judah said. "You're having *my* children. There is no dilemma. We will find Sidney an appropriate bride of his own. I'll lend him my tux, but nothing else."

Sidney put his palms up in surrender. "I'm thinner than you, so the tux wouldn't fit. However, I can see that Darla has made up her mind—"

"I haven't made up my mind," Darla said quickly, feeling bad for Sidney, "because what I'm trying to tell both of you is that none of this started out right with either one of you."

"I don't care how it started out," Judah said. "I'm pretty happy with how things are proceeding. But if Sidney tries to marry the mother of my children, I'll give *him* a concussion he won't forget."

"He probably would." Sidney stood, went to the door. "He's a caveman, Darla. And I'm a gentleman. But ladies have always been attracted to bad boys. I know when I'm beat."

"That's right," Judah said, and Darla glowered at him.

"You're not beat, Sidney," she said softly, "but he is a caveman."

"I just took you to Chicago," Judah protested.

Sidney kissed Darla on the forehead. "You guys have a lot to work out. I'll shove off."

"Both of you shove off," Darla said in annoyance. "I think you two have a lot to work out."

"What?" Judah asked. "You can't expect us to be best friends. We're both too manly for that."

"It's hard competing for a woman," Sidney said. "So I'll have to agree with him."

"Both of you go," Darla said. "Now."

They looked at her, neither one happy.

"And don't come back until you've resolved your issues. I'm not having any hard feelings over a day that should be the happiest of my life."

"But—" Judah started, and Sidney said, "All right."

"Now, look here," Judah said, "this game of yours of always being Mr. Nice is tiresome. I can be nice, too."

Sidney shrugged. "If you own that emotion, own it. No one's standing in your way."

Judah frowned. "He's not going to fight fair," he complained to Darla. "I don't trust skinny bronc busters. He's already tried to put one over on me about my nonexistent concussion."

"That was your own fault," Sidney said righteously. "Even you should know if you bumped your head or not."

"I've had other things on my mind," Judah said with a growl Darla's way.

"Good night," she said, closing the door on both of them.

"What about tomorrow?" Judah called through the door.

"Tomorrow is another day," Darla told herself, and went to bed alone, already wishing Judah was there to hold her in his arms.

"WE'RE GOING TO have to be careful," Sidney said. "She might find another guy to marry."

"What are you talking about?" Judah wondered if the top of his head was about to blow off. Was the doc crazy? In Judah's opinion, Darla loved no one but him—even if she hadn't realized it herself yet.

"If she has to choose between us," Sidney said reasonably, "she might opt for a third party."

They leaned against Judah's truck, chatting under the dark night sky as if discussing the stars. Judah grunted. "I'm not worried. I wouldn't let that happen."

"She's suffering with a guilt complex where you're concerned, so you might not have a say in the matter. Guilt doesn't make for an easy path to the altar."

Judah didn't care. "I'm getting her to the altar tomorrow. I have the rest of our lives to let her make up to me for all that guilt she's worried about."

"I don't know if that's the proper approach."

"You're my shrink now? My love doctor?"

"Someone's got to do it," Sidney said. "Look, I don't mind helping you, but I'm in a ditch. I need her, too. So don't push me."

"What's your deal?" Judah asked. "What's it going to take to get you convinced that Darla is not the bride you want? Because frankly, you're not going to have her."

"Remember I was first," Sidney said. "That flower arch in her backyard has my name on it, so to speak."

"What flower arch?" Judah's head turned like it was on a swivel. "I don't see an arch."

"Notice that all the little elves have been busy while you were chasing romance in Chicago."

In his haste to try to get past Darla's front door tonight, he hadn't noticed the lanterns strung along her porch, and candles wrapped with pink ribbons along the drive. "Okay, what's the plan? I'm open to suggestions right now. Because she returned the ring to me. And I heard she gave Sabrina some stupid magic wedding dress, not that I believe in magic." Judah thought about the wild horses that ran across the far reaches of Rancho Diablo. They hadn't been seen in a while. Maybe good luck had left him behind. "I do believe in magic," he said after a moment, "and right now, I need some."

"Yeah, me, too." Sidney nodded. "I was sent here tonight to break you two up."

Judah didn't let himself show his surprise. "So you're the villain in my fairy tale."

"There's nothing Bode Jenkins would rather see more than you and Darla calling things off."

"Over my cold dead body will that happen."

Sidney nodded. "I thought so. Anyway, that's why I came over tonight. Hope I haven't confused matters between you and Darla."

"What do you mean?"

Sidney shrugged. "Just in case she's in there right now having second thoughts. Third thoughts."

"She's not."

"Bode's determined to get at your family. I should probably keep my mouth shut, considering he holds some of my purse strings at the moment, but he's playing foul."

"Look," Judah said, "I don't know how to help you with your problem. I wish I did. But don't let Bode talk you into a wedding you don't want."

"Yeah," Sidney said, almost reluctantly. "I don't want it. And Darla doesn't love me, either. She's always loved you."

"Not me," Judah said, and Sidney said, "Yes, you. You're the only one who doesn't know it."

Judah blinked, considered whether Sidney knew what he was talking about or was trying to dig himself out of a pounding courtesy of Judah's big fists. "Did Darla tell you that?"

Sidney got in his truck. "You'll have to find out on your own. I've done all the repairs on my conscience I intend to. I'll be here tomorrow, waiting to move in if you don't do the job properly, though. And if you don't mind, keep this conversation under your big hat. I don't want Bode deciding to claim my inheritance. You have a trustworthy aunt who oversaw your affairs. Bode is a different proposition altogether."

Judah tipped his hat. "Be here with your tux on," he said. "I need a best man, and you'll fit the bill just fine."

Sidney looked at him. "Are we inviting gossip?"

"Just letting everyone know that the bride's a smart lady. She's got good taste in men. And you can show Bode he doesn't own you."

"He does, in a way, but that's out of my control now." Sidney backed his truck up. "Let me know if you come across an extra bride."

"By chance have you ever met Diane, Aberdeen's sister? She's not exactly looking for marriage, but you might change her mind. Anyway, good luck." He waved, and when the doctor's truck had disappeared, he marched to Darla's bedroom window. He tapped and a moment later she appeared, looking none too pleased to see him.

"Judah! What are you doing?" she asked through the glass.

"Serenading you."

She slid the window open. "Go away."

"I can't. We have to talk."

"So talk."

"Let me in, Darla."

She shook her head. "Not a chance, buster."

"What is it?" he asked, his voice innocent. "What's got my bride thinking less than happy thoughts the night before her wedding?"

"I'm not getting married tomorrow," Darla said, "even though everyone is conspiring to make it happen."

"I got blood drawn. I'm ready to rock," Judah said. "It looks like the decorating is done, and you've got a dress. We can go get a marriage license in the morning, and be ready to say 'I do' at sundown."

She shook her head. "I'm not a girl who rushes in to things."

Judah put his hands on the window ledge and hauled himself into Darla's bedroom. "Whew, I'm getting too old for this," he said. "I hope you plan on being a more agreeable wife than you are a fiancée."

"I'm not your fiancée. And you're not supposed to be in here." Darla closed the window and pointed a finger toward the den. "Go out there if you want to talk."

"It's dangerous for you out there, too," Judah said. "I like variety."

She didn't reply, but he could tell she wasn't exactly rejecting his suit. "So back to this guilt thing," he said. "I don't care if Creed's stupid condoms failed. I'm going to have the most beautiful babies in the world. And I don't care about Doc trying to give me the shove. I like him. He's entitled to want the most beautiful woman in

Diablo, too. So," Judah said, crossing to take her face between his hands, "can we put all this guilt business behind us? Because you really, really want to marry me, and frankly, putting me back out in the stream to be fished by other ladies is a move you'd always regret."

Darla closed her eyes, allowing herself to relax in his grasp. "Let's sleep on it. I'm too tired to think tonight."

"I've waited a long time to hear that. Come on, love, let me put you to bed."

He pulled Darla toward the bed, pressing her down into the sheets. He lay down next to her, tugging her up against him spoon-style, and rubbed her back until she fell asleep. Once she was breathing deeply and he could tell she was out like a light, he cupped a palm under her tummy—under his boys—and fell asleep himself, feeling like a million bucks.

Chapter Thirteen

Darla would have liked to pretend that she surrendered, but when she stood at the altar the next evening after a whirlwind of last-minute preparations, she knew she was marrying Judah because she'd always dreamed of it. Whatever they were letting themselves in for, he was going to be her husband, and she was going to be Mrs. Judah Callahan, exactly what she'd always wanted.

She wasn't strong enough to resist her dreams another day. She couldn't imagine not marrying him. In that, Judah was egotistically right: she didn't want to return him to the dating pond for other women to catch. She wanted him all to herself.

Maybe he wasn't the marrying kind, but she had to take a chance that he was.

Everyone was happy, smiling at the wedding. The evening was lovely, the air sweetened with romance. Judah was breathtakingly handsome and sexy; she couldn't believe he was actually going to be hers.

"Are you ready?" Jackie asked, coming to her side.

Darla nodded. "Thanks for being my maid of honor."

"I'm happy to have a sister." Jackie hugged her. "Judah's out there pacing. If we don't get you down the aisle, he's going to come get you."

Darla smiled. He'd been gone this morning when

she'd awakened, but he'd left a note on her pillow telling her that she was the luckiest woman in the world, and she'd always be the envy of every other woman in town.

Typical Judah.

"I'm ready," Darla said.

"Just a small warning," Jackie said, "so you won't be surprised. Bode's here."

"I didn't invite him." The news did nothing to calm her nerves.

"Bode is like the troll that no one ever invites, but he manages to hang around. I vote ignore him, and completely ruin his day. Fiona told him that if he did one thing to upset you, she'd have him tied to a cactus. And I won't tell you what Judah said about it."

Darla felt better. "Let's hurry before something bad happens. I distinctly feel an urge to speed this along."

Jackie waved to Diane, who was in charge of overseeing the music. Diane motioned for the harpist to begin, and serene music filtered through the air, joined by a traditional piano wedding march. Darla took a deep breath and headed down the aisle as Diane's little daughters scattered rose petals from white baskets along her path.

Judah was smiling at her, eating her up with his eyes as she walked to the beautiful altar. An excited tingle shot up her spine. This sexy man was about to tell the world that he was making her his wife. It was all her dreams come true.

A shot rang out, and in front of Darla's horrified eyes, Judah fell back against Sidney, who helped him to the ground. Guests cried out, scattering, and the wedding march ground to a halt. The little flower girls ran to Diane, and suddenly, Darla was grabbed by big strong Callahans and dragged away from the altar—and Judah.

She protested, wanting to be at his side, but Sam held her back, keeping her out of danger.

Darla shrugged Sam off and ran to Judah's side. She could hear Sidney calling for an ambulance as he worked to stop the bleeding in Judah's arm.

"Judah," she said, kneeling down next to him, despite the hands trying to pull her back, "don't you *dare* die on me!"

He gave her a weak smile. "I've been shot before. This is just a flesh wound. Don't get my babies all upset over nothing."

"How do you know it's a flesh wound? Sidney, is it a flesh wound?" She didn't wait for an answer. Her heart was painfully tight in her chest as she watched the blood oozing from him. "What do you mean, you've been shot before? You never told me that!"

"Hunting accident," he said. "Anyway, it wasn't important. We had a lot more important things to talk about."

"That's it," Darla said. "As soon as you're patched up, you're moving in with me. I'll make sure you stay out of trouble."

He closed his eyes, and Sheriff Cartwright's men surrounded the wedding party, moving everyone away in case the shooter was still out there. "Go," Judah told her, "I don't want you getting shot. Do what the nice lawmen tell you. Isn't that right, Doc?"

"That's right," Sidney said, and Darla said, "Shut up, both of you. I'm not going anywhere until I know you're not exaggerating about your flesh wound."

Sidney waved to the Callahan men, who were standing around helplessly. "Get him inside," he said, "not near windows, until the ambulance arrives."

But that wasn't necessary. The ambulance pulled

up, its sirens wailing, and two EMTs jumped out to take over from Sidney, who looked gravely concerned.

"I know we've had our differences, but I hope you know I didn't do this," Sidney said.

"I know you didn't," Judah said.

Sidney watched protectively as Judah was placed into the ambulance. "I'm going to ride with him."

"I'm going, too." Darla shoved her way into the vehicle behind Sidney.

"All this stress isn't good for the babies," Sidney warned, and Judah said, "Stay here, Darla."

She shook her head. "My children would never forgive me if I didn't stay with their father when he'd been shot."

"More guilt," Judah said, and Darla said, "That's right. Now just lie there."

"I'm going to love being married," Judah said, his face creased with a smile even though he closed his eyes wearily.

"I'm hoping this wasn't your way of getting out of marrying me," Darla said, and Judah's eyes snapped open.

"Not a chance, sweetheart. Not a chance."

Darla looked at the blood on her wedding dress and wondered if she should have worn the magic wedding gown, after all. She'd definitely seen Judah standing behind her in the mirror. He'd been smiling, handsome, tall and virile. Not shot by a sniper. Gooseflesh jumped onto her arms, and she rubbed them, not able to rub away the unease as the ambulance raced to the hospital.

"YOU SEE WHAT I MEAN," Sabrina whispered to her sister, Seton. "There's a dark cloud over Rancho Diablo."

Seton nodded. "I've been keeping an eye on the Jenkins's place, but I have to be honest with you, I don't think the old man did it. He seemed shocked when Judah got hit. Not displeased, necessarily, just shocked."

Sabrina blinked. "Who else would have done it?"

"Maybe the best man set it up. Weren't they romantic rivals?"

"You'd have to get to know Sidney to understand that he wouldn't hurt anyone," Sabrina said. "The man is gentle. He's a healer." She could see that in his peaceful aura, in the kindness in his eyes. He'd never borne any ill will toward Judah, and she knew Judah liked the doc, too. "No, it wouldn't have been Sidney."

"Any other ideas?"

Sabrina shook her head. "The Callahans are well-liked in the town, as you might have been able to tell by the number of guests who showed up to the wedding. And that was for a wedding no one thought would actually happen."

"Well, it didn't." Seton glanced around Darla's property, watching the guests help clean up the yard and put away chairs. "The thing that puzzles me is that whoever shot Judah either wasn't a practiced assassin or didn't mean to kill him."

"Why? What are you thinking?"

Seton shrugged. "I think someone just wanted Judah—or the Callahans—to know he was out there. Scare them a little bit. Or, and the possibility is remote, it could have been a random misfire from a hunter. But I don't think so. It didn't sound like a large firearm."

Sabrina sighed. "Hold that thought. Bode and Fiona are having a row, and since I've been employed by both, I'd better see if I can run interference."

"I'm telling you," Bode said angrily to Sheriff Cartwright as Sabrina walked up, "I didn't have anything to do with the shooting. And she hit me! That's assault. And I want to know what you're going to do about it, Sheriff."

"Not much, Bode, and you're not, either." The sheriff rocked back on his heels. "Do you have an invitation to be here?"

Bode's mouth flattened. "One doesn't need an invitation to attend a wedding of a local favorite. It was known by all that a wedding would take place here today."

Fiona looked at him. "Bode, one day, things are going to turn out badly between you and me. I suggest you keep your dealings with my family on the professional level, and quit being such a pest."

Bode didn't reply and Fiona left, with Sabrina following her. "Fiona, let me drive you to the hospital. We'll check on Judah and Darla."

Fiona nodded. "I'd appreciate that. They don't need me at the hospital, I'm sure, but if I stay here, I'm going to have more fighting words with that scoundrel."

"We don't want that." Sabrina steered Fiona toward the van, waved at Burke so he'd know they were leaving, in case he wanted to ride along. He did, and so did Seton, which made Sabrina feel better, having her sister around. Diane said, "I'll hold down the fort," and Fiona shouted, "Thanks!" out the window, and off they went to see how Judah was surviving his big day that hadn't turned out the way anybody had hoped.

"I'M FINE," JUDAH said for the hundredth time, thinking that having a nurse for a fiancée had its blessings and its curses. Darla hovered over the nurses, she hovered over the doctors, she hovered over Judah. No one escaped her watchful eye. He reminded himself that this was one of the things he'd known about her, that she was efficient and businesslike.

But he was a man, and he didn't want to be fussed over. Not about a gunshot wound, anyway. The truth was, dark thoughts kept running through his mind, torturing him, and he wanted to reflect on them.

What if the bullet had hit Darla?

What if his babies had been injured?

His blood ran cold, keeping him shivering, as the worries punctuated his blood loss.

"If you're cold, I'll get a heated blanket," Darla said, and a small redheaded nurse said, "I'll get it," anxious to stay out of Darla's path. She was as protective of him as a lioness, and Judah closed his eyes, not wanting to think about how much he wanted to marry her.

He was glad now that he hadn't.

"Darla," he said, as they began to wheel him toward an operating room, "today was not our day."

Tears jumped into her eyes. He hated to see her cry. If he had his way, a tear would never form on his behalf in her eyes, ever again.

"We'll have another day," Darla said. "We'll work something out."

He gave her a small grimace of a smile before he was wheeled to the O.R. so the bullet could be removed. He didn't care about the bullet. He cared about what had been taken from them today, which was romance and innocence.

It made him angry. Worse, the shooting had given him crystal-clear perspective. Until today, he hadn't really thought through what he was doing to Darla by marrying her.

But now he remembered. And now he knew what he had to do.

Chapter Fourteen

Sam waited until Bode walked up the drive of the Jenkins place before he launched himself at him, landing on top of the elderly man. Bode cursed, trying to throw a punch, but Rafe caught his hand.

"Mind your manners, Jenkins." Rafe held him down and Sam took a seat on the man's back.

"*My* manners?" Bode spit some dirt out of his mouth. "I'll have the law on you so fast it'll made your head spin if you don't get your ape of a brother off me. You Callahans have never been anything but trouble, you and your crazy aunt, too."

"Crazy!" Sam said. "Brother, did you just hear him insult our aunt, who raised us when no one else would have?" He leaned over from his seated position on Bode's back to look him in his eyes. "Bode, we're curious just how far back your animosity goes."

"It goes back years. Why the hell wouldn't it?" Bode demanded. "If you need a carbon dating, you could probably date it to the time your parents arrived here."

"We wonder what really happened to our parents," Rafe said as Jonas walked out of the neatly manicured bushes around Bode's property.

"There's no one here and Julie doesn't appear to be

home," Jonas said to his brothers. "You're free to conduct yourselves as you see fit."

"And you call yourself a lawyer," Bode snarled in Sam's direction. "Get off of me, you hooligan. All of you are insane, like your silly aunt."

"Ah," Rafe said with a sigh, "I'm just dying to hit him."

"But we won't," Sam said, "because that would be against the law. We're just having a chat with our neighbor." He bounced on Bode's back, drawing another snarl.

"I don't know what happened to your parents," Bode said. "That I swear."

"Your word's not really good with us," Jonas said, "if you don't mind me pointing out the obvious."

"What do you think I would have done with them? And if you really want to know, why don't you ask Fiona?" Bode tried to get up, but Sam was too heavy to be budged. He patted Bode on the head, comforting him like a child, and the old rancher cursed at him.

"Someone shot Judah tonight, and no one would do that but you. You're too clever to get caught," Jonas said, "so you hired some punk to do it. Luckily for you, Judah isn't dead, or you'd be joining him in pushing up daisies."

"Why would I want to kill your brother? Why don't you suspect the man he stole Darla from?" Bode demanded.

"That's too easy," Sam said. "First of all, Doc wouldn't hurt anybody. Second, you want us gone, scared off. When the ballistics on the bullet come back, we're going to have Sheriff Cartwright search your house for a match, and any records for a weapon that's been sold to you, licensed to you, ever fired by you at a tin can."

"I didn't do it. I really don't want any of you boys to come to harm. I swear it."

Sam bounced on Bode's back a little harder, and the rancher *oofed* into the dirt. "You say that now, while we've got you cornered. But we know you sneaked into our house and locked Pete in the basement. You threaten us constantly, and our aunt. So we know to come to you when we so much as find a piece of bread missing from the pantry."

Bode shook his head. "I'm not talking any more until I have a lawyer and the sheriff here."

"Why? We're not arresting you, Bode. We're just asking a few friendly questions. The truth is, we want to save you from yourself," Rafe said.

"How so?"

"Because you really don't want to be the jackass that you are," Jonas said. "We know deep inside you beats a heart that doesn't want to harm anyone. Isn't that right, Bode?"

"I want your land," Bode said. "And that's it. But I can figure out a hundred ways to get it besides killing people. I'm too smart for that."

Sam glanced around at his brothers, then got off Bode and rolled him with his boot so that he faced three angry Callahans.

"Bode," Jonas said, "just so you know, we'll do whatever it takes to keep you from owning one inch of our land."

"It's too late," Bode said, the corners of his mouth lifting with glee. "Your aunt is broke. She has no money. She made bad investments, and it's only a matter of time before I put all of you out on the road with nothing but your belongings. And I look forward to that day, boys. Your aunt and Burke, too, and all those hobos you take in."

Jonas sighed. "Pride goeth before a big-ass fall, Jenkins. Just remember I told you that."

"Maybe," Bode said, "but some of us don't fall."

"We'll see," Sam said, and the brothers walked away.

"THERE'S GOING TO be war on the ranch," Fiona said to her friends as they sat in the back room of the Books 'n' Bingo shop. "It may not be quite full-blown war, but I'm really afraid it's coming."

Mavis stared at her. "How can we help you?"

"I need help plotting more than anything else. There's got to be a way to think myself out of the box I'm in." She sipped her tea, and glanced around at the faces of her three best friends. These women had been with her through thick and thin from the day she'd arrived in New Mexico. Their friendship had strengthened and sustained her over the years at Rancho Diablo. Now she needed it more than ever. "The worst part is that the wedding had to called off. I'm so sorry about Darla's big day," she told Mavis.

"I'm confused," Corinne Abernathy said. "First I ordered a tea set for a wedding gift to give Darla and Dr. Tunstall, and then I had to change the card to make it to Darla and Judah, and now I don't know what to do!" Corinne blinked. "I think I'll take it back to the store. It's not a lucky tea set, for certain."

"I suppose you could give it to one of your nieces," Nadine Waters suggested. "Seton or Sabrina might like it."

"Don't worry," Mavis said. "Darla might be my late-in-life child, but she's always quick to resolve her dilemmas. And that tea set is lucky, I'm certain, Corinne." She patted her friend's hand.

Fiona sighed. "This is all my fault."

"There is no fault." Mavis shook her head. "It's just that Bode Jenkins can't leave well enough alone."

"I beaned him pretty good with my purse at the wedding. And it had Burke's pocket watch in it, too, which as you know is no light thing. I heard it go thump on Bode's thick skull."

"Why were you carrying Burke's watch?" Corinne asked.

"Sabrina had taken it somewhere to get it cleaned a couple months ago. She knew of a person who specializes in antique pocket watches. Burke does so love his timepiece," Fiona said with a sigh. "That watch has been running for over half a century now."

"Like you," Corinne said with a giggle.

"That's true," Mavis said. "Hope you didn't mess up the watch by using it as a nunchuku."

Fiona shook her head. "The watch has a gold case. It's like a rock, a lucky Irish rock." She looked around the sitting room of the Books 'n' Bingo shop, taking in all the volumes of beloved books, the various teapots lining the walls for decoration and for use, and sighed at the coziness of it all. "I just wish everything would settle down for just a little while. Mostly, I want Darla and Judah to get married. I want you to be my in-law," she told Mavis. "Even though you're all my sisters, I was really looking forward to adding one of you to my family tree. And I do so love Darla. She's just always so nice to me. Everybody in our family likes her so much."

Mavis blinked. "To be honest, as much as I think Sidney is a great doctor, I was really pulling for Judah.

I think those two have been making secret cow eyes at each other for years."

Corinne nodded. "At least you'll be getting more grandchildren, Fiona. That's more than I can say for myself. Goodness knows neither Seton nor Sabrina are interested in being altar-bound."

Fiona contemplated that over a sugar cookie. "I was just positive it was a stroke of brilliance for me to hire Sabrina to light a fire under my boys, since they have no idea you have nieces, Corinne. The fortune-teller bit was priceless. And it's a bonus that Seton is a private investigator, because now I can spy on Bode to my heart's content."

"But none of it's working," Nadine said. "Bode's still being ugly, and only two of your boys jumped at the chance to own the ranch. I mean, I think Judah will still make an excellent groom, Mavis," she hurriedly said, "when he gets over being shot."

"Being shot does slow a groom down." Fiona threw out that last bit to comfort Mavis, but the truth was, she feared that a wedding postponed might be a wedding canceled for good. "I'm all for striking while the bride is hot, though."

Mavis gasped. "Darla will always be hot! There are good genes in our family!"

"I meant iron," Fiona soothed. "You know Darla is a silver-blond beauty, Mavis. Don't get in a twist. I'm just so nervous and rattled my mouth is running off like a rabbit." She did feel completely rattled, and it wasn't fair. She didn't like not being in control. "I've always pushed my boys to do what I believed was best for them, and I want Judah right back at the altar before Bode figures out a way to…to—"

She couldn't bring herself to think about the fact

that Bode had tried to kill her nephew. "You know, they said the bullet was small, not meant to do anything more than incapacitate, but I don't believe that. Even a .22 can kill."

"Shoot, even a BB gun can kill a person," Nadine said morosely. "My husband used to shoot varmints with BBs, and you'd be surprised the damage they can do."

"I don't want to think about it," Fiona said, swallowing against a rush of coldness seeping into her body. What would her brother, Jeremiah, and Molly say if she let something happen to one of their sons? She had to keep the family whole and together—and at Rancho Diablo. "Judah will go home from the hospital tomorrow, and then we'll see what he's planning."

"I hope he's planning another wedding," Nadine said, and Fiona nodded.

"Me, too. I've about run out of lures to convince these boys that marriage is the holy grail." Fiona put down her teacup and pursed her lips for a moment. If Bode had gone to the trouble of harming Judah, basically scaring him away from Darla, then her plan of getting the boys married off was working.

She just didn't know why. "Why wouldn't Bode want Judah to marry Darla?"

"Because your family is growing and his is not, and he's a jealous old coot," Corinne said with some heat. "You don't think he'll ever allow his daughter, Judge Julie, to leave his house, do you? So while you've got grandkids popping out all over, he has no hopes whatsoever of having any at all. Because he'll never allow Julie to leave his home to marry someone. And pity the poor man who ever does try to take her off Bode's hands."

Fiona snapped her fingers. "That's what we need to do."

"What?" Nadine asked, lost. "What are we doing?"

"If we find a beau to hang around Bode's, eager-beaver for Julie, Bode won't have time to be in my business!" Fiona said with delight. "I believe the shock would almost end his ability to do harm to anyone on the planet."

"Except for the poor suitor," Nadine said. "You couldn't pay a man to date poor Julie."

Fiona blinked. "There's that."

Corinne nodded. "For every plot, there's a twist."

"But maybe the best way to declare war," Fiona said, "is to take it right to his door."

"We don't know a bachelor brave enough nor stupid enough to... Why are you looking like that?" Nadine asked. "Fiona, it appears as if someone turned a light-bulb on over your head."

Fiona smiled. "I have three nephews left, and all of them are very brave, and not stupid in the least."

Her friends stared at her.

"Can you imagine how upset Bode would be if one of my nephews started coming around his place? He wouldn't be able to focus on anything but Julie, and we could plan another wedding!" Fiona clapped her hands. "I just knew we'd come up with an answer if we brain-stormed enough!"

"It could work," Corinne said. "In fact, it's impressive. I do see one tiny problem, however."

They all looked at her expectantly. Corinne shrugged. "Which one of your nephews would you sacrifice to the dragon, Fiona?" Just as she posed the question, the store bell tinkled and Darla walked in, locking the door behind her.

"Darla!" Mavis exclaimed. "What are you doing here?"

Darla accepted a cup of tea from Fiona and took a tufted chair in the circle. "This is the only place where I can come and have a good...I don't know. I don't want to cry, but I definitely want to talk to women who've been through everything."

The four women looked at her carefully, and Darla felt comforted by their interested perusal. If anyone could give her solid advice, it was these four.

She hoped they had some advice.

"Are you feeling all right?" Corinne asked.

"The babies are okay?" Nadine inquired.

"Did you just come from the hospital?" Fiona demanded.

"Yes, yes and yes," Darla said. "Judah is raising Cain with the doctors to release him, so he's in peak form."

"As I expected." Fiona nodded with satisfaction. "All the Callahans are tough nuts."

Darla nodded in turn. "Tougher than you think. Judah broke off our engagement."

"What?" The women exclaimed as one and began offering sympathy in huge doses, which Darla needed.

"That scoundrel," Fiona said. "Honey, he didn't mean a word of it. You just give him a day or two to cool off, and he'll be throwing himself at your feet again, if I know my nephew."

Darla's heart was heavy as she shook her head. "I don't think so this time. He said there are too many things that endanger me and the children for him to marry me. He said there are too many family ghosts, and until they're laid to rest, he can't put me in jeopardy."

"With two little babies on the way he doesn't want

to marry you?" Mavis asked, proud mother coming to the fore. "Fiona, I don't think your nephew is being honorable."

Fiona puffed up like a small bird. "If there's one thing Judah is, it's honorable, Mavis Cameron Night." She leaned toward Darla. "It sounds like shock to me, Darla. We have no family ghosts, not really, not of the variety that would harm anyone, anyway."

Everyone stared at Fiona. Darla said, "I'm not afraid of ghosts. He is."

"Silliest thing I ever heard," Nadine said. "Ghosts at a wedding, indeed. Fiona, you tell Judah to buck up."

Darla's heart hung heavy in her chest. After all of Judah's romancing her through her own case of cold feet, she had never expected to hear him say that the wedding was off.

He felt that she was safer without him.

It broke her heart.

Fiona looked uncomfortable. "I think there's been a miscommunication."

Darla shook her head. "After the surgery, he distinctly said, 'I can't marry you, Darla—'"

"Pain pills," Nadine sniffed. "Sounds like they fed him a handful, and I wouldn't listen to a word he said, Darla. You were a nurse. You know how drugs can make people time travel right out of their normal dispositions. I've never seen a man crazier for a woman than Judah is for you."

"He said it's not safe," Darla said, not drawing any comfort from their words. "He said that in order to keep me safe, he has to keep away from me."

"I don't understand," Fiona said, blinking. "It's like he got shot with the opposite of Cupid's arrow."

"Yeah, it was called Bode's bullet," Mavis said.

"Oh, dear," Fiona said. "Darla, I'm so very sorry. Surely this will all pass after my renegade nephew gets out of the hospital. He was never very good with injuries, you know that. Look at the last one he had. He thought he had a concussion when he didn't. I'm not saying Judah's a wienie, but he's not a patient patient, and—"

"It's all right," Darla said, even though it wasn't. Her heart was shattered.

"Well, it just shows you should have married Dr. Tunstall," Mavis said hotly. "Dr. Tunstall wouldn't have put you through all this nonsense. He's a steady man with a good income, and no one would shoot at *him*."

Fiona stiffened. "That's my nephew you're calling unsteady, Mavis."

"That same nephew who can't be bothered to read a big-ass label that says Party Condoms on the side," Mavis returned, her cheeks pink.

"Prank Condoms," Darla said. "And it was just as much my fault as is. I seduced him."

The women went quiet, staring at her.

"I did," Darla said. "I've been wanting to for years, and I'd do it again in a heartbeat. In fact, I'd seduce him tonight if he didn't have an injury. But it really doesn't matter. Judah has vowed to stay five miles away from me until all the ghosts in your family have been laid to rest. That's what he said, and I could tell he meant every word."

"What are these ghosts, Fiona?" Corinne asked. "I don't remember anything phantasmagoric hanging about your place."

Fiona cleared her throat. "I think Judah means the whole Bode problem."

Darla shook her head. "He muttered something about aunts who keep secrets."

"Well," Fiona said uncomfortably, at her friends' curious perusal. "Pain pills are powerful."

Mavis gathered her teacup and purse. "You'd best talk to your nephew, Fiona. We have another suitor in the wings, and we're not going to wait around for Judah. To be frank, it sounds like the man got a case of winter-cold feet. Darla shouldn't be dumped and humiliated—"

"Mom," Darla said, "I'm not humiliated."

"You will be when your children are born and people wonder why you and Judah were getting married and then didn't." Mavis glared at Fiona. "This is what happens when you meddle, Fiona. Clearly, you hurried a man along who wasn't ready to accept his responsibilities. Getting shot is no excuse. Darla's a nurse, for heaven's sake. If anybody could nurse a man back to health, it's her."

"Oh, dear," Nadine said. "We need more tea. And cupcakes."

"Ladies," Corinne said, "I vote we adjourn our chat before fur really begins to fly, and words are spoken that can never be taken back."

"Goodness," Fiona said, "this is all a tempest in a teapot."

"A cracked pot, if you ask me. Come on, Darla," Mavis said, and swept from the store.

Darla blinked, then hugged Fiona goodbye. "It's not your fault," she whispered. "I always knew he didn't really love me. Not the way I was in love with him."

Darla followed her mother. "Mom, you shouldn't have said those things to poor Fiona. It's not her fault someone shot Judah."

"She raised a back-sliding nephew," Mavis said, "and it's high time she get her house in order over there."

Darla sighed. There was a house that needed to be put in order, and it was her own. Her mother wouldn't want to hear that right now—she was too upset over everything that had happened, and Darla understood. Everyone was upset. People would be talking in Diablo for weeks.

But she didn't care. All Darla knew was that Judah had pursued her, finally convincing her that she was the only woman for him. Even if it had been all about the babies, he'd still pursued her.

Now she intended to pursue him. She owed it to her children, and to their father, to make certain that they all ended up as a happy family, no matter how many ghosts Judah thought he had to protect her from.

She was in love with him, and he was just going to have to deal with that. *And I've never been afraid of ghosts, or anything else that goes bump in the night. What I fear is losing the one man I know in my heart is a good man, the right man, the only man, for me.*

Chapter Fifteen

The next evening Fiona walked into the bunkhouse and gave her four nephews, who were trying to resurrect their lagging game of Scrabble, a baleful stare. "Judge Julie's got herself quite the conundrum," she said. "She's trying to get that longhorn you brought from El Paso untangled from the fence, and she's wearing a tight dress and fishnets. I guess that's what a beautiful judge wears under her black robes." Fiona bleated a pitiful sigh—theatrical, to Judah's ears—and said, "I never knew why you boys had to have that longhorn, but if I was you, I'd go save it from the judge. Julie looks fit to slip it on the grill."

Jonas, Rafe and Sam abandoned Judah on the double, as Judah was certain Fiona had hoped they would. She looked at her nephew. "Why aren't you at the main house?"

"I'm fine here," Judah said.

"Usually when you boys have some kind of issue, you stay at the house."

"I don't have an issue," Judah said, not about to be lured by coddling.

She put her hands on her hips, staring at his arm, which he'd propped on a pillow. He preferred that to wearing the sling the doctor had given him. The sling made him feel like an invalid, and Judah wasn't giving in to any weaknesses when he most needed to be strong.

"You do have issues," Fiona said. "What in the world did you mean by telling Darla about ghosts?"

Judah shook his head, in no mood to be questioned the day after his wedding had taken a sinister turn. He leveled a wary eye on his aunt. "You should know about ghosts, Aunt."

"Well, I don't. I've never seen a ghost in my life," she snapped, and he grunted at her truculent tone.

"I don't know what all you've been keeping to yourself, Aunt Fiona. All I know is that Darla might have taken a bullet that was meant for me. And until I've got everything figured out, I'm not putting her in harm's way."

"The only harm that's going to come is when she decides not to wait for your silly butt." His aunt glared at him. "You do not take a bullet and then use that as an excuse, a pitiful one, not to marry the best woman that's ever been placed in your path. Trust me, even a woman who owns a shop full of wedding regalia doesn't put on the old satin-and-lace lightly. You should rethink your situation when you're not chock-full of hallucinogens."

"I haven't taken any pills," Judah said. "I don't like pain pills. So don't worry."

"You're not thinking straight, and I hate to see you make the mistake of a lifetime. You're going to look quite the ass when Darla marries Sidney."

"She won't," Judah said, though he didn't admit to a twinge of unease. But Darla's safety had to come first. "I'd almost rather she marry Sidney. Then I'd at least know she's safe."

"What?" Fiona exclaimed. "Don't talk like a quitter! I can't stand quitters!" She sank into a chair across from him. "One thing I won't have people saying is that I raised a bunch of lily-livered, weak-kneed men." She passed a hand over her brow, rearranging her hair a little, as if that would help reorganize her thoughts.

"There's been nothing but craziness around here for a while. I'm sorry to say it, Aunt Fiona, but your plan has definitely not been conducive to communal calm."

Tears jumped into her eyes, brightening them as she stared at him remorsefully. "I just want the best for you and your brothers."

"I know you do," Judah said softly, "but you don't give us all the facts. You wouldn't even have told us you and Burke were married except that we figured it out."

"You boys were so young when your parents…well, you know." Fiona sniffled into a tissue for a second, then stiffened. "Burke and I made the decision that we didn't want to confuse you. He always loved you boys, but he knew he couldn't take the place of your father, nor could I take the place of your mother. We felt it was best if we always were just aunt and bodyguard to you."

"Bodyguard?" Judah frowned. "Burke isn't your bodyguard."

"He was quite the fighter in his youth," Fiona said. "A street fighter for the cause. Things changed for us when we came over here to take care of you boys. We had to make fast decisions. Maybe we didn't make them the best we could, but I stand by them." She wiped at her eyes and put her tissue away. "I'm not going to say we didn't make mistakes. But there's a lot we didn't want to burden you children with."

"We're not children anymore."

"True," Fiona conceded. "Which is why I don't want you babbling about ghosts. You just marry Darla and raise your babies, and that'll be more than your parents were able to do for you." She sighed heavily. "People don't always get the chance to do what they really want to do."

Judah felt as if a knife had been stabbed into his gut. Never had it occurred to him that his father had been unable to raise him and his brothers. It was almost like an unbroken chain of missed parenting, he realized. The shock of being shot at, and being determined to keep his little family safe, had made him think that the best thing to do would be to let Darla have a life far away from Rancho Diablo and its spiraling misfortunes.

But should one bullet keep him and Darla apart?

He thought about the cave, and the secrets he knew were there, and the silver bar that had been in the kitchen, and the ancient Native American who visited their home every year. He thought about Sam coming after their parents were gone, as Jonas had pointed out years ago, and he wondered if it wasn't family ghosts he should fear, but far-reaching skeletons that had never rested comfortably. "I don't know," he murmured. "This isn't the way I envisioned a marriage beginning."

"That should be up to Darla, I would think. But you do what you think is best. Heaven only knows I'm all out of ideas."

Fiona left the bunkhouse, hurt and unsure, and Judah felt bad for the words he'd spoken to her. But then he got thinking about Darla for the hundredth time that day, and wondered if all his brave words about breaking up with her to protect her were really based in the fact that he'd never known a father growing up—and maybe he didn't know what being a father actually meant.

NOT THIRTY MINUTES LATER, Judah's jaw dropped when Darla wafted into the bunkhouse, wearing a blue dress and looking like something out of his most fervent dreams.

"This is the simplest decision you've ever made," Darla said. "Get up and get in my truck, Lazarus. Where's your overnight bag?"

"I'm not going anywhere," he said, just to test her, and she looked at him with a patient, determined gaze.

"Yes, you are," she said sweetly. "Because if you don't, I'm staying here, and I'm pretty certain a lady isn't welcome among bachelor men in a bunkhouse."

Darla would be. His brothers would welcome her with open arms. They liked Darla a lot, and they would feel that if she wanted to coop up here with the father of her children and the man she'd nearly married less than twenty-four hours ago, that was certainly her priority. Shoot, they'd probably roll out a red carpet and the family crystal.

But he could think of a bunch of places he'd rather Darla be than holed up with his brothers. As a crew, they were a fairly unimpressive group. They played Scrabble, and sometimes bridge. Some of them read books by foreign authors, and sometimes they watched movies in French, not to learn the language of love so much as enjoy it. They were basically nerds, and if there was one thing Judah didn't consider himself, it was a pencil-carrying nerd. "Where are we going, and for how long?" he asked, grumbling to show her he didn't appreciate being taken charge of, though secretly he thought it was sexy.

"Just get in my truck and you'll find out."

He shoved himself off the sofa. "Did Fiona put you up to taking me off her hands? She's worried about me."

"Everyone's worried about you because you've gone

weird. But Fiona doesn't know I'm rescuing you from yourself."

He blinked, hesitating as he tossed some random clothes into a duffel. "I don't need rescuing. I don't need nursing, either," he said stubbornly.

"Good, because Jackie can't take care of you and three babies and her husband, and she's the only nurse in the family I know of who'd be willing to take care of you. Can you carry that duffel or should I?"

He glared. "Only one of my arms was shot, thanks." Actually, he'd hang the bag around his neck like a Saint Bernard if he'd been shot in both arms. A man could stand to look only so weak in front of his woman.

"Good. Then come on. There's no time to waste."

"Why?" Judah strode after Darla, getting in front of her to open the driver's door for her. "What's the rush?"

"Would you believe me if I said I can't wait another minute to get my hands on you, Judah Callahan?"

He smirked. "Now that's more like it," he said, and closed the door. Tossing his duffel into the truck bed, he hurried around to get in the truck. "What took you so long?"

"So long to what?" Darla backed down the drive, waving at Sam and Jonas as they loped back to the bunkhouse, looking a little worse for wear. "What have they been doing?"

"I think they rescued Judge Julie from our long-horn." Judah squinted at his brothers, noting torn and dirty pants on both of them. "I'm kind of glad I didn't make that rescue. I wonder if they left Rafe for dead."

Darla turned on the main road. "Why would they?"

"Depends on how dead he was, and if an angel was smiling on him." Judah focused his attention on Darla, not worried about his harebrained brothers. "Anyway, what took you so long to realize you couldn't keep your hands off my rock-hard body? I should make you wait for playing hard to get." He tweaked her hair. "It would serve you right."

Darla laughed. "My, you talk big, cowboy."

Judah leaned his head back and grinned, happy to let Darla drive him to her house. "But I can back up every word, sweetheart."

"This may not be the kind of visit you think it's going to be. As you pointed out, I need protection, and so protection you're going to be," Darla told him. Judah waved at Judge Julie as they went by, and at his brother Rafe, who was lying on the ground, probably looking up the judge's tight dress—if Judah knew his brother, and he was pretty sure he did—and thought life was sweet when you had a hot blonde like Darla who was gaga for your lovemaking. Of course, if she wanted to pretend it wasn't all about the loving, and that she needed a bodyguard to keep her warm, he'd be her muscled protector—just for tonight. He'd rather keep an eye on her than listen to his brothers argue over words on the Scrabble board.

And he wouldn't be lying if he bragged that he could make love with one arm tied behind his back.

TWO HOURS LATER, Darla parked Judah in a room at the StarShine Hotel in Santa Fe. He'd protested, but he ceased his halfhearted carping when he saw that she'd reserved the honeymoon suite. She detected a fairly enthusiastic gleam in Judah's dark blue eyes, and a certain curiosity at what the little woman might be up to now.

The cowboy was in for a surprise.

"Why are we here?" he asked, in a tone that suggested he already knew, and Darla smiled at him blithely.

"It was the only room big enough for the both of us," she told him, her voice ever so sweet.

He raised a brow. "I mean, why are we in Santa Fe?"

"Oh." She waved a hand. "I knew you were worried about me being at Rancho Diablo in case someone tried to kill you, and I knew you'd be worried about being at my house in case someone tried to kill you, so I thought it'd be best to bring you someplace no one would be able to try to kill you. You know. In case someone tries to kill you." She smiled at him. "And we never planned a honeymoon, so this seems as good a place as any. I always wanted to stay here," she said, slipping off her shoes and coat. She noticed she had Judah's attention, so she pointed to the bed. "Why don't you make yourself comfortable while I take a bath? Be sure to prop that arm up."

"You didn't bring your nurse's uniform by any chance, did you?" he asked, his tone hopeful. Trust her guy to be the one with a nurse fantasy. Darla headed for the bathroom, planning to lock herself in and draw a nice, full tub.

"I'm sorry. I'm off duty. But you don't need anyone to take care of you," she called. "You just relax and let me know if anyone comes to the door."

"Are we expecting someone?" Judah asked.

"No. But just in case someone does come and tries to, you know, shoot you or something. I don't want to be in the tub when it happens."

She thought she heard him mutter, and smiled to herself.

Thirty minutes later, when she came out of the bathroom, Judah was sound asleep, which had been her plan all along. She grabbed her robe and her things and slipped into the room across the hall, locking the door behind her.

JUDAH AWAKENED TWELVE hours later, if his watch was right. He thumped on it to make certain it was still working. Apparently it was, because it corresponded to the clock radio next to the bed, which Darla had tossed a towel over for reasons he couldn't decipher.

Had he made love to her? Was that why he'd slept so long? Nope, he hadn't had so much as a kiss or anything pleasant like that. He passed a hand over his stubble, testing his arm. It was sore as hell, but not so sore that he couldn't pleasure Darla to the depths of her being.

So what had gone wrong with his little lady's seduction?

He felt the bed beside him, patting around for a soft, round body. There was time enough before checkout to give Darla a rousing dose of what she'd clearly wanted last night. After all, he was a stud, not a dud.

There was no sexy, warm female next to him, and the bed felt suspiciously undisturbed on her side. He flipped on the bedside lamp, realizing that not only had he not made love to Darla, she hadn't even slept in the room.

He tapped his watch again. No, twelve hours really had elapsed, and she hadn't spent them with him.

Which made him wonder if he'd said something to upset her. "Bath," he said, "and I fell asleep. Possibly I should have offered to bathe with her, but she seemed determined to be alone."

So that wasn't the problem.

"I'm pretty sure I shouldn't have been sleeping alone," he muttered, and went to find Darla. There was a door that looked as if it connected to another room in the suite, so he banged on that, and a moment later she opened it, wearing a stunner of a white nightie. His breath left him.

"Yes?" Darla said, and he frowned.

"Why are you in there?"

"Where else would I be?"

He took in her pretty pink toenails, and sweet lace in a V down her front, almost to her belly. In fact, if she shifted just right, perhaps he could see a little bit more of Darla. The peekaboo effect really had his attention, so he decided to play it soft and smooth. "Shouldn't you be with me? In that nice comfy bed?"

She shook her head. "No, that's a honeymoon suite. I'm not on my honeymoon."

"Oh," he said, "*that's* what this is about. You're annoyed." He had a sneaking suspicion he was caught in a plot, which shouldn't be happening in a honeymoon suite.

Other things should be happening, like lovemaking.

"Any chance I can convince you to let me order you breakfast in bed?"

She smiled. "I'd like that. Ask them to bring it to the B suite."

He glanced over his shoulder. "Am I in the A side?"

"Yes," she said, her tone like cotton candy. "A is for ass."

He blinked. "Oh. This isn't a weekend for seduction. This is about showing me what I'm missing out on."

"I always knew you were smart, cowboy." Darla smiled at him, and his gut tightened. "We could be on a honeymoon, but we're not, because of a tiny bit of lead. We could be making love, but we're not, because you broke up with me, because of a fractional piece of lead. And so," she said, "I'm sleeping without a husband, which I hate, because I really had my sights set on a certain cowboy. And so my children will be born without their father's last name, all because of a teeny weeny, miniscule—"

"That's it," Judah said. "If you went to the trouble of getting a honeymoon suite, you probably also went to the trouble of making certain there was a justice of the peace around who would marry us after you drove me insane with that bridal nightie."

Darla smiled. "Maybe."

"Did you bring a dress and all the rigmarole a bride needs? I'd hate for you to marry me without feeling like a real bride." Ten years from now, would she look back on their marriage as a quickie, low-budget affair? He tried to buck himself up to hero status in her eyes. "If you're determined to do this, we could fly to Hawaii."

She handed him a menu. "Order breakfast. You'll need it to fortify yourself for giving up your bachelorhood. Fiona packed your tux. You'll find it hanging in the cabinet. I can't wait for Hawaii, Judah, because you might get shot. Although I can get you a bulletproof vest for under your tux, if you're worried."

She closed the door.

"I'd like to think she's worried about me being shot," Judah muttered, "but I think she's trying to tell me something."

He went to order breakfast and then locate the tux the little woman had thoughtfully commandeered on his behalf. Who was he to tell a lady wearing a white lacy nightie that he wouldn't run through a hail of bullets for just one night in her bed?

Chapter Sixteen

Fiona peeped in after Darla closed the connecting door between suite A and suite B. Jackie followed, as did Aberdeen, and Darla's mother, Mavis, with Corinne and Nadine waiting behind them. All her friends were here, and for Darla, sandbagging Judah like this couldn't have been more perfect.

"Is he gone?" Fiona asked.

"With his marching orders," Darla said. "Come in."

"We'll get you into this beautiful gown post haste," Jackie said, "though I'm not afraid Judah's going to change his mind."

Darla wasn't afraid of that, either. Not anymore. If she'd learned anything, it was that her man was stubborn and opinionated, and if Fiona said he really wanted to be caught, because he was too worried about the danger to Darla to go willingly, then maybe she was on to something.

"Judah did say once that he'd never be caught dead at an altar," Darla said as Jackie eased her into the magic wedding dress, and Fiona said, "Well, he nearly was dead at the altar, so he was almost right, for once. We're just not going to tempt Fate a second time."

"If it wasn't for the children," Darla said, "getting married wouldn't matter to me so much." But the instant she said the words, she knew it wasn't true. The magic wedding gown sparkled on her, drew in light, making her catch her breath. "I love him," she murmured. "I always have."

"I know," Jackie said. "That's why this time we're not taking any chances. It's all about the gown."

It was true. The moment she'd waited for was here, and right. Deep inside herself, she knew Judah wasn't afraid of marrying her, he was afraid of hurting her. "Thank you all so much for helping me," Darla said. "I treasure your friendship more than you can ever know." She hugged her mother, and then, hearing Judah pound on the door adjoining their rooms, said, "You hide in here until we've left."

The ladies concealed themselves in the large bathroom and the huge walk-in closet, and Darla opened the door. Judah, just as handsome as he'd been last night in his tux, stared at her. "New gown?"

"The one from last time had a few bloodstains on it," Darla said. "I thought I'd wear something else for good luck."

"The luck is all mine. Wow." His eyes glittered as he took her in. "We could see how fast I can get you out of that gown now, and then go to the J.P."

"No, thank you," Darla said quickly, more than aware of the listening ears concealed in her room. "I'm not sure what time the office closes."

Judah nodded. "That's probably a wise plan, but you know, you could change my mind. I'm easy."

"I know." Darla was blushing all over, and if she ever got the nerve to tell Judah where the wedding guests had been hiding, he would probably blush, too.

Or maybe he'd just be proud of himself.

"Then I guess we're going to run this route," Judah said, "if you're sure you want to marry me."

"I'm not one hundred percent certain," Darla said coyly, "particularly as you once told me that marriage was for whipped men, and you wouldn't be caught dead doing it."

"Got you into bed that night, didn't I, though?" Judah kissed her hand as Darla blushed again. "I knew you were the kind of girl who just couldn't resist a challenge."

"Come on," she said, knowing that later on she was going to get a lot of teasing from her lady friends—and heaven only knew what her mother thought about everything she was hearing. Fiona was probably shocked, too.

Judah smiled at her. "You're the most beautiful bride I've ever seen."

"Really?" Darla asked. "Have you seen many?"

"My fair share," her sexy rascal of a man said, "but somehow, you're the only woman who's ever made me feel like getting married is magical."

"Let's go before the magic wears off, then," Darla said, and Judah just smiled as he took her hand. He walked past the closet and banged on it, and then the bathroom door and banged on that, too, and said, "Ladies, don't be late to the wedding!" and Darla wondered if he'd just played hard to get to see if she wanted him enough to drag him to the altar.

He was the most infuriating man she'd ever known—and she was head over heels in love with him.

JUDAH WASN'T CERTAIN why he knew this moment was the best of his life, but the second that Darla Cameron said "I do" he felt like a new man. A better man. He couldn't have explained the emotions that swept over him as he watched her face while she spoke the words. All he knew was that something he'd waited for all his life had just agreed to be a part of him forever, and it was a very precious thing. He couldn't imagine not having Darla beside him at this moment and every other, and when he slipped the ring on her finger and she gazed up at him with wide, beautiful eyes, he just knew the moment was magic.

And he wanted it to last forever.

WEEKS AFTER THE WEDDING, gifts were still arriving at Darla's house, which now contained one cowboy husband and a bunch of well-wishers. Of course, everyone in Diablo wanted to know why she and Judah had married out of town. Darla simply told everyone that they'd decided to take a leaf from Aberdeen and Creed's wedding manual. Folks were satisfied with that, except that they were dying to see a wedding at Rancho Diablo.

Her house had become a shrine to weddings and babies. Darla had never seen so many presents. "These children will lack for nothing," she told Judah, and he grinned as he unwrapped a pair of tiny pink snakeskin cowboy boots.

Then the smile slipped from his face. "Wait. Why are these pink, Darla?"

She glanced over at the boots. "I don't know, but they're darling."

"I know that." He studied them, mystified. "But they should be blue. Blue is for boys. My sons will not be wearing pink boots, even if they're in a cradle where I can cover them with a blanket."

Darla laughed. "Babies don't wear cowboy boots in a cradle. They're for later on. Toddler age."

"We'll have to take these back."

Darla put down the crystal bowl she'd just unwrapped and went to look at the card. "The boots are from your brothers. Every single one of them signed the card. And there are two pairs of boots." She giggled. "I never realized the Callahans are so into gag gifts."

"I'm tired of gag gifts," Judah grumbled.

Darla looked at him. "What do you mean?" she said, wondering if he was referring to the gag gift that had brought them together in the first place.

Judah dropped the boots back into the box. "Uh-uh," he said, "you're not going to catch me that easily. I love gag gifts. I love my brothers' insane sense of humor." He kissed her cheek, her neck, finding his way to the buttons of her dress, which he casually popped open. "Don't worry that I meant the original, granddaddy of them all gag gift, because I didn't."

"You'd better not." She pulled away from his interested perusal of her cleavage. "Keep unboxing. We have a lot of thank-you letters to write."

"This house isn't going to be big enough for all of us and all this stuff," Judah pointed out.

Darla smiled. "Jackie and Aberdeen warned me this conversation would come up."

"Why?" He shook his head. "By the way, I'm not writing the thank-you letter for these pink boots. You can do that one."

Darla ignored his anxiety over the baby-girl boots. "Because somehow Jackie and Aberdeen said they found themselves eventually moving out to Rancho Diablo. I intend to hold firm, however."

"But it's such a great place to live." Judah held up a fluffy white baby blanket embroidered with a pink giraffe. "Why are we receiving pink things, Darla? Am I the last one in town to know something?"

She giggled. "It would be both of us. Unless my doctor has dropped a hint…"

They stared at each other.

"He wouldn't have," Darla said.

Judah shook his head. "No. Doc Graybill wouldn't."

"Unless Fiona wormed it out of him," Darla said.

Judah started to deny the possibility, then closed his mouth.

Darla sighed. "Let me know if anybody gives us something blue. But you see, there are reasons not to live at Rancho Diablo while we're still getting to know each other, Judah."

He gave her a look of innocence. "Did I ever hint that I wanted to move to the ranch?"

"You just claimed my house is too small."

"It is," Judah said, "but I like being as close to you as possible, Mrs. Callahan. In fact, I'd like to be a lot closer. Let's downsize and get a smaller house and a much smaller bed." He grabbed her around the waist, lifting her so that she had to put down the gift she'd been unwrapping, after which he carried her to the bedroom.

Darla laughed, enjoying her husband's antics, thinking that there was nothing more wonderful than making love with Judah on a summer afternoon in August. But then pain sliced across her belly, and she doubled up. Worried, Darla waited for the pain to go away.

"What happened? Are you all right?" Judah asked, leaning over her as she took deep breaths through her nose, trying to stay calm.

Another cramp racked her. "Probably just a little baby kick or two. Maybe we're having dancers. I don't think it's something I ate."

"We had oatmeal," he said. "Plain organic oatmeal with a tiny bit of brown sugar, nothing exciting, so that means, Darla, my love, that you get a trip in my chariot to see the doctor. We'll let him tell us if you've got garden variety gas cramps. Or just a lot of baby fun going on in there."

"I think you're right," Darla said, letting Judah lead her past the presents to the door, feeling her whole world shake around her.

"I'M NO COWARD," Judah told his brothers, who'd gathered around him to wait at the hospital, where Darla had been instantly sent by her concerned doctor, "but I'm shaking like a leaf right now. And if somebody doesn't come out of that room soon and tell me something about my wife, I'm going Rambo."

"Easy," Jonas said. "Darla needs you in a Zen state, not all whacked out. Everything's going to be fine."

"You're a cardiac guy, what the hell do you know about that end of the female body, anyway?" Judah snapped, appreciating his brother trying to ease his fears, but unable to do anything but bite down on any hand that reached out to comfort him. Like a feral wolf. That's how he felt: feral, primitive, caged. This is when he ran. Always separating himself from fear, anxiety, doubt.

This time he couldn't. He had to sit here and wait. Darla wasn't far enough along to be having the babies. He knew that, though Jonas hadn't proffered any professional opinion. Judah had seen his brother hanging around the nurses' station, ferreting information out of them. Medical terminology was way over Judah's head at the moment. He wanted a simple "your wife is fine, your babies are fine."

He wanted to be with Darla, but Darla had said she wanted him to stay in the waiting room. Had insisted.

The anxiety was killing him. He wondered why she hadn't wanted him with her. Shouldn't a wife want her husband? If he didn't hear something soon, he was going to make everybody mad by barging into his wife's room, and damn the consequences. Of all people, Darla knew best that he wasn't a patient worrier. He wasn't patient about anything.

At least he had his brothers with him to wait this agony out. "So, you guys are butts for giving Darla and me pink cowboy boots."

"You're having two babies," Sam pointed out. "We thought it was a priceless idea. Rafe came up with that one. I was rooting for pink baby dolls, but then Rafe suggested pink ropers and we immediately ordered them."

Judah grunted. "Why not blue?"

His brothers smirked at him.

"Why would you be the one to have the boys in this family?" Creed asked.

"A precedent has been set, if you haven't noticed," Pete said, "and we figure gambler's odds on pink being the order of the day."

"We'll see about that." He'd be happy to have babies of either sex—babies born healthy and yelling the ears off the nurses, though not tonight. They weren't quite ready to come out of the maternal oven. "What could be taking so long? Darla was just having a bit of a stomach ache."

The brothers turned their gazes to Jonas, who shrugged.

He was saved from answering by the doctor coming out. "Mr. Callahan?" he said, and all the brothers said, "Yes?"

"Sorry," Rafe said, "we're strung tighter than guitars. This is Dad." He pointed to Judah, who stood, with nervous pangs attacking him.

"I'm Darla's husband," he said. "These are my brothers."

"Why don't you step back here so we can talk, Mr. Callahan?" the doctor suggested. "I'm Dr. Feske."

"Can I see my wife?" Judah asked.

"You can, but let's talk first." They settled in a small room, and from the unsmiling expression on Dr. Feske's face, Judah knew the news wasn't good.

"Is Darla all right?"

"Your wife is fine. Your daughters were born prematurely—"

Judah tried to bat back the small specks of blackness dancing in front of his eyes. "Prematurely? They've hardly had time to grow."

"The success rate with preemies is quite good, though they'll be in the hospital for some time."

"Is something wrong?" Judah pressed his palms together, trying to keep his hands from shaking.

"We're running tests to make certain everything is as it should be, in the range for the amount of time they spent—"

"Doctor," Judah interrupted, "is Darla all right?"

He nodded. "Mr. Callahan, the prognosis is good for your entire family. Yes, the babies are young, but they seem well-developed and within the norm for what—"

"I'm sorry," Judah said. "But I can only take in about half of what you're saying, and I really need to see my wife." He wasn't certain he'd ever felt this desperate in his life. Fear gnawed at him, driving him crazy.

"I understand, Mr. Callahan. Would you like to see your wife, or visit the neonatal—"

"Darla," Judah said. "I need to see my wife."

The doctor led him to Darla's room. She was pale, and had a sheet pulled up to her neck.

"Hey, beautiful," Judah said. "How do you feel?"

"Like I've been through a washer." She looked at him as he tucked a strand of her hair behind her ear. "Have you seen the babies? What do you think?"

"I came to see you first." Judah kissed her forehead, then her lips.

"Well, apparently your daughters were anxious to see you," Darla told him. "They get their impatience from the Callahan side of the tree."

He tried to smile for her sake. "Everything's going to be fine."

"I know," Darla said. "They're Callahans. They're tough."

Judah nodded, his throat tight. He hoped so. God, how he hoped so.

Chapter Seventeen

When Judah saw his daughters ten minutes later, he honestly thought his heart stopped. He felt for his chest, wondering if he'd imagined a skipped beat. His daughters weren't tough at all. They were tiny, half the size of footballs maybe, with more tubes than a baby should endure taped to teeny appendages.

He wanted to cry. Pete's daughters had gone longer in the womb than these, and at their birth, Judah had been totally unnerved by those tiny little babies. He was overcome now by the urge to hold his daughters, but he knew he couldn't.

He had to stay strong for Darla.

"You're as beautiful as your mother," he told his twin girls through the glass. "You don't know this now, but she's a nurse. She can help you grow big and strong."

Then his shoulders began to shake, and he started to cry, wondering what he could have done differently to help his tiny babies grow. The doctor didn't have to lie to him. Judah could tell that these babies might not make it, and if they did, they might not be strong, barrel-racing, boot-scooting cowgirls. "You've got me on your team," he told them, "and I'm a big, tough guy. Daddy won't let anything happen to you. Nothing at all."

But he thought they needed guardian angels, too.

"Don't worry," a voice said next to him.

Judah turned, startled to see Fiona's Native American friend standing at his side.

"Do not worry," he said, his black eyes sure and calm as he met Judah's gaze. "These are blessings, and they are meant to be here. They are meant to make you strong."

Judah blinked. "You mean, I must make them strong."

"No." He went back to perusing the tiny bassinets.

After a moment, he surprised Judah by taking out an iPhone and snapping a picture. "I will say prayers," he told Judah, and then ambled down the hall.

Judah stared after the man, who disappeared around the corner before he had a chance to say anything else, stunned as he was by the sudden visit. Then he glanced back at his daughters, his gaze searching, but strangely enough, he felt calmer now.

"I'm going to go take care of your mother," Judah told his daughters. "But I'll be back. Every day you'll see my face at this window. For now you just rest, and when you're ready, I'll be here to hold you. Daddy will always be around to hold you, until finally it's your turn to take care of me."

Judah loped off to find his wife. It was just beginning to hit him that he was a father now, for real. Those tiny bundles were his, and he felt as if he'd just been handed the world's biggest trophy and the shiniest buckle ever made.

"HE'S CHANGED," FIONA told Burke a week later. "I don't know what's come over Judah, but he's seems in permanent 'ohm' mode. Have you noticed the calmer, more relaxed Judah? When he's not at the hospital, that is."

"Guess he likes being a father." Burke put away the last of the dishes and smiled at her. "He just didn't know how much he would, maybe."

"He's different." Fiona considered her nephew with some pleasure. "Nothing rattles him anymore. He never even mentions being shot. I've got the ballistics report from the sheriff, but Judah never talks about what happened that night, so I'm sure not going to bring it up."

Burke shrugged. "The shooting wasn't important to Judah, as long as Darla was fine. I think he believes it was an accident, and if it wasn't, Sheriff Cartwright'll let him know. All Judah cares about is that he married Darla with no static from next door, and he has his daughters. That's all that matters to him." Burke looked over Fiona's shoulder at the paper she held. "So what does it say?"

"That the gun was a .38. It's not registered to Bode or anybody else in this town. Likely it was black market." Fiona frowned, her thoughts moving from the pleasant aspect of her two new great-nieces to the rumblings on the ranch. "Which scares me, because it means we don't know what we're dealing with. It's a new element. I was hoping it was Bode," she said, "because we could have easily handled him."

Burke frowned. "Does the sheriff have any theories?"

"They found no footprints, and no new vehicles coming through town that they noticed that night or since. No one's been in town asking questions, and nobody has contacted the sheriff's office with any tips. And everyone knows about the shooting, because most of Diablo was there. So if somebody strange was hanging around, Sheriff Cartwright would get a call in a hurry."

"Why would someone we don't know want to take a potshot at Judah?" Burke asked.

Fiona and he looked at each other for a long time.

Then they turned back to cleaning the kitchen, both to their own tasks, without saying another word.

SINCE DARLA HAD REQUIRED a C-section, her mother and all her friends wanted to come over and take care of her. Judah found he didn't have as much time alone with his wife as he wished, thanks to the steady stream of callers. He'd asked Darla if she'd like for him to start screening her visitors a bit, trim her social time, so she could rest—and so he could spend some time with her.

Darla had said she enjoyed the company and knew he needed to be working, so he might as well go do what he had to do and let everybody else look in on her if they wanted to. He'd tried to act as if he had a whole lot he could be doing, but the truth was, his brothers were covering for him, and shooed him away from the chores if he ever came to help.

It was getting depressing. There was nothing for him to do at the hospital except stare through the glass at his daughters, and because he was there so much, it seemed to him that they never grew. He didn't detect any changes at all, which gave him the nearest thing to a panic attack he could ever recall having.

In fact, staring at his babies and not being able to do anything to help them was worse than a bad ride. He'd rather be thrown any day of the week than be helpless, as he was now.

And Darla didn't want him hanging around. That much was clear. She said she had "lady" moments he couldn't help with, which he'd decided was code for

I'm trying to figure out pumping breast milk, so I need Jackie and Aberdeen more than you right now.

Although he would have been more than happy to help with that. He was pretty sure Darla's breasts were a lot bigger right now, and he wouldn't have minded re-acquainting himself with them, which he supposed was a chauvinistic thought, except that he missed his wife and wanted to feel he had some connection with her.

He felt like a roommate. He wasn't even sleeping with her, having banished himself to a guest room so she could rest, and so he wouldn't accidentally turn over in the night, forget and reach for her, and crush her stitches or something. He didn't know if she had stitches. He wasn't certain how a C-section was performed, exactly. He did feel that his wife was in a fragile state right now, and the best thing he could do was not roll over on her in his sleep.

But she hadn't invited him into her room, either.

Forced away from chores on the ranch and outnumbered by females in his house, Judah slunk off to the bunkhouse to try to center himself. He flung himself onto the leather sofa and closed his eyes in complete appreciation of the quietude.

Which lasted all of five minutes before the door blew open on a strong gust of wind. Judah didn't open his eyes until he realized the door hadn't closed.

He sighed upon seeing his visitor. "It would be you, Tunstall. An ill wind blows no good."

"Your brothers said I'd find you here," Sidney said. "Mind if I talk to you?"

Judah sat up and motioned to the sofa. "Sit."

He waited for Sidney to unload. Hopefully, this was about anything other than Darla. Right now, Judah wasn't in the mood to discuss his wife, or his life, or much of anything. He didn't even want company.

"Congratulations on the twins," Sidney said.

"No doubt you wish Darla was married to you. Probably, you figure that as a doctor, you could care for them better than I can," Judah said sourly.

"Problems?" Sidney asked.

"Do I look like I'm having problems?"

"You always look like you're having problems, Judah." Sidney smiled. "Your daughters are going to be fine."

Judah crooked a brow. "Do you think so? Or are you just blowing smoke up my ass for your own nefarious purposes?"

"Now, Callahan," Sidney said. "Darla told me you were having a few little worries about your girls. I just came to reassure you."

Judah grimaced. "Because you're a pediatrician or a wizard, and know so much."

Sidney shook his head. "Look. I know all this animosity isn't because of Darla. I know you're worried. Darla loves you. She just wants you to lighten up so she can quit worrying about *you*."

"Did she send you to tell me this or are you applying for a job as a marriage counselor?" Judah couldn't have said why he was so ornery. Pretty much anything Tunstall said was going to rile him. His brothers could give testimony to the fact that just about everything annoyed Judah lately. "Okay," he finally said. "I'll admit I'm a little worked up. But that doesn't mean I want you here ladling out advice and words of comfort I don't need."

Sidney nodded. "All right."

"So you can go." Judah waved a hand toward the door.

"I haven't finished."

Judah raised a brow. "Then would you get on with it? I don't have all day to listen to your clichés."

Sidney laughed. "You really have it bad, don't you?"

"Have what bad?" He frowned.

"Never mind," the doctor said. "Listen, what I wanted to ask you is…" He lowered his voice, even though there was no one else in the bunkhouse. "Well, I've been talking to Diane lately. And I was wondering—"

Judah held up a hand. "No. You can't marry her to fulfill the terms of that inheritance that's hanging over your head. Diane isn't Darla. Darla was being…well, she was trying to be helpful because she's like that, and you caught her at a difficult time in her life, and…I don't want to talk about it."

"I wasn't talking about Darla. You were," Sidney said. "All I want to know is if you think Diane is ready to date. I didn't say I wanted to marry her. Jeez."

Judah lowered his eyelids, considering him through slitted eyes. "You're kind of a snake in the grass, aren't you?"

"I resent that!"

Sidney really did sound riled. Judah grunted, realizing he'd drawn blood, when he hadn't drawn any with all the other barbs he'd flung at the doc. "All right. Why Diane?"

"I like her," Sidney said with a sudden flush of his angled cheekbones. "I like her little girls."

"Those are Creed and Aberdeen's little girls, too," Judah said. "And Diane is… I don't know about Diane. Why the hell are you asking me?"

Sidney shrugged. "I'd like to do this right." He stood. "Anyway, sorry to take up your time. Good luck with the twins and—"

"Hang on a minute," Judah said, motioning for him to sit back down. "Don't go off all offended."

"I'm not offended," Sidney said. "You're always a little rude, but I understand why."

"I am not rude," Judah stated. "I pride myself on being a gentleman."

"Whatever," Sidney said. "As long as Darla sees that side of you, I don't care how you are."

Judah took a long, hard look at his one-time rival. "Diane had a difficult road to hoe. If you ask her out, you take good care of her. Which I know you will," he said generously. "You're an okay guy, and I'd probably feel all right about you if you hadn't tried to marry my girl."

"Darla wasn't your girl," Sidney said, "and as I recall, at that time you had your head so far up your ass you couldn't see daylight. Darla didn't want to be unmarried and pregnant. This is a very small town, and everyone knows her and her mother, and that's why she was willing to help me out. But it had nothing to do with love or sex or anything but a bargain between friends. You were not her friend, you were a butthead, and she wasn't going to sit around and wait for you."

Judah listened to Sidney's soliloquy, then shook his head. "I've been in love with that woman for years."

Sidney's eyebrows shot up. "Are you serious?"

Judah nodded. "Yep."

"Does…Darla know this?"

"I don't think so," Judah said, trying to remember if he'd ever gotten around to telling her that she'd held his heart for so long he'd sometimes thought he might not ever get it back. "Things have been moving pretty fast."

"Yeah, well." Sidney walked to the door. "If I had a prescription to offer you, it would be to sit down and talk to your wife instead of hiding out over here. You don't want to be in the bunkhouse, you want to be with Darla."

Judah nodded. It was true, and the fact that he didn't want to stomp Sidney's head in for implying he wasn't handling his love life very well was a great sign. "Hey, good luck with Diane."

Sidney smiled. "Thanks." He disappeared out the door.

Judah got to his feet, took a deep breath and turned off the lamps.

It was time to go home. It was past time for some honesty between him and the lovely Mrs. Judah Callahan.

If he could shoo all the well-meaning friends and family out of the henhouse.

Chapter Eighteen

When Judah entered the house, Darla was surrounded by about sixteen ladies giving her a baby shower. He walked in tall, dark and handsome—and Darla could tell at once that something was wrong with her man.

He looked darker than usual.

"Hi, Judah," Darla said.

"Have some punch, Judah," Fiona added, handing him a crystal cup filled with pink liquid.

"And a cucumber sandwich." Mavis passed him a plate with tiny, triangle-shaped, crustless sandwiches. Judah looked perturbed, as if he didn't know what to do with such insubstantial food.

"And a petit four," Corinne Abernathy said. "The frosting is so sweet it'll give you a cavity on contact. But it's so good!" She put two on a tiny dish she stacked on the other plate he was holding.

Nadine Waters handed him a pink napkin. "We decided to decorate the nursery. Which meant a shopping spree! And of course, a small party."

Darla smiled at Judah. He looked overwhelmed, ready to flee. And she didn't want him to go anywhere. She wanted him to stay and relax for a change. He never relaxed around her; he never relaxed *here*. She was pretty certain he had complete fish-out-of-water syndrome in her house.

"Let me show you what the ladies did for our nursery, Judah." She got up, and Judah practically dropped all his plates, plus the crystal cup, rushing to press her back down on the sofa.

"Don't get up. You're supposed to be resting," he said. "In fact, I'm not sure all this excitement is good for you."

"I'm fine," Darla said with some exasperation. "I'm not made of china."

"I can find the nursery myself," he said, tipping his hat at the ladies as he escaped down the hall. He'd left his food untouched on the table, and Darla suspected he was happy to be away from all the females.

"Excuse me," she said to her friends. "I have to go tend to my husband. I hate to cut this short—it's been lovely—but I need to settle him down or he'll never feel like this is home."

Fiona grinned. "We completely understand. We'll clean up in here, and you go calm a cowboy."

"Thank you." She looked around at her friends. "I can never thank you enough for everything you've done. And the nursery is a dream come true."

Corinne touched her hand. "We'll be quiet as mice, so don't mind us at all."

Darla went down the hall. Judah wasn't in the nursery; the door hadn't been opened. She found him in the guest room, sitting on the bed he'd commandeered for his own. "Hey, husband," she said.

"Hi." He glanced up morosely. "You should be resting. Not having company all the time."

She sat down next to him. "Judah, I can take care of myself."

"I'd like to take care of you."

She gingerly put her face against his. "You need to work. The ladies are happy to keep me from losing my mind while my babies can't be here."

"I can be here." Judah allowed her to stroke his cheek, then caught her fingertips and pressed them to his lips, kissing them. "I want to be here."

"And I want your life to go on as it was, unchanged, until our daughters come home. I want you to stop worrying. There's nothing you can do here, Judah. I'm learning about my body, and healing, and figuring out why some parts of me work differently than they used to. Some of it's a little strange. I'm a bit embarrassed by it all."

"Why?" He lay down, pulling her alongside him and cradling her head on his shoulder. "I want to get to know my wife."

"All right. No more company. You can do everything for me from now on. You can help me pump breast milk—"

"You're not scaring me."

Darla smiled. "And you can watch me while I nap, which is a lot of excitement—"

"I can do that."

"And you can help write our thank-you letters for all the wedding and baby shower gifts."

He leaned down to kiss her. "We don't have to go all crazy."

Laughing, she pushed him away so she could recline on his shoulder again. "You don't want to be stuck here all the time. You'd be bored out of your skull. You're a man of action, not a couch cowboy."

"True," he said, "but if I can talk you into being

naked, and just the two of us watching soaps together, I could learn to like being king of the couch."

"Ugh." She closed her eyes. "I'm not going to be the queen of the couch. I can't wait to get back in my jeans so I can ride my horse."

"Let's move out to the ranch," Judah said. "There's a bunkhouse that we're not using for anything right now. We could call it home. Then I wouldn't be away from my job. You'd be there and I'd be there, and we'd have more room, and the babies would have all the family and friends around they could stand."

"I thought the ranch might be sold."

"Maybe," Judah said, "but I've got faith in Sam. He's got a lot of aces in his boot. But even if it was, we'd still be together."

"Just homeless," Darla said, loving the fact that she and Judah were lying together, dreaming about the future, comfortable with one another. This was how she wanted it to be. She wanted them to slowly grow together and bond.

"Do you doubt me, wife?" Judah cuddled her, kissing her neck—but not touching her.

"I won't break if you hold me, Judah."

"You can't lure me that easily. The doctor said rest, and rest you shall do." He nipped her neck lightly, then moved back to her lips. "Quit avoiding the subject."

Darla gave a small moan, wishing she were healed and that she could make love to her husband. "What subject was that?" she asked, distracted with lust from all Judah's kisses. *I could fly, he makes me feel so light, so gauzy.*

So in love.

"Do you doubt my ability to provide for you?"

"No," she said. "When were we talking about that? I never asked you to provide for me."

He sighed. "Typical new-age female."

She kissed his forehead, troubled but not sure why. "Typical old-fashioned male."

"Darn right," he said, and then Darla drifted off to sleep, vaguely aware that she'd missed something important, but not sure what.

WHEN DARLA AWAKENED, Judah had slipped away. The sun was shining brightly outside, and birds were singing, and—

"Heck," she said, and hopped from the bed. She remembered what they'd been talking about. He wanted to move to the ranch. She'd been giddy with lust.

"Yes, Virginia, females lust. At least I do, for Judah," she muttered, and jumped in the shower. She bathed carefully around the stitches, glad that Judah wouldn't ever see her like this—she wasn't about to let him—and then put on a comfy, oversize pair of shorts and a T-shirt that she would normally only wear for cleaning.

She went into the nursery, doubtful that Judah had even glanced in here to see the ladies' handiwork. He wasn't coping well with the fact that his daughters had come early. None of it was real yet—or he was scared. Men like Judah avoided what bothered them.

But it was a beautiful nursery now, all pink iced confections gracing smooth white furniture. She couldn't wait to bring her daughters home. Their new room was like a music box, and—

Judah hadn't looked at this room because it wasn't real. In fact, this wasn't his home. He wasn't comfortable here, and he never would be.

She was going to have to fix the situation, if they were ever going to truly be two halves of a whole.

FIONA WRINKLED HER NOSE and hung up the phone. "Judah Callahan, what have you done to that wife of yours?"

He blinked, caught in the act of lifting a piece of pound cake from the covered glass pedestal as he headed out to the barn. "Let me think about it." Squinting, he took a bite of fragrant cake, sighing with happiness. "Haven't done anything to my wife. Doctor's orders."

"That's not what I meant," Fiona said. "Corinne just called and said Darla is listing her house with her."

"Listing her house?"

"As in preparing to sell it." His aunt put her hands on her hips. "When we left that house last night, you two were supposed to be cozy as bugs in a rug."

"We were." Judah raised his cake to her. "This is delicious."

"Then why is she selling her house?"

"Beats me." He shrugged. "I've never understood the mysteries of the female mind. And that includes yours, Aunt." He kissed her cheek. "Though I do love you."

She brushed him back. "If she moves farther away from me, I'll be annoyed with you. You go over there right now and be a gentleman. Tell her you don't want her to move."

"I can't," Judah said. "She has a mind of her own."

"Did you tell her you wanted her to move?" Fiona shot him a suspicious glance.

"Yes, but..." He stopped, put down the cake. "But she wouldn't do that for me." Would she? "I asked Darla to move to the ranch, and she'd said she didn't want to in case we lost the place, and then I asked her if she doubted my ability to provide. And that was that," he said. "Honest. Moving barely came up."

Fiona glared. "You can't guilt your wife into moving when she doesn't even have her babies home from the hospital, Judah. She hasn't recovered from giving birth!"

He felt like a heel. "I admit it probably wasn't the right time to bring up the topic."

"And now she's listed her house." Fiona shook her head. "You need to tell Darla that she doesn't have to sell it."

"Why?" Judah asked. "Isn't it a good thing that she's willing to make me happy?"

Fiona closed her eyes for a second. When she opened them again, she just shrugged. "Nephew, you'll have to figure this one out on your own."

Which didn't sound good, if Fiona wasn't in the mood to dish out wise counsel. It sounded as if she was adopting a new, mind-my-own-business strategy, and Judah knew that could only mean one thing.

He had stepped in it big time.

"Hey," Jonas said as he walked by.

"Hey." Judah fell in beside his brother. "If you might possibly be in the doghouse with your lady, but you're not sure, and yet you don't want to be in the doghouse if you're not actually there—"

"Jeez," Jonas said, "I haven't had my coffee yet. Could you speak in some other format besides riddle?"

"I'm not sure if Darla is making a big decision because of me," Judah said, following his brother into the barn. "I don't want her doing something she'll regret. So I'm wondering how to approach this. Is it a flowers situation? Or a turquoise bracelet situation?"

"Boy, you're dumb," Jonas said. "The fact that you're

even asking shows that you have no idea of the work-ings of the female mind. What did you do to Darla?"

"I didn't do anything to her!" Judah was up-to-here with everyone assuming that he'd done something to his wife. "All I said was that we should move out to the ranch. Next thing I know, she's put a call in to list her house. I hear all this from Fiona. Darla didn't tell me."

Jonas slumped on a hay bale. "The problem is that you're slow."

Judah hesitated. "Slow?"

"Slow to figure things out." He waved a hand ma-jestically. "Obviously Darla thinks you're an ape and is moving as far away from you as possible."

Judah's heart nearly stopped. "I did not do anything to upset my wife!"

"Did you ask her?"

He shook his head. "No."

"If you did, she'd probably tell you that she liked her little house, but since you used faulty condoms and got her pregnant, now she's going to have to sell her house and live out of a cardboard box with you."

"Cardboard box?" Judah blinked. "Rancho Diablo is no cardboard box."

"Yeah, well, that's if it doesn't become Rancho Bode." Jonas shrugged. "I guess she's taking a leap of faith that you'll provide."

That's what he'd asked her: if she doubted his ability to provide for her. Judah felt a little guilty about that.

"So, I'm guessing turquoise bracelet, huh?" Judah asked, and Jonas sighed.

"I'd go ahead and make it sapphires," his brother said. "And make good friends with the jeweler. I have a feeling your marriage is going to require a frequent-shopper discount."

Judah snorted. "Why am I asking you? You've never even had a girlfriend," he said, and stomped off.

Jonas was wrong.

But just in case, maybe it wouldn't hurt to make a quick stop on the way to Darla's.

WHEN JUDAH GOT TO Darla's house, the place was empty. No note, no nothing. A shiver ran across his scalp. He didn't even have her cell phone number.

Jackie did. He could ask her, but then everyone would know that he and Darla hadn't gotten to the point of even exchanging information, and he'd look pretty much a dope, which was how he felt at the moment.

He didn't know if she was at the bridal shop or the hospital. "She's not supposed to be out of the house," he muttered. "Doctor's orders."

Fear jumped into him, and he hurried to his truck. What if she'd had a problem? What if something had gone wrong and he hadn't been here to help her? After he'd sent her friends and family away, and made a big deal of how he could take care of her, he hadn't even bothered to ask for her cell number.

He tore down the driveway and nearly collided with Jackie's truck as she was pulling in. Darla was in the front seat. He was relieved, but still plenty unhappy.

He hopped out of the truck and strode to Darla's window. "Where have you been?"

"What?" she said, while Jackie stared at him, almost gawking. "What do you mean, where have I been?"

Judah tried to cool his jets so his blood pressure wouldn't pop out of his head like a fountain. "You scared me. I didn't know where you were."

Darla blinked big blue eyes at him. "I had my two-week doctor's appointment, Judah. Goodness."

"Oh." Sheepishly, he stepped away from the window, and the mirth in Jackie's eyes. "Sorry about that. Hi, Jackie. Thanks for driving Darla."

"Hi, Judah," Jackie said. "Mind moving your truck so I can get by?"

"I'm going." Okay, he was going to be the laughingstock of the town. He'd just made a superior ass of himself. He backed up, parked, then followed the ladies to the house. They didn't pay a whole lot of attention to him as they went inside. Darla slowly seated herself on the sofa, and Jackie got her a glass of ice water.

"I'm going now," Jackie said to Judah. "Think you can handle it from here?"

"Yes," he said, his tone gruff, his gaze drinking in his tired wife. "Thanks, Jackie."

"No problem. She has another appointment in a couple of weeks, so put that on your calendar so you don't give yourself a coronary." His sister-in-law smiled at him and waved goodbye to Darla as she popped out the door.

"Sorry," Judah said. "I've lost my mind."

Darla sighed. "I didn't think to tell you because it wasn't important."

"Yeah." He took a seat beside his wife. "I won't always be like this. I don't think so, anyway."

"You won't," Darla said, "or I'll put you back in the pond, toad."

"Speaking of ponds," Judah said, "Fiona told me you might be looking for a new one."

She closed her eyes, leaning her head back. "It's as good a time as any, I suppose."

"I thought we talked about the fact that you're not supposed to be doing anything, not even so much as moving one of those tiny, pink-painted piggies of yours," he said with a frown.

"Judah, I only made a phone call. I didn't lift weights or pull a truck." Darla sighed. "Are you always going to be difficult and overbearing? Because I'm not sure I saw this side of you when I let you sweep me off my feet."

"Who swept who?" He brought her hand to his lips and kissed it, then took the plunge. "Are you thinking about moving out to the ranch?" He ran a lock of her silver-blond hair between his fingers, mesmerized by the silkiness of it, as he waited for her to give him the answer he wanted so badly.

"I've always wanted to live in a renovated bunk-house," Darla said.

"Have you really?" Judah asked, and she said, "No. But I'm willing to give it a shot."

He grinned, the happiest man on earth. "Thank you," he said. "If you're sure."

She rolled her head to look at him. "I'm not completely sure."

"Oh." He didn't know what to make of that. He just knew he'd feel better if she was at the ranch, where more eyes could be on her, and on his daughters.

"But I've always been practical." She gazed at him. "Something tells me my downside risk is minimal."

"Can I have your cell number now that I've talked you into moving into a run-down bunkhouse with me?" he said, and Darla smiled.

"Exchanging cell numbers seems like a very serious step."

He kissed her nose. "Commitment is fun. You'll see."

THE NEXT MORNING, Judah was feeling slightly better about things. He and Darla had spent a pleasant evening together, even sleeping in the same room. It was a milestone for him. He was becoming less afraid of hurting her, and the future seemed pretty rosy. One small step at a time, baby steps, he told himself, whistling as he went to the barn. *And soon my babies will be coming home, too.*

"Hey, did you hear the big news?" Sam asked from the barn office. Jonas and Rafe were sitting in there with him. They all wore half-moon grins.

Judah paused. "I never hear any news. What's the news flash?"

They all laughed, practically waiting to pounce on him *en masse.*

"That you got your wife's cell phone number!" Sam said, guffawing like a pirate. "You're really slick now, bro."

Rafe nodded. "Jackie told us all about it. She said you were in a panic when she brought Darla home from her appointment yesterday. That you were breathing like a woman in labor."

"I was not." Judah slung his hat onto the desk. "I just...I mean, what the hell was I supposed to think?"

"We're just ribbing you. The news is that Sidney and Diane eloped," Jonas said.

"What?" Judah's jaw went slack.

"Yep," Sam said. "Just think, if Sidney had married Darla, he'd probably have had her cell number by now. But that's okay. We're not embarrassed by you or anything. Every family's got its runt in the love department."

"No one has to tell me that the small details have been known to get by me." Judah looked at his brothers. "Is this good news about Sidney and Diane?"

They all shrugged.

"It's not bad news," Sam said. "It's just news."

"I guess." Judah sank onto a chair. "But it's so fast."

"Maybe for you," Rafe said. "But not every man is frightened of women."

"I am not—oh, hell. Why do I bother?" He was a little afraid of Darla, he supposed. He definitely had her on a high pedestal, keeping her out of reach. "I don't feel like I'm standing in knee-deep mud. It feels like I'm running pretty fast."

"But you're not getting anywhere." Sam nodded. "We understand. We're trying to help you."

"I don't need any help." Judah got up. "We get plenty of help. More than we need."

"But Sidney bagged his female and is off on a beach in Hawaii, while you're making your wife move into a little-used bunkhouse," Rafe said. "We think your romance quotient is low. We've been theorizing about where you went wrong."

"I haven't," Judah said, heading off to the stalls, wondering if he had gone wrong, when he wanted everything to be so right.

Chapter Nineteen

"So the ballistics showed that the bullet was from a .38," Fiona told Judah as she swept out the bunkhouse. "Sheriff Cartwright doesn't think it was a random hunter's bullet."

"I could have figured that." Judah watched his little aunt getting the bunkhouse ready for his brood to take over. "What can I do to help?"

"Stay out of my way," Fiona said cheerfully. "I think I'm going to have to take down these red-and-white gingham curtains. They're too bunkhousey for a new family. I know Darla will want to decorate your home, but she doesn't have any time right now, and this can all be changed later. So I think we'll do plain white lace curtains Darla can replace."

Judah helped his aunt move some furniture. "You work too hard. Let me have that broom."

"You just take care of your arm. Don't think I haven't noticed that you bark at Darla but haven't exactly been taking care of yourself."

He shrugged. "It was a scratch."

Fiona sighed. "Judah, remember when you found the cave?"

"Yeah." He pushed the furniture back and waited for Fiona's broom to land in a new spot so he could try to help her. "If you tell me what needs cleaning, I can do this, Aunt Fiona."

"You're not paying attention." She wrapped a rag on the end of the broom and gestured to the overhead fans for him to dust. "You didn't mention the cave to anyone, did you?"

"No. Not even my daughters, whom I spend every waking moment with when I'm not with my wife." He grinned. "They're making good progress. And the doc says in a month or so they'll be over five pounds and can come home."

His aunt smiled. "Maybe home will be here, if Darla doesn't change her mind."

"Why would she?" He frowned but didn't look at Fiona as he dutifully moved the broom around the wagon wheel chandeliers and fans.

"I don't know." She watched him with an eagle eye to make certain no dust was missed. "Anyway, if we can keep to one subject, Burke and I have been talking it over, and we think there's possibly a connection between you getting shot and the cave."

Just talking about it was making his arm hurt. Or maybe reaching for dust and cobwebs was doing that. Judah ignored the pain and kept dusting, wanting everything perfect for Darla. He was so happy she was willing to live here that he could hardly stand it. And then, in time, he'd build her the house of her dreams.

Their family would begin here, at Rancho Diablo.

"Did you hear me?" Fiona asked, and Judah snapped his thoughts away from Darla.

"Yes, dear aunt. You said the cave is the reason I got shot. But that makes no sense, because Bode doesn't know about the cave, and he wouldn't shoot me at my own wedding, anyway." He handed the broom back to his aunt. "Clean enough even for a nurse."

Fiona looked at him. "Bode didn't do it."

She had his full attention now. "How do you know?"

"A feeling I have."

Judah snorted. "You don't act on feelings. You've always been too practical for anything but data and hard evidence. Even when we were kids, you didn't believe anything you heard about us until you saw proof that we'd painted a neighbor's goat for the Fourth of July, or that we'd been smoking in the fields outside of town."

Fiona's lips went flat. "If I'd believed every rumor I'd heard about you kids, you would have been doing chores for the rest of your lives."

Judah shrugged. "So it makes no sense that you'd be dealing in hunches now."

"Except that it's not really a hunch. There are things I can't tell you—"

"Why?" Judah demanded. "We're all full-grown men, Aunt Fiona, not little boys. You don't have to bear the burden of protecting us any longer."

"I know." She nodded. "I'll tell you eventually, as soon as I know the time is right. And I know that time is coming very soon. I knew it the night you got shot."

"I just don't understand what it has to do with the cave. I know someone would love to help himself to the silver. But why pick me?" He looked at her for a moment. "Because I found it and whoever it was didn't want me to?"

She didn't say anything. Judah's blood began to run cold. "You're not trying to tell me that Darla and the girls might be in danger, are you?"

"I don't know," Fiona said. "I didn't expect anyone to try to harm you. Frankly, I'm scared to death."

He sank onto the old sofa in front of a fireplace that hadn't been used in years. "What does Burke say?"

"That you should be careful," Fiona said simply. "We don't know what we're up against now."

"But it has nothing to do with Bode trying to run us off."

She shook her head. "We think Bode is the type of man who tries to buy everything he wants, or cheat people of it, but he wouldn't kill anybody. I know I cracked him with my bag that night, but once I cooled down, I realized how unlike him it would be to use foul means. He's too much about the thrill of destruction. He likes being able to take people down legally, and sometimes a little bit under the law. I'm not saying he'd bring us a loaf of bread if we were starving. He'd enjoy watching a family be run off. But he wouldn't physically harm any of us. He wouldn't want Julie to see him in a bad light."

"So you're telling me I'm bringing my wife and kids here, and we have a murderer running around?" Anger assailed Judah as he thought of what he would do if anybody ever tried to harm Darla and the babies.

For the first time, he knew he was capable of harming another human. And it scared him. But he knew he would protect his family at all costs. It made him keenly aware of how Fiona must have felt all these years about the family for which she'd been responsible.

"We were at Darla's for your wedding that night," she said softly, reminding him. "We weren't here."

His throat went dry; blood pounded in his ears. "You're right. I've always thought of Rancho Diablo as the unsafe place because of Bode." But Fiona was correct. Whoever shot him—if it had been on purpose— had followed him to his own wedding, a time when he would have had his guard down completely. It felt like a warning.

"Darla's alone at the house," Judah said, and ran for his truck.

DARLA LET OUT A SCREECH when the back door crashed open. As Judah burst into the living room, she wanted to bash him with the baby name book she was holding. "What in the world, Judah?"

He slowed down, his eyes crazy, his dark hair blown and wild around his head. He was, unfortunately, handsome as all get-out, but she wanted to slap him silly. Maybe she would as soon as her heart slowed down.

"What are you doing?" he demanded.

"What does it look like I'm doing? I'm trying to pick baby names. For heaven's sake, Judah, you frightened me!" She glared at him. "I thought we talked about this. You were going to calm down." She worked herself up into some righteous anger. "You just can't keep acting like a madman. You've been crazy ever since you found out I was pregnant, and it's only gotten worse." She bit her lip, then said, "Or maybe I never really knew you."

"Of course we didn't know each other," Judah replied. "I could never get you to even talk to me."

"Well, I'm talking now, and I swear, if you don't calm down…" She looked at him. "Why did you come in here like you were running from the devil, anyway? What is your problem?"

He put his good arm around her, holding her. She could feel his heart beating hard in his chest, ricocheting in panic. "What is wrong with you, Judah?"

"I don't know," he said. "Actually, I do know, but some things are better left unsaid."

She pushed him away and went to stare at him from

the sofa. "I don't know that I can live with a crazy man. You literally frightened me out of my wits. I didn't know who was coming in the house." She frowned at him. "Why did you use the back door, anyway?"

"I overshot the driveway," he said, a little embarrassed. "So I came in the rear. I was in a hurry." He gathered her to him once more, ignoring his wounded arm. "I worry about you, I guess. And did you know that Sidney and Diane eloped?"

She pushed him away a final time and said sternly, "The driveway is not a speedway. You nearly hit Jackie's truck the other day." Darla gave him a long look, thinking it was a shame that her handsome husband had such race car driver tendencies. "Look. Is there anything I can do to make you feel less insane?"

"I don't think so," Judah said. "I think it's the new me."

She sighed, trying to be patient, which wasn't easy. "You can't be jealous if Sidney and Diane have eloped, so what's bugging you now?"

He shrugged. "I wouldn't say I'm done being jealous of ol' Sid. Sometimes I wonder what women see in that bony bronc buster. But as far as what's bugging me, it's not Tunstall. I haven't figured everything out yet, to be honest. It's a work in progress."

"So maybe you're always going to be a fat-headed ass?" Darla was in no mood to let him off the hook. "You're going to have to get a grip."

He would, but not today. He'd been a dad for only four days—and as far as he was concerned, he had over a month to change. He could do it. "Keep the faith, wife."

ON THE FIRST OF AUGUST, Judah could honestly say that "Coming Home Day" was the best day of his life. "Miss

Jennifer Belle Callahan," he said proudly, laying daughter number one gently in her bassinet, "and Miss Molly Mavis Callahan." He placed his second daughter near her sister in a matching bassinet.

Instantly, both babies began to cry. "They don't like their names," Judah said, feeling helpless.

"They want to be together." Darla sat up in bed and motioned for him to hand her his daughters. Gingerly, as if he was handling small, fragile pieces of china, he passed the girls one by one to their mother. Darla made sure their blankets were wrapped properly, then put the girls side by side next to her on the bed. Instantly, they stopped fussing, and Judah's nerves stopped jumping.

"I don't like it when I don't know what they want."

"You'll learn. We'll learn. Right now, I'm sure the girls just want to feel like they did in the womb."

He nodded. "Looks good to me. Any room for Dad?"

"Come on." Darla motioned to the other side of the twins.

"I don't know," Judah said, hanging back. "I read that it was bad for Dad to sleep in the bed with babies."

"It might be, but you're not going to sleep," Darla said. "I haven't seen you sleep for weeks. Do you ever?"

He thought about it. "Now that you mention it, I don't think so."

Darla smiled. "Just don't roll over on them, and everybody will be happy."

He stared down, wanting very much to get in but not sure it was safe. The bed seemed so big, for one thing. And it was full of females. While this was normally a good thing, these females were all in a very delicate state. "I think I'll wait until everyone is a little more, uh, ready for company," he said, backing away. "I'll sit over here in the rocker and watch you ladies enjoy having the bed to yourselves. It won't last forever, so take advantage of it while you can."

Darla shook her head at him. "You're afraid of your daughters."

"Sometimes I'm afraid of you. I'm not ashamed to admit that." Judah waved his hand and then reached for a pink baby blanket to roll up behind his head. "The guy who can't admit the truth isn't much of a man."

"That's nice. Did you make that up?" Darla asked. "I've never known the philosophizing side of you."

He yawned. "I think so. Then again, I might have plagiarized it from somebody smarter than me."

And then he fell asleep.

Darla looked at her knocked-out husband and smiled tenderly down at her babies. "He's going to be better now, I think, girls. Bringing you home was the best thing that could happen to him." It was true. The moment he'd held his daughters and brought them home, she'd sensed a change in him. He wasn't frantic or rattled up anymore.

Judah seemed content.

Darla kissed each of her daughters on the head, falling in love with all the new people in her life, and the magic she could feel binding them together as a family.

WHEN JUDAH OPENED his eyes, he found Darla and the babies gone. Pushing himself out of the rocker, he went to find his family. They were quietly nursing on the sofa in the den, and he was amazed that he'd apparently slept through baby calls for breakfast. "Sorry. I guess I was tired. What can I do to help?"

"Hold a baby," Darla said with a smile, and he thought he'd never seen her look more beautiful. He found himself literally gawking at his wife.

"I want to marry you," he said, and Darla laughed. "We are married."

"I know. But I'm afraid you'll get away from me. Maybe I'll marry you once a month just to make sure you're holding tight to our commitment." He sank onto the sofa and trailed a finger over his daughter's face as she nuzzled her mom. "Remember when you used to talk about our marriage as something you wanted to do until the girls were born?"

Darla nodded. "Is that what's making you all nervous and weird?"

"No, this is my natural state now," he said, and she nodded.

"Probably." She handed him the daughter who'd gone to sleep on her breast.

"So," he said, taking the baby tenderly, "if you don't mind, I'd like to make this a solid, no-holds-barred commitment. I have a feeling you're going to like being married to me."

Darla laughed. "Well, confidence isn't your short suit."

"So, I'll go rustle up some breakfast. What are you in the mood for, little mama?" The least he could do was grab some grub, since she was doing all the work—and as lovely as that work was, she didn't seem to need him all that much.

"Fruit," Darla said. "I'd kiss you for fresh fruit."

"Really? Does a truckload rate more than a kiss?"

Darla smiled at him, and Judah tried to ignore the fact that she hadn't said a whole lot about staying married to him longer than the time it took to give his daughters his name.

Which was now.

"Oh, that reminds me," he said, "speaking of gifts and whatnot—"

"We weren't," she said. "We were just talking about breakfast."

"Well, I know, but a guy has to work in opportunity when it presents itself." He handed her the jeweler's box he'd picked up in town. "It's not a banana or an apple, but it's something."

She indicated the baby on her breast she was supporting with one arm. "Would you mind opening it for me? My hands are full at the moment."

Okay, so maybe his timing wasn't all that great. Judah told himself it didn't matter—timing wasn't everything.

Or maybe it was. He snapped open the lid, and Darla gasped.

"Judah!"

He laughed when she freed a hand to grab the box so she could look at the sapphire bracelet more closely.

"It's gorgeous," she said. "But what's it for?"

He chuckled and took the box back. "To thank you for my babies? To work my way out of the doghouse I land myself in occasionally? I don't know. Maybe it's because I love you."

She looked at him, cornflower-blue eyes assessing him. "Do you?"

"I might," he said, putting the sapphire-and-diamond bracelet on her wrist. "Maybe. When you're ready."

She looked at the bracelet, then smiled. "Thank you. It's the most beautiful thing I've ever owned."

"I don't know about that." Judah stroked his daughter's tiny head. "Our babies look like their mom. So they are the most beautiful things I own."

Darla's eyes sparkled, and then she broke eye contact. "Thank you," she murmured.

"You're welcome. So," he said cheerfully, feeling better about his place in the world already. "Bananas? Apples? Peaches?"

"All," she said, looking back at him, "and when does the moving truck arrive?"

Chapter Twenty

"About that moving truck," Judah said. "I think it's too soon, don't you?"

Darla touched the lovely bracelet he had given her, and wondered why he was so worried about every little thing. She was fine; their daughters were fine. He'd asked her about making a real commitment, and that commitment was best made in a home they started out in together. Maybe Rancho Diablo was just so much a part of him that he couldn't relax until he was there.

"If you're worried about me, Judah, don't be. I've waited a long time for us to be a family. You don't have to stress out all the time."

"I do," Judah said. "It's a new husband, new dad thing."

"All right," Darla said. "But the sooner you're not feeling like a fish out of water, the sooner you'll de-stress."

"I don't know. I'm accepting stress as my due in life at the moment. But," he said, clearly trying to take all the blame for his unease, "I would feel better at the ranch, although not for the reason you assume. I'm not unhappy here with you, Darla. If things were different, this house would be fine for a month or two. At least until our daughters start needing some elbow room."

Darla gazed down at their diminutive babies. "I think that'll be a while, don't you?"

"Nah. They're going to be tall like their mother and father."

"That's probably true, but I don't think it'll happen overnight."

"The way they're chowing, I wouldn't underestimate them," Judah said enviously, eyeing his breast-feeding daughter.

Darla smiled. "So what's the reason?"

"What reason?" He appeared momentarily disoriented from staring at her breasts, and Darla shook her head.

"The real reason you want to move to the ranch, if it isn't for a bigger house to raise your family in."

"Oh," Judah said, bringing his gaze back to her eyes. "I don't know."

She frowned. "Yes, you do. You're a pretty practical guy. You know why you do things. So quit hiding it."

"Uh, I have to get breakfast for my love right now," he said, edging toward the door. "Don't you worry about a thing while I'm gone, and when I get back, I'll watch babies so you can shower."

He escaped out the door, and a second later she heard his truck roar off down the driveway, no slower than he'd driven in. He was always in a hurry. Darla looked down at the bracelet on her arm, mesmerized by the twinkling diamonds and deep blue sapphires, and wondered why Judah wouldn't just tell her what he was thinking.

"Maybe he's one of those men who keep everything inside," she murmured to her daughters. "The strong, silent type. Which will be hard to deal with since I'm not a mind reader."

She knew he'd wanted her out at the ranch yesterday—but he'd just said it wasn't because of building their life together in a bigger house. Darla closed her eyes after a moment, deciding to relax and not think about her mysterious man. Judah was Judah—and he moved to a drummer that only he seemed to be able to hear.

"WELL, LOOK AT YOU, making the doughnut run," Bode Jenkins said as Judah loaded the groceries he'd grabbed onto the checkout counter. Bode glanced over his purchases. "Hungry wife?"

Judah grunted. "Bode, mind your own business."

"Hey, that's no way to talk to a neighbor."

Judah ignored the comment, paid his bill with cash and departed. Bode followed, trying to keep up with Judah's long strides.

"I mean to give you a wedding gift," the older man stated, and Judah said, "Don't bother."

"Callahan," Bode said, his voice changing to a more insistent tone, "you really ought to be nicer to me."

"Why?" Judah asked. "Nice really isn't my deal, but most especially not to you. And I don't have time to chat this morning, Bode. If you have a complaint with me, lodge it with someone who cares." He got in his truck, tossing the groceries on the seat next to him.

Bode stood at the window. "Listen, I think I know who shot you."

Judah hesitated in the act of turning on the engine, surprised that Bode had brought up the shooting, and wondering if he should even bother to listen to anything the old man had to say. "If you think you know, why don't you tell the sheriff?"

"Wouldn't you rather I tell you?"

Judah scrubbed at his morning growth of beard, wishing he had a magic club he could beat Bode over the head with and make him disappear. "Jenkins, if you knew anything at all you'd be shouting it from the rooftops, not trying to keep me from my family when you can see I'm on a mission." He started the truck. "To be honest, I don't care who shot me. You can't scare us off our land, Jenkins. Callahans don't scare."

"It involves your aunt, and some other things I think you'd be interested in."

"All right," Judah said, "spit it out so I can get home to my hungry wife and kids."

"Ask your aunt," Bode advised, and Judah said, "What?"

"Ask your aunt who likely shot you."

"Jump, Jenkins," Judah said, "'cause this truck door'll swing open in two seconds and knock you flat to the ground."

Bode jumped away from the vehicle and Judah drove off, swearing under his breath. He cursed colorfully, using words he rarely said, and told himself it was against the law to back up over an old man, even if Bode deserved it. Judah pressed the pedal down, peeling out of the parking lot, eager to get home. Never had he been more anxious to see his wife and children.

DARLA HEARD JUDAH'S truck roar up the drive, and was mentally ready when the front door blew open with a great sucking sound. "Shh," she said, "the babies are asleep, Attila."

"Attila?" Judah handed her the bag of fruit. "Who's he?"

"He was a man who was always on a conquering mission. You've just about conquered my driveway and my door frames. I'm going to need to have everything Judah-proofed."

"Sorry," he said, and she sighed.

"You were going to start acting like a human being?"

He shrugged. "Maybe it takes a while."

"Hmm." Darla went to the kitchen and got out plates. "Thank you for the fruit. It's beautiful."

"Babies are beautiful." Judah threw himself onto the sofa, looking rattled even for him, Darla thought. "Fruit is just appetizing. Or not."

She shook her head and cut the fruit into two bowls. "Are you all right?"

"Yeah." He got up, went to her fridge. "Any beer in here?"

Darla's eyes widened. "At eight o'clock in the morning?"

"Maybe just a fruit chaser." He found a Dos and opened it gratefully.

"That's older than you want, like from a picnic last summer. How about some coffee instead?"

"I'm jacked enough already." He opened the beer and took a swig, made a face and sucked down another swig before pouring the rest down the drain. "That was just what the doctor ordered."

Darla shook her head and handed him a bowl of fruit "Are you all right?"

"Never been better," Judah said, but Darla had the strangest feeling he wasn't being honest.

And it wasn't the first time she'd felt this way.

She heard a tiny cry from one of the babies, and set her bowl down.

"I got it," Judah said. "Eat."

She hung back in the kitchen as he'd told her to. It would be all right. Judah would call her if he needed help. No sound came from the other room. She chewed her fruit halfheartedly, listening, and when she still heard nothing, she peeked around the corner.

Judah had both babies on his chest as he lounged on the sofa. He peered down one baby's back, hooked a finger in her diaper and peeked. "Nothing there, Dad," he said, talking for the baby, then hooked a finger in the second diaper. "Nothing here, either, Dad," he said, still being a baby ventriloquist.

Darla smiled and brought him his bowl. "What do you know about changing diapers?"

"Just that it needs to happen often or everybody's unhappy." Judah smoothed a hand over tiny heads. "And I did a lot of babysitting in high school. Fiona was a big believer in us working whatever odd job came our way. Babysitting, wrangling, bush hogging. Didn't matter. She said it was good for us to respect a buck."

Darla didn't know where to put herself. She wanted to sit next to Judah, but something held her back. "If you're good with the girls, would you mind if I grab a shower?"

"Go. The babies and I are going to watch an educational flick." He turned on her television, flipped channels with the remote and chose the movie download. "For our first foray into intelligentsia," he told his daughters, "we're going to examine the societal differences between *Little Women* and *Gone with the Wind*. I'll expect spirited discussion during intermissions."

Darla laughed. "Oh, you'll get spirited discussions, but they'll all be concerning dinner."

"Switch out the lights, please. We must have the proper surroundings to begin the study of our topic of females in society."

"Okay," Darla said. "By the way, your aunt will be here in thirty minutes."

"Why?"

"You'll see," Darla said with a smile, and left the room.

"When you become literary bra burners," Judah told his daughters, "please remind yourselves that men don't like surprises." He said it loudly enough for Darla to hear in the next room, and she rewarded him by saying, "Men like spice, girls. Never forget the spice."

And then Darla put tape on the final packed box in her room, sealing it and marking it "Darla and Judah's bedroom."

We'll see how well my husband handles surprises.

THIRTY MINUTES LATER, Judah had just gotten comfortable watching *Little Women* when the door banged open.

"We're here!" Jonas called out. "Darla, we're here!"

"Hi," Fiona said, poking her head into the living room. "What are you doing here, Judah?"

His brothers and Burke piled in behind Fiona.

"Have you guys ever heard of being quiet so as not to wake sleeping babies?" Judah said with a growl.

"Not those two. They sleep like puppies." Fiona came to kiss each great niece on her downy head.

"Anyway, what do you mean, what am I doing here?" Judah didn't appreciate the inference that he might not be where his wife and daughters were.

"Well," Sam said, "we thought you'd be off doing something stupid, like trying to solve the universe's problems. We're trying to give you a surprise party."

"Party?" Judah raised a brow. "What kind of surprise party? I don't like surprises."

"And yet it's been one after another for the past several months. Good morning, girls," Rafe said, touching a palm to each of his niece's tufts. "Miss me?"

"No, they don't," Judah said. "We are trying to have a literary discussion."

"Oh, your favorite movie." Jonas laughed, and when Darla came into the living room he told her, "Judah always wanted to be Laurie."

"Didn't happen, though," Sam said. "Judah was never polite enough to be Laurie."

"True. He's been a little on the crabby side lately." Darla smiled, and Fiona said, "Are we ready?"

"Everything is boxed up." Darla took them back to her room, and Judah tried to spy down the hall to see what they were doing. He couldn't move the two tiny bundles on his chest, however, because they were so warm and satisfied right where they were.

"What's happening?" he demanded as Burke went by with a wheeled dolly.

"We're moving your wife and girls to the ranch," Jonas said. "Surprise!"

Chapter Twenty-One

Once they had Darla and Molly and Belle moved into the bunkhouse, Judah really did feel peace come over him. There were so many people coming and going all day long at Rancho Diablo that he knew his ladies were safe.

Which meant it was time to talk to Fiona. He caught her heading to the basement, her favorite haunt besides the kitchen. "Whoa, frail aunt, let me carry those for you."

She sniffed and gave him the box of party lights she'd hung in June. "I'm not frail. You're frail."

"In what way?"

"You're making your wife do all the heavy lifting."

He stared at Fiona as they made their way down the stairs. "What lifting?"

"She's making all the sacrifices."

It was true. "Not much I can do about that right now."

"You could take her on a honeymoon. Let me keep the babies."

He hesitated. "Uh, she's breast-feeding."

"True, but trips aren't planned in a week, nephew. Good ones, at least. There are logistics involved. And I'll probably have to fight Mavis tooth and nail for baby time, so I want to get my request in first."

She sniffed again, and Judah said, "Catching a cold, Aunt?"

"No. I'm merely allergic to bone idleness."

"I suppose you have the name of a travel agency you prefer?" he asked with a sigh.

"I do. But I refuse to pick a destination. You'll have to ask Darla what she wants. I can't do everything for you."

He smiled. "Thanks for thinking of it. I'd forgotten."

"You've had a lot on your mind." She showed him where to shove the box, and pointed to another she wanted.

"I thought you were going to have a monster garage sale and get rid of all this."

"I might, if we ever have to move. But right now, Sam's doing a bang-up job. I'm only fifty percent worried these days. And Jonas has become quite the financial investor, something I was never aware of before. Guess he has to have something to do now that he's not cracking open people's chest cavities."

Judah winced. "Aunt, speaking of cracking things open…"

"Oh, let's don't," she said. "I hate to think of it. Only eggs should be cracked open."

His gaze slid to the dirt patch that was unlike the rest of the basement floor. They'd asked Fiona about it when they were younger, and gotten some water-seeping-in, covered-over-mold story. The boys had told each other ghost stories about the dead body in the basement, but these days, Judah wondered if he could dismiss any tale about his fey aunt.

"What about safes? Safes get cracked open."

"No," she said dismissively, "not unless one is a thief,

and we have none of—" Her gaze met his, and then slid to the floor where he'd been looking. "Now, nephew," Fiona said. "Don't go odd on me just because you're lacking sleep due to your darling daughters. In fact, you should go—"

"Bode says I should ask you about who might have shot me," Judah said quietly, and Fiona stared at him.

"Bode's a fool. Why would he say such a thing?"

"You tell me."

She put her hands on her hips and glared at him. "Whose side are you on, Judah?"

"Callahan side, ma'am," he answered, "but why are there sides?"

She pursed her lips. "I always think of everything that's happened as Jenkins versus Callahan. That's all I meant."

"Do you have a theory as to who shot me?" Judah was determined to know just how much Fiona was hiding.

"I have theories," she said, "and they're about as good as any that are floating around. I've had people ask me if you accidentally let your own gun go off."

"Why would I be carrying at a wedding?"

"See how much sense it makes to listen to gossip?" She moved to inspect her rows of pickled vegetables, breaking eye contact. "I've heard that it was Bode. That it was a hunter. That it was Sidney." She shrugged. "We're probably never going to know, Judah."

And yet he sensed she was holding back on him.

"And who else might it have been?"

She looked at him for a long time. "Put those boxes on the dining room table, please," she said, and marched up the stairs, leaving him in the basement, knowing that something wasn't adding up.

"TONIGHT'S FAMILY COUNCIL is necessary," Fiona said, "because lately I've noticed a lack of faith among my nephews in the job I've been doing. Not that I blame you, because I alone got us in the mess we're in."

The six brothers and Burke watched Aunt Fiona as she struggled for words six hours after Judah had tried to talk to her about Bode down in the basement. Of course, he'd known that Bode was intent on stirring up trouble. Yet it was his aunt's lack of heat in the denial that had sparked his curiosity. Now she was calling a family council, and his curiosity was even greater. They had these meetings at least once a month to discuss family and ranch business, but this one had been called out of schedule.

Now they sat in the wood-paneled library. Burke passed out square cut-crystal glasses of fine whiskey, and Judah drank his gratefully.

"First, Burke and I want to tell you that we're married," Fiona said, "just so you know that I'm walking the walk and talking the talk when I try to set you boys up for lifetimes of happiness with someone you love. I know you already know, have known for a while, but I'm making it official."

The men applauded, congratulated Burke and Fiona, acted surprised, as if they hadn't figured it out years ago.

"Now I'm here to answer any questions you might have," Fiona said, "and I know that, based on a discussion I had with Judah this morning, that you have some. Anything we can clear up, Burke and I are here for you. Always."

The brothers glanced at one another. This was new, Judah thought. This new transparent Fiona was an unexpected metamorphosis.

And yet she'd specifically told him never to talk about the cave's existence. He wondered how far this transparency would go.

"All right, I'll bite," Judah said. "Where are our parents buried?"

The room went deathly silent. Fiona's gaze leveled on him, seemingly dazed, and then, without any warning, she fainted.

"SHE SCARED THE LIVING daylights out of me," Judah said as he lay in bed that night with Darla and their two angels. "I really thought I'd killed her."

Darla giggled. "It's not funny, I know, but it kind of is. You know Fiona is tough as cowhide. I don't think you can hurt her, Judah. Don't worry."

He winced. "I do worry. She's not so much cowhide as she once was. I feel terrible about the whole thing." His brothers had piled on, telling him that Fiona's offer had been more rhetorical and polite than anything, and was he trying to give her a stroke?

"Don't worry. Fiona knows you love her." Darla gave a contented sigh. "I love living in this bunkhouse," she said, and Judah's attention was totally caught.

"Are you being serious?"

She nodded. "Much more than I thought I would. It's really ideal for a growing family. There's so much storage space. And Mom and her friends came over today and set up the nursery just the way they had it at my house." She smiled at Judah. "It's perfect."

"I'm glad." His tone was gruffer than he meant it to be, but so much emotion was flooding over him that it practically choked him. "Thanks for being okay with this, Darla. I feel better with us being here."

"Yeah, Sam told me." Darla closed her eyes, enjoying

the peace. "He said that ever since you got shot, you've been a bit of a wienie."

Judah sighed. "He's probably right."

"And he said that this is your place. Your piece of the universe." She rolled her head to look at him. "I didn't really have a piece of the universe. I loved my house, but it was just a house."

You're my home, he thought, *my whole life. My real universe.*

"Want to honeymoon?" he asked, and Darla grinned at him.

"Maybe the Bahamas," Darla told Jackie the next day when she came to see the new digs and bring a house-warming gift. "Judah says I can probably find a white skirt and he'll wear a white shirt with palm trees on it, and we'll have vows said under some kind of coconut tree or something." Darla smiled. "He's gone all romantic since we moved into the bunkhouse."

"Rancho Diablo suits these men." Jackie pulled out wedding dress vendor photos for two years out. "I figure we might as well start looking these over."

"And I need to decide what to do with the magic wedding dress," Darla said. "I suppose we should sell it. Sabrina says the magic has to keep moving."

"Do you really believe all that stuff she talks about sometimes?"

"I don't know," Darla said, "but I do know that I'm happier than I've ever been, and if a dress can bring a little luck, I'm all for sharing it. I'm a romantic at heart."

"So am I." Jackie looked at the photos and drawings. "You're still okay with the wedding dress shop, partner?"

"Why wouldn't I be?" Darla was surprised by the question.

"I thought Judah didn't want you to work."

"Well, not while the babies are so tiny." Darla stiffened. "I didn't mind changing houses, but I would never give up my shop for a man. Not Judah or any other guy."

"Just checking."

Darla frowned, not sure where all this was going. "You've got triplets, so why wouldn't I keep working, too?"

Jackie shrugged. "Pete doesn't mind me working."

Darla wondered if Judah cared if she worked. If he did, he was going to get a fat lip. "This dress shop was my brainchild, and I wouldn't give it up for him. I don't think he'd ask, either."

Jackie nodded. "I was pretty certain you'd feel that way."

Tickles of unease ran over Darla. "You're not telling me everything. What happened?"

Jackie sighed. "Judah came to me and offered to buy out my half of the shop."

"What?" Darla couldn't believe what she was hearing. "Why?"

"Well, Pete says Judah was planning on giving it to you as a wedding gift."

Darla thought about that. "But I don't want to own the whole store. I like the way we have things set up." She frowned. "How dare he?"

"I think Judah has your best interests at heart, Darla," Jackie said calmly. Her efforts to soothe her weren't working, however, because Darla was practically quivering with anger.

"Why?" she asked her friend. "Why do you think that?"

Jackie's face wore a how-do-I-get-myself-out-of-this expression. "Pete says if you own the whole store, you can sell it and have more time for the babies."

Darla began to quiver again. "I haven't even thought that far ahead. Why would Judah think he has to be involved in my business?"

"Because he's a man, and because he's a Callahan, and because he honestly thinks he's doing the right thing."

"By thinking for me?" Darla soothed Molly and Belle, who were beginning to get restless from the angry tone of their mother's voice.

"He says he doesn't want you too tired out." Jackie nodded. "And you know, Darla, when we bought the shop, we were single women, and now we're married with children, and your babies are very delicate—"

"Don't give me that. You don't want to sell your half," Darla said. "I know you too well."

"No, but if it's best for you—"

"It's not," Darla said, her tone dark with finality. "Just forget my husband ever brought this up."

"Oh, dear," Jackie said. "I don't want to cause trouble."

"You didn't. Judah did."

And the moment her man got home, he was going to get his chauvinistic tendencies trimmed way back. There was a difference between diamond-and-sapphire bracelets and buying out one's sister-in-law—a difference her handsome husband was about to learn.

"Storm brewing to the east," Rafe told Judah as they put away the last of the horses. "We'll pull the barn doors shut when we go."

"Okay." Judah glanced over his shoulder at the

bruised sky. Winds were swirling the clouds, sending them scudding across the dark heavens. "When's Diane coming back?"

"She and Sidney return tonight. They'll take the girls to their new house in Durant, where Sidney lives." Rafe put his saddle away, and Judah did likewise. "I'm going to miss the heck out of the little girls."

"Whoa," Judah said, an arrow of sadness shooting through him. "I guess I should have expected that." The girls had been going back and forth from Jackie to Fiona to Aberdeen while their mother was gone, with Aberdeen keeping them at night. Still, Judah was going to miss the sound of their young voices.

"It's sad, but nothing stays the same. Eventually, all little birds fly away," Rafe said.

"We didn't."

"Our jobs are here," Rafe reminded him. "But you tried to fly. You just got your wings clipped."

"I think of it more as if I got my wings retooled. They're better now." Judah was proud of how he was handling his new settled life. He couldn't wait for the big All's Clear from the doctor—he was going to make love to his wife until he gave out. "Life's great. You should try marriage."

"Not me," Rafe said. "I don't do relationships."

"Neither did I," Judah said, pretty cheerful about the new him.

"So, about the other night," Rafe said. "What made you ask about our parents?"

He shrugged. "I'd like to know. Wouldn't you?"

"I don't know. I'm a year older than you. I understand that there are some things we'll never know. At twenty-nine, you decide it's too late to know some things."

"When you're looking down the barrel at thirty, you

mean?" Judah shook his head. "Not me. I'll always want to know what happened. How did they die? Where were they?"

"They died," Rafe said, "of some funky illness."

"I thought it was a car accident." Judah frowned. "You know, it's not that hard to request a death certificate. Sam probably has done so a thousand times for clients."

Rafe turned to look at him. "Do you think Fiona would have told us, if we really wanted to know?"

"You mean we don't want to?"

Rafe shrugged. "Do you?"

"I—yeah."

"Then order the certificate." Rafe walked out of the barn into the storm, leaving Judah to wonder why he was the only one in the family who asked questions.

Finding out more about the cave was going to be first on his to-do list, Judah thought. After exiting the barn, he turned to slide the doors shut behind him, and suddenly felt a splitting pain in his skull, followed by blackness.

INSIDE THE KITCHEN, Fiona had the entire family scattered about, perching wherever they could find space. "This is our last meal as an extended family," she said over the din, "because tomorrow night our three little ladies go to their new home in Durant. So I cooked their *faborites*—" she stressed the word, imitating the little girls' pronunciation "—SpaghettiO's. Real sauce and real pasta shaped like Os." She kissed them on their heads. "And now, Judah will lead us in the blessing. Since he's the most newly married, he may have the honor. Judah."

No one said anything. Fiona glanced around the room. "Darla, where's your husband?"

Darla shook her head. "I haven't seen him all day. And if someone does, will you tell him I want to talk to him?"

Everyone hooted at that. Fiona shook her head. "Someone please call his cell phone and tell him it's rude to be late to the little girls' going-away party, especially when their aunty has made them a pink-and-white cake with kitties on it."

"I will." Jonas rang his brother's phone, then said, "No answer. He'll be along soon enough."

Rafe said, "I left him in the barn, so maybe he went to do something else."

Rain pelted the windows. Fiona glanced outside, shaking her head. "All right, I guess we'll eat without him." But she wasn't happy about it.

They were all eating, deep into the spaghetti, when the kitchen door opened. Judah stumbled in, blood running down the side of his face.

Darla screamed and ran to her husband. She waved everyone away as he sank to the floor. "What did you do, Judah?" she asked, grabbing a wet paper towel from Jonas, who hovered near his brother, looking over the wound.

"You've got a mighty big goose egg back here, son," Jonas said. "You're going to need a few stitches. Maybe even a staple. Rafe, check the barn, since you were out there last. Sam, go with him. Look for…look for things," he said, with a quick glance at Fiona.

Judah groaned and slumped toward his wife, and Darla knew at once that everything he'd been worried about had been real. There was trouble, and he didn't want her to know, but was carrying the burden himself.

Her heart grew cold with fear.

"DON'T MOVE," DARLA said two hours later, after Jonas brought Judah home from the hospital with a bandage tightly wrapped around his head. "You stay right in that bed. And no TV until I can ascertain that you aren't going to have latent swelling or something. You just sit there and don't move." She was being unreasonable, but she couldn't help being afraid.

"Yes, Nurse," he said. "But will you at least put on a crisp white nurse's uniform with a real short skirt if I have to put up with your bossing me?"

"You're trying to joke about what happened, but it's not funny. First you get shot—"

"Just some kids playing with their daddy's gun, for which they owe me three months' hard labor on the ranch. And I intend to work them harder than my brothers and I ever worked, not to mention mucking. We've got sixteen horses, you know."

She ignored his effort to make light of the situation. "But then you took a knock on the head, and teasing about it just isn't funny right now." She burst into tears.

"And I'm not laughing, either, my love." He patted the bed. "Come over here and let me look down your blouse, and I'll feel ever so much better. The medicine I need is a little naked wife."

Tears streamed faster, so she grabbed a tissue. She hated crying, but couldn't quit. "You scared me!"

"Darling, I scared myself." Judah perked up. "Was it a two-by-four? It felt like a house. Tell me it was at least a really big board."

She nodded. "Sam found it out by the barn. What

were you doing, getting in the way of a thick, long piece of lumber?"

"I don't know. Silly of me, wasn't it?"

"Yes! Because you said that if we moved out here, we'd be safer, but clearly you're not!" Darla shrank onto the bed and curled up next to her husband so she could indulge in a little crying on his shoulder. "And you tried to buy Jackie out of her half of the wedding shop, so I really wanted to be angry with you, but now I can't because your head's all bandaged up, so I'm really upset!"

He laughed and tugged her closer. "Now there's the bright side."

She sniffled. "It was horrible when you came into the kitchen all Lon Chaneyish. Never do that again." Darla hiccupped, which she hated to do. But once it got started it always took a while to stop, so she sat next to Judah and hiccupped, aware she sounded pitiful.

"Your daughters aren't as needy as you are," he teased, and Darla stated, "I know. They're angels."

"About the wedding dress shop," Judah began, but she said, "I don't want to fight right now."

"We're not going to fight. I was just trying to buy it for you to help Jackie out. Pete says she's overwhelmed with the triplets right now."

"Oh." Darla thought about that for a few seconds. "Pete told Jackie you were a chauvinist pig who didn't want his wife to work. Not in those words, of course. Those are my words."

"I'll put my brother in the corner with his dunce cap on later. You were really going to tell me off, weren't you?" Judah asked, planting kisses against her hair, and Darla smiled through her tears.

"Yes."

"But since I'm not a chauvinist pig, I get to see you naked for a reward?"

Darla kissed him on the forehead. "The jury's still out on the pig part. Although you're starting to look more like a prince all the time." She got up to go check on the babies, who were nestled in their tiny bassinets.

"Hey," Judah called after her, "what does a guy have to do to prove to his wife that he loves her even when she's not properly dedicated to his nursing care?"

Darla popped her head back in the room. "What did you say?"

"I said..." Judah tried to remember what he'd said that had made Darla return so quickly "...uh, what do I have to do besides take a beating with a two-by-four to get some attention from my wife?"

"Go on," Darla said.

Pain was throbbing at the base of his skull. His long hair had been shaved off in back for the stitches, and his pride was pretty bent about that. Still, Judah tried hard to think. "Oh," he said with a grin, "you're trying to get me tell you that I love you."

"No, I'm not." Darla shook her head. "I'm not trying to get you to *do* anything."

"I love you, Darla," he said. "I loved you long before you ever sneaked into my room and made wild love to me."

"You did?"

She sounded genuinely surprised. Judah nodded, feeling better already. "Why else would I have failed the condom test? I say it was all subconscious."

She advanced on him, her gaze lit with mock anger and a lot of laughter. "When were you going to tell me?"

"When I was certain I'd caught you." He held a pillow in front of himself for protection from his wife. "I love you madly, Darla Callahan, but it was darn hard waiting on you to finally leave your slipper in my path."

She got on top of him, straddling him, and he tossed the pillow away. "Mr. Callahan, are there any other surprises you'd care to share with me?"

He shook his head. "I just want you to know that you're not the only one capable of keeping one's cards to their chest." He gazed at the front of her blouse reverently. "Or breasts, even." He caught one finger in the top and tugged. The blouse fell open, and he sighed with pleasure. "Nurse, I have a terrible ache."

Darla smiled. "I can help you," she said, leaning over to kiss his lips, "but you'll have to undress so I can fix that ache."

He kissed her all over, so passionately that Darla knew she was the luckiest woman on earth. Which was really no surprise at all, because she was married to the man she'd always loved, with all her heart.

Epilogue

"Sheriff says you've had some bad luck," Darla told Judah once they'd taken out the stitches a few weeks later. "He says you shouldn't get in the way of flying boards like that. The storm really kicked up some things."

Shingles had been ripped off the roofs of some houses. Fences had blown down. One of their cows had mysteriously moved onto Bode's property. He'd returned it promptly.

"Don't want you calling me a cattle thief," he'd said, and Fiona had humphed at him.

Judah was glad it was just a board that had hit him, and not one of his brothers, his aunt or his wife. "There are worse things to be in the way of, I guess. Are you packed, wife? Itty-bitty bikini and everything?"

Darla laughed. "There will be no bikini. Just a one-piece."

"One-pieces are great. Lots of leg." He rubbed his hands together.

"Did you bring your swimsuit?" Darla asked. "I want to see hunk for the whole week."

He puffed out his chest. "I'm your hunk, darling."

Darla laughed. "Shall we go say goodbye to the girls?"

Judah's face fell. "I'm not sure if I can. I'll miss them too much."

It was true. They were up with him at the crack of dawn when he ate breakfast. He'd make bottles for them, since he'd talked Darla into changing to bottles a bit before their trip. The girls had grown by leaps and bounds. They might have started out slow, but the pediatrician said they were catching up quickly on the growth chart. He said it was amazing. Judah thought it was his wife who was amazing.

Even he was flourishing, living with her.

"When we get this lawsuit settled," he told Darla, "I have a surprise for you."

"Tell me now, just in case," she said, and he grinned at her. "Nah. I like making you beg. It's so much fun."

She swiped at him. "I thought you didn't like surprises."

He swept her into his lap while they waited for Rafe to drive them to the airport. "Well, once I realized surprise was your game, I decided to turn the tables on you."

Darla smiled. "So tell me."

"I'm going to build you your own house."

His wife stared at him for a moment. "Here, at the ranch?"

He nodded. "I don't want to get your hopes up, in case we do lose the ranch."

She kissed him. "I love the bunkhouse, but thank you for thinking of such a wonderful gift. I love you, Judah Callahan."

"I know, Mrs. Callahan. I feel it every day."

"And you know something else?" she said, wrapping her arms around him so she could pull him close, to tell him something she'd long been wanting to tell him, for his ears only. "I had a dream about you last night."

He perked up. "You did? Did it involve naked you and whipped cream and maybe even some cherries?"

She kissed him on the lips. "Even better," she said. "I think we're pregnant."

His jaw dropped.

"Surprise," she said.

Judah laughed and pulled her into his arms, the luckiest, happiest man alive.

When they had put their suitcases in the car, and Rafe was driving them away from Rancho Diablo, Judah saw the Diablos running like the wind, faster than the wind, disappearing on the painted horizon.

And he knew he'd found all the wealth and happiness a man could ever hope for, because the only treasure that truly mattered was love.

* * * * *

SPECIAL EXCERPT FROM

HARLEQUIN®

American Romance®

Read on for a sneak peek at
CALLAHAN COWBOY TRIPLETS
by USA TODAY *bestselling author Tina Leonard*

Available September 2013
from Harlequin American Romance.

Tighe, the wildest of the Callahan brothers, is
determined to have his eight seconds of glory in
the bull-riding ring—but gorgeous River Martins
throws off his game!

Tighe Callahan sized up the enormous spotted bull. "Hello, Firefreak," he said. "You may have bested my twin, Dante, but I aim to ride you until you're soft as glove leather. Gonna retire you to the kiddie rides."

The legendary rank bull snorted a heavy breath his way, daring him.

"You're crazy, Tighe," his brother Jace said. "I'm telling you, that one wants to kill you."

"Feeling's mutual." Tighe grinned and knocked on the wall of the pen that held the bull. "If Dante stayed on him for five seconds, I ought to at least go ten."

Jace looked at Tighe doubtfully. "Sure. You can do it. Whatever." He glanced around. "I think I'll go get some popcorn and find a pretty girl to share it with. You and Firefreak just go ahead and chat about life. May be a one-sided conversation, but those are your favorite, anyway."

Jace wandered off. Tighe studied the bull, who never broke eye contact with him, his gaze wise with the scores of cowboys he'd mercilessly tossed, earning himself a legendary status.

"Hi, Tighe," River Martin said, and Tighe felt his heart start to palpitate. Here was his dream, his unattainable brunette princess—smiling at him as sweet as cherry wine. "We heard you're going to ride a bull tomorrow, so the girls and I decided to come out and watch."

This wasn't good. A man didn't need his concentration wrecked by a gorgeous female—nor did he want said gorgeous, unattainable female to see him get squashed by a few tons of angry luggage with horns.

But River was smiling at him with her teasing eyes, so all Tighe could say was "Nice of you ladies to come out."

River said, "Good luck," and Tighe shivered, because he did believe in magic and luck and everything spiritual. And any superstitious man knew it was taunting the devil himself to wish a man good luck when the challenge he faced in the ring was nothing compared to the real challenge: forcing himself to look into a woman's sexy gaze and not drown.

He was drowning, and he had been for oh, so long.

Watch for
CALLAHAN COWBOY TRIPLETS
by Tina Leonard

Available September 2013
from Harlequin® American Romance®!

WIN *Vegas*
A **TRIP** TO

& **TICKETS**
TO CHAMPIONSHIP
RODEO EVENTS!

Who can resist a cowboy? We sure can't!

You and a friend can win a 3-night,
4-day trip to Vegas to see some real
cowboys in action.

Visit
www.Harlequin.com/VegasSweepstakes
to enter!

See reverse for details.

Sweepstakes closes October 18, 2013.